Castles Made
of Sand

CASTLES MADE
OF SAND

GWYNETH JONES

The right of Gwyneth Jones to be identified as the author of
this work has been asserted by her in accordance with the
Copyright, Designs and Patents Act 1988.

http://www.boldaslove.co.uk

First published in Great Britain in 2002 by
Gollancz
An imprint of the Orion Publishing Group
Orion House, 5 Upper St Martin's Lane, London WC2H 9EA

This edition published in Great Britain in 2003 by Gollancz

A CIP record for this book
is available from the British Library

ISBN 0 575 07395 0

Typeset at The Spartan Press Ltd,
Lymington, Hants

Printed in Great Britain by
Clays Ltd, St Ives plc

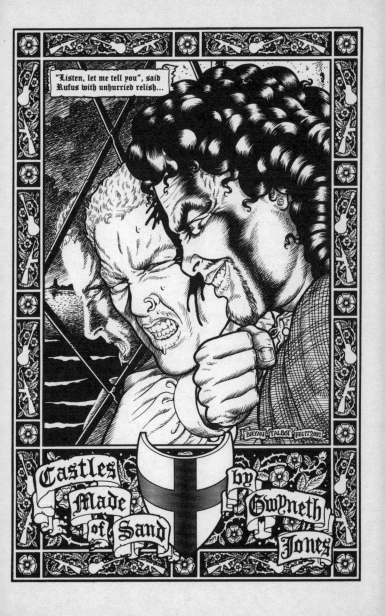

Here begin the terrors
Here begin the marvels

ACKNOWLEDGEMENTS

Acknowledgements, Dedications, Bibliography, Discography, Commentary and contact details can be found at http://www.boldaslove.co.uk

Castles Made of Sand, Locations and Sources (Short version)

LITERARY SOURCES:
Ma Bohème, Arthur Rimbaud (*Arthur Rimbaud Collected Poems*, tr. Oliver Bernard, Penguin Classics); *Led Zeppelin From Early Days To Page and Plant*, Ritchie Yorke, Virgin Publishing; Verses from the Qur'an, A. J. Arberry, *The Koran Interpreted*, London 1955 (quoted in *Night, Horses and the Desert*, an anthology of classic Arabian Literature, Robert Irwin, Allen Lane); *The Ancient Celts*, Barry Cunliffe, OUP; *West Kennet Long Barrow Excavations* (The Avebury Monuments DoE official handbook, HMSO); *The Bone Cave Excavations* Alveston, Gloucestershire (Time Team investigations); *The Mabinogion* tr. Gwyn Jones, Everyman; *Arthurian Romances*, Chrétien de Troyes, tr. D. D. R. Owen, Everyman; *Le Morte D'Arthur* Vol II, Sir Thomas Malory, Everyman; *Mistress of Mistresses*, E. R. Eddison, Ballantine; *Lord Jim*, Joseph Conrad; *Uncle Vanya*, Anton Chekov, ed. David Lan, RSC; 'Green Tea', Joseph Sheridan LeFanu, and 'The Facts In The Case Of M. Valdemar', Edgar Allan

Poe (*Great Tales of Terror And The Supernatural*, ed. Wise & Wagner, Hammond and Hammond); 'The Scarlet House', Angela Carter (*A Book of Contemporary Nightmares*, Michael Joseph). Special thanks to Betty Gwilliam and Jim McLaughlin for Irish dialogue.

LOCATIONS:
South Lakes Wild Animal Park, Dalton in Furness, Cumbria; Swadlincote, Derbyshire (courtesy of Miss Ann Halam); *Lonely Planet Guide to Washington DC*; *The Rough Guide to Amsterdam*; Padstow and District, North Cornwall; Ross Castle, Kilarney, Co. Kerry; & *Focal Buiochais* to the people of Baltimore and Inis Cléire, West Cork.

Watch out for **The Annotated Castles** feature on the Bold As Love site, for Ax's playlist, and a full chapter-by-chapter breakdown of sources and acknowledgements.

http://www.boldaslove.co.uk

About four a.m. Fiorinda and Sage decided they'd better leave the Disabled Toilet, fond as they had become of the place. They woke Ax up and persuaded him that this was a good idea. Cleaners, Ax. Folks with brooms and buckets; you don't want to meet them. The Rivermead Centre seemed deserted, blank corridors echoing with departed revelry. In the car park (ominous clanging noises from somewhere, no other signs of life) Sage hugged them goodbye and set off into the dark. But almost immediately he came loping back, hands in his pockets, shoulders forward, a dearly familiar tall silhouette, to where they were standing bereft, not knowing what to do with themselves. No, no no, he said. This is wrong. We stick together. C'mon, come back to the van.

They crossed the ghostly arena with its shadow-buried rainbow of towered stages and marquees and headed into the campground, still smashed enough that even Sage found his own back yard a puzzling wonderland. They could have gone on forever; they probably did go round in circles once or twice, sometimes on access lanes, sometimes threading their way by paths only staybehinds used, between rows of tents that lay like sleeping animals: hand in hand, leaning together or in Indian file, brushing past spider-pearled thickets of Traveller's joy and Michaelmas daisies; discussing their route in rapt whispers. It would have been paradise to go on forever, walking like this through the chill, river-misted night . . . no need for a house or a home, sleep under a hedge somewhere with the stars rustling overhead.

Instead, they reached the van, which turned out to be full of people, most of them unknown to the proprietor (as far as he could tell). They tiptoed past a couple of staybehind women who were having a hushed, early-hours conversation, stepped over the bodies on the floor in Sage's room (the boss's actual bed had remained sacred), and slept again, in the midst of the crowd. Many hours later Ax and Fiorinda woke alone, fully dressed, surrounded by digital hardware, and followed the scent of frying bacon to the kitchen – where they found Sage and his brother Heads, George and Bill and Peter, all four of them skullmasked as usual, with George Merrick's wife Laurel, Bill Trevor's posh girlfriend Minty LaTour, plus a grab-bag of Heads crewpersons, all engaged in cooking and eating a huge fried breakfast. Sage was cheerful and sweet, but a certain distance had been re-established, perhaps inevitably.

From there it was straight back to business as usual. The newly inaugurated Dictator and his girlfriend had to get to London and start establishing a *modus vivendi* with the suits. The Heads zoomed off to Truro, where they'd promised a free gig for the Cornish (most of whom had no tv reception at present, so they'd missed the big concert). The show must go on, while none of the ongoing emergencies let up. The three leaders of the Rock and Roll Reich didn't have another chance to examine their private life, all through the winter. But at last there came a pause, an equilibrium. At last a chance to take stock, count the bruises, relax a little. A dangerous time.

ONE

Sweetness And Light

'What's that?'

'Haydn. Okay?'

'Yeah, fine. Cruise, Sage.'

'Tisn't working.'

'I wonder . . .' muttered Ax. The Heads reckoned their boss was only safe to drive unaided when he was so wrecked he *knew* he was in trouble, which was not the case this morning. But there was a lot more room per vehicle on the roads these days, despite bomb-crater-sized potholes and long stretches where the surface had been hacked off by the righteous and never replaced. The van's erratic glide wasn't going to meet much opposition. Let him do without the autopilot, if it makes him happy. This is a holiday.

'I think I fell in love with you,' he said, 'the night we did the concert at the end of the Islamic Campaign. You remember?'

'Nah.'

'Sage, you are having me on. Cast your mind back. Bradford Civic Centre, end of January last year. Arabian Nights décor, inadequate stage crew. We'd been running around the Yorkshire Dales with a bunch of hippy guerrillas for three months, playing live-ammunition wargames with the Islamic Separatists. I sell my soul to make peace, we agree to do an armistice gig for both the armies.

I

No bands, just you and me: Aoxomoxoa on noise, stunt-dives and horrible special effects, Ax Preston on guitar. Worked out pretty well, considering.'

'Yeah, yeah, yeah. I didn't mean, *I don't remember*. I meant, what, only then, Ax? Now you have hurt my feelings.' The living skull turned to him, grinning in blithe affection.

If truth be known, he'd rather have had the guy's natural face today but—

'*Shit!* Watch the road—!'

Unfortunate that they should have hit a patch of traffic at that moment. Horns blared. A woman with a horse and cart was left yelling furiously . . . Well, strictly speaking, horse and cart rigs should keep to the left hand lane but—

'Sage, I think I'll drive.'

'No, no, no. *My* van. *I* drive.'

'Fuck. How old are you? Three and a half? Listen, if we were in a sports car I think I might let you kill me, but you could take out twenty innocent bystanders with this thing. I'm going to drive. Stop the van! NO! (he corrected himself, urgently), PULL OVER! Get off the roadway, *then* stop the van. DO IT, Sage—'

But when the great grey space capsule was parked on the hard shoulder (Sage having accomplished this feat without incident), Ax stayed where he was. They smiled at each other, while the cab filled and brimmed with stately, joyful music.

'Nah,' said Sage at last, 'can't be true. You can't have fallen for me only that night. I have never felt more *understood* in my life than I did that time, first time on stage with you. You must've been practising.'

'Maybe it was love at first sight.'

'Hahaha. I *don't* think so!'

In the lost past they had not been friends. They'd had one of those personality-clash feuds beloved of the music biz media: Aoxomoxoa, of Aoxomoxoa and the Heads,

2

shameless commercial techno-wizard (otherwise known as Sage Pender), always picking a fight with Ax Preston, the modest, critically acclaimed guitar-man.

'Okay, not love,' Ax conceded (though from this vantage point, all of it looked like loving). 'Intrigued at first sight. Or from an early date. Remember when I took you out drinking after you'd been slagging off my band on the tv? *Complacent nostalgia wank-aid for dreary little left wing acne-suckers*—'

'It all comes back to you.'

'Oh, I remember every word. That was when I first really looked at this—' He reached over and traced the eyesockets and cheekbones of the skull. 'There're a lot of digital masks around. This is something else. It's a serious piece of coding, and an amazing work of art.'

Sage kept very still, very happy to be touched. The avatar mask, that phenomenally expressive veil of coherent light, grinned between sheepish and self-mocking—

'I didn't believe you bought it off someone you met in a bar, either. Not one of your more convincing yarns. So then I started noticing how much got done, behind the drunken oaf cover. The bit-by-bit slog that goes into those immersions of yours. You and the Heads touring like maniacs, and a stage act you couldn't *survive* if you weren't in constant training. It nagged at me. If he made that mask, and if he's secretly so focused and organised, he's not stuck for inner resources. Why does the stupid bugger feel impelled to spend half his life *so fucking hammered* just walking across the room is a great big adventure?'

'Bored, bored, bored.'

'Not so bored now? Not so smashed so often, anyway.'

'Can't fit it into my ministerial diary, Sah. I never have the time to get decently trolleyed these days, I'm too busy being a workaholic bureaucrat. It's a disgrace.'

They collapsed into giggles. The situation they were in was so *ridiculous*.

'You ever going to tell me why you used to pick on me like that?' said Ax. 'Mr rich-as-fuck multi-eurobillionaire megastar? It was a mystery to me why you bothered.'

'Oh . . . Yeah, okay. I'll tell you. We were a pair, in the Indie music biz: equal and opposite. Ax Preston gets the critical acclaim and the cred, Sage gets the filthy money, and everyone's convinced that's just the way it ought to be. I was jealous.'

Ax looked amazed (he'd clearly been imagining some slightly more grown-up grievance all this time). 'Is that what it was? *Really?*'

'Really.'

'Well,' said Ax, after a moment, 'now I know your stuff better, I can't say I blame you. But it wasn't my fault. You should've *behaved* more like Leonardo da Vinci.'

'Ax, I'll never beat you at this game.'

'What game?'

'Forgiving, understanding. Maybe the game is being good.'

'Oh, I'm not good,' said Ax. 'I think *you* are good.'

They listened to the music for a while.

'We don't need the van,' said Sage at last.

'Nah.'

'Don't know why I brought it out.' He tapped the phone implant on his wrist. 'George . . . Hi, George, when you get to this, I've left the van by the road—' George Merrick was the second-in-command of Sage's band. Pause, while Sage looks out of the cab, peers around and finds nothing in the shattered concrete vistas of Reading's urban freeway that he can fix in his mind. 'Well, it's somewhere. Not far. Take it back to the Meadow, will you? Thanks.'

The van belonged in the Travellers' Meadow on River-mead Festival Site, where thousands of staybehinds had been living like Bangladeshi slumdwellers since Dissolution Summer, three and a half years ago. It wasn't as

4

bad as it sounded. In ways, the campers, in their lo-impact, alt.tech hippy squalor, were better off than the people of Reading town, now that the economic crash had really begun to bite. They got down and stood checking each other over: tall Sage with a living skull for a head, and skeleton-masked hands to match. Ax Preston, the Dictator of England, in his old leather coat, milky-brown skin and smooth dark hair of non-specific non-white origins, looking a little lost without a guitar attached.

Maybe the absence of guitar's the cause of the uncertainty crisis he's suffering, a worried frown in his pretty brown eyes—

'Are you still up for this, Sage? No second thoughts?'

The skull grinned at him. 'Not much option now, is there? Eh, Teflon-head?'

'Oh. Oh yeah, right.'

'Hahaha.'

They began to walk.

'You know, Ax, I can always tell when you are completely out of your tree.'

'Oh really, how is that?'

'You become convinced you're sober, an' you start ordering me around.'

'Do I? I'm sorry—'

'Nah, it's okay. I like it.'

Ax had driven down from London very early. He'd left his car parked near the Caversham Bridge to avoid getting hassled by Staybehind Gate Police over private transport hypocrisy. As they walked into town, passing empty plate-glass windows (where plate glass had survived) and the burnt-out gaps that had been fast-food chains or car salesrooms, they discussed going to look for it. But they reached the station first so they settled for the train, and the quiet intensity of sitting side by side among strangers: touching hands, brushing shoulders, traversing the crowds at Clapham Junction with that magic thrill in the blood – barely speaking, occasionally sharing a smile of delight.

'For once we can just enjoy this,' Ax said.

'Yeah. But it was there all the time.'

'I know.'

By mid-afternoon they were in Brighton. Neither of them knew the town, but the gazetteer on Ax's warehouse implant (though out of date) helped them to fool around. It was so bizarre, such a treat, to be idle together, the strains of their own music not infrequently washing over them as they prowled the fashion shoplets: two stunningly recognisable faces (one face, one mask) so studiously unrecognised it was like a cloak of invisibility. The Dictator and his friends never had to worry about invasion of privacy. That had been established very early on: Stone Age Fame, Fiorinda called it.

So this was Ax's England; this is the way we live now. In Reading town the violence of change was more obvious. Here, in a town which had always been Countercultural heartland, it looked more permanent. The music and video that acted as urban décor were cutting-edge, but the Shopping Mall Generics had vanished, taken over by farmers' markets. Personal cars had gone, or turned up ingeniously recycled. Asphalt and brick and concrete had been torn up to let weeds and wilderness flourish in the streets. There were marks of privation. The 'see a queue, join a queue' mentality of Eastern Europe prevailed. But the wandering crowds were peaceful; there were buskers but no beggars, and there were no weapons in sight. Considering the events of the last few years, that last was definitely a triumph.

At sunset the only street lighting was by ATP patches: cell metabolism energy, bio-activated by the fingertips of passers-by who had taken the treatment, Sage among them. They ate (Ax ate. Sage, typically, ignored some food), and went down to the beach, between the two piers. Evening crowds flowed on the promenade behind them, but they were alone on the shingle.

It was cold, the air was still, the sea murmured in the tawny dusk.

Sage folded himself, cross-legged, in one of his giant pixie poses. Ax sat wrapped in his leather coat, trusty old friend, examining an antique ring on his right hand. It was a birthday present from Fiorinda; he wasn't used to wearing it. The carnelian bevel had an inscription in Arabic: *this too will pass*. She gives me Solomon's ring . . . and is that a threat or a promise, my Fiorinda? I think it's a promise. Everything will pass, but not your love for me, my love for you. It was the twenty-first of February. He was just twenty-nine years old. He'd been Ceremonial Head of State for six months, the official leader of the English Countercultural Movement for a little longer.

In Dissolution Summer, when Mainland Britain was preparing to become, officially, three nations again, Paul Javert, the then Home Secretary, had set up what he called his Countercultural Think Tank: a sanitised alternative to the real eco-warriors, who were becoming such a scary force throughout Europe. The Westminster government had been planning to appoint a funky Green President to replace the departed Royals. Mr Javert had secretly decided to improve on that idea, blow away the real candidates and install his own hippy-rockstar puppet in the job. But his chosen figurehead had turned out to be a monster, and the situation in the country more volatile than anyone had guessed. Paul Javert's night of the long knives, when murder and mayhem invaded a government reception for the Think Tank, had marked the start of the green revolutionary Blitzkrieg that became known as the Deconstruction Tour, and a wild rollercoaster ride of a year, including a small war, and the death of the European internet by a demon virus . . . Through force of nightmare circumstances, none of Ax's choosing, the suits had found

7

themselves depending on Ax Preston, with a battle-hardened hippy army at his back, to keep the peace.

They'd been only too glad to offer him the Presidency, but he'd refused to let them call him President. The title he'd insisted upon gave him some bitter satisfaction.

Ax had wanted to be a leader. He'd seen the crash coming and he'd vowed to be one of the people trying to hold things together. He'd never expected anything like this.

'Times and times,' he said, turning the ring. 'I prayed to God we'd make it this far, and I didn't see how we could. Now I know that everything that's happened since Dissolution was the easy part. Now we have to keep it all going. Fuck.'

'No need to think about it tonight. Take the evening off.'

'What did we do with the shopping?'

'Can't remember. Something. Does it matter?'

'Not at all.'

He didn't eat, thought Ax. He never eats enough. Not a gram more than he has to, to keep that fabulous body in shape. But I am not going to nag. He took one of the skeleton hands and measured it against his own, the virtual fingers and the real ones. This was Sage's left hand, missing the fourth and fifth fingers. The right was worse off, having lost index and second finger and half a thumb. He thought of the ten-month-old baby, couldn't even talk, with meningitis and septicaemia, poor little scrap. They put him to sleep, he woke up and *what'd happened to his hands*? The little boy who refused to eat, because he couldn't stand the clumsiness of those maimed paws. Ah, God. Unbearable pity.

'How d' you decide how long to make the missing fingers?'

'These are my real hands.'

'What?'

8

'The masks are based on my bones the way they would have been. It's not hard to work out. Now ask me why I never wear fake normal hands, like a normal person would.'

'You can't fake anything. Remind me not to try and turn you into a diplomat.'

'Ha. I can lie. I do it all the time.'

'You can talk bullshit. There's a subtle difference. I wish I'd known you before.'

'You did. You didn't like me much.'

'I mean long ago. My life has had its ups and downs, but tonight it strikes me forcibly that you must have been horribly unhappy, for *years at a time*. I never put it together before. I wish I'd been there, to stop things from hurting you.'

'I deserved most of it,' said Sage. 'Not the meningitis, obviously, but the rest. If you'd known me when I was a teenage junkie you would not have liked me, Ax. But I know what you mean. Me, I have a desperate need to time travel somehow and punch out the playground racists – that you've never told me about, but I know the fucking south-west of this fucking country. You couldn't have missed them.'

Ax was from Taunton, Sage was from Cornwall. 'I'd have liked you,' said Ax firmly, 'if I'd known you. We should have been together; total waste of time that we weren't.'

'Never leave me, Ax.'

'I won't.'

They laughed, dropped the handclasp and looked away from each other, smiling. 'The racism didn't bother me,' said Ax. 'I was okay with it by the time I was ten. I resign myself to work around stuff like that.You write horrors like the *Arbeit Macht Frei* immersions, as you told me once, because you want *to see the world as hideous and miserable and terrible as it really is, and still find it loveable—*'

9

'Did I say that? God. I must have been pissed.'

'Pissed enough to trust me, briefly, on that night out. Then you were straight back to giving me unmitigated shit, any chance you got . . . But you'd changed, next time our paths really crossed, in Dissolution Summer. Still winding me up the whole time and habitually plastered, but you didn't seem to be finding the world such a difficult place to love. If you don't mind me saying so.'

Sage nodded. 'Yeah, well, that was Fiorinda. I'd met Fiorinda, the year before all of this shit started. In March, in Amsterdam . . . She turned everything around.'

When the three of them had joined Paul Javert's Think Tank (not even Ax having any idea what was really going on), Fiorinda had been sixteen. Sage had been playing the big brother, waiting for her to grow up, but he'd waited too long. It had been Ax who'd made the crucial move. It had only gradually dawned on him, through the terrifying months when his old enemy was becoming his best friend, that he'd cut Sage out . . . that Aoxomoxoa the bouncing sex-machine, the laddish fool you'd think couldn't deceive a fly, was secretly, passionately, permanently in love.

The problem was on the agenda, the unspoken agenda of this day and the drug they'd taken. But the right words wouldn't come. They looked at each other in silence, sad and helpless, the skull's frontal bones glimmering with a faint silver light. The look moved into a kiss, hard to say who initiated that, and then, irresistibly, into plenty more than a single kiss. Ax caught an alarming glimpse of what it might be like if he *ever really* had to fight this supple giant.

They flung apart from each other, breathing hard—

'*Don't ever do that to me*', snarled Ax.

'Do what?' demanded Sage, lying with an arm flung across his face. 'Who? Did what to whom? You absolutely sure that wasn't your idea?'

Ax chucked a couple of pebbles at the sea. 'Okay,' he said, 'sorry. Two sides to it.'

He heaved a sigh, moved over and shifted his friend's arm. The mask looked up at him, doing a heartrending line in *alone, conflicted and confused.* 'Hey, stop that. Not the whipped puppy dog. Knock it off, you're scaring me.'

'How do I know what's the right face to make? Me, crass, oversized, blundering oaf.'

Ax lay down, settling his head on Sage's shoulder. 'Huh. If you are so lost in the complex world of grown-up human emotions, maestro, who made the mask? Hmm?'

'Doesn't mean anything. A lot of that mapping, join-the-dots stuff is pre-conscious. Wood ants could build an avatar mask.'

'*Wood ants.* Tuh.'

The sea swooshed in and out. They stayed like that for a while, very happy.

At last Ax sat up and fetched out his smokes tin.

The cocktail party on West Pier, the gig that had brought them down here, was in full swing, all that lacy, artfully restored old ironwork lit like the Titanic on ghost-crab legs: a beached starship. Tinsel-faint wafts of music reached them, escaped from the sound-proofing. 'Now listen,' said Ax, lighting the spliff and handing it, 'we're going to Allie's party, and I put it to you that we walk in there tonight, we're the two coolest dudes in the *known universe.*'

'I thought you didn't like being famous.'

'Usually I don't. But this isn't celebrity culture, this is undeniable fact. Far as our island nation goes, right now, we fucking *are* the two coolest dudes in the known universe. Just for once, why don't we get some fun out of it? You up for that?'

'And no sarcastic rock and roll brat around to make her deflating little remarks. Yeah, let's go for it. Fuck, what is in this? It's blowing my head off.'

'That's because you've hardly eaten a thing all day. I've been watching you. It's only Bristol skunk . . . and you couldn't leave the street lighting alone, could you? You cannot drain your cell metabolism like that, and then not eat—'

'What would you know about it, *fogey*? I like draining my cell metabolism, it gives the world a nice edge, also like getting my head blown off—'

'Sage, pull yourself together. Coolest dudes. Can you do it? No falling over things?'

'Coolest dudes. I will not to fall over anything. But now I need a shit.'

'Oh, God. Trust you. Well, you can't do it here. You cannot shit on a public beach.'

'Why not? This would be a Rivermead GM turd, with unzip bugs. Be gone in an hour. Okay, okay, if it worries you. Ax, how you got to be the leader of the outlaw unwashed I will never know. I'll be dead suburban, I'll go and shit in the water. I hope a terrible wave doesn't come and drown me.'

'Then I'd be sorry—' Ax stopped laughing. He could see this wave. 'Hey, be careful.'

'Calm down, there is no terrible wave. Maybe you better come and hold my hand.'

The party was being thrown by Allie Marlowe, Queenpin administrator of the Rock and Roll Reich, and a Brighton local. There was quite a crowd: the Few and friends, core members of the Rock and Roll Reich, mingling graciously with south coast Countercultural luminaries, favoured media-folk, non-Few rockstars, other useful people. Ax and Sage walked in and caused a satisfying stir. They presented themselves to their hostess (an ill woman to cross, Allie: better make sure and be polite), who congratulated them for turning up. They then forgot about being the coolest dudes and made for the bar, where they stood, forgetting to drink and ignoring everyone, talking about Fiorinda.

In Dissolution Summer she'd been the Indie babystar with a past: a teenage vagrant, recruited off the streets by DARK, infamous Teesside dyke-rockers – and then outed by the music press as the daughter of Rufus O'Niall, veteran Irish megastar. Ax had known the ugly story behind that connection and admired the kid's courage, but had not been inspired to check out the music before she was his girlfriend.

'I knew what DARK were like, and I knew *you'd* taken her under your wing, which I'm afraid did not give me confidence. I had to get hold of *No Reason* and listen to it when she wasn't around, to find out whether she was total crap—'

'Hahaha. Then you got a surprise.'

'*Yeah.*' Ax shook his head fondly, remembering. 'She blew me away. She was fantastic. But you knew that—'

No Reason was the debut album DARK had made with Fiorinda. It had transformed the band's fortunes. Without her, they'd been a disaster with flashes of genius. With her, they were extraordinary: mind-blowing rough diamonds, though still fully as volatile.

'I knew,' agreed Sage, the skull grinning sweet and rueful. 'Oh yes. She was like that the first time I saw her on stage. Fourteen years old, screaming like a banshee, having distinct difficulty singing and playing a guitar at the same time—'

'Well, it's a situation I try to avoid, myself.'

'But she was the business—'

'Dunno why I bothered, looking back. It was about a year before she condescended to turn up at a Chosen Few gig—'

The Chosen Few, now generally known as the Chosen, because *the Few* meant something else, was Ax's band, comprising two of his brothers and his ex-girlfriend Milly Kettle on drums. They didn't play a big part in the Reich, preferring to stay in the background and keep out of politics.

Fiorinda stories from long ago, some of them new to Ax even now. Her epic fights with Charm Dudley, DARK's rabidly bad-tempered front woman. Her cut-crystal in-your-face management style with the government suits. Her secrets. (Have you ever caught her writing a song? Nah. Nor me. Always happens when I'm off the premises.) The shock of her intelligence. How much they missed the arrogant, oblivious, cruelly damaged teenager they had known. How much they loved the person she had become.

The party chattered on. Across the room, above a frieze of heads, a big screen was showing tv coverage of the Armada concert, finalé of the Boat People tour last summer. They paused to watch. Fiorinda and DARK with Ax Preston as an emergency stand-in guitarist, quite a change in demeanour for the Chosen's sober, reserved virtuoso—

'Did you plan to carry on like that?' asked Sage. He'd been elsewhere that night.

'No! I planned to blend in with the wallpaper, so that Charm would not hate me—'

'Nyah. Not worth worrying about. Charm hates everyone, regardless.'

'But with DARK, blending in means—'

'Go for it 'til you fall down bleeding at the nose and ears.'

'Yeah. So it just happened.'

The rock and roll brat, meanwhile, in her tight-waisted red and gold Elizabeth dress, red curls falling around her face, was simply standing there: no can-can kicks, no cartwheels. This they didn't like so much as the sight of Ax thrashing it up with a bunch of deranged dyke-rockers. They knew what a feat of alcohol and raw courage was keeping her upright. But how the cameras loved her. They gazed, absorbed: turned away again as soon the scene changed.

'You know,' remarked Sage, 'I really don't like Charm Dudley. She's mean and deranged and I stand by that judgement. But it must have been a hell of a thing. All through Dissolution Summer I kept thinking, I'm fucking glad that firestorm of a brat didn't happen to *my* band.'

They laughed and talked of other things, only for the pleasure of coming back to Fiorinda in a little while. Ax was launching an education scheme: futuristic-Utopian training in the arts and crafts, for the children of the revolution. He needed to convince the media people, and the great English public, that this was a brilliant idea – without arousing the suspicions of the Ancient Brits. The Ancient British tendency (who now called themselves 'Celtics' and were aligned with the Pan-European Celtics across the Channel) were anti-science, anti-recovery, covertly racist and dangerously attractive.

It was a hijack. You didn't hear Ireland, Scotland and Wales calling themselves the 'Celtic nations' much any more – they did not wish to be associated. And yet, needless to say, the sinister romantics had their fans among the suits. Neo-feudalism sounded very good to some of the bastards in mainstream government. How to combat the Celts? Definitely not at the cost of a civil war in the Counterculture. They talked it round, planning the moves together the way they'd planned guerrilla actions in Yorkshire . . . Masterclasses in music tech; rock and roll history in hedgeschool kindergartens. Involve the rest of the arts, bridge the gap between the CCM and the rest of the country. Get some irresistible albums out—

The music meant something different now. Crowd control. Psychological landscape. Connection with the modern world, which was their lost past—

'I wish you'd sing more,' said Ax. 'You have such a great

voice. There are songs I'd love to hear you do, and so would the punters, if they only knew it—'

'Nah.'

'But no, you prefer to hide behind those hardman circus stunts that scare me to death, and I'm sure you're going to kill yourself—'

'I am not going to kill myself. Knock it off, Ax. Look, if I sing, I have to take care of the voice, an' taking care of *the body* (yeah, go on, laugh, my stock-in-trade) is enough of a time-consuming hobby. Why don't *you* sing for them?'

'Because I can't.'

'Now that is *nonsense*—'

But the pauses became longer. Sentences broke off and fell into pools of engrossing silence. They left the spot where they'd taken root, went out on deck and stood leaning against the rail, backs to the water, elbows touching, breathing slow, sinking deeper and deeper into the feeling—

'Sage?'

'Ax.'

'Let's go home.'

Fiorinda had had the flu for Christmas, gone back to work too soon and succumbed to an attack of bronchitis. The after-effects were enough to keep her indoors on a chilly, damp February night. Well, she wouldn't have known where to put herself at Allie's gig, in the circumstances. So this is what happens. You are poorly, so your boyfriend abandons you to spend the day with his best mate, and they're going to your best girlfriend's party out of their heads on *hideous mind-destroying drugs*—

She'd planned to go to bed early. At midnight she was sitting up reading, drinking red wine and trying not to worry. When friends take oxytocin, the intimacy drug, things have been known to go horribly wrong. Especially when the friends are the same sex, and heterosexual (or more or less heterosexual, darling Ax . . .) Fiorinda hated modern drugs anyway. Taking massive doses of enhanced human biochemicals for fun sounded to her like feeding cows on dead cows. You don't need the details; if you have any sense you *know* it's a terrible idea. They'll be okay. Sage will be in charge, because it is drugs. Or Ax will be in charge, because Sage loves that. Anyway one of them will be in charge. They always do that, very clever; or maybe it's genetic, a male thing, to avoid—

The entryphone chimed.

She had to go down and let them in.

'Sorry,' said Ax, on the doorstep, 'couldn't find my key.'

'You don't have a key, idiot. You look at the ID thing with your eyes. What are you doing back here, you futile creatures? You can't have a pair bond with three in it.'

'We're not interested in any other kind,' said Sage, and kissed the tip of her nose.

'DON'T kiss my nose! I HATE it when you do that!'

But he had followed Ax upstairs, laughing.

In the big living-room they were walking around, beaming weirdly. Ax had taken off his coat and Sage his outer scummy sweater. Fiorinda returned to her book. She'd been asleep when Ax left for Reading (actually, pretending to be asleep, to signal her disapproval). 'Is that what you were wearing at Allie's party? She *will* have been impressed.' There was nothing wrong with Ax's dark red suit except that it was a little shabby, which should be a virtue these days. Sage was wearing his beloved slick, Imipolex, one-shouldered black dungarees (easy for hosing down), over a dreadful Hard Fun Tour hoodie, the Heads itinerary dates illegible with age. It might once have been grey. Or maybe mud-brown.

'Uh, yeah?'

'Are we not modish enough? Maybe that's what was up with her.'

'She didn't say anything—'

17

'I don't remember whether she said anything. But I received tetchy vibes.'

'Oh, surely not,' said Fiorinda. 'She would not have wasted her fire.'

Fiorinda was occupying one couch, along with Ax's cat, who was fast asleep on a cushion. They took the other: Sage stretched out, Ax propped against it on the hearth rug, in front of the old flame-effect gas stove. 'Is this room warm enough?' asked Sage. 'Can we turn that up? You have to keep warm, Fee.'

'I am very cosy. Leave the stove alone, both of you. The state you are in, you will do yourselves a damage, or set the place on fire. So, is it turning out the way you expected?'

Sage looks at Ax, Ax looks at Sage. They have a little staring match: probably breathing in synchrony. She's not going to get an answer. Either they've forgotten the question, or neither of them is going to be the first to back down and say yes, or no.

'What's it *feel* like,' she asked (her attitude softened by the fact that nothing seemed to have gone horribly wrong), 'doing oxytocin?'

'Depends who you are and who you're taking it with,' said Sage, disengaging from the stare to grin at the ceiling: a skull in a soppy dream. 'If you're me, and taking it with Ax, it feels not unlike being three years old and spending a happy day pottering around, doing nothing much, with your mother.'

'I'd go with that,' said Ax, smiling at his huge infant. 'Only different.'

'I may throw up.' She wondered about Allie's party. 'Could you behave normally if you wanted to?'

'Oh yeah,' said Ax. 'It's very mild, really.'

'Are we not behaving normally?' asked Sage, and both of them started laughing like fools: then stopped, gazing at each other with such grave happiness—

'Maybe I'll go to bed and leave you to it.'

But she did not throw up, or go to bed. She stayed, pretending to read, unable to tear herself away. They didn't seem to mind. Ax went and fetched an acoustic guitar, sat down and made sure it was in tune. He started to play, looking at Sage expectantly. She was so flustered by the situation, it wasn't until Sage began to sing that she realised Ax was playing 'Stonecold', Fiorinda's own paradoxical, teenage-vagrant anthem, her first big hit, her first *big* song. What on earth's going on?

She hid behind her book, wishing she hadn't tied up her hair, depriving herself of her usual retreat behind a mass of tangled curls. They played the song through, then they stopped and discussed the chords, the key-changes, the melody, laughing about the time last year when 'Stonecold', along with Fiorinda's solo album, *Friction*, had wiped the floor with the opposition, Ax and Sage's bands included. So life goes on, and people keep buying music, in the midst of catastrophes. Fucking babystars, they said, grinning sweetly. Makes yer sick. Thank God she never did that aerobics video. Then the song again, word perfect, note perfect, and 'Stonecold' is a *good* song, not a forced rhyme or an off syllable: her own music that still gives her goosebumps, the shivering feeling of power running through her—

'Is this okay?' said Sage, as if suddenly realising they had an audience.

Fiorinda nodded, keeping her nose in her book.

When they'd finished with 'Stonecold', they did 'Rest Harrow': Fiorinda gets ecological (and she'd never realised how much of Sage there was in that song, hayseed, plough boy, until she heard him sing it). Then another, less familiar track from *Friction*, and another. Song after song, getting the same intense, loving attention, Ax adding to the guitar part, how could he not, but never taking over, always staying close to what she'd written.

This oxy must be good stuff. They didn't steal her wine,

or either of them even light a cigarette, they just went on playing and singing Fiorinda's music. She'd had *no idea* they could do this. She forgot to be embarrassed and simply listened, and watched them. They were so beautiful together, locked into each other, her tiger and her wolf.

A longer pause. What next?

It was 'Pain', the original Fiorinda-song, with the stupid monochrome tune and the ridiculous teen-angst words, that she had never released, and never would, though fans yelled for it at gigs and sometimes got it. The song she had scribbled in the middle of the night, under a 40-watt bulb in a hostel dormitory, when she was a lost, desperate, bitter little kid, wanting to tell the world what it's like when pain is all there is (as if the world didn't know) . . . that she'd screeched out like a crazy prayer from the stage, all through Dissolution Summer; and put behind her, and been ashamed of – and here it was restored to her by Ax's skill and Sage's voice, the way it had felt when she wrote it, but totally different; made beautiful.

> Live even in the pain, deep inside the pain . . .
> Live for this moment . . .

Tears stung her eyes. She turned a page with shaking fingers: invaded, heartwrung, overwhelmed, staring at the print and seeing nothing, until the music ended.

Ax put his guitar aside. There was a pause, then Sage said he thought he'd go to bed. He'd sleep in the music room, as usual when he stayed. They had a spare bedroom, but it was unfurnished (they'd only moved into this place last May) and full of junk.

'You want me to sort you out a duvet and stuff?' said Ax.

'Nah. I know where to find things.'

Sage prowled halfway to the door, big and graceful, but undecided, as if he'd forgotten something but couldn't remember what it was . . . not an unusual state of affairs for the perfect master of short-term memory loss. He came back, dropped on one knee beside the couch and kissed Ax gently on the lips. 'G'night . . .' He started to get up again, then changed his mind. The mask vanished. Sage's natural face appeared, blue eyes wide and dreamy, that big soft beautiful mouth between solemn and smiling—

'I've been wanting you to do that all day,' said Ax.

'I know,' said Sage, and kissed him again, this time both of them getting into it, a deep kiss, a soul kiss, Ax's fingers locked in Sage's close-cropped yellow curls.

Sage stood up.

'G'night Fee,' he said, and left them.

'*God*,' said Fiorinda, fascinated. 'Why don't you go after him?'

Ax laughed, leaned back on the couch and stretched his arms.

'Because, little cat, in the morning I'll be sober, and so will he.'

'Perhaps more to the point,' suggested Fiorinda demurely. Ax could be a bit of a chameleon. Aoxomoxoa, despite the wishful dreams of the nation's gay community, was definitely one way only. In normal life. She peeped at her boyfriend over the top of that useful book. 'If we go to bed and fuck now I am going to feel extremely weird, knowing I'm supposed to be six foot six with a curly blond brush-cut.'

'Hahaha. Lay off. Have respect for a man's drug experience.' Ax sighed, and smiled. 'What happened with Sage's mother? If I ever knew, I've forgotten.'

'She quit when he was ten or so. Got sick of the hippies-in-a-cottage drop-out dream, I think. He didn't see her for years. He sees her now, sometimes. He says it's like another incarnation. She's someone else. She's not much interested and neither is he. He says.'

'Oh. Sad . . . Still, it's something to have had a happy

childhood. Which I think he did, in spite of his hands and all that. Unlike you or me, or most of the people we know. It grounds him, rock steady. Makes him someone . . . very safe to be with. Don't you think?'

'A lot of people wouldn't instantly recognise Aoxo-moxoa from that description.'

'Oh.'

'But I do. Yes.'

About noon the next day Ax came into the kitchen of the Brixton flat and found Sage, masked, eating toast and reading the broadsheet newspaper that Ax (such a fogey!) had delivered to the door. Elsie the cat was on the top of the fridge, disgruntled. She didn't like Sage. The feeling was mutual. Sage didn't approve of pet animals.

'Hi,' said Ax, looking at the door of the fridge.

'Mm,' said Sage, concentrating on the paper.

'Sleep okay?'

'Yeah . . . She's well again, isn't she?'

'Oh yeah, she's fine. All better.'

This was a relief. Bronchitis doesn't sound like much, but it had dragged on and they'd been scared, though they'd had to hide it from the babe. Some fantastic futuristic medicine survived in Crisis England, but simple things like effective antibiotics were gone. But she's tougher than she looks . . . thank God. The fridge made no sudden moves. It was old-fashioned whiteware, though green enough in its habits, unlike the fridge in Sage's van, which was a futuristic womb-like thing with a superb energy audit. Ax picked off a magnet and replaced it carefully in line with the chrome door handle.

'Want to take back anything you said yesterday?'

'Nothing I said, and nothing I did.'

He risked a glance around. The living skull was giving him a look he'd never seen before, kind of a tender, outgoing mix of *enigmatic smile*. Sweet trick.

'We have to talk,' said Ax.

'Yeah. But not this morning. Got to get to work. Later.' And off he went.

Fiorinda was back at her desk in the Office at the Insanitude, the Rock and Roll Reich's London head-quarters. It was freezing (the San's righteous building management refused to turn the heating up). She was wearing two cardigans (the top one fluffy and orange, which clashed splendidly with her hair) over a fifties antique party dress in indigo moire satin, looking like the dawn of a stormy day and feeling energised and cheerful. She had an office of her own, and a secretary too, but she rarely visited them in person. She preferred the buzz of this big, gaudy, shabby room with the view over the Victoria Monument, Allie's admin staff chatting, people wandering to and fro, the familiar irritating album-hopping on the sound system.

The political Counterculturals, staybehinds on the Festival sites, urban communards, looked after them-selves, and accepted their supposed rockstar government as a useful fiction. The barmy army, Ax's military, had their own organisation. Fiorinda's business was with the real drop-outs, the huge dangerous mass of people (nominally green, really just hopeless) who had simply given up, in the economic collapse, and taken to the roads. Keeping track of them, keeping them fed and sheltered and feeling good about themselves, was quite a job. But it must be done, or there'd be hell to pay.

She checked on various situations, cursing under her breath as she ran into Ivan/Lara bulkheads that separated the Insanitude network from the Westminster government departments. The data quarantine imposed by the Internet Commissioners, US-based firemen of the data networks, was ruthless. They'd cut the undersea cables, fried the earth stations; they policed the airwaves and all physical

traffic to make sure nothing in Europe could get out . . .
Allegedly, total hygeine would mean time off for good
behaviour, but how would the situation benefit from
ridiculous paranoia about a network (the Insanitude network) that had actually *never been infected*? Oh well. She
would have to go and visit the DETR in person; that
usually sorted them out.

More greenfield campgrounds. Fuck. The Reich was
fiercely opposed to countryside camping. They tried to
keep their nomads on wasteground, on brownfields, but
the demand for unskilled agricultural labour was making
that impossible. Long gone were the days when Fiorinda
had had to scratch around for harmless work that her
healthy drop-outs could handle. Luckily they enjoyed
being a Land Army, and they were getting better at it.

She did what she could, and then checked the Magic
Scrapbook, a bulletin board on the Volunteer Initiative
intranet where her staff posted *strange phenomena* stories:
ghosts, ghoulies, animal transformations, talking trees.
Faith healing, Celtic rituals and prophetic dreams . . . A
lot of these reports were perfectly genuine, alas, but she
was glad to see that the level of action was still piddling, no
different from what you saw in the mainstream media.
Anne-Marie Wing, the Few's token hippy earth-mother,
said the emergent psychic powers of the English were
being blocked by an unknown force. Fiorinda, whose own
psychic powers would have caused quite a blip on the
graph, just hoped they would stay that way. She had a very
low opinion of strange phenomena.

'Magic is no friend to civilised society,' she murmured.

But there was nothing to worry about, not yet . . . She
shut everything down, peeled off her throat mic, tipped
her earbead into a paperclip tray and sat back. On either
side of the central doors to the Balcony stood pasteboard
blow-ups of two of the photographs that had been used
on the New Year's postage stamps. One was a brilliant

montage of Ax on stage with DARK and Fiorinda, at the Armada concert. The other was the famous photo of Sage spinning Fiorinda above his head, in the Battle of the Sexes Masque at Reading last September. She smiled at them. My tiger and my wolf.

The oxytocin serenade was still running through her head. And what will come of that night? She didn't know, not yet. But she was sure it would be something good.

She picked up her saltbox – the only memento she valued from her hated childhood – dropped the polished birchwood apple into her bag and went to join the others.

At the other end of the room the Few were gathered around the circle of battered schoolroom tables where they traditionally held conclave. These were the survivors of the original Countercultural Think Tank, and Mr Dictator Preston's closest associates. The atmosphere was informal. Wine was being drunk, spliff passed, sodium chloride-free snackfood from the works canteen disparaged. Roxane Smith, ex-man and veteran music critic, had put hir feet up, wrapped hir Dantesque velvet robes around hir and was resting hir eyes. Kevin Verlaine, Rox's young boyfriend, and Chip Desmond, Ver's partner in an esoteric techno duo called The Adjuvants, were plaguing the Dictator, trying to get him to divulge his pulling techniques . . . from before he was famous and didn't need any. Felice Hall, Cherry Dawkins and Dora Devine, aka the Powerbabes – vocalists and horn section from the Snake Eyes Big Band – offered helpful jeers.

Rumour has it Ax Preston used to be a *smooooth* operator—

'Sorry,' says Ax, grinning, 'it's been a long time. I can't remember.'

'You should be going after Sage,' advised Felice, senior Babe. 'He's the sex machine.'

Her fellow Powerbabes greeted this with some wicked snickering.

'Nah, Sage is useless,' said Verlaine, pushing back his silky brown Cavalier ringlets (today topped by a dashing Jimi Hendrix hat). 'We've observed his crap methods. He just bounces up to the babes and goes "Hey, I'm Aoxomoxoa, wanna fuck?"'

'If it stops working,' said the king of the one night stand, unmoved, 'I'll let you know.'

Rob Nelson, Snake Eyes front man and boyfriend to the Babes, wanted to discuss a scurrilous sketch in the latest issue of the staybehinds' vidzine *Weal*. Rob had been a music-biz political activist before the crash. He didn't like being called a member of a fascist junta. It hurt his feelings.

'Rob, dear boy,' said Rox, opening half an eye, 'if you must read your reviews, try to see the good in them. The piece was very flattering about the Few's actual music.'

'I don't blame *Weal*. They have a right to insult us, we're successful aren't we? I just don't want to be taken out and shot in the next blood-fest, because some slimy crypto-Celtic hippy freelance gave us a reputation we don't deserve.'

'I would *hate* that,' agreed Sage.

'It's an arms race situation,' said Fiorinda, coming up from the admin end and taking her usual place between Ax and Sage, Fiorinda's bodyguards. 'If we react, we're just helping the bastards to get better at fucking us up. And you have to admit, it was our beloved leader's own idea to call himself Dictator.'

'What can I say?' said Ax. 'It seemed like a good idea at the time. Relax, Rob. We're getting into education. The coup-merchants will see that, realise we're pathetic losers and leave us alone out of pity.'

'Hey,' announced Chip, sweet black angel style-victim in

retro-punk-chic, his hair a tiny rug of green and blue spikes on the top of his head. 'Fiorinda's back! Cool!'

The rock and roll brat was cheered and toasted. She was invited to take a bow, but she wouldn't; her saltbox was passed around to enliven the pondweed crackers.

'Fiorinda,' said Chip, gallantly, 'you're our survival tool.'

'Thank you so much. Give me my box back.'

'Hippy insults don't worry me,' said Dilip Krishnachandran, the slender, doe-eyed mixmaster general: pushing fifty and still beautiful. 'It's the glamset I'm afraid of. The shiny people love the green revolution, they want to be part of this, but what do we have to offer? Community Service? Free concerts where every bedraggled outlaw also has a backstage pass? I don't think so.'

None of the Few, except for Aoxomoxoa and the Heads, had been exactly famous before Dissolution Summer. They'd spent the chaotic years since then mostly on the road, slogging their guts out beside the army and the police, struggling to keep the peace. It was disconcerting to come down from that long, strange trip and find celebrity England carrying on as usual (except that ultra-green was the new shade of opinion) and eager to fête the leaders of the Reich.

'The Few only want to be with the Few. That's the accusation, and they are right. But how can we help it?'

'We could try to make it less fucking obvious,' muttered Allie Marlowe, who was sitting beside Dilip, head down, ostentatiously catching up on some paperwork. The tetchy vibes were not in doubt.

'Genuinely sorry about that, Allie,' said Ax.

'Don't worry, Ax,' said Allie darkly. 'I know *whose fault it was*.'

'Remind me,' sighed Roxane, opening half an eye again, 'what outrageous rock and roll behaviour has Sage committed this time? The casualties? The damage to property?'

'Shit, Rox,' Chip rolled his eyes. 'You were there. You saw him. He failed to mingle!'

'The unforgivable crime,' sighed Dilip, taking the spliff Chip passed to him.

'I don't know why you're all blaming Sage,' said Fiorinda. 'The oxy was Ax's idea.'

'This is true,' said Ax. 'I led him astray.'

'Nah. I claim equal responsibility,' declared Sage. 'And I too am truly sorry. Turning up mildly drugged to a cocktail party, shit, my, my. What was I thinking of—?'

Everyone laughed. 'You can all fuck off,' growled Allie. 'That stuff is important.'

Yeah, yeah. We know. We need the support, we have to play the game.

Fiorinda noted the covert relief in her friends' laughter, the Few very glad to know that Ax and Sage's big night out had Fiorinda's seal of approval. Sigh. Who needs paparazzi with this lot breathing down your neck? But she accepted the inevitable. The real core of Ax's organisation was many thousands strong, a network of like minds – some of them police officers and soldiers, some ordinary punters, even a few government suits – who had worked together, over and around the criminially insane, understanding how bad things were, knowing how much worse it could still get. But it would always come back to this handful of people here: Ax and Sage and Fiorinda, Rob and the Powerbabes, Dilip and Chip and Verlaine, Rox and the Heads. They had to stick together, imprinted on each other.

It's okay, she thought, silently addressing her *de facto* family (the only kind of family she would ever acknowledge. Fiorinda hated blood-relationships). The situation between the three of us may look dodgy, but it's okay. We can work it out.

Shortly, Sage's brother Heads turned up, bringing with them a couple of illustrious non-Few musicians. The mainstream media folk arrived and the press conference began: live radio; live terrestrial tv for the parts of the country that had reception. The Few played merrily with the concept of Rock and Roll as a culture. For we have our rabid rulers and our huddled masses, we have our scientists and our artists, our dynasties and our battlefields, our liberal bourgeoisie and even our sufragettes. Peter Grant for Bismark, and Jimmy Page for zee Kaiser! Jimi Hendrix is Einstein, and Eric Clapton is Rutherford. Everyone knows Bob Dylan is Shakespeare, but we could have, say, Thom Yorke for Thomas Hardy, Polly Harvey for Virginia Woolf! Madonna as the Margaret Thatcher of Rock!

Then Ax came in with the serious message. If someone doesn't teach the children of the drop-out hordes *something, someway* there's going to be an appalling problem in ten, fifteen years' time. We think we can reach them. We're going to teach them our craft, but we're also going to tell them about the history of this music, and the grassroots Utopian movement that has been entangled with it. The good and the bad, the betrayals, the triumphs. It's important for kids to have a framework, a context for their lives.

And yeah, before you tell me, it's artificial. We're going to be offering this from above. But that's the way things work. Culture is naturally artificial.

'Will the Counterculture buy it, Ax?' asked the EBC radio front man. 'Aren't your citizens going to say, *you're* okay, Ax, and we love your guitar. But rock and roll isn't a native tradition. Aren't they going to say this is from the heart of the evil empire?'

'For the record, I don't see the US as an "evil empire". I hate that line. But no nation has a monopoly on rock and roll. The music goes around and around, high culture into pop culture and back again . . . England, Ireland, West Africa, USA, Asia. Our roots are everywhere.'

'So is the Utopian thinking,' added Roxane Smith. 'You know, Anil, the original arts colony at Woodstock, New

York State, where tradition now says the Woodstock concert was held (of course, that's not quite the case) was founded by followers of John Ruskin, the art critic, in imitation of the English arts and crafts movement? A movement which was influenced itself by the nineteenth-century Utopians of India and Pakistan—'

Anil was the radio man, and a highly influential journalist these days. Radio tends to survive when newspapers and tv and the internet vanish.

'Paul Javert had his own reasons,' said Ax, 'when he picked rockstars for his team. But it works, because this music genuinely is the art form of our times. It's folk, and futuristic. It embodies the idea that cutting-edge technology can be used, without harm to the environment, to express universal human emotions. To make us more ourselves—'

'A boy's relationship with his electric guitar,' murmured Fiorinda. 'That's the universal human nature of the Rock and Roll Reich—'

'Thank you, Fiorinda—'

'But wasn't all that primitive sixties idealism naïve and corrupt?'

'For sure,' said Sage. 'We just said that, cloth ears. Bad stuff, good stuff. Being naïve and corrupt is a vibrant part of our cultural heritage, which we fully acknowledge.'

'You were always into the history, weren't you?' remarked Dian Buckley, favoured media babe. 'Snake Eyes and their "post-Motown" sound. Sage and his Dead fixation—'

'A lot of musicians are into the past,' said George Merrick, with dignity. 'A grounding in the classics can be very useful.'

'You learn things,' explained Peter Stannen, 'that you didn't know before.'

The term *Celtic* was never mentioned. No need to spell it out. These were tame media folk, they knew what was going on. They were happy to collude with Mr Dictator in his war of ideas . . . The discussion was lively; the Few played their usual parts. Some of the admin staff left; others stayed, while London grew dark outside; the session broke up in music, as Ax's media briefings generally did.

The Triumvirate lingered until they were alone in the room.

'Did you talk to Jordan?' asked Fiorinda. 'Has the baby got a name yet?'

Milly Kettle, the Chosen's drummer and Ax's ex-girlfriend, had been Jordan Preston's girlfriend since a short while before Ax and Fiorinda met. Their first baby had been born in November, but remained nameless. Communication with Taunton, under Crisis conditions, could be difficult.

'Yeah, I got through eventually. Nah, no name. My dad is still fucking with their heads, trying to get them to call the poor kid something idiotic. I have once more vetoed Slash, and I hope my voice will be heard.'

'But Ax, you should be pleased. I-am-a-Hard-Rock-Idiot Preston Mark Two. What could be more fitting?'

Ax looked a little hunted. 'Please don't start. The media folk have left the building.'

'I'm not going to start. I think your education scheme is a wonderful idea. The drop-out kids will ponder on the chord structure of *All Along The Watchtower* the way children of yesteryear studied Ox Bow Lakes, and who is to say which knowledge is more useless? Not me . . . Whose idea was Marlon, Sage?'

Marlon was Sage's twelve-year-old son. He lived in Wales with his mother; Sage didn't often see him. Mary Williams had been Sage's girlfriend when he was a teenage junkie with a taste for domestic violence. She was tough on visiting rights.

'Mary's. But I like it. I think it's after a Welsh god. Or it might be something to do with the kindness of strangers, I don't know. I've never cared to ask her.'

Smalltalk ground to a halt. Fiorinda studied the mackerel patterns on her indigo skirts. She looked up and found them staring at her with such doubtful, solemn intensity that chills went up her spine. Sage had taken off the mask.

'What's the matter?'

'Nothing,' said Ax. 'Nothing at all. We were wondering if you'd like to get down to Cornwall for a few days, for a break.'

Cornwall meant Tyller Pystri, Sage's cottage on the North Cornish coast.

'We can take the time off,' said Sage. 'And you need some fresh air.'

'Okay,' said Fiorinda slowly. 'Good idea. Count me in.'

The Heads had been down in Cornwall doing some filming (for a project that was being kept very firmly under wraps). They'd stayed at the cottage. Everything was clean and tidy, but there was a faint spoor of alien presence: in the stone-flagged kitchen, in the dusky living room where Sage's big bed stood, in the freezing bathroom with the ancient pebble-patterned linoleum, in the bedroom that Fiorinda and Ax used. Fiorinda walked around, discovering things out of place and setting them back where they should be. On the upstairs landing, with the windowseat over the garden and the bookcase full of childrens' classics, icy rain spattered the windowpanes, drowning the last of the light. She stood listening to the roar of the little river Chy in its miniature gorge. Stupid. Tyller Pystri doesn't belong to you. This is not home. You've only been here twice . . . She leaned her forehead against the dark glass, feeling almost frightened. What am I doing here?

Down in the kitchen Ax was frying eggs, while Sage put together a plate of chicken salad for himself from the cold food Mrs Maynor, his housekeeper, had left ready. They stopped talking when she came in. 'Hi Fee,' said Sage, with false bonhomie. 'Lemme give you some wine. What d'you want to eat?' He poured the wine, precariously, with his awkward right hand; she knew better than to take the job away from him.

'I'm not hungry.'

She lifted a small piece of chicken from his plate and nibbled it.

'Hey. Do you have to do that?'

'What's the matter?'

'She does it to me too,' said Ax. '*I'm not hungry*, then nibble, nibble . . . Drives me nuts. Say the word, I'll make you a fried egg sandwich, Fiorinda. All of your own.'

'Okay, fuck it,' said Fiorinda. 'I said I'm not hungry. Keep your crummy sandwich.'

They looked at each other, two men and a girl, an abyss suddenly opening. Does this work? Are we far too old? Is she too young? Do we even *like* each other?

Fiorinda went to tend the living-room fire.

Sage and Ax followed her and ate their food, making stilted conversation, while she stared at the flames and drank her wine, wondering what the fuck had gone wrong.

'Shall I put on some music?'

'Nah,' said Ax, getting up quickly and hurrying to the dead media wall, which was stacked with a collection handed down by Sage's parents. 'I'll do it. You don't know what you're doing with this catalogue, and you'll scratch the vinyl.'

'Thanks for reminding me how old you both are. Practically thirty. Wow, how weird that must feel. Jimi Hendrix was *long dead* before he got to your age.'

'I didn't mean—'

'Wasn't he? Not that I would know, of course, being a girl and totally ignorant.'

Ax spent ten minutes dithering over the antiques, and

was impelled by some kind of death wish to put on Ry Cooder, which he knew Fiorinda hated. Sage fetched a jigsaw from the games cupboard. They sat on the floor, sorting straight edges for what felt like hours, in a painful attempt to recapture the mood. Last year, when Tyller Pystri had been their haven, when this firelit room had been a bittersweet paradise . . . At last Fiorinda fetched her book and another glass of wine and settled on the edge of the fender, leaving them – she hoped – to improve their tempers.

'Do you have to sit right there, little cat?'

'Yeah, do you mind? Could we see some fire?'

'Ah, let her alone,' said Ax, 'she can't help it. She's an obligate fire-hogger.'

'She's finished the wine too.'

'She always does that. Let's make her get another bottle.'

They laughed, exchanging very weird looks of guilty complicity.

Fiorinda stood up. 'Okay. *Enough.* I don't know know what the fuck's got into you two. I don't know why you're being so horrible, but I'm going to bed.'

They stared at each other in panic, jumped to their feet and rushed to block her way.

'Oh no, Fiorinda! Don't leave us! Stay just a moment!'

'Fee, please, please don't go—'

They led her, unresisting, to the battered sofa. She must sit down, while they knelt, on either side of her, holding her hands.

'Fiorinda,' said Ax, 'please don't be pissed off. We're clumsy but we don't mean any harm. W-we want to ask you something.' His voice was shaking.

'Yeah,' said Sage: and what's this? Sage, her best mate, her dearest friend, doubly unmasked, looking at her the way he's *never* looked at her. She stared back at him, and then at Ax. Ax smiled, and kissed her cheek, and then they

34

were both kissing her – chaste, delicate, thrilling kisses, showering on her eyelids and her brows, her ears, her fingers, the blue veins in her wrists. Her sleeve was pushed back so Ax could kiss the inner skin of her elbow. Sage's soft mouth traced the neckline of her dress, brushing the hollow at the base of her throat—

She said nothing, she didn't respond; she remained passive, pliant, staring at them.

'Fiorinda,' said Ax, drawing back. 'We want to ask you if all three of us can be lovers. We wouldn't ask except we think you want it too.'

'In spite of us being so old,' added Sage (that one obviously still smarting).

Silence from Fiorinda.

'Well, um, what do you say?' asked her boyfriend at last, looking very worried.

Sage's blue eyes were telling her everything's going to be all right.

She kept them waiting for so long they'd have been terrified – except that she was still holding their hands, and the charge of those kisses was glowing in her eyes. 'Dearest Ax,' said Fiorinda. She leaned over and kissed him on the angle of his jaw.

'Darling Sage.' She kissed him too, at the corner of his mouth.

She removed her hands from their grasp and folded her arms.

'Alphabetical order. Well, this is very formal. So this was your big plan, was it? You decide you want some group sex, so you cunningly kidnap me and lock me up, miles from anywhere, sneer at me, ignore me and be totally horrible to me. And then when you think you've done a fine job of softening me up—'

'Sheer nerves,' said Ax hurriedly.

'Frightened stupid,' explained Sage. 'It just came out that way.'

'Tell me, does this approach *succeed*? Is this how you romanced all those sheep?'

'I knew we'd get to the sheep. I'll be hearing about those sheep to my dying day.'

'*Sheep?* Huh? What sheep?'

'All those sheep we met in Yorkshire, Sage. Surely you remember.'

'Oh.' Sage's turn to look worried. 'Er . . . well, in that case. Maybe this is the moment when I ask for, um, a few other sheep to be taken into consideration.'

'I don't think you'd better tell me how many,' said Fiorinda bitterly. '*Not that I care.* My God. If either of you really thought this would work, then I am sorry for you.'

She took Sage by the shoulders, tugged him close and kissed him on the mouth, long and strong, tongue in it, first time ever. Then she let him go and did the same to Ax.

'That's reverse alphabetical order. And I'm still going to bed.'

Left alone, they sat on the sofa with their ears ringing, silent for a decent interval to allow tumescence to subside. 'So much for that,' said Sage. 'Shall we go after her?'

'I don't think we should, not tonight. But I don't think it went too badly—'

'No. Not considering what a fucking mess we made of the intro.'

Sage got up and started to prowl around, so wired, so electric Ax expected sparks to rise from anything he touched. Finally he went and softly closed the door to the stairs, which Fiorinda had left open.

'Why d'you do that?'

'Because I'm going to kiss you. I want to find out how it feels without the drug, and I don't want Fiorinda by any chance walking in on us. Could be misunderstood.'

'Kiss, not fuck.'

'Absolutely.'

Ax sat waiting for the threat to be made good, thinking he wished to God the three of them had fallen into this arrangement as an act of casual lust years ago and had the difficult emotional dynamics sorted by now. But things happen as they must. Sage came and sat down again beside him.

'Ax—'

They kissed, for a long time. When they finally tore themselves away from each other, Sage leaned back, staring at the ceiling, making up his mind. 'Oooh. I think I could live with that.'

'Good. I suppose we might as well go to bed.'

'You going to stay down here with me?'

'If you don't mind. It seems like the right thing.'

They made the room ready for night: the rituals of Tyller Pystri, where ancient electric lamps have to be switched off one by one, black vinyl put away in cardboard sleeves, the fire made up. They stripped, got into Sage's nice big bed and lay listening to Fiorinda stomping about overhead. It sounded as if she was moving furniture.

'Maybe one of us should stay awake.'

'What for? You think she'll come down and take an axe to us?'

They nearly choked themselves smothering hysterical giggles, which would not sound good at all upstairs. 'You can stay awake,' said Sage. 'Since you're going to anyway.'

The room was cold, despite the fire. The rain had stopped. There was a black frost out there beyond the thick walls, the deep-set mullioned windows where the night looked in, the icy dark stretching out forever.

About an hour later the stairs creaked. Ax felt a surge of movement rousing from beside him, like something much bigger than Sage. *My God*, he thought, *what have I unleashed?* The door opened. Fiorinda came into the room, her fiery hair tumbled on the shoulders of a brown and gold shawl, a candle in a china holder in her hand. She sat on the edge of the bed and stared at them, pale as the candleflame. The shawl fell back. She was wearing a nightdress, a long slip of cream satin with narrow shoulder straps.

'Most of our friends are convinced you two are having a secret affair. Are you?'

'No!'

'We were waiting for you,' said Ax.

She nodded. 'Well, okay . . . Okay, I knew this was coming. Of course I did. I've known for a long time . . . Fact is, from the night you did the oxytocin, I knew it had gone too far. No more pissing around, I just had to have you both.' She saw them startle. Ha! Nice to give them a view of the situation they had not really taken on board. But she wished she could stop shivering, all gooseflesh; she felt such a kid. 'Only . . . I don't know how it works. I w-want to, but I don't know how? Who do I turn to? W-which of you two am I with? Which of you—?'

Ax got out from under the covers and put himself behind her, a wall at her back, hugging her close. Sage took her hands. 'Don't worry about it. Anything you do is right.'

'If *anything* feels wrong,' said Ax, kissing her hair, 'at *any point*, you say the word, and you and me go back upstairs.'

'Everything will be like before,' said Sage. 'No damage. We promise.'

'And don't, fuck's sake, worry about the secret affair. It won't happen. Will it, Sage?'

'Of course not.'

Fiorinda shrugged. 'Fine. W-why all the fuss, anyway? It's just sex. It's not a big deal.'

'Yes it is,' said Sage.

'Yes it is,' said Ax.

She sat there for a moment, her heart beating hard against Ax's arm. Then she freed herself, picked up the skirts of the satin slip, tugged it over her head and tossed it. Instantly Sage pushed back the quilt, so they were naked together. All three of them sighed then, involuntarily: a sigh of profound relief, we're over the edge, we've done it. Fiorinda leaned back against Ax, how warm he feels, and held Sage's maimed hand to her breast, ah, what a rush. 'This'll never work,' she said, her whole body sweetly burning. 'We'll fall out, and it will be awful.'

'It's worth a try,' said Sage, trying to sound level-headed.

'It'll work,' said Ax. 'As long as we're careful at the start, and make an effort—'

She moved her head gently from side to side so her hair caressed Ax's throat, the way he loved. 'Nothing's supposed to be an effort in the Good State. Or it won't last.'

'But we're allowed to concentrate on one another,' said Sage. 'I remember that.'

They were quoting from Ax's manifesto, the one he'd pitched at his friends three years ago: a plan worth living for, in the dark on the other side of the end of the world. In the Good State we will only take time off from having fun, from making art, from *being ourselves*, to concentrate on each other, like the social animals—

She's flying, into Sage's arms, Ax falling after her—

Well.

That was very good. What a rush, how overwhelming, how frightening, to tell the truth, to lie naked between them, these two big fierce male animals. But from the moment they both had their arms around her, kissing her, whispering, *sweetheart, is this really okay? Are you okay Fee?* it had been nothing but good and wonderful. Oh, there are problems, I know there are problems. But we truly love each other, and the sex is brilliant. Surely we can sort out the rest. Someone was walking around. Sage. She opened her eyes and saw him in the icy grey morning, dressed in biker leathers, sitting down to pull on his boots. There wasn't anyone in the bed with her.

'Where's Ax?'

'Gone for a walk. He'll be back soon.' Second boot on. Snap the closures.

'Where are you going?'

He came and sat on the bed. 'I'm going back to Reading.'

'Why? What's wrong?'

'Because I can't do this threesome thing. I'm sorry, baby. I can't.'

She sat up, pulling the covers around her, suddenly very young, suddenly a shamed and frightened child. 'W-was I no good?'

'Oh God. Fee, it will be all right. I'm still your Sage. I *love* you. I will be your best friend, forever and ever. But I can't do this.' He didn't touch her. She didn't dare reach out to him. 'So I'm going. The keys are on the kitchen table. Leave them at Ruthie Maynor's. You can push them through the letterbox.'

Ax had walked towards the sea, along the unfenced track that crossed the clifftop grassland, then taken a turn along a field line, beside a hedge. Before the crash he'd had a data chip implanted in his brain, holding a huge stack of information about this country. He'd thought it would come in useful. He could review Sage's estate in several scales of detail: twelve acres of dry granite pasture, a portion of the Chy; not much cover except for the gorge, which would be a trap. A standing stone. A patch of oak trees. Odd set-up for megastar seclusion, but there you go, that's Sage. He was now on National Trust land from here to the South-West Path; the cliff's edge, the Atlantic.

God, it was cold. He took shelter under the thorn hedge, his back to the coast, the wind fingering his spine through tangled branches. He was thinking of the strange, strained conversation he and Sage had had, the day after they took the oxytocin, in the Fire Room at the Insanitude – an old retreat of theirs in the North Wing. At present it was an island of Few territory in the Boat People accommodation; but still a good place to be private.

What they were asking of Fiorinda wasn't easy. When she was twelve, this amazing girl was pregnant in horrible circumstances. When she was thirteen years and three months old, she saw her baby die. She's only eighteen now. She's so brave, but inside she's still a damaged child. How could they risk hurting her, risk adding to that damage in any way? They'd agreed that they were sure enough of their love, and of her desire, to ask the question. If she said yes then they'd take it carefully, be ready to back off at any moment. They'd agreed that the three of them must be lovers, equal partners, not two rockstars sharing the girl. Fuck that! On the oxytocin showing, Ax and Sage should have no problem getting physical, to some extent, have to see how it goes.

Are you really okay for that? Ax had asked.

Oh yeah, he says, the grinning mask almost as blank as Hallowe'en. I took the drug with you, didn't I? And then he stalks off without once touching me. Weird.

So far so good on that aspect. *Sage!* What a storm of soft ferocity. Like being assaulted by a giant albino tiger cub. A giant tiger cub that loves you very much, but still—

Sage's greater size and strength must never become an issue, have to watch that.

His brave girl, leaping into Sage's arms as if into deep water.

He saw himself walking with her: a beach, a street,

41

doesn't matter, holding her hand, shall we do it? We love him so much, we must make Sage our lover. They would have been very happy and very sad, saying goodbye to what they'd had: *why didn't I do that?*

He hadn't had the courage to face what he might see in her eyes—

The sky was ironbound. The branches of the thorn were covered in half-unfurled fists of green, ice crystals hanging from them, sometimes a bud encased in a crystal sphere. Every time he took his hands out of his pockets to wipe his eyes and mop his nose, the wind burned them. He had to stop crying so he could go back to Tyller Pystri before they started to worry, but the tears kept coming. She loves me, I know she loves me. She'd never leave me, but she loved him first, only she was a kid and she didn't realise . . . I've known it for I don't know how long, and *this is the solution.* But she won't be my little cat anymore. She'll be Sage's baby now.

He knew he had found the only way to save himself from unimaginable pain, but he just *couldn't stand it.*

He heard a motor bike and thought nothing of it, not attuned to the rarity of such a sound out in the Cornwall countryside, three years after the end of the world.

At last Ax realised he'd have to go back anyway. He let himself in, went to the bathroom and splashed his face. It was the wind. It made my eyes water, fucking cold out there . . .

Very quiet in here.

Fiorinda was sitting on the bed, wearing her orange cardie over the red and blue chiffon dress and skinny faded denims, same as she'd been wearing last night. Her hair was a mess. She looked half-asleep, almost dazed.

'Where's Sage?'

'He's gone. Back to Reading.'

'What? Did something happen? Did Allie call?'

42

'No. He's just gone.'

'But how?' said Ax, fixing on the practical impossibility. 'The car's still here.'

'He took his bike.'

'Oh, God.' He looked at the windows, as if he might catch a glimpse of Sage's Triumph careering away down those narrow, ill-kept lanes. 'I hate that fucking bike. There's black ice everywhere—'

He came and sat beside her. 'Fiorinda. What went wrong?'

She shook her head.

'Okay,' said Ax, with reserve, 'if there's stuff you don't want to tell me, I understand.'

'*No!*' wailed Fiorinda. 'He said, "I'm going back to Reading because I can't do the threesome thing", and then he left, and now you know as much as I do.'

'Shit. Do you think that was really the first time he ever got sexual with another guy?'

'Yes. But.'

There wasn't a single thing she could say that would be true to both of them.

He put his arms round her and they clung to each other, heartbroken. 'Sssh, ssh. Don't cry. It'll be nothing. I'll talk to him.'

'You can try,' said Fiorinda. 'It won't do any good.'

They drove to Reading. Sage wasn't there. He'd been and gone.

'Sage?'

'Hi Ax,'

'Sage, can we talk?'

'We're talking.'

'Fuck. Sage, *please*. This is horrible.'

'It's not horrible. I tried your idea, I can't do it, that's all. Everything's fine, everything goes back to normal. Now leave me alone, I'm working.'

Silence.

The big cluttered room at the top of the converted warehouse that was the Heads' London stronghold, filled up with this pitiful silence—

'Okay,' said Ax's voice at last, 'I'll call you later. Sage, I love you.'

Gone.

'Yeah, yeah, yeah,' said Sage. 'I love you too.'

He genuinely had been working. He pulled off his eyewrap and spun his chair away from the boards so he could stare out of the long window that overlooked Battersea Reach. I was all right, Ax, I was fine. I was living with my situation. I was even *happy*. Until you came along with your damned very generous offer, Sah.

Now every thought of her is poisoned.

I don't think you'd better tell me how many . . . her grey eyes flashing on him that glance of hurt reproach. Totally outrageous, totally unjust reproach, what was I supposed to do, brat? But oh how sweet. But he must not think of her, because he could still taste the scent of her skin, he could feel her teeth and tongue, the small, warm weight of her little breasts. Thinking of her, of the *details* of Fiorinda, which had been his consolation, would only bring on the maddening, humiliating, adolescent problem of an erection he could not will down.

Damn you, Ax.

Testosterone's a good drug if you have something hard and positive to do with it. If not, well, a no-brainer, blocked power surge, foul irritability. He could dose himself out of this state, but he would not. Masking the symptoms is a fool's game. It'll pass.

He thought of putting his fist through the window.

But he'd only feel like an idiot, and then have to get it fixed.

What a crappy, adult way to think. Shame on you, Aoxomoxoa.

He probably couldn't break the glass, anyway. It was supposed to be bulletproof.

TWO

Unmasked

This was the year that the imported fuel crisis hit rock bottom. European fossil fuel reserves were in dire straits, and renewables came nowhere near bridging the gap. Travel of any kind was a nightmare; powercuts lasted for weeks, and the effects of data quarantine kept on dealing further blows, major and minor, to the remains of modern life. ATMs, coming back online at last after Ivan/Lara, doled out new currency notes with even less spending power. The proverbial major credit cards had vanished. Alien or long-vanquished diseases were defying public health measures, the British Resistance Movement pursued a nagging terrorist campaign in the rural hinterland, and there was a serious campaign to make witchcraft once more a criminal offence.

But Ax Preston's solution to the CCM threat was still a miraculous success. While violence and civil unrest smouldered and burned throughout Continental Europe, while governments fell and democracy was abandoned, the English lived at peace with their green revolution. The other nations of the former UK, who did not admit to having an eco-warrior crisis, had nothing but respect for Ax's hybrid régime. The party atmosphere, the glamour and the optimism of the Rock and Roll Reich prevailed over hardship, and even those people (the vast majority, outside the CCM) who were living the simple life because they had no option, shared the buoyant mood.

It was just as well the public were not aware that their most sacred icons were in trouble. The Few themselves didn't know exactly what had happened, only that a trip to Cornwall had been cut short, and suddenly there was something badly wrong. The three were professional about it, no open rift, but the warmth and reassurance that had radiated from that charismatic friendship was gone, and everyone was scared. If the Triumvirate failed, how long could anything in this fragile house of cards survive?

In April, the week after Fiorinda's birthday, they had their regular meeting with Benny Preminder, Parliamentary Secretary for Countercultural Liaison – the only suit on the original Think Tank team who had survived Massacre Night.

Benny Prem had been safely elsewhere when the gunmen opened fire because he'd been implicated in the conspiracy up to his neck. But the investigation at the time hadn't touched him, and Ax had decided it was easier to leave him in place, in the harmless niche he'd created for himself, rather than try and open up that can of worms. He had no connection with Ax's Ceremonial Head of State role, or with the working relationship between the Rock and Roll Reich and Westminster. All he had to do was sit in his well-appointed office, pretending he had the ear of Mr Preston, and providing (at these monthly meetings) a valuable supply of unofficial information.

Today it was national surveillance. The countrywide system, much battered by green violence, had been run since the Deconstruction Tour by the barmy army, Ax's militarised hippies, in co-operation with the police. Benny knew some people who'd like to take over the management of this resource. He'd been approached, and if

Ax was at all interested, he was prepared to broker a deal . . .

Ax said it wasn't his concern, it was Home Office business, but he believed the hippy netheads and the police were getting on fine.

'Carn't argue with the barmy army,' drawled Sage, stretched at insolent length in one of Benny's armchairs, the skull doing between scary great oaf and bored stupid. 'We don't interfere, 'less we have to. Tha's the way it works.'

The mainstream government of England was not in a very stable state. Standards of legitimate behaviour had never really recovered from Massacre Night. There had been a string of covert plots to remove the ruling coalition by more or less nefarious means. Ax refused to get involved, but Benny kept trotting out these dodgy offers, convinced that Mr Dictator was just waiting for the right deal.

Luckily I hate birthdays, thought Fiorinda, who was sitting in another of Benny's armchairs, bare feet tucked up, staring out of the window. She left the talking to Ax and Sage on these occasions, and got away with it because Benny was convinced the girl in the Triumvirate was only there for decoration. The sky over Whitehall was sullen and low, weighed down by the fumes of wood and coal fires. Ten days ago it had been the anniversary of the Act of Dissolution, London en fête in the rain. She'd had to sing her loss-of-habitat song, 'Sparrow Child', to accompany ceremonial plantings of hedges and ivy through the concrete jungle. God, what a waste of time. The civilised world is finished. How can people be so cheerful, so hopeful? Why can't we all just let go?

Benny had accepted his rebuff calmly. He'd been paid to ask the question, it didn't bother him if the answer was no. Now he was marvelling over the latest figures, predicting that the drop-out movement was going to affect thirty per cent of the population of Western Europe. Isn't that awesome? I mean, wow, fucking weird!

He gazed at the three with his wistful, uneasy smile.

'But who's counting?' said Sage, studying the ceiling.

'Maybe it's the natural climax vegetation of global capitalism,' said Fiorinda, still looking out of the window. 'Like peat bogs. People think of forests as climax vegetation, because the trees look big and successful. But the final result of all that explosive boom and bust has to be a flatline. Stands to thermodynamics, really.'

'Thermodynamics? I'm afraid I don't follow.'

'It doesn't matter. Just nonsense.'

Benny's attempts at being matey fell very flat with Sage and Fiorinda, and he always seemed genuinely bewildered. You'd swear he *didn't remember* that he'd helped to organise that killing spree. And Benny was right. It really didn't matter anymore. This is a new world, with new rules . . . At last the allotted twenty minutes were up. Fiorinda, who had been watching the clock when she wasn't staring out of the window, put her boots back on. Benny made his usual attempts to prolong the chat, gave up in the face of more than usual resistance, buzzed his secretary and stood to usher them out.

'I'll see you all at Beltane, then.'

They stared at him.

'Beltane?' repeated Benny, with his trademark uneasy smile. 'Isn't that what we're calling it now? At Reading? You famous rockstars will be on stage, but I'll be there.'

'Oh,' said Ax, 'you mean the Mayday Concert. Sorry, Benny. I'm not up on the Ancient British calendar. It's not my style.'

'Shit, Ax,' said Fiorinda, when they were outside. 'How could you turn him down? There was probably a timeshare on a villa in Tuscany in that CCTV thing.'

'I read the small print.'

'*Beltane*,' said Sage. 'I don't like the sound of that.'

It was annoying, the way the mainstream world had latched onto Celtic terms. Trust Benny to have caught the bug.

'That's exactly why it's good to have him around. Benny tells us more than he ever realises about what's going on over here. I'll explain to him about avoiding neo-primitive language. He'll understand. He's committed to us, in his weird way—'

Fiorinda sighed in exasperation. 'Benny Prem is committed to the main chance. Someday soon he won't be subtly letting us know about the latest plot. He'll be telling the coup-merchants how to get rid of *us*.'

'Well,' said Sage, 'I got code to write. Talk to you later.'

Lengthening that deliberate stride he zoomed away, leaving them standing.

This was Sage's idea of 'getting back to normal'. He did what had to be done, he turned up for all his gigs, and never came near them otherwise.

Someone peeked out of an office door, and quickly closed it again. There was a hiss of whispering voices, suddenly cut off. All the suits around here were madly envious of Benny. They calibrated the time that the Triumvirate spent in his office by the second. The dim-lit Whitehall corridor was like a wild wood: alive with feral eyes and stealthy movement. Ax and Fiorinda looked at each other, personal heartbreak and appalling responsibility merging.

Without Sage, the burden of what they had to do was impossible.

The cultural history idea had taken off. It wouldn't have much direct effect on the drop-out kids; or on hippy politics. The Volunteer Initiative had been running hedge-school kindergartens since before the Inauguration, and the former Ancient Britons weren't going to be defeated so easily. But it was colourful, and it was fun. The punters liked it, and at least the media folk had something else to talk about besides the thrill of forbidden sacrifices at Stonehenge and the romance of head-to-toe tattooing.

Rob Nelson and Ax attended a musicology seminar at Goldsmiths and returned, by the vagaries of Crisis Conditions public transport, to the Lambeth Road. The Snake Eyes urban commune, a hotbed of music radicalism since Dissolution Summer, was still going strong. It had expanded, taking over the house next door and one across the street. Key members of the Big Band, with crew and families and hangers-on, were permanently in residence; it was loud and crowded, full of new sounds and constant arguments. But the basement was quiet that evening. They settled with beers and spliff and spent a while chewing over the absurdities of rock and roll academe.

'*Snake Eyes* means losers,' sighed Rob. 'That's all we meant. Nothing Foucault in it. We were the beautiful losers, that was our thing. Righteous, non-star, never-going-to-sell-out Black music. And now look. You've made us into the establishment, Ax.'

'Sorry,' said Mr Preston, gloomily. 'It just happened.'

Rob, inspired by beer and nostalgia, and the terrible feeling that everything was out of joint, decided he had to tackle the issue. Ax bottles things up, that's his problem. When he found out about Milly and Jordan he never dissed either of them, he didn't confide in anyone. He made up his mind the band must come first, and carried on as if the change of partners was all in a day's work.

But the Chosen Few hadn't been the same after that.

'You know, Ax, Sage is a great guy, and I love him—'

'Oh yeah?'

'But he's *white*. It makes a difference. There's nothing wrong with being white, but he has a different attitude to life, and, er, relationships, and all that shit. You can't handle him the way you would a brother—'

'Milly's white,' said Ax, narrow-eyed. 'So is Verlaine, and

Rox. Fiorinda, as you may have noticed, looks white, as long as you keep her out of the sun. What's your point?'

'Huh? No offence—'

'I suppose you'd prefer it if I didn't do guys at all. That would be more politically correct, wouldn't it? For a *brother*.'

If there was one thing Rob disliked more than being called a fascist, it was being called homophobic. It was simply not true. He just didn't happen to know any exclusive homosexuals – except Chip and Ver, and Rox, if a post-gendered person qualified. He had never felt *any* unease about Ax! He was about to protest when he realised what he'd just been told. Oh, fuck.

'Hey, I'm sorry. Uh, I didn't know it was like that. I didn't mean . . . Shit, the Babes *told* me, but I didn't believe them—'

Ax was thinking of the nights he'd spent in this basement in Dissolution Summer, his first nights with Fiorinda, and finding the memories poisoned by cruel loss. He couldn't care less what the Babes had told their unobservant boyfriend. Rob, chunky and dark and earnest in his sharp green suit, sat there all gobsmacked concern, and Ax, who hated violence, had difficulty refraining from punching him out—

'Well, now you do. Rob, I never thought I'd have to say this to you.'

Rob braced himself. He knew he was in deep shit. 'Yeah?'

'Mind your own business.'

Olwen Devi, the Rock and Roll Reich's chief scientist, was ready to white-label her latest invention. Ax went down to Reading to talk about it, knowing that Sage would be on the Festival site. If he could catch his friend alone, off guard (and, let it be said, without Fiorinda) he knew he'd be able to turn this hateful situation around.

The Zen Self tent, the eau-de-Nil geodesic dome that seemed curiously larger on the inside than on the outside, had its usual crowd of staybehinds and day-trippers, trying out the neuroscience rides. Zen Selfers in Welsh red and green moved among them, offering help and advice. He passed through and found Olwen Devi in one of the inner labs, wearing an immaculate lab coat over a festive sari of gleaming emerald silk, a scarlet tilak mark on her smooth, ageless brow and flowers in her hair. She looked as if she'd been called from a wedding to attend some kind of medical emergency; she was probably getting ready for a workshop. Olwen was a performer, in her way. She knew the value of looking the part, and Ax liked that. No use having the big idea if you're not prepared to go out and sell it.

She had been running her experiments in human consciousness in Reading arena since Dissolution summer, and providing Ax Preston with alt.tech spin-offs from the Zen Self quest, in return for his protection from the anti-science mob. He did not fully understand why she had decided to work for him, or why she had left Wales, where her parent company was still based. But she had believed in his vision of the future, when his career had been at a very low ebb, and he counted her among his most trusted allies.

They discussed the ATP situation. Cell-metabolism energy sourcing was doing well. The punters, Countercultural and otherwise, were lining up to find out if they had the right genes to take the treatment. (For a percentage of the population the gene-manipulation didn't work in its present form.) But they didn't want to move too fast. The aim was to get these new and strange developments *out into the world*, but do it quietly. Take no risks. They agreed they would pull back. No more new treatment centres, and no more projects like the Brighton street lighting: not right now.

They moved on to Olwen's new baby, the bi-location phone, which thankfully involved no transgenic tissue infusions. Ax – who had never taken the ATP treatment and never would – had his demonstration, and enjoyed the bizarre experience of being in two places at once: slightly like looking into a mirror, and also being the person looking out . . . In the long term, he was dreaming of industrial-scale applications for this one. Your muscle power and part of your conscious attention can be in one place, doing some kind of dull, necessary work, while you are somewhere else, enjoying life. (His imagination baulked at the idea of more than one doppelgänger, though Olwen said there was theoretically no limit.) But that was far in the future. In the meantime they had a medical application, and an intriguing novelty mobile phone.

Olwen had a handful of severely disabled people (whose health otherwise checked out A1, a rare breed) signed up for the trials. Other white labels would go to influential hippies, mainstream opinion-formers with the right sympathies, and trusted media folk. She advised against the term 'living ghost'. No 'clones' either. Definitely not!

'Okay, so what are we calling it? Bi-location presence is a mouthful.'

She showed him her right hand, and the ring with a large milky-golden stone that she wore on the middle finger. It looked like a jewel; in fact it was the Zen Self mainframe computer. 'Serendip can make copies of herself – apparently physically separate copies – that remain entangled with her, so there is still just one Serendip. We call that a facet. Something logically similar is happening in the bi-location phenomenon. It's a possibility that's long been implied in the theory of memory transcription, where we know that in effect a different virtual self is created for every moment—'

'Right,' said Ax, cutting it short before she lost him completely. 'Facets it is. Nice and neutral.'

He looked around the green-tinged, light-filled cell, vaguely recognising brain science equipment. What goes on in the Zen Self experiments? Sage and the Heads were involved, along with Chip and Verlaine and Dilip: Olwen's rockstar labrats. Ax had never been interested. Know your limits. Seeking for some kind of technologically mediated Nirvana was not for him. But Sage was a fool for all that. He wanted to use the bi-location trick for cheap space travel. Send your little receiver off to the moons of Jupiter, and bi-locate to it, why not? A facet doesn't need life support—

He'd been silent too long. He thought he could read, in Olwen's kindly eyes, that she knew all about the bust-up. The Zen Self guru and her A student had had a brief fling at one time, and they'd stayed close. Olwen probably knew more than Ax did about what had gone wrong at Tyller Pystri . . .

He'd been planning to linger, in the hope that Sage would turn up. It would be better than going to knock on the door of the van. Instead, he left quickly. In the outer tent he spotted Kevin Verlaine, parting company from a couple of Selfers, and on an impulse followed him into the arena.

'Hi.'

'Oh, hi Ax.'

'What're you doing down here?'

'I've been buying illicit drugs,' said Verlaine proudly. 'Well, not exactly *buying*—'

Neurologically active compounds sometimes exited the Zen Self tent without Olwen Devi's cognizance, and Olwen would not strictly approve. Verlaine left the sentence hanging and discreetly showed Ax his loot: half a dozen translucent golden capsules in a twist of green paper.

'What's that?'

'Snapshot. It's something we use in the experiments. It

aligns your firing patterns so that the scanner can take a snapshot of the global state of your brain. But when it does that, for an instant your mind gets freed from the middle dimensions and you enter the sum of all possible states—'

'I see,' said Ax, grinning. 'What's in it?'

'—and you get these amazing visions. You'd have to try it . . . What's in it? Well, acetylcholine, I know *that*.' The labrat looked a little crestfallen. 'Er, a lot of things. Cadherins. I don't really know.' He brightened. 'You want some? It doesn't take any time, not normal time. You're *Whoosh! Pssht!* You're there, then you're back.'

Ax was not a hardened NDogs (endogenous psychotropics) abuser. He usually preferred classic drugs, but he hesitated only briefly. Talking to Olwen had left him feeling embittered, sidelined and reckless, and anyway acetylcholine sounded okay. He knew Sage used that stuff all the time.

'Go on then.'

It was mid-afternoon. The towered stages were bare, the marquees empty or playing host to staybehind concerns. They had stopped under one of the camp council's THIS IS A SPACESHIP banners, behind the main sound stage. LITTER LOUTS WILL BE KILLED. Ax saw the young man's face, its frame of light brown ringlets, wisp of brown moustache, the kid's last-moment uneasiness. He was sharply aware that he didn't have a guitar case slung over his shoulder. See Ax Preston, see guitar, Fiorinda used to say. He'd given up the habit, afraid it was getting to be an affectation, but he missed that weight—

'Are you feeling calm? You're supposed to be calm.'

'Hit me.'

Two young hands with bitten nails and puzzle rings, snapping the capsule under his nose . . . and he was wakening from sleep, with Fiorinda beside him. But what's this? Fiorinda is sixtyish, the dark red curls all silvered.

Feeling very peaceful and blissfully happy, he propped himself on one elbow to look at her. She's too thin, his little cat still not wasting much of her time on stupid body-fuel, but my God *how beautiful* she has become. He realised that the change was in himself, not in his girl. For Sage, Fiorinda had always been beautiful (they'd never talked about this, but Ax knew). For Ax, dearly, dearly as he loved her, she had stayed the skinny white girl, not his physical type, that he'd first taken to his bed. Occasionally he'd catch a glimpse of the face that was there for other people. But now he could see it. He could see her soul, her courage, her steadfast heart, all the perfection of his darling . . . *Well*, he thought, with great joy, *I will get there* . . . I will have it all. How pale she is. She's white as paper, and what's this sticky wetness seeping from her place in the bed? Has she pissed herself? Can't be. Fiorinda never sleeps that deeply, no matter how smashed she gets. What's wrong? He moved, and felt a strange reluctance in his joints (but that makes sense because if Fiorinda is sixtyish Ax is over seventy). Not really frightened yet, but . . . Hey, Fiorinda? Oh God, she's not breathing. OH GOD. OH GOD. NO!

—and he was staggering on the green grass, under the THIS IS A SPACESHIP banner, his body thundering, a steel claw clutching his chest, the arena exactly as before, the whole vision having taken less time than it takes to say *cardiac arrhythmia*—

'Ax! Oh, shit. *Ax*, are you okay?'

'Yeah,' he said. 'I'm fine.' The world was dark and shaking; he could hardly focus on the kid's scared face. 'I know what I meant to ask you. D'you know where Sage is?'

'Yeah,' said Verlaine, eyes big as saucers. 'Sage. I better get Sage, I'll get him. He's teaching. You stay—'

'No thanks. I'll find him myself.'

*

Aoxomoxoa, in sharp black and white as if for a stage performance, and with the skull at high contrast, was holding his class in a quiet spot by the Blue Lagoon marquee, a slew of wireless hardware spread around him. He had the kids looking at animation on their cellulose-based-plastic slates and he was talking to them about how their brains worked.

What a privilege to minister to the awakening of these young minds.

'You see, whatever you "see", whatever you "hear", whatever you "touch", et cetera, what your brain experiences is a pattern of fire. See that? How it washes over the whole brain, like, mm, a cloud of sparks? When I write my immersions I copy those patterns, and make your brains believe they've had the experience. I do it visually, and I'll explain why that works best in a moment. I write the code, and I deliver it on a carrier wave of visible light. I don't even have to fake the patterns very *well*, because brains love being fooled, yeah, what?'

'Did you always want to be a rockstar?'

'No. I wanted to be a dancer, or a gymnast. But I'm far too tall, and I have weird hands, so I had to give up the idea and be a rockstar instead.'

So much for delusions of grandeur.

This was not an Aoxomoxoa masterclass. He'd started those as well, but this was merely a celebrity warm-up for the hedgeschool kindergarten. No one expected him to teach the kids anything. He only had to turn up, looking like Aoxomoxoa, move the mouth, do some tricks, and make the children (and their teachers) feel included in the new idea. Just because they'd broken up, he was not going to let Ax down. He would carry on, doing everything that was asked of him, though it was cinders and ashes . . . Ah well, back to the Sanskrit.

'Okay, now all the visual information that registers in your eyes, mostly at this little spot called the fovea, ends up here, in the bit of your brain called the middle temporal cortex, which is right in the middle, appropriately enough, of where the rest of your senses are handled. When I send the fake information on my carrier wave, the MT starts thinking it's having an experience. It goes through its cache, looking for a real experience it might be having. This alerts the hippocampus (little thing allegedly shaped like a seahorse, down in here), and triggers the whole brain to get involved, *whoosh*, with emotions, sensations, the whole thing. That's when the punters get convinced that what's happening is totally real, because insofar as a brain knows reality, it *is* real. Sharks biting them, clouds of butterflies, flocks of seagulls, ravening werevoles, what-ever. It isn't incredibly hard, if you use the right hooks—'

The children gazed at him like sponges. 'Oh,' said a girl in the front row, about ten years old, a toddler dozing on her knees, '*MT*. That says Em Tee! Is that why the other track on *Morpho*, besides 'Morpho', is called 'The Empty Zone'?'

Morpho was the Heads' first album, the first immersion record in the world. They'd lost the rights when they broke up with their record company, which had for years been a very sore point. But eventually you see reason. *Morpho* had been written and released before this child was born.

'Yeah,' he said. 'You got it—' suddenly feeling that this was indeed a privilege, and also feeling like a, like a talking trilobite. Fuck. I am *ancient*. I am the first page of their history books. Or would be, except most of them can't read. Over the kids' heads he saw Ax coming towards him. What's he doing here? No way to escape, so he waited in silence while Mr Dictator came around the children and sat down.

''Scuse me,' said Ax, 'I need your teacher. Sage, do you mind?'

He was grey in the face, hands visibly shaking.

'Okay, class dismissed.'

The children scattered. 'Sage. Do you think you'll live to be old?'

'Oh yeah,' he said, judging that *live fast die young* was not what Ax was looking for. 'Very old.' He spoke slowly, gently taking Ax's wrist in his left hand. 'I reckon I'll quit gigging when I'm a hundred, before it gets undignified, an' I'll take up gardening. Or I'll keep koi. I like fish. Ax, what the fuck have you been doing to yourself?'

The pulse was not good.

'I don't know. I met Verlaine. He gave me a, stuff called snapshot. Oh God, *Sage*—'

'Sssh. Let's see.' Sage touched his righthand fingertips to the sweat on Ax's upper lip and put the taste in his mouth. He had enough of the drug left in his system that he might be able to get some idea of what had happened—

'Oh,' he said sombrely a moment later. 'Unlucky, Ax. You have to be careful with snapshot. It goes for the jugular, if you give it a chance. Well, it seems I can tell you two things. What you saw is further off than you think. And I will be there.'

Ax's heart gave another terrible leap. He was in a garden, and this old man was crying in this other old man's arms. Oh God, those arms, still hard and strong, carrying with them such a freight of memory, of conviction, of *reality*, oh God, *unbearable*—

Wrong thing to say . . . Sage saw Ax's eyes widen in horror and had to catch the falling body. 'Ah, no. Ax, babe, I didn't mean to sound like that, I'm a bastard, you caught me off guard . . . Hey, *it doesn't last*, it's a bad dream, it'll be gone, few seconds, hang on—'

But Ax was out. Sage laid him down, slapping his phone implant—

'George! George, get over here. *Now*. Bring the First Aid . . . *Shit*. Where is that little fucker? I will *kill* him.'

Ax came to lying in an outdoor passageway backstage of

the Blue Lagoon. George Merrick was beside him, with the white picnic hamper that was the Heads' First Aid kit open on the grass. Bill Trevor was sitting on a plastic chair, between the two of them and the world, casually on guard. There was no one else around. He took a deep breath and sat up. He didn't know if he'd walked here or been carried here. Some fleeting memory of a dream, gone the instant he tried to focus on it, and *what happened*? I took some brain candy from Verlaine that nearly gave me a heart attack.

'Hi, George,' he said. 'What's the screen saying?'

George took a pull on a fat joint and handed it over. 'You'll do.' He peeled the telltale from the back of Ax's hand, stowed it and shut the box. 'Looks like snapshot's not your drug.'

'I would agree,' said Ax, with feeling. 'Ah, shit, my head. Got any painkillers?'

'You're not supposed to take that stuff except in lab conditions . . . You c'n have a half an aspirin. Pain is a warning, Ax. It's there 'cos you need it. You driving?'

Head Ideology occasionally bears a suspicious resemblance to Primitive Methodism at its most hardnosed. If you're meant to suffer you suffer, fuck it. But George and Ax had had that conversation. Never argue with a Cornishman about his religion.

'No, I'm not driving. I'll pass on the aspirin. Where's Sage?'

George and Bill exchanged a glance. George decided Ax didn't need to know what was probably happening to Kevin Verlaine right at this moment.

'I think 'e went back to his class.'

'Right,' said Ax, who had clocked the glance. He leaned over to give the joint to Bill, and decided he would make no more pathetic attempts at reconciliation. Enough is enough. In future he would play this exactly the way Sage wanted it.

*

Life goes on. Fiorinda recorded her vocals on the Heads' new album (still under tight wraps) at the Battersea studio; and though she didn't pretend she was having fun, you'd never have known it from her singing. Sage and Ax went to Yorkshire with the Chosen for a one-off gig at Bradford Civic Centre, where they debuted the immersions Sage had written for 'Blues In C#', and for Ax and Jordan Preston's 'Dark Skinned They Were And Golden Eyed' (diluted to visuals for a concert hall). The crowd included Sayyid Mohammad Zayid, the premier leader of English Islam – the man who'd received Ax into the Faith. The Dictator and his Minister spent time with Mohammad and other Islamic leaders afterwards, reinforcing the peace, as if there was nothing wrong. Sage also went on supporting Ax (as one or two people knew) in his secret and delicate investigation of the limits of data quarantine.

But the rift showed no sign of healing. At the Reading Mayday concert, which was a huge success, the crowds went crazy for the Heads' dance mix of 'Little Wing' with Ax Preston on guitar. Silver and Pearl Wing, Anne-Marie's nine-year-old and seven-year-old little girls, whirled around on stage, dressed as butterflies, each convinced that Ax Preston had written this song, and Aoxomoxoa mixed it, just for them. Techno-green Utopia was the message; Celtic bonfires were discouraged. At the end of Sage's masque (Sage's multimedia masques had become a tradition) the Dictator and his Minister did Hendrix's 'Third Stone From The Sun', with the spaceship dialogue and some truly amazing immersion effects . . . and then walked off stage in opposite directions, without having exchanged a word that wasn't scripted.

Fiorinda was having nothing to do with either of them. If rumour could be trusted, she spent the night of the concert in one of the hospitality benders with Cafren Free of DARK and/or three or four husky and thrilled male crewpersons.

It had to be only a matter of time before things went horribly public.

The last Saturday of May was invite-only Dance Night at the Blue Lagoon. Snake Eyes were playing; the Few were to be there in force. It would be a private gala, and everyone was hoping it would be more fun than Mayday. Ax called Fiorinda in the afternoon to say he wasn't going to make it. She decided to go down by herself, went by train and took a taxi from Reading Station, dressed in her best and feeling defiant.

'I had that boyfriend of yours in the back of my cab the other day—'

Oh yeah, thought Fiorinda. Which one? The one who dumped me, or the one who's too busy saving the world? The people of Reading were honorary Counterculturals; they didn't have to pretend the Few were invisible. Equally, the Few didn't have to be polite. The driver met a stony, glacial stare in his rear mirror and shut up until they hit Richfield Avenue.

'Blue Gate, Fiorinda?'

'No,' she said. 'No. Drop me here.'

The taste-free Leisure Centre buildings were being demolished, to make way for something . . . not yet fully worked out. The tented township stretched into the distance, drainage ditches twinkling, nylon hummocks and teepees, turf-roofed shanties and lake-village platforms, the firetowers with their banners standing out like marker buoys on a rainbow sea. She took off her shoes and walked barefoot through the site gates, where chickens scratched and every conceivable support was festooned with tomato vines.

What a *hideous mess* we made here, in Dissolution Summer. Dear Lord, we reached new depths. My God, the mud, my God, the cans, the trashed cars, the plastic fires, the streaming middens of human excrement. What a way to start an eco-friendly revolution. Yet there was logic in it. The kids came to the rock festivals like trusting little lambs, and had their own souls sold back to them, bubble-packed, and I remember what a feeling it was to break out of that damned production loop. No sense, no reason, no ideology. Just NO, actually. No, I won't shuffle obediently into the slaughterhouse, not today, thank you. There's this plate-glass window saying *throw a chair at me*. It was mad and stupid, filthy and infantile, nothing built on it can possibly last, and I'm still glad I was there.

In the arena she stopped to put her shoes on and stood for a moment gazing: the Counterculture's rockstar Titania in a froth of cream tulle over gilded net petticoats, peacock feather mandalas scattered over her bodice and skirts. Her subjects parted around her, smiling and respectful. She didn't notice. She was trying to see this place as it had been one evening in July, years ago. A sunset, red and gold. A road-worn, angry little girl, too scared to use her backstage pass, lost in the crowd, looking for a friend.

The sky over the Thames Valley was pale and mild, with rafts of lemony cloud. Another rockstar party had arrived, moving through the staybehinds. In the midst, like a prince among his courtiers, strolled a very tall, blue-eyed blond, magnificently built, yet slender, hands in his pockets, moving like a dancer, and wearing an extremely beautiful suit, sand-coloured, with a glitter of gold in it.

The Heads saw Fiorinda and came straight over. They lined up: Sage in the sand-colour, George Merrick big and broad and ruggedly goodlooking in slate-blue, Bill aquiline and sardonic in rose velvet, Peter in crumpled dark brown linen: an owlish post-modern gangster. They gave her a twirl and a bow, and launched into a short burst of the synchronised dancing. The onlookers clapped and cheered. Sage faced her with a smile that was like a plea for mercy. Under the suit jacket he was wearing a white teeshirt, a little too small, bearing the timeless message: *I'm naturally blond, please speak slowly*—

Fiorinda made a swift, pragmatic decision to accept the peace offer, even if it was only for tonight. It would be a fucking pleasant change, to be with him in public and not have it be a hateful, publicly awful experience.

'You finished it,' she said, smiling back.

She knew about the suits. She was in on the secret of the *Unmasked* album.

'Yeah. Finished the master about four o'clock this afternoon.'

'Are you pleased?'

He shrugged. 'Oh, as I ever am. God knows what the punters will think.'

It was a shame things had had to turn out this way. *Unmasked* had been planned as a surprise present for Ax. Something that would make him laugh, but he would also really love it. It featured the grandmasters of techno-weirdness not only unmasked, but singing classic covers, and dancing like an apotheosis of Take That.

'He's pleased,' said George. 'It's fucking good. You wait.'

Sage glanced around. 'Where's Ax?'

'He isn't coming.'

'Huh? Where is he?'

'I don't know. Oh, don't panic—' (Sage had looked alarmed.) 'I don't know where he is, because I didn't show enough interest, but he's with some barmy army netheads. He hasn't been kidnapped by terrorists, not yet, he just isn't going to get here, okay?'

'Okay.'

They looked at each other for a long moment, then turned together and headed for the marquee, Bill and George and Peter forming up around them.

Sage suddenly realised it had been much easier than usual to look Fiorinda in the eye.

65

'Hey.' He grinned at her, sidelong. 'Nice!'

'Enjoy it while you can,' said Fiorinda cheerfully. 'Until I break my ankle. There's a way to walk in spike heels, but I can't never get my head around it.'

'Ah, you can lean on me.' He slipped his arm around her shoulders. She hesitated for a split second, then leaned close, and they walked into the Blue Lagoon like that.

This was the third version of Reading arena's major covered venue, which had been destroyed twice, once by arson and once by storm damage. It had a sprung floor of fireproofed reclaimed timber and a classic rock-fest décor of marquee membrane, naked scaffold and coloured lights. Tonight the tent was laid out cabaret-style: a dancefloor in front of the stage, tables by a bar. Cigarette girls and boys in fancy dress were sashaying about, proffering trays of spliff and Meanies (the lethal Reading Site dance pills). The floor was hopping with campers, dancing to the resident DJs; the rockstars and friends were busy socialising. Fiorinda, Sage and the Heads joined the crowd and were instantly surrounded. Fiorinda had to repeat countless times that Ax was tied up and wasn't going to make it. A stream of people came up to congratulate Sage and the band on their new baby. Everyone was fascinated by the suits, the naked faces, the whole concept. 'Is this the way it's going to be?' Dian Buckley, the media-babe, wanted to know. 'Have the demons of techno morphoed into an elderly boyband?' The Heads declined to commit themselves. 'We're takin' it a day at a time,' explained George. Sage admitted he had a copy of the master in his pocket, but no, it wasn't going to get played.

Even Allie admired the suits, though she deplored Sage's stupid teeshirt.

'Yeah,' said Bill, maliciously. 'Shame 'e couldn't get it in his right size, either—'

Friends, acquaintances, schmoozing strangers came and went. Fiorinda and Sage stayed put, maybe both of them afraid to move, afraid to break this bubble. It could have been a night of long ago: Aoxomoxoa and his brat, with the Heads as a protective guard, drinking hard, talking nonsense, entertaining everyone with firework towers of repartee. And if Fiorinda's sallies were a little barbed tonight, nobody blamed her, least of all the boss, who took his licks like a gentleman, grinning sweetly, and not making the slightest attempt to retaliate.

Rob and the Powerbabes went off backstage with their bandmates. The inner-circle group diminished, and still all was well: until Laurel Merrick, and Minty LaTour, Bill's posh girlfriend, came back from a socialising cruise and took George and Bill off with them. Fiorinda suddenly realised that Peter had slipped away too. The cabaret was still crowded, a sea of chatter and bright clothes and body paint, but somehow she and Sage had been left alone.

The merry banter had died, she wasn't sure just when. Probably the moment they'd realised they had no audience. She stared at the tabletop, almost wishing he would jump up and flee. How terrible to be with Sage, and struggling to think of something fake and anodyne to say. She had lost him forever. Such a pain in her heart—

She looked up to find a pair of blue eyes watching her, so contrite and so tender she forgot everything she'd been trying to script and just said, 'You look amazing.'

'So do you.' He reached over and brushed the froth of tulle at her shoulder with the tips of his crooked righthand fingers. 'I *love* the dress. Wanna dance?'

'Yes.'

He took her hand; she followed him to the floor. They began to dance the way they'd often danced together: not touching, just loving the rhythm. But maybe everything had been decided in that moment outside the marquee. Their eyes met in the music, question and consent. They moved together and began to dance like a man and a woman, first time ever.

. . . and this was so intoxicating that they just couldn't stop, except for pauses to refuel the blaze with alcohol and Meanies, until finally, some glorious while later, Sage had the idea of bounding up on stage and romancing Felice (Snake Eyes' bravura Trumpet Strumpet had a soft spot a mile wide for Aoxomoxoa) to lead the band into Swing. Rob attempted to remonstrate, *Hey, you get off of my stage*, but he had to give it up. He didn't want to cause a scene, and frankly, the situation, the fabulous pair they made, those two, was hard to resist, even for Ax's staunchest defender . . . Sage leapt down, caught Fiorinda by the waist and then it was no holds barred, they were lindyhopping all over the shop, a few couples crazy enough to keep up, the crowd clearing out of the way with yells of admiration, the rock and roll brat, red curls and gilded petticoats awhirl, feather-light, almost as acrobatic as her partner—

They had to take several bows, laughing (saved by the habit of performance), before they escaped. Fiorinda found a scaffold pillar unoccupied and propped herself against it. Sage was beside her, looking down, not touching, but very close.

Two minds with but a single thought, and the thought goes something like this:

Don't fucking care. Devil take tomorrow. I am NOT going to pass this up.

'You're not even breathing hard.'

'Yes I am. That's a beautiful shade of lipstick you're wearing.'

'Isn't it? Best colour I ever found. It's called pomegranate flower.'

'It's very—'

'Let's get another drink.'

The backstage bar called Bartoli's Hideout was deserted; everyone was in the tent. Fiorinda sat on a stool at the bar, a pint of lager in front of her, Sage's arm around her. She played with his right hand, biting gently at the web between the surviving joint of his thumb and his palm, folding the two crooked fingers and rubbing them against her cheek. From the mirror below the optics his natural face looked on (the blunt nose, wide high cheekbones and big mouth: a blue-eyed faun, an elemental, definitely odd) with a tender, possessive, *fuck tomorrow* smile. She wondered if it was late or early. She'd lost track.

'You coming back to the van?'

'Yes.'

'How about now?'

'Sounds good to me.'

'Okay . . . Okay, stay there. *Don't move.* Got to talk to George.'

And he's gone.

'Aw, *Sage*,' wailed Fiorinda, banging her head on the counter, 'how can you do this to me? How can you!' But he was back almost at once. She jumped down from her stool, bristling. '*What the fuck* did you have to go and talk to George for?'

'I had to tell him,' Sage explained, distinctly, as they left the bar, 'that if anyone asks, he doesn't know where I went, and no one is to come near the van tonight. That's *no one*,' he repeated, stopping to look into her face. Sage is being gallant, making sure she's not too smashed to know what they are doing.

Fiorinda nodded, and laid a finger across his lips. No more of that.

The night was dark, overcast and warm. He noticed, as they began to walk, that the top of her head had reverted to its normal position, about level with his breastbone. Wonder when that happened? It must have been long ago. Sometimes she has delusions of being a supermodel, but this brat can hardly walk across a room in high heels.

'Fiorinda, where are your shoes?'

'I don't know. Somewhere. I'll find them in the morning.'

'I'm gonna have to carry you.'

'No, you are not.'

'Fee, you can't cross Reading arena barefoot at this time of night. Think what you'll be treading in. Broken glass, bloody sharps, knocked-out teeth, pools of piss, vomit, turds, steaming diarrhoea, dead rats, dead cats, discarded body parts, oozing viscera—'

'Nonsense. That was years ago.'

'But this *is* years ago. Didn't you realise? It's Dissolution Summer. We went dancing, my brat, I'm takin' you home: and look there's a fucking *lake* of vomit, right now—'

'Carry me.'

He carried her to the west entrance, at first trying to kiss her as he walked, but that didn't work, too much, he couldn't do both. Out into the township, and why stop here, why not keep hold of this sweet burden, she isn't complaining, all the way to Travellers' Meadow? There was no one about when they reached the gate in the trees, not a sign of the hippy watchmen. Fiorinda, stirring out of a tranced stillness, reached down and lifted the latch. Sage carried her through, set her on her feet and shut the gate.

'Kissable,' he whispered, stooping, mouth against hers, as she stood on tiptoe—

They slipped down, kissing, into the scent of honeysuckle and heavy elderflowers, into the cool embrace of the meadow grass. He meant to take her there, Fiorinda very much consenting, but just when he couldn't hold back any longer, when he *must have her*, she pulled away, jumped to her feet and ran—

He had to give chase, cursing and laughing. She was waiting at the door of the van. She slapped the lock, they fell into the kitchen and she leapt into his arms, legs around his waist, all he could do to get his cock free and safe inside. Instantly they were fucking like hammer and tongs, her skirts crushed between them, her heels in his back, gasping, babbling, stumbling all over the place, seemed to go on forever, sorely unromantic (you horrible brat—) but wonderful, flat out, total discharge—

Finished?

Yeah, she's nodding her head, teeth and claws relaxing; the little vixen is finished for a while. He slid to the floor, back against a cupboard door, hugging her on top of him. 'Fiorinda,' he said, 'Sweetheart—' the words coming out slow and spent, his left hand gently massaging her spine, 'what was wrong with the meadow, hmm? Why did I have to get up and run, an' be in real danger of putting come stains on my beautiful new trousers, probably ruining them forever?'

'I hate al fresco sex.'

'C'mon, you weren't going to be the one getting rocks in your back. You know that.'

'Well, all right. I wanted it to be in here, because I love this place.'

'Ah, she likes my van! . . . Don't you like my cottage?'

'The cottage was different. Anyway, what are you whining about? You're happy now, aren't you?'

'Oh yeah. I'm happy now.' He sighed. 'I'm happy, but . . . I'm not comfortable. How about you let me get up, hm? Lemme get out of these clothes, let's get to bed—'

He stripped off. Fiorinda, a warm shadow-girl in the darkness, was having trouble locating her side zip. 'Oh no. We keep the dress. I *love* it, it's like fucking a Barbie doll—'

'Oooh, you shouldn't have said that! Off with the dress. There—'

'Ah, Fiorinda, please. Let me have you in the frilly dress, please please, *please*—'

'Fucking pervert. Oh, all right. You can have Barbie in her underwear. It's a very pretty outfit, except I don't know what happened to the knickers—'

'They're in my pocket. Okay, let's see this—'

He touched the wall. ATP light rose, pearly-white, and there was Fiorinda, sweat-blackened curls plastered to her brow, smiling up at him, her eyes like stars. He forgot to clock the lingerie because he just had to hold her; it felt as if he was folding something bigger than the whole world into himself, this fragile girl, wriggling like a fish now to get her arms free and fling them round his neck—

'Let's get to bed. I want you in my bed, where you belong.'

'Yes.'

But when they lay together on Sage's silver-grey quilt, in the room with the walls of hardware, their mood had changed. He'd been showering her face with such kisses as they stumbled through the van, she'd wanted to tell him, I'm *not* a doll, Sage. I can kiss back. I have as much loving as you to fit into this one night. She hadn't had the heart, because he was crying: tears on thick golden lashes, salt tears on her mouth when she managed to get a kiss in edgeways.

'Sage,' she whispered, 'I want to tell you something.'

He smiled, wiping his eyes. 'Shoot.'

'This goes back a long way,' she said, wiping tears from her own eyes with her fingers. 'Back to the day you and Ax came home from the war in Yorkshire. Do you remember? I met you on the platform at St Pancras, and told you about Pigsty getting arrested.'

'Yeah. I remember.'

The first Countercultural President had turned out to be a child killer: a revelation that had been the downfall of his brutal hippy régime.

'I was telling that story. You were both terribly shocked that I'd had to be involved, and I was thinking, you are so wrong, because I'm not the delicate flower you two think I am. I'm just what people say Fiorinda is. I'm hard as nails, and my world is very small. As long as I had you two back

72

safe, nothing could hurt me, not poor Pigsty or anyone. But my best friend Sage was looking at me . . . You were looking at me, I don't know, in a different way. My eyes were opened. I knew that you were in love with me, and I was in love with you too, and I had been for a long time, only I hadn't known it. But it was too late. It's too late, Sage. It didn't happen. It can't happen, because I love Ax now. I love him with all my heart, and I could never, ever hurt him.'

'I think I loved you the first night I met you,' said Sage. 'I know I've loved you more every night and day since. And I love Ax – oh, differently – as much as I love you. But I can't do the threesome thing. I need you to be only mine. Nothing else will do.'

She stroked his hair, combing her fingers through the lamb's fleece. 'I know, my sweetheart. I understand.'

'Oh Fiorinda, how can you forgive me?'

'What's to forgive? I'm the one who fucked up. I'm the one who ruined—'

'Ah, *no*—'

He kissed her to silence her and they lay quiet, looking into each other's eyes, for so long that Fiorinda felt herself slipping into the place or state that she had discovered in the terrible year – the year when she'd got pregnant, and her baby had been born, and he had died. She had that Escher feeling, the impossible perspective, the world and Fiorinda moving into phase, becoming one. Aeons passed. Then she was back, and nothing had changed, except for a faint, extraordinary smile at the corner of his beautiful mouth. But wherever she had been, and for what immeasurable time, she knew that Sage had been with her there.

Nothing was spoken. There was nothing to be said. Such a moment just is.

He moved in closer.

'Hey. Want some more?'

*

Shortly before dawn three Heads came quietly into the room, deposited Fiorinda's shoes and her bag and stood looking at their boss and the babe. 'If the length of courtship is related to the length of his sexual relationships,' remarked Bill, 'they should be together for about a thousand years.'

'I told him to do that *five years ago*,' sighed George. 'The kid's wearing the yellow ribbon, she's not interested in sex, which does not stop other blokes doing her. He says he can wait, she's too young and too hurt. I say don't be a fuckin' idiot. Be nice to her, romance her a bit and take 'er down. Do it now or you'll miss your chance. You'll be forgiven, any fool can see. But would he lissen? He never lissens.'

'Hell to pay when Ax finds out,' said Bill.

'Yeah. Well, at least they had their big night out. Can't honestly grudge 'im that.'

'Sometimes the cards aren't worth a dime,' said Peter, 'If you don't lay them—'

The other Heads groaned softly and hauled him away.

Fiorinda didn't mind them coming in. If things had turned out the way maybe they should have turned out, no doubt she'd often have opened her eyes in this bed, in these arms, to find three brother Heads looking kindly down. She pressed herself closer against Sage's side: so happy in this moment, so completely, hopelessly without any solution for the morning, that really, now would be a good time to go to sleep and never wake up.

But if you have to wake up, in a disaster movie on the wrong side of the end of the world, and with a bone-crushing hangover, it helps, *it certainly helps* if you can arrange to do so with the Minister for Gigs wrapped around your back, his lovely mouth nuzzling your spine. Eyes closed, without leaving the soft chemistry of sleep, she turned in his arms, skin warm against skin (she'd been allowed to take off her underwear eventually), and slid her knees up around his ribs, so she could take his cock inside in one smooth rush—

The spurt of a struck match.

Ax was sitting on the end of the bed.

'How did you get in here?' gasped Sage.

'Talked to George. He wasn't happy about it, but I persuaded him.'

'Oh bugger,' said Fiorinda. 'We forgot you would be able to do that.'

She had grasped in one icy, drowning instant that the only possible way to handle this was to see the funny side. But no. Not a chance. The two men stared at each other, sheer murder on the one side, sheer horror on the other.

'I suppose I have only myself to blame,' said Ax. He stubbed out his newly lit cigarette in the ashtray he had carefully provided for himself, jumped off the bed and slammed out of the room.

Sage was dressed in twenty seconds and about to fly out of the door before he spun around. Fiorinda was hunting for her clothes, set mouth and averted eyes saying she'd always known it would be like this. Always known it, and now she's finally been added to Aoxomoxoa's *mille e tre* of course he's going to leap up and run. No big deal.

'Ah, *shit*.' He flew back, grabbed her, hugged her tight, '*God*. Fee, darling, it'll be all right. Stay here. *Don't* be frightened. I'll talk to him, I will sort it. I *will*.'

It was raining. When Sage caught up, Ax was storming along a staybehinds' footpath through the fields that bordered Travellers' Meadow, head down, hair flying in dark wings around his jaw. He gave Sage one savage, naked look and kept going.

'Ax, hey *Ax*, listen to me. Look, we were drunk, these things happen—'

'Fuck off.'

'*Please*, Ax. It was a drunken night, nothing serious. *Talk* to me—'

'*Talk to you?* Where the fuck have you been since March, you bastard?'

The path led through pasture where cows were grazing, indifferent to the weather, among the unburied corpses of cars that had been trashed in Dissolution Summer, awash now in grass and flowers, and then swerved into the back lot of a scrapyard on Richfield Avenue, where pieces of Rivermead Leisure Centre were lying around, waiting to be recycled. No way to go except onto the road. Betrayed, Ax turned in fury and sat on a lump of concrete, staring ahead of him.

'I couldn't help that.'

'Oh, fuck. Not the fucking giant toddler line. You knew what you were doing. You had it all calculated. You let me give you the spiel, you pretend to go along, because you'll get to sleep with her, and then you're off. King of the one night stand, and I don't care about me, but *how could you do that to her*—'

'I did not! That's not! That is NOT what happened!'

'If you didn't plan to leave the next morning, what was your bike doing there?'

'*What?* Ax, that is fucking *paranoid*. *Look*, the bike was there because I rode the bike down when we did the filming, and then I came back in George's car. *Fuck's sake*—'

Ax refused to look at him. The rain fell fine and straight. Sage walked around in a caged circle, wanting to leave, unable to leave: finally sat on another chunk of concrete.

'Oh God. Ax, listen. When I said yes to you, I meant it. I desperately wanted that to work, but I . . . I love her too much. I couldn't stand it. I DID NOT plan to leave like that. I didn't plan to behave the way I've been behaving. I thought I'd be okay. But it was so fucking . . . painful. I've been *trying* to get back to being normal . . . Fuck, last night I—'

He didn't know why he'd come chasing after the guy. This wasn't going to help Fiorinda. The only way he could truly help Fiorinda was by bowing out, leaving them both the fuck alone. Unfortunately that's impossible, *we're the Triumvirate.*

'Shit. I don't feel like getting into this discussion; you don't want to know, it's useless, it leads nowhere.' He doubled over, head propped on his hands to hide the tears. 'I can't talk to you. I don't know why the fuck I'm trying.'

Ax had come to Reading straight from a very tough night, to find the whole site buzzing with the exploits of the nation's wild-cat glamour puss and the amazingly transformed Aoxomoxoa, with Ax cast, in their flashy piece of MTV, as the dull, controlling, workaholic cat who has to be away so these fabulous creatures can play. He was cruelly wounded, mortified, furious, and in no mood to be merciful.

'I suppose I should be grateful the show you put on last night wasn't being *televised.* At least I was only publicly humiliated in front of every single person I know.'

Sage's head came up, indignant. 'Publicly humiliated? You what? By me dancing with Fiorinda? Oh, fuck that—!'

'Yeah. When you've hardly spoken to me for six weeks. You can say what you like. Nobody who was there last night was in any doubts about what was going on.'

Sage glared at him. 'Ax, if you were even wondering, let me assure you it was a one-off. She made that very clear. The way you found out was rough, and I'm sorry for that. We were pissed, we didn't think. But don't talk to me about . . . Oh, *I know she's your property.* I've had that well shoved in my face. You tell me I can play with her sometimes, you let me get into bed with you, but I have to kiss her, this girl I love more than my life, *for the first time,* under your supervision. I can't say a word to her of my own. I have to, to m-make love to her, for the first time, *with you looking on*. What was that about humiliation? Tell me again?'

'*One off?*' Ax curled his lip. 'Oh give it up. I know how she feels about you. Of course I know, you stupid fuck. That's not an issue. What d'you take me for? D'you think I'd have ever *suggested* the fucking threesome if I hadn't known she loves you—? And don't tell me that night was no good, you destructive shit. *I was there.*'

'It felt like playing golf with the boss.'

The words sank into Ax like poison darts. He tried to tell himself Sage would say *any nasty thing* right at this moment, as long as it would hurt Ax. But all he could hear was the awful pain in Sage's voice, and all he could see was himself on that morning after, crouched under the frozen thorn hedge crying his eyes out, because he knew he had to share his darling and he couldn't bear it—

'Anyway,' said Sage, viciously pursuing the advantage, 'I don't know why this is all about me. What about the way *your property* was behaving? The Dictator's girlfriend surely must not act like that. Why aren't you blaming Fiorinda?'

'Because *Fiorinda is never to blame*,' said Ax, in a terrible voice.

Sage's turn to back down, defeated by the self-evident truth. 'Ah, fuck it. Last night was nothing. It's you she loves, first and last. I'm just a bit of rough trade. I know that.'

'Don't whine, Sage. It doesn't suit you. '

They fell silent. Fiorinda, in her peacock mandala frock, was coming across the field, barefoot through the rain, looking like a somewhat bedraggled fairy of the Christmas Decorations Plant. She came up, and saw the tears on both their faces.

'Well,' she said. 'At least you're not fighting.'

'That'd be a short contest,' said Ax bitterly.

She sat down on the wet grass. 'Listen. You two said

let's be a threesome, and I agreed. I remember that. I don't remember where I signed anything saying, if I fuck Sage Ax has to be in the room, or vice versa. Correct me if I'm wrong. You both love me, I love both of you. Any fool can see you're madly in love with each other, or you wouldn't be sitting out here sobbing like broken-hearted fools. When we all had sex together it seemed to work. One of you tell me, *what is the fucking problem?*'

'There's a problem,' said Ax. 'There's a problem with this manipulative bastard, rewriting history.'

'*Me? Manipulative?* How the fuck do you make that out?'

'Oh God. Well, I don't care. I've got a *pitiful* hangover, I feel sick and I can't keep my head up. I'm going to lie down here for a while in this puddle. Wake me up when you've finished yelling at each other.'

Fiorinda suited her action to her words. The rain started getting heavier. The Dictator and his Minister sat on their lumps of concrete. 'Good sex?' said Ax at last.

'Brilliant.'

'She's amazing, isn't she?' said Ax, deliberately.

Their eyes met. There's nothing either one of them can claim for himself alone. No secret thing she does that she might not do with the other. It's horrible. Sage nodded. Yeah, brother. Got the message. They stared at each other, for once contemplating this disaster, this terrible thing that has happened to them, without any colouration, in its naked truth. There is no way out. It can't be fixed. There is *no solution*. Unsmiling, but with a strange lessening of tension, they looked away.

Several minutes passed.

Sage wiped his nose with the back of his hand. 'God, Ax. I've *missed* you.'

'Wasn't my idea.'

Silence.

'Okay,' said Ax. 'I accept that I fucked up. To some extent.'

'I shouldn't have run out. But there was provocation.'

'So what now? Are we going to try and force her to choose between us?' *And break her heart*, he added, by means of a glare she couldn't see.

'I don't think we can,' Sage answered, looking down at Fiorinda. Her eyes were closed, but of course she was listening to every word. 'I think she'd quit us both. I'd have tried to take her off you years ago if I hadn't spotted that.'

'Well, thanks.'

'No problem.' He wanted to draw Ax's attention to the shadow under her lashes, the lovely angle of her cheekbones, to the reckless curve of her sweet mouth, the natural rose-madder still traced in clean scarlet, pomegranate flower. 'Why stop at two?' he said fiercely. 'Every man in the world should worship her. She's a *miracle*.'

'Hm. Maybe we should remember this is purely a diplomatic coma.'

'Don't care.' He poked the rock and roll brat with his foot. 'Hey. You are amazing and wonderful and wise, and the best fuck in the universe.'

'Yeah,' said Ax. 'All true. Fiorinda? You can wake up now.'

But Fiorinda had grown attached to her coma, and refused to stir. They headed back to Travellers' Meadow, Sage carrying the babe. 'So where were you last night, anyway? I brought a copy of *Unmasked* to the party for you, er, kind of a peace offering—'

'But then, ironically, decided to nick my girlfriend instead. Makes perfect sense. I was in Hiroshima.'

'*What?* Oh God, you did it!'

'Yeah.' Ax grinned wearily. 'Yeah, we bust the quarantine. Using my chip, and your code, and I don't know what the difference was but this time it worked. It was fucking exhausting, and *could we talk about it later?* After I've had about thirty-six hours' sleep?'

'You're mad,' said Fiorinda, opening her eyes. 'You're both insane. You're going to get nicked, and then things will be a million times worse. Put me down, Sage.'

They'd reached the van. She stood looking from one to the other. 'Well, what's the verdict? Have you two decided you can handle sharing *the meat*?'

'Ouch,' said Ax. 'I think I deserve that. I'm sorry, little cat. I'm just a jealous guy.'

Most unexpectedly, Fiorinda burst into tears and flung herself into her boyfriend's arms crying, '*Oh, Ax. I'm sorry too.*'

At four in the afternoon Sage and Fiorinda were sitting outside the Continental Breakfast Bar in the arena. They'd just struggled through brunch in the hospitality benders with Dian Buckley, an informal get-together they'd apparently agreed to attend at some point during the night before. Needless to say, they'd forgotten about it until Ax told them. In normal circumstances they'd have stood Dian up, no question. Favoured media-babes ought to know better than to prey on helpless drunks. After the way they'd behaved, they'd felt they had to go and mend some fences.

Before that, they'd been organising the getaway, Ax having tearfully refused to organise anything, as he was so crap at it and had fucked up so badly last time. They'd left him sleeping in the van, while they arranged for Allie to look after their diaries, fixed for someone to go to the Brixton flat and pack bags for Ax and Fiorinda, fixed for someone to drive the Volvo down (Ax had arrived by train this morning). As soon as the car arrived, the three of them were going back to Cornwall, to try again.

They'd ordered coffee and bread and jam (neither of them had touched the brunch), but they couldn't eat. Sage kept catching startled glances from passers-by, who couldn't believe he still wasn't wearing the mask. Fiorinda was sitting in a foul miasma of patchouli. She'd had to borrow some clothes from Anne-Marie, who lived in the hospitality area with her brood, or she'd have been chatting to Dian in the mandala frock.

Her head felt broken and empty, a tub full of useless chemical fragments that didn't know what the hell to do with each other. She wrapped her icy hands around her coffee bowl, trying to get them warm. The Continental Bar coffee was Crisis Blend, mainly ground roasted dandelion roots. It didn't taste too bad, but it smelled like nothing.

'Sage.'

'Hm?'

'Last night when we were alone, you told me you couldn't do the threesome, no chance, never. You talked to Ax and now it's happening. Could you explain that?'

'Don't you trust me?'

'No. I think you and your boyfriend will probably run off and leave me.'

If he'd been wearing the skull she'd have called the look she got *weary forbearance*, with a mix of *bleak resignation*. 'You can trust me. I finally realised, you and your boyfriend are making me the best offer I'll ever get in my life. I'm sorry it took me so long to grasp the concept.'

'Hey.' She took his hand (Sage so lost to vanity he was sitting out here in public not even hiding them: he *must* be feeling rough). 'Knock that off. I love you both the same. Don't you ever believe you come second. Don't you *ever believe that*.'

Sage thought of the vision that Ax had forgotten. He had forgotten it himself: snapshot glimpses don't last, they *vanish*. Yet he could guess where they had been, though he remembered nothing. What will happen to Olwen Devi's quest? Is it impossible? Is it even desirable? The Zen Self had seemed so important, when he had nothing else. Now the reversal of his fortunes overwhelmed him: the straits he'd been in, even last night when he held her in his arms; the *terrible* look of that long lonely road ahead. He wanted to kneel at her feet.

'Fiorinda.'

'Now what?'

'About those other sheep . . . I will be true to you.'

She stared at him, amazed. Then she laughed. '*Funny* Sage.'

'I mean it.'

'Give me a break. Aoxomoxoa monogamous? Don't be silly.'

'*Fuckit*, Fiorinda. Why will you never, *ever* take me seriously—?'

'Oh! Shit! Did we arrange for someone to feed Elsie?'

'Yeah, we did. The cat will be fed, don't change the subject—'

The people of Reading arena passed by. She kept on holding his hand, feeling like driftwood, floating, her heart filled with golden light.

George and Dilip had been visiting the Leisure Centre deconstruction, which had become a Reading sideshow: recycling robotics, seething tanks of plastic-disassembling slime moulds, all kinds of interesting stuff. They came out in time to see the black Volvo getting handed over, in the alt.tech builders' yard that used to be the car park. Ax had just arrived. Fiorinda hugs her boyfriend, Sage hugs him too. Ax chivvies them into the car, refusing to be distracted by some last-minute tale they want to tell—

'Sweet,' said Dilip.

'You shoulda been at the van this morning,' said George grimly. 'Fuck. I thought there'd be murder done.'

Dilip stared at him. 'I don't believe it. Sage would never lift his hand to Ax.'

'Maybe not. That's not the way round it was going to be.'

For a moment they faced each other – big George and

83

the fragile mixmaster, no taller than Fiorinda – like duellists' seconds, but with loyalties the opposite from what you'd expect. Then they shrugged and resumed watching the departure.

Fiorinda in the back, Ax and Sage in the front. Off they go.

'It'll end in tears,' sighed George.

'Because it always does,' agreed Dilip.

But secretly they were hopeful. This isn't your average no-brain rockstar ménage à trois. This is the Triumvirate. Nothing is beyond their powers.

When they reached Tyller Pystri, long after midnight, it transpired that Sage had forgotten to call Ruthie Maynor. The house was dank and cold. There was no electricity, and no water coming out of the taps. They made up Sage's bed, crawled between the sheets and slept, clinging to each other like refugees in a burnt-out cellar.

The next day Fiorinda woke in sunlight. For a while she watched them, asleep in each other's arms: Sage unmasked, Ax's hair spilling in a dark, gleaming fan across the pillow. And how often do you see that? How often is Ax Preston relaxed enough to sleep in *Fiorinda*'s arms? Huh. Well, she thought. That's the size of it.

She got up and went out (remembering to leave them a note). In the garden she found a bed of wild strawberries. She picked all the ripe ones and carried them off down the footpath that led to the stepping-stones across the Chy and the short-cut to the village. Red berries, blue sky, yellow sun; the little river rushing and shining beside her, the larches and the hazels and the oak trees every shade of tender green.

Later they joined her at the pub called the Powdermill. There wasn't going to be any electricity for at least a week: North Cornwall Renewables was having trouble with the wrong kind of waves. The spring-fed water pump was a separate problem. Ax reckoned he could fix it, and arranged to borrow some tools – but not today. They stayed at the pub until evening, drinking beer and eating bread and cheese (the only food on offer, alas, no crisps, no Bombay Mix), and then headed back by road. Sage and Ax tried to convince Fiorinda that Ax's visit to the Pan-Asian Utopians had not strictly broken the quarantine, he'd just harmlessly proved that the quarantine *could be* broken . . . Fiorinda had heard this kind of doubletalk before, and was not impressed.

'Just don't do it again,' she said. 'Or if you do, I don't want to know.'

We have bottled water. We have firewood, we have oil for the lamps. We can live here. The water in the Chy is not safe to drink (*giardia*); but we could boil it if we were stuck . . . A little shy with each other, they settled in the living-room. Fiorinda lit a fire, because the house was still cold. Ax and Sage started to work on the jigsaw they'd begun on the last, abortive visit. Fiorinda fetched a book from the landing and curled in an armchair to read. The room grew warm and dusky. The two men abandoned the puzzle and sat back, leaning against the sofa.

'Fiorinda,' said Sage, 'tell me something. Did you eat my strawberries?'

'Yes.'

'Told you,' said Ax.

'Oh, for heaven's sake. What's wrong with me eating the strawberries? If you didn't happen to be here, the slugs would have had them.'

'Not so. Ruthie packs them up and sends them to me.'

'God, that's pathetic. You're such a *baby*.' She ditched her book and jumped on him.

Ax watched them giggling and tussling and felt a momentary pang, *hey, unhand my girlfriend* . . . Then he remembered all the times the three of them had been together, and Sage and Fiorinda not allowed to touch each other. Sage's pain, and Fiorinda's pain, that he couldn't even bear to think of. *This is how it has to be.* There's no other option.

He leaned over and cut in.

'God, that feels weird,' he complained. He was kissing a freshly stripped skull.

Sage had put on the mask to go down the pub. Fiorinda couldn't care less, but Ax is such a fogey—

'Sorry, I forgot. Is that better, Sah?'

'Yeah,' said Ax. 'Much better.'

How strange that three should be so different from two. The difference between a line from A to B and the whole world.

The sex was as good as last time, in fact, mysteriously, it made last time better, reaching back to undo the knots of tension in that remembered night. They kept going for a long time, very practical, greedy, instinctive, mostly silent, only laughing and talking in the pauses between takes. At last there was a longer pause, the three of them lying on the bed in an exhausted, sweat-greased tangle of limbs.

They moved into an easier configuration. 'Was there some wine?' mumbled Sage.

'I'll get it,' said Fiorinda.

The two men turned instantly to watch. Fiorinda walking away from you, naked in the firelight, there can't be enough chances in a lifetime. Shoulder to shoulder, they glanced at each other, sharing the delight: and how appalling now to think how differently this could have ended: Ax not here in this room tonight, Sage with some other woman—

'Oh. I'm afraid it's a touch more than chambréed. Anyone for claret soup?'

'Never mind, bring it here.'

She brought the warm wine. Ax went and found some glasses. They toasted each other and settled again, Fiorinda curled up between the two men, her head on Ax's ribs.

'Anyone hungry?' said Ax after a while.

Fiorinda giggled. 'Ax is hungry.'

'Okay, guilty. Ax is hungry. Sage, is there anything in that kitchen of yours that can be eaten, like, easily? Without any soaking of lentils or scraping of roots?'

'There's whatever we bought in the garage shop last night. Bread, butter, bacon. Can't remember. Tomatoes? There are tins. I don't feel like doing anything about it.'

'I fetched the wine,' said Fiorinda.

In the end they all got dressed, or half-dressed, and made the expedition together: Sage carrying the babe, because the stone flags were cold for her little feet, or some such excuse. He set her on the counter by the fridge and tracked down the groceries, which they'd secured by knocking up the garage shop people in the middle of the night. Bread, butter, a pan for the bacon, check the gas cylinder, light the gas, slice some tomatoes, the tomatoes are a little frisky, but it's not beyond him . . . He looked over his shoulder. Ax and Fiorinda were kissing, Fiorinda still on the counter, her slender ankles and rosy heels locked in the small of Mr Dictator's beautiful, copper-coloured naked back.

'Hey. Why am *I* doing this?'

'We don't know,' said Fiorinda, winding a strand of Ax's hair around her fingers and giving herself a silky dark moustache. 'Why are you?'

'Carry on,' said Ax. 'You're doing fine.'

'Tuh.' He carried on, but he couldn't stop looking at them, kept casting envious glances: finally he deserted the frying pan and came raiding.

'Let *me* have him. *I* want him—'

Sage takes possession, but these two can't snog quietly like normal human beings. They have to start racketing

87

around Tyller Pystri's old-fashioned, perilously cluttered kitchen, laughing, falling against the dresser, the table, the chairs, the things hanging on the walls, both of them delighting in Sage's size and strength, as if it's one of the greatest glories of the universe—

'Out!' yelled Fiorinda. 'Get out of here! You're going to BREAK things!'

She finished cooking the bacon, made the sandwiches, put them on a tray and brought them back to the living room. Sage and Ax were on the bed, naked, still grappling furiously. Are they fucking or fighting? Looks like a bit of both. 'Idiots,' murmured Fiorinda. She set the tray by the fire, knelt beside it and took a bite of sandwich. God. *Delicious.* The best bacon sandwich *in the world, ever.*

Better give them space. Hopefully they're not going to hurt each other, but these are two big fierce male animals, and they're not holding back. Fiorinda watched for a little while, put down the sandwich, pulled her dress over her head, tossed it and got up on the bed. What she meant to do was quietly masturbate, eyes closed, lying in the penumbra of their heat and movement. Instead she was captured, a hand gently covering her eyelids: ooh, I'm not supposed to know who? Come on. You are not exactly identical twins . . . But it didn't matter. They were all three lost in a blind world, reaching a new, incredible peak of three-in-oneness, for ever and ever and ever, feels like as far as anyone can go, without never coming back at all—

When she opened her eyes they were looking at her anxiously.

'Are you okay Fee—?'

'Maybe that was too much, maybe we won't do that again—'

'I'm fine. I loved it. What do you want me to do, turn cartwheels?' Then she decided she *did* feel like a fragile, broken flower: deliciously broken, but absolutely finished.

She burrowed under the duvet. 'I'm fine and now I'm going to sleep.'

'Hey, Fiorinda,' crooned Sage, 'don't you want to smoke a cigarette with us?'

'I keep telling you, little cat. It's guys who are supposed to do that.'

'leavemealoneI'masleep.'

'Spliff?' said Ax.

'Yeah.'

They put their trousers on again before they moved to the hearth: not so much to mark a line between sex and friendship, as from a futile sense that they ought to be prepared. Being naked feels so vulnerable. 'I have post-traumatic stress,' confessed Ax. 'Always, everywhere, at the back of my mind, I'm waiting for a bunch of gunmen to burst into the room and start blazing away.'

'And not a thing we can do about it,' agreed Sage. '*Yeah. Me too.*'

This is the enduring legacy of Massacre Night, the night the civilised world ended, and their bizarre afterlife began. They'd seen worse disasters since, and higher body counts. They'd been to war and become soldiers, dealing out death themselves. But nothing compares with the memory of the first time, the first sight of violent death; the first horror of their helplessness.

'Nah,' Sage decided, after a moment. 'We're safe. If they were going to burst in tonight, they'd have been here 'bout half an hour ago.'

'And that would have been a real shame.'

They grinned at each other. 'Wrong on both sides?' offered Sage.

'Wrong on both sides.'

A hand clasp on it.

They shared the spliff in peaceful silence. Sage went out to take a piss. Ax moved around the room, mending the fire, tidying things, putting out the lamps (fucking lucky we

89

didn't smash one). Sage came back and stood gazing down at the hearth, enraptured. What's he looking at? A mouse-nibbled bacon sandwich.

'You're soft in the head about that girl, Sage.'

'I certainly am.' And about you too, babe, he thought, but I plan to try and keep the extent of that to myself. You push me around quite enough as it is. 'The sky's cleared. Good stars. Want to come out in the garden? We could choose a few of the best ones, an' pull them down to put in her hair?'

'Yeah. Good idea—' But no . . . 'No, I can't. I can't leave her.'

Not for five minutes. Sage came to the bed to see what Ax was seeing: a tangle of red curls, a creamy shoulder, the tip of her nose.

'Sage, do you have guns in the house?'

Sage hesitated, knowing Mr Dictator's opinion on firearms. 'Er, yes.'

'Thought so. Within easy reach?'

'You want to get sorted now?'

Ax shook his head, disgusted that he felt better for knowing they could defend her. She doesn't want that kind of defence. She wants the world where she was free and my equal, which is lost forever, that's how she sees it, and *I can't give her that.*

'No. Just wanted to know.'

'Hey, Ax, knock it off. Stop looking like that.' Sage hugged him, and it's strange how much more vulnerable, yet also (thank God) more *protectable* Mr Dictator feels in his arms than that fragile girl . . . 'Sssh. Live for the moment. I love you, Fee loves you, let's get into bed and I will be your teddy bear.'

'Looks like Fiorinda's bagged the middle.'

'We can work around that.'

Fiorinda was not quite asleep. She was thinking: Tyller Pystri must belong to all of us. The Brixton flat is Ax's territory, Sage has the van. Shit, this is not tenable. I will have to have a place of my own. She couldn't remember, right now, why the idea filled her with dread. But things happen as they must . . . and drifted into soft oblivion, to the murmur of those two West Country voices, the one from further west a little deeper, a little sweeter: but really, on the edge of sleep, almost impossible to tell them apart.

Fiorinda and Ax had fun mending the water pump. Sage refused to take them to Tintagel, for fear of tourists, but they visited the standing stone and the waterfall pool, and climbed down the cliff path to the cove at the end of the track, but couldn't swim there for masses of very un-romantic stinking kelp. It's usually like this in the summer, said the native son smugly. Keeps the tourists at bay. (There aren't any tourists, but this doesn't get through to him.) On the last day before they went back to London they walked for miles along the South-West path, the sea like another country laid out in silver and turquoise beneath the cliffs, larks shouting in the sky; the turf under their feet glowing with yellow trefoil, rustling with hare-bells. They came to a headland where there had been an Iron Age fort, climbed to the end of the promontory and sat down among the flowers.

'I wonder what Rivermead will be like in a hundred years' time,' said Fiorinda.

'It will be part of the city,' said Sage, 'with a futuristic forcefield dome over the arena, tent-inspired architecture and all our wild and free ephemera set in stone. Reading will probably be the capital by then. London's shrinking, you know.'

'That's if Ax wins his game,' said Fiorinda. 'If Ax loses, the watermeadows by the Thames will belong to the otters and herons again, except for a few smoky huts. Might will be right, women will be property and the peasants will be revolting, just the natural way things ought to be.'

'It doesn't have to be like that,' said Ax stubbornly. 'We can stay civilised *and* get back to the garden . . . But I'm sorry I got you into this, both of you. It's not your fight.'

'Don't be sorry,' said Fiorinda. 'We're volunteers.'

'We're with you, Ax.'

They clasped hands and stayed there for a long time, looking into the west.

Back in London Benny Preminder missed his monthly Liaison meeting. No picture postcard for him, nothing but a curt message, hardly an apology, from Ms Marlowe. At the appointed time he sat in his office, smarting. What are these people, after all? Nothing but popstars, and Benny remembered when they'd not even been famous.

I *made* them. But of course no one remembers that now.

He took out the dossier from its drawer. (No big secret, why shouldn't he keep a Triumvirate scrapbook? Doesn't everyone?) He had some beautiful pictures of Fiorinda that he knew were fakes; but he kept them anyway. A thrill went through him as he gazed on the forbidden. And here are the notes, brief and concise. *April.* (Cuitos.) Mr Preston remains in final control of law and order in this country. *May.* (Giamonos.) They are secure in power. The only threat to the Rock and Roll Reich is the instability of the Westminster government . . . What was his news this time? *June.* (Samivisionos.) The Triumvirate took a holiday. What is the message here?

Back at the start of this Countercultural adventure, long before Ax Preston made himself Dictator, Benny had explored the wilder shores of extreme green ideas. He'd been disappointed, finally, by people who were all talk. Then he had found himself keeping this dossier. For a while he had been very puzzled, but he had come to understand the situation. Once, Benny had seen himself as a kingmaker. He didn't crave the limelight. To be the guiding hand behind Ax Preston, or some other local hero, would have suited him very well. He felt that he had grown since those days. He no longer needed to be in control, he could *flow*. He was protected, he was blessed (Benny Preminder leads a charmed life!); and he would see downfall of those arrogant bastards.

Sometimes emotional satisfaction is worth more than power.

He didn't know who his secret master was. It could be someone he met every day, it could be someone not even in the country. He'd decided it would be wiser not to try and find out. He'd been offered a chance to get in on the ground floor of a strange, exciting, new opportunity; and he had taken it. Leave it at that. Presumably he would know more when he needed to know more. The plan would become clear. Meanwhile, all he'd been asked to do was to keep this blameless record, and wait for the fullness of time.

He knew that presence he felt was in his mind, but it seemed to fill the room.

The dossier meant nothing, and everything. It was a ritual, a focus, an outward sign . . . He had locked the door against his secretary. He was safe from any orthodox spying eyes. The Rock and Roll Reich is an anti-surveillance culture, but he swept this room for bugs regularly, using his own expertise, just to be sure. He trusted his master to protect him from any – shall we say, unorthodox interference?

He put the book away, took out his little box of props and lit the incense-studded candle. He should be naked, but better not, just in case of interruption. What message must I send? He didn't fully understand, but *he knew*. Kneeling by his desk, he looped the knotted cord around his wrists in token of submission. Bowing his head, he whispered, in the ancient language that Ax Preston was trying in vain to suppress.

Come, master, come lord. Come soon. The fruit is ripe.

THREE

Car Park Barbie (Was: Sweetness and Light)

Unmasked, Aoxomoxoa and the Heads
(whitemusic.)
NME **album of the week** ★ ★ ★ ★ ★

Classic Rock Music, with its unique blend of magic-tech and untrammelled human expression, is the essential soundtrack of techno-utopian revolution, and anyone who needed to be told that by the high culture authorities makes us puke . . . but political correctness is a poor excuse for this fearless stunt-dive into a collection of tasteful ditties for the over-sixties. How the king of weird could make such anodyne choices leaves us reeling in the years, and finding Aoxomoxoa's Desert Island Discs . . . The black vinyly respect-fest is only relieved by two new tunes and a plaintive a capella rendition of 'The Diarrhoea Song', that, frankly, the world could have done without. Yes, that's Fiorinda on the vocals on 'Ripple' and 'Atlantic Highway' and also (uncredited) playing guitar on 'Scarlet Begonias'. The antiques are unspeakably predictable, (Psychokiller), sometimes need (ahem) no explanation (Son Of A Preacher Man; Mighty Real), and guess what, there's too much Grateful Dead. George Merrick rules the sound with aplomb, Bill Trevor turns in a cool tenor solo or two, and my, my Peter Stannen, you handsome devil you, all the girls will be swooning now! But you're going to buy it anyway, so we'll unashamedly leap onto the bandwagon. The lads can sing, the dancing is a proper treat, and at least there are fewer opportunites for irritating Cornish bits. Don't forget to press a copy for your gran.

The Triumvirate returned from Cornwall with a new body language, a new collection of private jokes, and Sage was staying at the Brixton flat. It was Festival season. The night before the Few's lumbering caravan of a roadshow set off, into the wild unknown of Crisis Conditions, they gathered at the pub by Vauxhall Bridge which had been one of their watering holes since Think Tank days. Rockstars, crew, hangers-on, filled the premises and spilled out onto the warm, dusty pavement.

Chip and Verlaine, Triumvirate-soap addicts, decided this was their chance to snag some prurient details. They accosted Fiorinda as she came in from the street to get her round in for the girl-talk table. Sage's Barbie Doll collection is a concept, says Chip, and wild strawberries we can get our heads around. We feel we have a handle on the sheep, adds Verlaine . . . But you have to explain about the bacon sandwiches. The rock and roll brat breezed by them. 'It's like a Mars bar party,' she told them, over her shoulder, grinning like a very sexy Cheshire kitten. 'Only different.'

Mr Dictator and his Minister, drinking at the bar with Doug Hutton, the Few's security chief, simultaneously choked on their beer.

Oh my. Wait till they get her home.

In the second week of July the circuit brought them back to London, for the gala opening of an urban exterior art show called 'Stairway To Heaven: The Virtual Counter-culture'. The day was warm and humid. Immaterial art-works filled Trafalgar Square, glittering with colour and causing consternation to the pigeons. The great and the good and the media people stood about nattering; the PA played a medley of the Few's greatest hits.

Ax, a guitar over his shoulder because he'd been busking for the cameras, stopped to talk to the Reading Site barefoot-architects, who were here with a maquette of their new Rivermead building. The building – multi-coloured and crinkly, a kind of lo-rise Barcelona Cathedral

– was constructed out of reclaimed car-bodies and mulched plastic waste. It was genuinely cheap, unlike some recycling options; and people would get used to the way it looked, (you have to be patient with architecture). Ax was less happy to see that the flood-proofing scheme, which involved pumping a layer of CO_2 *under the whole Festival site*, had reappeared. Tempting though it might be to envisage the Rock and Roll Reich kept afloat on a sea of dry ice, the expense would be ludicrous.

'But Ax, Rivermead's yer showcase,' insisted the team leader, a rotund lunatic white guy with a beard like a bramble bush, known to his pals as Topsy. 'This is hot tech for the flood countries, we have to *be there*, you got to see that.'

'Fuck. I'm just a vapid materialistic rockstar, you're the eco-warriors. If you can't live with the river, move away. What happened to listening to Gaia?'

'What if we can get funding from the government?' asked a barefoot-architect henchwoman, at which Topsy glared at her furiously.

'What if we pretend you didn't say that. Do you really want Rivermead part-owned by the suits? I don't care what they told you, they have no money: but if they had, we wouldn't take it. I said no, and I mean no. Forget it.'

Silver Wing and her sister Pearl, wearing their butterfly dresses from the Mayday concert, were competing to hammer on the button that made the model heave up and down in its cellulose case. '*Stop* that,' said Silver, 'you're breaking it.'

'You stop. I was touching the button first.'

'*Stop it* or I'll tear your fucking head off.'

Time to move on. Anne Marie had a charming habit of simply letting her rugrats loose on Few occasions, taking it for granted someone she knew would have to pick up her childcare. Breaking up their fights was ugly work. Let the hippies do it.

Fiorinda was walking around with her gran. The old lady had no interest in rock music and never came to gigs, but there was a much-hyped portrait of her granddaughter at the exhibition and this had moved her into a rare sortie from her lair in the basement of the cold house where Fiorinda had been brought up. Gran had expected a limousine, and probably a motorcyle escort. She'd refused the modest, green alternative of Fiorinda fetching her in a taxi, and come along with some neighbours, who were now mingling with the crowd, mildly fascinated to be in the highest company, the most VIP enclosure in the land.

'You're behind the times, Frances dear,' said Gran. 'Sainsburys sells magic now. You can buy cantrips in Boots. Why shouldn't I use my little powers?'

Gran was a witch, a Wiccan. She'd been plying her trade for years, on the quiet, but these days it wasn't so funny. Fiorinda had been getting a worrying report on the old lady's antics. 'Just stick to the herbal remedies,' said Fiorinda. '*Please*. Promise me that.'

She ignored the irritating reappearance of her original name. She hadn't called herself 'Frances' since she was eleven. Gran knew that. She was just being annoying.

'I'm not doing anything wrong,' said the old lady. 'You shouldn't listen to tell-tales.'

They stopped in front of a voluptuous, virtual purple female with fuschia-pink parted lips, crouched upon a gravestone in a midnight churchyard. Ah, poor Ax. So much for the futuristic Arts and Crafts movement.

'You know what I'm talking about, Gran.'

Gran had grown smaller, the way old people do; but her button eyes were bright as ever. 'You're the one who should be careful how you use your powers, my dear. Which are far greater than mine. You can't go on suppressing nature this way. It isn't right.'

Fiorinda returned the sly, challenging look and grinned, unabashed.

'Oh no? *Watch* me . . . Come on, you said you wanted to see the portrait.'

'Isn't this it?' said Gran, maliciously, affecting old-lady confusion and peering at the purple Metal Calendar Girl. 'It's very nice. Atmospheric, I would call it.'

'No, Gran. You know I never wear pink lipstick.'

Fiorinda and Allie took a break, sitting on the broad, black back of one of Landseer's lions, sipping frosted sherbert. It was fortunate that this wasn't a party where one would want to get drunk, because sherbert was the only nice thing on offer. The fake champagne was vile. Above them a collar of shimmering perturbation (unoriginally titled 'Untitled') circled Nelson's column, as if that massive limb of ribbed stone was sporting a mauve and silver ballet tutu. A party of Islamist elders strolled by, casting a tolerant eye on the infidel excesses, and bowed to Ax's lady. 'I like the tutu,' said Allie. 'They should keep it. And Whistlejacket is amazing. I haven't seen a single other thing I can stand.'

'Fucking unicorn-merchants,' agreed Fiorinda. 'It's embarrassing.' The show featured a few masterpieces, rendered in virtual 3-D for the first time (Stubbs, Constable, Turner: had to be English, of course). The rest of the stuff was like that Calendar Girl – school of hippy market stall, faithfully imitated by currently famous names.

She sighed. 'Bad news—'

'Sage has punched someone from NME.'

'Hahaha. No! The only problem with that review is that Peter is now afraid to go out without a mask, in case he gets mobbed. Otherwise Sage thinks it's fine. He says. The bad news is my gran. She's fallen out with her lodgers again.'

'Oh God. She hasn't hexed them?'

''Fraid so. Mrs Mohanjanee says she's been acting confused. I don't believe *that*. She's putting it on because she knows she's in trouble. But she's nearly eighty, and she's not a *young* eighty—'

'Is she a real witch? I mean, can she do things?'

Fiorinda shrugged. 'I suppose we have to admit that it can happen, these days. I don't think she's very effective at it, thank God. But that's not the issue.' She stared into her glass and sighed again. 'The issue is that you grow up, and then your past returns to haunt you. Family things. *Fuck.* I thought I had dumped all that.'

'What about sheltered housing? You could find her a really nice place.'

'And throw away the key,' agreed Fiorinda, with feeling. 'It's a plan. Nah, I couldn't do that to her. What she needs is someone to live in that house, not obviously a nurse or a warden, who'll get on with her and keep her under control. What she *wants* is me. She wants me to move back there, the way I did when my mother was dying.'

'Has she asked you?'

'I won't let her. I sneak out of it. But I know what's on her mind. Fuck. What would I do? Have Sage and Ax visit me at weekends, huh?'

'No one expects you to do that,' said Allie quickly. 'Don't even think about it!' (Allie making a mental note to warn Ax about this bright idea. Fiorinda must not go back to that place, the scene of her horrible childhood. Not even part-time!)

'Don't worry, I'm not tempted. But . . . I don't know what to do. It's not going to be easy to find a keeper she'll tolerate.' She prepared to slide down from the lion's back. 'I'm going to be polite to the artist-bloke. I said I'd talk to him when I'd seen Gran off, and that will be my last mingle, okay?'

The artist was standing beside his much-hyped picture, talking to Chip and Verlaine. Faced with his subject's undivided attention he didn't last long: just muttered a few platitudes and melted away. She was left looking at the portrait while a small crush of people, held back behind an invisible line by her presence, looked at Fiorinda.

She Feeds And Clothes Her Demons. It was a 3-D image of a picture in a frame, oils on canvas, photorealist. The figure was nearly life-sized, the frame antique. The original would be taking up residence in the City Art Gallery in Birmingham. A tired, pallid young woman with red hair, wearing a tattered green dress, crouches among the roots of a fallen oak. Livid little Hieronymous Bosch nightmare creatures are crawling out of cracks in the bark, from holes in the ground, buzzing in the air. She's feeding them cupcakes, sweets, chocolates, and giving them clothes out of a tapestry bag.

The bloke had worked from photographs. He'd wanted to borrow the green silk dress, the Fiorinda dress from Dissolution Summer, but they hadn't been able to let him. That dress had fallen into rags and been *buried*, like a pet hamster (only way Fiorinda's friends could stop her from wearing it) in Reading site boneyard; it wasn't going to be exhumed. She reached out, to see her fingers go through the frame: which was something everyone was doing to the virtual art.

'Do you like it?' asked Chip, looking over her shoulder.

'I think it's creepy,' said Fiorinda softly. 'They're not *demons*, if he means the drop-out hordes. There's no need to feel too sorry for most of them; to an extent they've made their own luck. But they're not *demons*.'

She rubbed her bare arms, thinking about the shape of things to come. Are we doomed to be sacred icons, public property, for the rest of our lives . . . ? The radio bead in her ear – a routine security precaution – was letting her eavesdrop on several conversations. She could hear Anne-Marie, on the other side of the square, giving some media folk the benefit of her Countercultural Feminism (all men are scum. Any woman who doesn't live in a bender with sixteen kids is denying her true self . . .).

Suddenly, AM's manifesto was cut off:

Doug, saying the Triumvirate are wanted urgently at Blue Gate.

They met in the crowd. Sage was wearing his beautiful suit, but skull-masked, as was appropriate for a digital art show. Ax had been talking with the PM, a social obligation his Triumvirate partners had callously avoided. 'Maybe this is it,' said Fiorinda, only half-joking, thinking of Massacre Night. But they would never be caught like that again.

'Nah,' said Ax. 'I don't smell trouble.'

'It'll be nothing.' Sage pressed his fingertips, virtual and real, together, and pulled them apart, drawing out a skein of vivid blue sparks. Nice trick.

'Where'd you get that?' asked Ax.

'In the workshop. Want some?'

Ax and Sage were right. At Blue Gate ('Blue Gate' at an event like this, was code for wherever the Few's own security had their command post), outside the iridescent screens that closed off the square from public access, they found the crew chatting to a raw-boned ginger-haired bloke in grimy jeans, silver rings in his ears, wearing a blanket round his shoulders. So, a normal Countercultural citizen, one of thousands; but Fiorinda thought there was something familiar about his seamed, alcohol-ruined face—

'Hi folks,' said Doug, grinning. 'Got someone here wants to thump Sage.'

'Hey, Sage,' said the ginger-haired bloke, 'told yez I'd be back.'

'Fergal!'

Ax laughed. 'What are you doing here, you crazy Irishman?'

The stranger gave them a gap-toothed, blackened, charming grin. 'What would I be doing? I've defected, comrades. I've come to serve the cause. If ye'll have me.'

So that was why he looked familiar. This must be Fergal Kearney of the Playboys, the Belfast band who'd been over for the Rock The Boat tour last summer. Fiorinda hadn't met him, she'd been on a different line-up on the tour, but Fergal was a living legend. A fine musician, real contender, who had destroyed himself with drink and drugs; a stage compadre people spoke of with affection and respect, in spite of his fucked-up career . . . Oh great, she thought, standing on the edge of the conversation. Another of those music biz guy relationships, that I don't understand because the world ended before I could get trained in how to react, so now I'll never get it. She was prejudiced against the Irish.

Fergal turned to her. 'This is Fiorinda?'

'Yeah,' she said, 'this is Fiorinda.'

'Jaysus,' said the Irishman, staring at her intently but not offensively. His eyes were blue-green, in cruel contrast to his pocked, scarlet complexion. 'Y'er even lovelier than yer videos . . .' He gulped. 'It's a great pleasure. No, it's an *honour.*'

He groped under the blanket, which she saw was really some kind of Celtic mantle. A couple of police liaison officers, not quite as happy as Doug with this situation, made a half-move. Fergal brought out an Irish harp, most of the gilding gone but all the strings in place. 'I saw yez first on the tv, Dissolution Summer. I've never missed a chance since. Ye're the bravest girl I ever saw, an' a queen of the music. Ye'r worth ten of Ax Preston, which I hope he knows, and ten hundred of this focker Aoxomoxoa: and now I've told ye, which was half me plan in coming to England. Here's me harp. I'd lay it at yer feet. But I'd only look a fockin' eedjit and embarrass ye, so I won't do that.'

She couldn't think of a response. Fergal's complexion grew even more scarlet. He cleared his throat. 'Uh, well, that's the business done. Now, Sage, me favourite fallen angel, is there anywhere here a man could get a drink?'

Being called a fallen angel pissed Sage off. It was a music media term for former global megabuck earners, trapped and impoverished by the data quarantine. But the living skull merely beamed affectionately. 'Ooh, I think we could arrange that.'

They crossed the square, Fergal gazing around in frank curiosity: taking in the VIP crowd, the armed police side by side with the hippy guards, the slick and gaudy revolutionary art. 'Fock, this is amazin'. I niver thought, this time last year, ye'd still be keeping it all going. An' how's the band, Ax? Shane and Jordan, and yer girlfriend. Sorry, I shouldn't say that. Yer ex-girlfriend. Lovely woman, I forget her name, yer drummer. Are they here?'

'They're not in London at the moment.'

'Oh, right so. You know, there's been rumours. I'd hate to think that the Chosen—'

'Nothing's wrong.'

'That's grand, because I can see how it must be tough, havin' yer frontman into focking government politics—'

'I'm not into government politics. I'm into Community Service, state ceremonies and putting on a few free concerts, that's all. Everything's fine, Fergal. Thanks for asking.'

It was months since the Few had had such an interesting visitor, and Ireland was outside data quarantine (having been judged innocent of the Ivan/Lara disaster); which made Fergal even more welcome. They abandoned the VIPs and took him back to the Insanitude. They gave him a tour of such of the old pile that wasn't Boat People accommodation – and then took him out to eat at their favourite Mexican. The English were hungry for news of the world they'd lost. The Irishman was flatteringly insistent that the Rock and Roll Reich was not forgotten out there. They were famous. They were the coolest thing in the wreck of Europe—

'Fock,' he kept saying, 'here am I among the legends!'

But of course he wasn't a stranger to the Reich. Last summer, when an armada of four hundred thousand refugees had come across the North Sea, through the worst storms in a century, the Playboys had been part of the chaotic mad panic as the Few and guests raced up and down the country, staving off anarchy with free rock concerts.

'Jaysus, that was the best hard fun I iver had on a tour, barring none. Dez ye recall that night in Manchester, or was it Preston, Sage?'

'Yeah,' said George Merrick. 'You bet we do.'

The Playboys, righteous traditional musicians, had taken offence against the Heads' set and heckled from the side of the stage, resisting the efforts of crewpersons to silence them, until Sage dropped out of his acrobatics and—

'Yer man, looking ten foot tall in that fockin' spaceman outfit, comes over and sez to me, "Will we give you bastards what you are asking for now or later?"'

'An' Fergal here,' supplied Bill, 'says, "We didn't know you do requests. In that case, we'll have, 'A Nation Once Again',", and then—'

'You left out, "If Sage can find his voice in those tin knickers",' put in Chip.

'Yeah, there was the tin knickers remark. Think that was from Pierce Lyon.'

'Aye, that's right. Because it was when Sage picked up our Peezy – he's a little man – and threw him off the stage, that the fockin' punters took it into their minds to get involved. An' it was pissing down, and there was mud fockin' *everywhere*—'

'Funny, I don't think I ever heard this story before,' said Ax, grinning. 'I fondly imagined we were all trying to keep the level of violence *down*—'

'Fergal, what are you doing to me?' protested Aox-omoxoa. 'Hey, it wasn't me, Sah. I was somewhere else.

It must've been my shadow. I don't remember any of this—'

'Oh Jaysus, I fergot, ye've turned over a big new leaf. Will it be okay though if I tell the story of that barney we had at Glasto, first time we ever met—?'

The story of the famous barney at Glasto, well-known but worth repeating. Stories abounding. Fergal Kearney, devouring red wine in astounding quantities, kept them coming. It was after midnight before they got back to the San, and he was still going strong, living up to his reputation for the highest quality *craìc* (Irish, verbal variety).

Dilip and Chip and Ver stripped to bodymasks and cache-sex and went off to dance, (it was melting-hot on the dancefloors in the State Apartments). The rest of them settled, regally, in the Bow Room chill-out lounge. The band who'd been playing live in the ballroom arrived to pay their respects, and were graciously allowed to stay. Sweaty, glittering clubbers made excuses to come up and say hi. Fiorinda chatted to the singer with the band, a brash overawed fifteen-year-old called Areeka Aziz, and found herself strangely distracted by the sound of that rambling Irish voice. It set her teeth on edge.

Areeka was supposed to be a Next Big Thing, and needed to be sounded out for Few associate status. So this is what we'll do now, thought Fiorinda. We'll recruit the new wave, the second generation. Me, chickenhawk.

At the other table Fergal had reached the garrulous stage and was explaining exactly why he'd 'defected' . . . 'Fockin' government sez there's no Countercultural Problem in Oirland, fockin' shite. Right enough it's not the Counterculture that's the problem, it's the fockin' bastards that are using it fer their own sinister aims, an' I know where it's heading. It'll be like the fockin' Catholic church all over again, and will the people rise up against the tyranny of it? Will they fock—'

That voice. She couldn't help it, she just didn't like that sound—

'Fockin' Irish, they're a race of political masochists, they love their fockin' chiefs and princes an' a strong hand belting them. It's like the man said in the play. *Abair an focal republic i nGaoluinn?*'

The Few looked at George Merrick.

'He says, "say 'republic' for me in the Irish",' said George, 'the point being, I reckon, that there's no such word.'

Fergal stared, his seagreen eyes growing brighter in the dim, chill-out light. 'Jaysus. I had fergot ye had the Gaelic. I shall have to watch me tongue—'

'There's no word for republic in Cornish either,' said George, grinning.

'I'm only glad there's a countrywoman of mine among ye to stand up for me.'

The Irishman cast a wistful glance towards Fiorinda, who was sitting with her straight back turned to him: still dressed for the art show, feet tucked up under her storm-cloud indigo skirts, a silver grey bolero jacket covering her shoulders, a little silver cap on her burning hair—

She looked around. 'I am not Irish,' she said, the cut-crystal vowels very apparent.

'Aye, well. Half-Irish, I meant to say.'

Chip and Ver and Dilip came in, dripping sweat and towelling themselves with sodden teeshirts. They stopped short, looking at each other in dismay. A *frisson* went round the whole party.

Fergal must know about Fiorinda and her father. What is he thinking of?

The rock and roll brat shrugged. 'Tuh. My father was born in Chicago.'

'It makes no odds. Ye can be Irish by adoption, 'tis a culture, not a race.'

Rufus O'Niall, veteran megastar. Born in Chicago of

Black and Irish American ancestry, raised in Ireland by his adoptive parents, a minor Hollywood movie actress and a Belfast businessman. Married twice, divorced twice. Had a daughter with London rock journalist Suzy Slater, a relationship that broke up when the child was four. When that daughter was twelve she was taken by her aunt, a procuress to the famous, to spend the weekend at Rufus's English manor house. The little girl was seduced by the star and later became pregnant by him. She had no idea he was her father. Opinion is divided as to whether Rufus knew what he was doing.

That's the story. Everyone knows it. *Shut up*, Fergal. But no, he can't stop digging—

'Yer dad's a black-hearted swine, Fiorinda, as yez don't need me to tell ye. He's one of the bastards I was just talking of. But I hate the whole fockin' Irish nation meself, an' I'm still an Irishman.'

'I don't follow your logic.'

'Jaysus, girl, I'm saying don't turn yer back on yer heritage, because one man did ye a terrible wrong when ye was too young to know—'

'What *I* want to know,' announced Chip, loud and clear, flopping down in an empty chair, 'is, when are we going to see some Gay Pride from Aoxomoxoa?'

'Oh come on,' said Rob, equally loud, lamming some of those art-workshop sparks at the insolent kid (Rob's were acid yellow). 'Leave the guys some dignity. You want Fiorinda to make you a video or something?'

'Hey, it's a plan. That could be a nice little earner.'

'The words tigers and Vaseline come to mind—' sighed Felice, rolling her eyes.

'He'd never do it,' said Allie, 'not after everything he's said about gays. He's such a hypocrite. Okay, we use a body double. Should be easy. I'll check my personal database.'

'Nah. Has to be the boss. We'll let 'im have his mask—'

'Why is it always *me*?' demanded Sage. 'Why don't you fuckers pick on Ax?'

'They can't,' said Ax, leaning back beside his Minister on the sofa they were sharing, grinning complacently. 'I'm the great dictator. They have to pick on you.'

'You're his bitch, Sage,' said Dilip. 'We thought you knew that.'

Fergal, looking confused, joined in the general laughter.

Fiorinda had escaped to the toilet. She stood clinging to the porcelain anchor of a wash basin, staring through the face in the mirror. The raffish splendour of the State Apartments didn't extend behind the scenes. Here there were broken tiles, ancient utilitarian fittings, dirt in the corners. Such is our small world. Such is the shabby little hothouse we call our Rock and Roll Reich, where everyone knows what you mustn't say to Fiorinda, where *everyone in the room* jumps a mile if someone dares to mention her father's name in her royal presence. Oh fuckit, get a grip, this is ridiculous, put it behind you, worse things have happened to plenty of stupid twelve-year-olds, *why am I fucking shaking?* Thank God Fergal Kearney would never know the abyss into which he had plunged her. Any luck, he'll just think I'm naturally rude and snotty—

Shit, what did I say to Areeka before I scooted out here? I was filthy rude to her too, I know I was. *Shit.* Have to fix that.

Now I'm going back, and I'll behave like a human being. I can do it.

She opened the door. Sage and Ax were waiting in the dark passageway outside (biological sex not an issue, but you don't invade the Ladies at the San unless you are *dressed* like a lady). Ax had her bag. 'Moving on,' he said, tucking it onto her shoulder.

'Raves to rave,' said Sage, kneeling to put her sandals on her feet.

'The night to explore.'

'What's wrong? What are you *doing*? I'm fine. Let's get back.'

'Not fucking likely,' said Ax. 'Fergal has had his audience with the great dictator. Let's hit the town.'

London was dark and motorised traffic scarce, but the night was warm and the streets were full of people: moving around in droves, carrying their own lights, looking for the party. Sage and Ax and Fiorinda joined the shadowy carnival. Some unmarked time later they were in a club called 69, on the Caledonian Road, behind King's Cross Station. Desmond Dekker, Marvin Gaye. Eyekicks of startled recognition in the fitful light, but no fuss: these are Ax Preston's children. At the back of the floor Fiorinda danced with Ax, easy and close, letting the bittersweet defiant mood of the ancient music lift her. It was *so wonderful* to be in his arms, and Sage right there (leaning against the wall, smoking a cigarette, choosing to watch his lovers rather than dance), not jealous, not hurting, loving this beautiful guitar-man as much as she did. How can anything be wrong, what does anything else matter, as long as I have my tiger and my wolf—

'Sage!' she whispered, over Ax's shoulder. 'I have to have this Ax. Somewhere private. Right now.'

'Is that so? What about you, Mr Dictator?'

'*Yeah.*'

'Okay. Leave this to me.'

He led them out the back of the building. There was a car park, dank and dark, by the Regent's Canal, buddleia and willowherb sprouting from the asphalt, almost empty except for a couple of rows of derelicts that might have been there since Dissolution. Sage lifted Fiorinda onto the bonnet of a flat-tyred Vauxhall, divested her of her pretty pants (he loves having her underwear in his pocket—) and stooped over her, the skull mask glimmering silver. 'My brat, but this is al fresco sex?'

'This isn't outdoors,' said Fiorinda, hugging him with arms and legs. 'This is an urban exterior, which is totally different, I *like* this—'

One deep kiss and he moved aside, saying All yours, Sah – a little atavistic ritual happening, part laughing and part strangely intense. Fiorinda took Ax, Ax silently powering into her, God, *wonderful*, while Sage kept watch at the end of the row. Then Sage was back, twisting Mr Dictator's hair in a silky rope, biting the nape of his neck, big cat style: *hey, brother, move over, I want her*, and it was Ax's turn to stand guard . . . The whole double act took about five minutes, and it was bliss.

They sat in a row, backs against the old motor, passing a spliff, the rain falling on them like cold kisses. The air smelled of railway grime; puddles glimmered on black, cracked pavement. Fiorinda, a warm wall on either side of her, looked up into the opaque sky and couldn't stop grinning. No one understands us, she thought. Not anyone, not our dear, protective, demanding friends, no one: because this is all we want. Nothing else, just this. Forever, ever, ever.

'Good car to drive,' mused Sage. 'After a war.'

'Very poky ride—'

'Cheap to run an' all. Couple of pints of snakebite and a handful of Bombay Mix, she'll go all night.'

'Lovely interior.'

'Mm, and great road holding—'

'You noticed that too?'

'Hohum,' said Fiorinda, pulling her hair across her face in two thick hanks of tangled curls. 'Fiorinda remains problematic role model for liberated young women of England.'

'Ah, no!' They grabbed her, swept her up onto the bonnet again and fell to their knees, pressing the cold, rosy soles of her feet to their faces, kissing away the gravel and rainwater and dogshit. 'Fiorinda, angel, empress, we're stupid drunks, we thought it was funny, we didn't mean—'

'Idiots. Let me down.'

They lifted her down and cuddled her close between them, but they were a little sad now, a little crestfallen. Sage leaned over and kissed Ax, a long kiss: rubbed his cheek against Fiorinda's hair and heaved a sigh. 'Ah, well. Me and my ruined fortunes.'

'Yeah. Me and my falling-apart band. Ouch, ouch, ouch.'

'He doesn't mean any harm.'

'Nah. Just not the soul of tact, our Fergal. It's not his fault we're caught in this trap.'

'As long as we can get pissed and fuck in a car park, in the pouring rain,' said Fiorinda, 'I reckon we have not lost the game of life.'

'I love you, Fee, because you are so wise.'

Sage went indoors to rescue Fiorinda's bag and sandals from becoming the objects of a cargo cult. They headed for home on the all-night Underground, the carriage almost empty and weirdly bright, Fiorinda curled up on Sage's knees, falling asleep. 'I wonder what he's really here for,' she mumbled. 'Fergal.' Sage and Ax exchanged a wry glance.

'I expect we'll find out soon enough,' said Ax.

Fergal Kearney came to the flat in Matthew Arnold Mansions, Brixton Hill, on a warm grey summer evening two days later. He was staying at the Insanitude, where the building management had found him a room. Mr Preston himself came down to let him in. Fergal followed the Dictator upstairs, into the living quarters, and stood looking around. He saw a big room, very simply furnished: a gas stove in an old-fashioned fireplace, a few pictures on the walls, a couple of good North African rugs. Tall windows at the back stood open to a brick terrace, with pots of greenery. You might call the style minimalist, but there's nothing precious about it. Just travelling light. Here, on a stand on a bookcase, is the stone axe, the famous Sweet Track Jade, the one they gave him when he was inaugurated. Here's a pair of car numberplates, AX1, which someone must also have given him. Mr Preston is way too arrogant for vanity plates, so they end up an ironic ornament. Here's an immersion cell, in a flat screen, Sage Pender's best work, Jaysus that's a pretty thing, and better not look at it too long for it will suck you in. Here's a framed piece of Arabic lettering, looks antique. He frowned. Ah, now, the Islamic question . . . The smell of cooking drifted pleasantly from somewhere further into the flat. Mr Preston is an excellent cook, that's also part of the legend. An open door gave a glimpse of a wide, low bed. A tortoiseshell cat crouched on one of the couches by the stove: poised, glaring at him, as if not sure which way to run.

He was trying to read the runes. How do they live together, these two beautiful, powerful men? How do things shake down between them: Mr Ax Preston, with the air of command on him that you could cut with a knife, and Sage, who surely to God (joking apart) is no feller's bitch—? He already knew, from the way he'd been greeted, to expect a little distance. Mr Preston at home is not going to be the same person as Ax, relaxed and half-drunk at the Insanitude.

There was nothing that suggested Fiorinda, and this caused him concern. Why does she leave no mark?

Ax, seeing his visitor preoccupied, had returned to the current jigsaw, and sat cross-legged beside it on the floor.

'You're alone?' said Fergal, at last.

'Yeah. So, what did you want to talk to me about?'

'Yez don't keep any staff here?'

'Fuck, no,' said Ax. 'I spend my life managing people. I come back here, I want to switch off. We have a cleaner three times a week because if we didn't, with the best will in the world, the place would get disgusting. Other than that we do our own chores. I don't know what anyone sees in domestic servants, it's a crap idea.'

'That's not exactly what I meant.'

Ax grinned. 'What did you mean? Armed guards?'

'Ax Preston is a very brave man,' said Fergal, somewhat sternly. 'That's part of the legend, an' I don't doubt it's the truth. But there's Fiorinda to think of. Fockin' Jaysus God, what if you was to come back here one day an' find her raped an' murdered? Would ye not be better with a few of yer barmy army fellers around?'

Brixton is my village, thought Ax. I run SW2 as my private fief. I don't need guards at my door when I own the neighbourhood. But Fergal probably didn't catch the last issue of *Weal* . . . and one day, yeah, maybe this shit situation will become too dangerous. It'll be time to get out, and take my friends with me. Hope I don't miss the moment. He smiled. 'The day we need to be protected from our neighbours is the day we quit.'

'Aye. Right so. But suppose you find out it's time to quit half an hour too late?'

Ax shrugged. 'Insh'allah. Please, make yourself at home. Sit down.'

The Irishman came over and peered at the jigsaw, which was a National Trust classic, featuring about fifty different varieties of British sheep. Fiorinda had bought it for them.

'You like sheep?'

'Very keen.'

'Hm,' said Fergal. He dropped the shoulder pack he was carrying and sat on a couch. His complexion had a dull, magenta cast today, and he moved with the deliberation of an old man, or a painfully sober drunk. 'How d'yer Islamic backers feel, about you and yer man—' He nodded significantly towards the bedroom door. 'Do they not find that a wee bit hard to take?'

'Jaysus fockin' God, Fergal. Don't be afraid to ask an awkward question.'

'I'm just trying to get a clear picture.'

'I think they might find the video hard to take,' said Ax, 'so we'll probably hold back on that, until we're really strapped for cash.'

'Fockin' wind-up merchants. Fock it. I knew that was a big leg pull.'

'Sure you did . . . Fergal, I converted to Islam to end the separatist war in Yorkshire.' Ax rifled the pieces and picked out a fragment of shaggy-brown big sheep. No, it's a piece of rock. 'They knew what they were getting. Some of the Faithful are appalled that I perform on stage with a stringed instrument. But they'll live with it, because I'm their warrior prince. I don't pretend to be conventionally devout, I behave with reasonable decorum in public, and it works. The leaders of English Islam are in this for the long haul. They see themselves heading for a golden age, England as an enlightened, multi-ethnic Islamic Caliphate. I'm a move on the board, a step on the way. They're not homophobic, they even believe in civil rights for women, and they don't give a toss for my dissolute lifestyle, if I serve their purpose.'

All true. It was also true that Ax's conversion had been genuine, but he didn't see why he had to discuss that.

'Ye know, I've never known a woman to really enjoy a ménage à trois. They put up with it if they have to, but they're naturally monogamous. Are ye sure she's happy?'

'Fergal.' Mr Preston was beginning to lose patience. 'I find it hard to believe that the Irish government sent you over here just to investigate my sex life.'

'Fock. I'm not working for the government.'

'So who are you working for? The Dublin chapter of the CIA?'

Footsteps on the stairs. The cat, who had partly settled, roused again and stared at the door. Sage came in; Fiorinda was behind him. 'Hi, Fergal,' said Sage, 'sorry, Ax, we should have called. I had to go and haul Fiorinda out of the DETR.'

'Environment, Transport and the Regions,' said Ax to Fergal, politely. 'The government department we mostly have to deal with. It's okay, the stew's taken no harm. I'll put the couscous on to steam now.'

'I'll do it,' said Fiorinda, quickly.

People who have a lot of pain and suppressed anger in them are often 'tactless': Ax had noticed this. As much as they want to please you, as much as they know they're self-destructing, the little back-bites, the totally unnecessary comments will come tripping out. Fergal Kearney, poor devil, was well known for his terrible habit of saying the wrong thing. But this was different. Even at the San the other night, Ax had felt that this was a man with a plan. The Irishman ate sparingly, fortified himself with several glasses of red wine and went on probing, crudely but thoroughly. He was sounding them out, like a political refugee indeed, dropping references, watching for reactions, testing the ground.

He also tried hard to make up to Fiorinda for his *faux pas* the other night, but she wasn't having any. She hardly spoke, and disappeared to the kitchen whenever she had the slightest excuse.

Fiorinda loaded the dishwasher (a very *green* dishwasher, but Ax refused to live without one). The three men moved to the couches by the stove, with a new bottle of wine. Giving Fergal Kearney spirits would be outright murder, but you had to accept that he needed his drug, in some form, beyond the point of no return.

'So,' said Ax, 'did we pass? Now can you tell us who you're working for?'

'I told yer,' said Fergal, 'I'm working fer the Rock and Roll Reich, Ax. If yez'll have me.' He gave them his sweet, broken grin. 'Be easy, I'm not planning to make a move on yer girlfriend. But I've fallen for her, that's the truth, an' I've parted company with the Playboys – don't know if you heard. Me life's near at an end. Why should I not follow the gleam? I've nothin' better to do.'

He picked up his glass, drank, and set it down half full. 'You know, it's a funny thing. The first time a doctor gave me a death sentence, I was terrible upset. I'd lie awake nights, grieving. Now it's on me, and I can't be focked to worry about it.'

This was chilling. Fergal was maybe ten, at most fifteen years older than they were themselves: and he was dying. He had been on the edge when they last met him, but now the marks were unmistakable.

'Yeah,' said Ax, after a moment. 'That's half the story. And the rest?'

'Aye, the rest.' The Irishman looked at Ax uneasily. 'You was saying, it's time to ferget conventional politics: concentrate on the culture, the lifestyle choices. Control the mob, and let the mob control the bastards in the suits. I hear ye have the army and the polis eating out of your hand an' all . . . An' that's all well and good, in *yer* hands, becuz ye're only using this classic game plan fer peace and preservation. But there's other people besides yerself, Ax, that sees this fockin' cascade of disasters as a golden opportunity—'

He broke off as Fiorinda crossed the room. Ax and Sage noted with approval that he'd waited for the third member of the Triumvirate to return before getting serious. Tactless maybe, but the Irishman isn't stupid. Fiorinda sat on the end of the couch where Ax and Sage were sitting. Fergal nodded to himself, and looked hard at his glass, but did not touch it. 'Mr Dictator, ye've got a problem.'

'I have several,' said Ax. 'Could you be more specific?'

'Aye, mm . . . How well d'you know yer Prime Minister? Mr David Sale?'

The three did not look at each other, but they became

more closely united. Oh shit. Here it is, whatever 'it' is. Here comes trouble.

'We have a good working relationship,' said Ax, sedately.

Fergal nodded, still with the air of someone weighing his words very carefully, hesitating over every step. 'But yez don't know him personally?'

'I wouldn't say he's a personal friend. No.'

'Did ye know he's a smack addict?'

Sage grinned. 'Yeah. He's a vegetarian an' all. We try to be broadminded.'

'It's not funny, Sage,' said Fergal, reproachfully.

'Addiction's a big word,' said Ax. 'I know David's taken to using heroin. But in England today, that's not really a problem, Fergal. Personally, I don't like it: but it's not a guilty secret.'

'Aye, well. What if I was to tell yez he was getting into something worse?'

Fergal reached for his bag, took out an envelope and drew from it several sheets of paper. He laid them on the coffee table that stood between the couches. A succession of lo-res monochrome images: groups of seemingly naked human figures cavorting in a dark background. Some of the heads were circled and highlighted.

Ax picked up the sheets, one after another. The face that was best enhanced, recognisable in each of the images, was clearly the face of the English Prime Minister.

'What is this about?' he asked, in a tone of cold reserve.

'This is about the Celtics,' said Fergal grimly. 'The folks that used to be called "Ancient Britons" in your country.' He touched one of the pictures. 'There's a lot of this caper goes on in Ireland now. The acceptable side of it, the pilgrimages to the High Places, the feasts and the bonfires, is somethen' they're saying we never really left behind. They're saying, this is religion returning to a state of nature, an' even the Catholic hierarchy, fer what their opinion's worth, says it's fine and dandy. And maybe so, an' maybe ye're going to tell me the English Cabinet is welcome to practise Pagan sacrifices, along with takin' hard drugs. But however that may be, according to my information, yer Mr Sale has progressed to the harder stuff.'

'What d'you mean?'

'Magic.'

'You mean, real magic?' said Sage, taking up the pictures and frowning at them.

'I don't know what yez understands by that,' said Fergal, after a pause for thought. 'I think the blood-sacrifice would be real. An' effective, in that they get closer to what they are asking for, which is the dark ages. How real do yez want it?'

Pagan animal sacrifice was one of the problems that kept Ax awake at nights. The hardline Celtics insisted they had a right to practise their religion, and it was extremely difficult for him to deny them that right while trying to keep the Celtics on board and avoid an open split. He had to leave it to the campground councils; he had to leave it to the hippies themselves to condemn the bloodthirsty extremists. But it was definitely *not* okay for the English Cabinet to go cavorting around the bonfires. Animal sacrifice was still seriously illegal. The fact that it happened, inside and outside the Counterculture; the fact that there were secret networks of punters who gathered for these blood-daubed raves, was one of the most scandalous, shocking features of the whole Celtic issue . . . Of course it couldn't possibly be *true*. David wouldn't be such an idiot! Then the real import of the pictures hit him, and his blood ran cold.

It doesn't have to be true. My God.

'Are you trying to tell me these are genuine snapshots of the English Prime Minister attending a so called "Celtic" animal sacrifice?'

'Aye.'

'Oh, for heaven's sake!' Ax dismissed the idea with a wave of his hand. 'Give me a break . . . I can see by looking at them the images have been faked to hell. I don't know who sold you this, but there's nothing in it. This isn't evidence!'

'I niver said anything about "evidence",' said Fergal, with dignity. 'I should think a public enquiry's the last thing ye'd be wanting. I said a problem.' He stared hard at the Triumvirate, as if still trying to decide if he could trust them. 'I can't tell yez how I got hold of these. I don't precisely know where they came from, meself. But the pictures aren't all. According to me informants, there's a place that yer Mr Sale knows of, where the fun goes beyond killin' animals. I can tell yez where and when: and yez can check it out fer yerself.'

They stared back at him, straight-faced. 'I don't believe you,' said Ax.

Fergal nodded. 'Aye. I can understand that. An' I can understand how ye'll feel about the messenger. But ye had to be told . . . Ye're not alone, Ax. I'm a sad old drunk, but everything I said the other night's the truth. I have the greatest admiration fer your achievement, and I'm not the only one. There's a whole world out there, wanting to believe Ax Preston's England isn't going to collapse into a pile of shite.'

'That's nice to know.'

'I was coming over to yez anyway. I wisht I hadn't had to bring this. Or I wisht you had laughed in my face an' said it was a pack of fockin' nonsense. But I see that's not how it is. An' now I'll leave the matter.' He stood up, delving in his pack again. 'Didn't bring me harp, I had a feelin' no one would ask me to play. But here's a present from Ireland . . . I couldn't carry much,' he added shyly. 'I tried to think what yez'd really be missing.' He put a gift-wrapped package beside the envelope and glanced diffidently at Fiorinda, who hadn't said a word through the whole exchange. 'Are they good to yez, these two? Jaysus, I hope they are.'

'Oh yes,' said the rock and roll brat, raising cool, merciless grey eyes. 'They take me for walks, and I have my own bowl with my name on it and everything.'

Ax and Sage went down to see Fergal out. They came back and stood considering their babe. She seemed to be okay. 'How about a guinea pig?' said Sage to Ax.

'People speak highly of those big furry spiders,' said Ax. 'Apparently they can be very companionable.'

'Sorry.'

'But what do you think of him?' said Ax, sitting down again. 'Truly?'

'I think he's genuine,' said Fiorinda. 'He puts my back up, but I have to admit, I think he means well and he really wants to join your rock and roll band. I hope to God somebody's using him to deliver loony disinformation. But I think Fergal himself is fine. Of course I could be wrong.'

'You could be, but you're not often. Well. Let's see what we've got.'

He opened the parcel. They had three cans of Diet Coke, a cellophane package of black peppercorns, and a bottle of genuine, hundred per cent agave, Mexican tequila.

Of all the countries subjected to the Internet Commissioners quarantine, in the wake of the Ivan/Lara virus disaster, the three nations of Mainland Britain suffered most, and England worst of all, having neither Scotland's connections with Scandinavia (where quarantine had already been lifted); or much benefit from the smuggling across the Irish sea. They'd lost not only e-commerce and financial services, but a crippling amount of their surviving foreign trade. In the midst of a global economic crash, with fuel wildly expensive, the punitive maze of anti-virus regulations had been the final straw.

They laughed. England was in more need of machinery parts than peppercorns. But even after the news he'd brought, it was impossible not to be touched by Fergal's bounty.

'I don't think we should do anything until morning,' said Fiorinda. 'I'm going to practise. Soundproofing on or off?' She often practised the piano late at night. It was the only way to find decent, solid time, and she liked the echoing secrecy of those hours.

'Off,' said Sage.

'Mind if we join you?' asked Ax.

'As long as you don't talk.'

Fiorinda played Bach, rapidly and carefully, frequently the same phrase over and over, obsessively smoothing out the kinks. Ax lay with his head in Sage's lap, watching her hands in the pearly glow of ATP lamplight. This room, with the piano, which was still their spare bedroom (are we ever going to get that guest room sorted?) was Fiorinda's territory. Her favourite dresses hung on the walls; other treasures of her life were scattered around: the red cowboy boots he'd bought her when they were first together. Her guitars (including that awful battered old acoustic). It isn't easy to give Fiorinda presents; those orange trees on the terrace, a triumph for Sage, but if you give her something and it gets to live in here, you know you're doing well . . . Most of Ax's guitars were still in Taunton. Will I ever move them up here? And if I move them, will Jordan see that as my final betrayal of the band?

Fiorinda was right. Don't start flailing around in the middle of the night. Wait, sleep on it. But he couldn't relax. He kept hearing Fergal's question again. No, Ax did not *know* David Sale. He had sometimes felt a great respect for the man. This was the chief executive who allowed the Deconstruction Tour to happen, without escalating the violence. Who had kept his head when Pigsty Liver was running riot; who had kept the regular troops out of the fighting in Yorkshire . . . Who had *created*, let it be said, the situation that had brought Ax to power. But Ax had kept his distance. He had never wanted to be in David Sale's confidence, because there was too much dirty water under that bridge. There was the question of how far the PM had been involved in the Massacre Night conspiracy. There were other questions . . . Things Ax had preferred not to find out.

He thought of their last meeting, at the artshow. David had been with a group of glamset green-revolutionaries, dressed in expensive 'Celtic' fashion. Ax had been sardonically amused, recalling the Think Tank era, when the Prime Minister and the Home Secretary had been so thrilled to be hanging out with rockstars. That's David. He has to be in with the in-crowd. That's his thing.

Oh, shit.

He'd brought the photographs to the music room, not meaning to look at them again, but . . .

He sat up and studied the images: turned them over and read the handwritten notes on the backs of the sheets. Dates, locations. Fuck. He pushed back his hair, rubbing his temples with calloused fingertips.

'I'm going downstairs to try and send a couple of faxes. I won't be long.'

Fiorinda went on playing. Shortly, she turned her head. Sage was watching her, hands in his pockets. He was wearing the mask less and less, but the hands still had to be hidden if at all possible. One long leg crossed over the other; a little sickle-shaped indentation by the left corner of his mouth, picked out very clearly by the lamplight. *He will be fifty*, she thought, with a shock. He will be this big, thin, middle-aged bloke, extremely used to getting his own way.

'What is it?'

'Fee, can you still do that trick of yours, with fire?'

Fiorinda's grandmother practises witchcraft. Sage had

accidentally discovered, about two years ago (or been allowed to discover, he wasn't sure which), that Fiorinda could do some strange things herself. She'd made it clear that she'd decided to bury her talent, or whatever you called it. He was not allowed to tell anyone. Not even Ax.

'You mean like this?'

She stopped playing and held out her right hand, palm upwards. A dot like molten copper quivered on her skin, and then a leaf-shaped flame was there: flickering red and orange. He even thought he could feel the heat. But the brain loves to be fooled.

'Is that an illusion?'

She moved her hand so the flame rising out of her palm connected with the corner of a sheet of music that was lying on top of the piano.

The illusion continued to convince his senses.

'Oh, *Fiorinda*—'

She resumed playing, having used her fingers to crush out the miniature fire. A wisp of smoke and the smell of scorched paper remained. 'Look. You've had genetic engineering done to you, that means you can pump out energy from your fingertips, enough to light a room or boil an egg. Ax has a piece of etched silicon or something in his head, that means he can tell me all the postcodes in Billericay, and exactly what the Ministry of Defence plans to do in the event of a nerve gas strike, without pausing for thought. I have something weird in my wiring that randomly happened, that I was born with. What's the difference? I don't see a difference. I don't know why you are raising the subject. I don't see how what I can do with fire has any connection with loony neo-Celtic ritual blood sacrifices.'

The word Fergal used was *magic*, he thought. But he wasn't looking for a fight.

'Of course not. Never said there was. You have to tell Ax, that's all.'

'Yes, but not now,' said Fiorinda, cunningly. 'Not *right now*. Let's get over David and the blood-cult thing. Then I'll tell him. As soon as there's a good moment. Honest.'

FOUR

The Grove

Two weeks after Fergal's visit to Brixton, Fiorinda was in the dead centre of England, on the border between Leicestershire and Derbyshire. She was on her way to an extra date on the Festival Season's royal progress, and taking a side trip to inspect a derelict property for the Volunteer Initiative.

The weather had changed. The sky was baking blue, and heavy with summer silence. She walked up the steps from the fishponds to the rose-terrace. The stonework was weed-smothered and moss-grown; the roses had vanished in a tangle of knotweed. The fishponds behind her were lost in reeds and rushes. She was half puzzled to find the place wasn't a ruin, half surprised at the neglect. A lot can happen in seven years, and yet it's not such a long time. She sat on the top step, her back to the apricot-tiled, ambling profile of the house. It was here, she told herself.

This is where it happened.

Roxane Smith came up the steps and sat down beside her, carefully arranging the summer version of hir trade-mark flowing garments. 'What were you expecting to find?' s/he asked, looking out over the briar-tangled woods, the hay-meadow lawns: all the romance of a lost domain. 'Ghosts?' A pity the countryside beyond was soul-free potato fields in every direction, but that's rural England for you.

'Nothing. Nix. Zero.' She grinned at Rox's frown of concern. 'I wanted to see it again, that's all. To prove something. I'm *all right*. Honestly.'

'Hmm . . . Is the manor still your father's property?'

They hadn't broken in; the gates at the road were falling apart, but they didn't have any keys. This was normal practice for the Volunteer Initiative. Time enough to trace the owners of an empty property if they decided the place looked useful.

'I'm not sure. It might even be mine.'

Chip and Verlaine were down by the swamp that had been Rufus O'Niall's fishponds. They were talking about Aoxomoxoa. Verlaine had not yet recovered from the incident when, in a moment of dire folly, he had given Mr Dictator Preston a dangerous neurological drug . . . and then Sage had come looking for him. It bothered him that he couldn't remember a word his hero had said. The encounter played in his mind like a sunlit, horrible silent movie. 'Don't you cross him, Merry. You think you've seen him angry, but you haven't. He didn't touch me—'

'Commiserations.'

'Lay off. You're the one that lusts after him, not me. My feelings are pure. He didn't touch me because he knew if he touched me he'd kill me.' He looked up at the terrace. 'D'you think she's okay?'

'Never in doubt. Look at them, aren't they great? Our court philosopher and the young queen, in stately conclave.'

'Cool,' agreed Verlaine. 'God, don't you *love* the way this is turning out—' A moorhen chugged from between strands of flowering rush, breasting mats of green. The water underneath didn't look too malarial; it was brown and clear.

Chip got interested. 'D'you think there are newts in there? Let's have a look.'

'It might be yours?' prompted Roxane, back on the steps. 'Oh? How's that?'

Fiorinda rested her chin on her hand, gazing ahead of her. 'When I started singing with DARK, and someone outed me as Rufus O'Niall's unofficial daughter (It's okay, Rox. I've forgiven you), I got a lawyer-letter offering me money. The deeds of this house were in it. So . . . The band helped me, because I hadn't a clue, and eventually his lawyers got a lawyer-letter back saying I don't want your money. With the deeds in it, torn up. Don't know what he did about that, I never heard anything more. I suppose you could say he was trying to make up, but I didn't feel like playing.'

'I was once raped by a stranger myself,' said Rox. 'A long time ago. As I recall, the hardest part was convincing myself that I could let it go. That I should forget, if I could not forgive, and get on with my life. It took me several years.'

'I wasn't raped,' said Fiorinda. 'I was just taken, like a piece of fruit.'

She was thinking that she owed Fergal Kearney a debt of gratitude. Two weeks ago she couldn't have been having this conversation. Now there was Fergal, for whom *Rufus O'Niall* was simply a name that was bound to come up, simply a big name bastard, with heinous right wing opinions, and the taboo was broken. It had been a nasty shock, that first night, but she was over that. A weight had fallen from her. Who's Rufus O'Niall, anyway? Just an ageing celebrity who did something to me long ago that is unfortunately public knowledge . . . and that's all. He can't hurt me now.

When she'd realised that investigating Fergal's story was going to bring her within twenty miles of this house, she had decided she had to come and see. So here she was, and it was fine. No ghosts, no panic attack. Not that she intended to make a habit of revisiting her past, no thanks.

But I'm glad I did this. She touched her throat mic and recorded, blandly, 'The house seems weatherproof, no gaping holes, no vandalism, grounds neglected but with plenty of level space, well-drained. However, the position makes this a wildlife refuge in a sea of essential agribusiness. It could be linked to the National Forest corridor. I think that's what we should be looking at, rather than moving campers in.'

Enough said.

'Rox, is Fergal really dying?'

Rox knew everything about everyone: s/he was worse than Ax and Sage in this regard.

Roxane understood from the serene, forbidding, very *Fiorinda* smile s/he was getting, that the subject of Rufus O'Niall was closed. One doesn't pester this young lady. Her confidences are a rare treasure. 'Ah, Fergal . . . Every time I meet him, I'm surprised he's still alive. He has a systemic cancer, and cirrhosis. The tumour suppressants make it difficult to treat the liver failure, and I'm afraid that's about it. But who knows? As long as he can keep himself supplied with modern medicine, he might have a few more years.'

'Can he play that harp? He seems to just carry it around.'

'He can play. Last summer, at least, he could still sing. I think you'd have to get him on stage. Prop him against something, turn on the lights, he might surprise you.'

The ever-infantile Adjuvants came up from the ponds and flopped down, duckweed to the armpits. 'Palmated newts,' said Chip, impressed. 'How about *that*? Enough to stop a motorway, if we had one planned. D'you want to come and see?'

'Pass,' said the philosopher and the young queen, in unison.

A bee hummed. A bird burst into song, one solitary voice, loud and sweet.

'What I can't understand,' complained Verlaine, 'is how

they can call it a revival. How do they know? I mean, where are the sacred texts? Where did they turn up the church liturgy of the ancient Celts? How do they know what they're meant to do?'

Magic and ancient ritual held no terrors for the Adjuvants. Nor Rox. They treated the whole subject with a very English sceptical affection. Hammer Horror and Narnia.

'They don't have to know,' said Fiorinda, 'if it's like Wicca. Wicca isn't old. Someone started it in about the nineteen fifties or something. According to my gran, anyone can do ritual magic. Get yourself sky-clad, get some candles, ball of red yarn might be handy: do whatever you think. Impro is positively encouraged.'

'Yeah, and I bet most of it absolutely sucks,' said Chip. 'Most people shouldn't be *allowed* to use their own material . . . er, present company excepted.'

'Wanker,' said Fiorinda, amiably. 'Talk about making a virtue of necessity.'

Notoriously, the Adjuvants rejected the concept of *original music*. Every scratch and sample and scrap of lyric that went into their daft compositions was previously owned.

The security crew had been left with the van out on the road. They started paging, complaining that they were bored. The party left Rufus O'Niall's manor house and drove on, twenty miles up the road, to the little country town where they might possibly find evidence of the Prime Minister's involvement in a bloodthirsty Pagan cult.

The Triumvirate had brought Fergal's 'problem' to a closed meeting in the Office. They'd banished the admin staff on the grounds that they needed to discuss their new recruit, which, in a sense, was the truth.

Before this meeting Ax had talked to Fergal again, but the Irishman had had little to add to what he'd first told them. When they'd taken him out on the night of the artshow, he'd claimed he had no recollection of his journey from Ireland; he'd been on a bit of a bender. Now he said he'd come over from Dun Laoghaire on a smuggler's boat and crossed into England from the South Wales coast without passing through a customs point. Fair enough. He could tell Ax nothing about the source of the information he'd brought. He'd been contacted as a likely courier, by people he trusted: he couldn't say more than that. He didn't know how digital images of the English PM had turned up in Ireland, on the wrong side of the data quarantine barrier. He'd been told the originals had been destroyed, but he couldn't prove it. He knew only what he'd been told to say.

'It's possible,' said Ax, 'that Fergal is telling us the simple truth, as far as he knows it. He was always a politico; I can see him having contacts in the Irish radical underground. I can equally see the Irish Intelligence Services using someone like Fergal, with or without his knowledge. The data quarantine isn't unbeatable. We can't make so much as a phonecall across the barrier, but discs and electronic devices and e-paper can be smuggled: we know it happens.'

The photographs were passed around those school-room tables. There was a feeling of dread, yet at the same time almost of relief, in the atmosphere, a sense that a long expected blow had fallen. Things had been quiet for so long, but no one here had believed the storm was over.

'But if the Prime Minister is into something like this,' protested Verlaine, 'he has minders. They would have to know. They'd have a file a mile wide. We'd have heard rumours. *You'd* know, Ax. Something would have had to slip—'

'It could be his minders are incompetent,' said Ax. 'That's not impossible. It could be they're covering for him very efficiently, maybe not even knowing what it is they're covering up.'

'But why come to you?' said Dilip. He rifled the blurred images and passed them on to Allie with a shrug. Anything can be faked . . . 'Whoever sent him, why send Fergal to us with this, and not the suits? What does that imply?'

'That's a good question,' said Sage.

'Maybe "they", whoever "they" are, have told the government as well,' said Fiorinda. 'That's another possibility.'

Everyone except his Triumvirate partners looked at Ax. 'I don't know. I've heard nothing.'

'But is there any truth in the story?' asked Roxane, cautiously. 'That would seem to be a significant issue, wouldn't it?'

'I have no idea,' said Mr Dictator grimly. 'I haven't a *fucking* clue how we can get hold of the truth, Rox. The Rock and Roll Reich does not have an intelligence network inside the Westminster government. I'm sorry, major oversight . . . I tried making a couple of enquiries, just checking whether the PM's whereabouts was accounted for on dates we'd been given. I realised – in time, I hope – that I was going to make people curious, because *I don't do that*. It's my policy to stay out of their business. I don't check up on the Prime Minister. I don't ever ask a single unnecessary question.'

'We can't investigate it down here,' said Fiorinda, 'because the moment anyone notices what we're doing, we risk launching the very scandal we're trying to avoid.'

'But there's got to be *someone*,' protested Dora. 'Someone we can trust, who could ask the questions, without—'

'Who do you suggest,' growled Sage. 'Benny Prem?'

There was a general mutter of disgust; and renewed silence.

'There are plenty of Celtic sympathisers at Westminster,' said Ax, at last. 'The worst bastards in mainstream government find all that neo-primitive, green-nazi romance very appealing, for their own reasons. But the hypocrisy of English politics is sufficiently intact that if this ritual-sacrifice story comes out, David will be forced to resign. If David resigns, the government will fall. If this government falls—'

'We are *fucked*,' said Sage.

The Heads were all masked. As long as Peter didn't want to appear barefaced, they would support him. The living skull's expression was as bleak as the Few had ever seen it. It crossed Verlaine's mind that he wouldn't like to be in David Sale's shoes . . . If he was guilty of this insane pissing around, and if Sage got hold of him.

'The only reason England is still in shape,' explained Fiorinda (unnecessarily, they all knew the score), 'is because we have what looks like a legitimate government, working in harmony with the CCM. That's the illusion that we've created, with our Rock and Roll and Community Service solution. But we're not independent of the suits. If the Coalition falls, there's no other party in Westminster that we can work with, and the Rock and Roll Reich is done for.'

'You said, "down here",' remarked Dilip, after another long pause. 'You said we can't investigate down here. Are you suggesting an alternative?'

'We have dates and locations,' said Ax. 'We have a date and an approximate location for an illegal ritual event that's allegedly coming off at Lammas, at a place called Wethamcote, in the East Midlands. There isn't a known hardcore sacrifice venue in the area, I was able to check that in police records, but that would figure. I presume the Prime Minister would be on some kind of exclusive, well-protected, blood-fest network, if at all. We want to go up there,' he glanced at Sage, 'with a good excuse to be in the area, and quietly check it out.'

'Wethamcote has an arts festival,' put in Fiorinda. 'They call it a Lammas Festival, but apparently it is *not* Pagan, or

Celtic, just a perfectly innocent picturesque summer fête. Theatre, folkdancing . . . The idea is that I visit the fest openly, get the local information and pass it on to Sage and Ax, who will be lurking in the countryside.'

Allie stared. '*What?* Fiorinda, you can't go up there alone! No one knows what the fuck's going on in the rural hinterland these days! They have a Pagan festival! They have blood sacrifices in the woods. They could be up to *anything*!'

The living skull looked (a rare sight) as if it thoroughly agreed with Ms Marlowe. 'Yeah, well. You talk to her . . . Fiorinda will be in the town, Ax and I will be with the barmy army. We can fix for the barmies to summon us to have a look at the British Resistance Movement situation in the East Midlands, which is a genuine errand, and then slip over to Wethamcote. If we find a hardcore ritual venue, that will be confirmation of Fergal's story. If possible we'll try to get a look at the ceremonies. Which apparently David Sale is down to attend.'

'What, you're going to *bust* him?' exclaimed Chip, round-eyed. 'Wow. Er . . . would that help?'

'We're not planning to bust anyone,' said Ax, patiently. 'If we find them, we'll try not to get spotted. If they spot us, we'll back off. Very sorry ladies and gentlemen, we thought you were rural terrorists, no, please, don't bother to get dressed, we'll see ourselves out . . . We have to try and manage this fucking thing without offending the Celtics, that's the other bind. We can't deputise it, it's too sensitive, but I can't be seen to be hunting down Counter-cultural ritualists. If we do find them, we have to hope we can make it look like an accident.'

'But what if he's there?' protested Chip, 'What if *he's there*? What will you do then?'

'We won't know if he's there or not. From the look of those pictures – which must have been taken in infra-red, if there's anything in them at all – he wears a digital mask.'

The pictures were with Rob. He nodded. 'Oh, yeah, I get you.'

The skull-masked Heads nodded too. 'We've been caught like that,' said George.

'I will have to take this to David,' Ax continued. 'The bottom line is, the pictures exist. If the story's true, someone else could out him at any moment. If the story's a hoax, then someone's deliberately trying to destabilise our government—'

'Hohoho,' muttered Fiorinda, 'As if—'

'Yeah, as if it was necessary . . . That would be another problem, and it's going to have to be addressed, which is David's business, not mine. But I don't want to tackle him until I know what I'm talking about.'

'Lammas is the first of August,' said Allie, opening her laptop, 'isn't it? That's two weeks . . . Shit. Okay, well . . .' She tapped keys and checked the screen. 'Fiorinda is *not* going to go alone. I will be calling for volunteers. Ax, this is going to fuck you up worst. You're supposed to be playing with the Chosen at—'

'I know,' said Ax, cutting her off. 'Yeah, thanks. I spotted that.'

Ax had been playing with the Chosen since the start of the Festival circuit. As his friends and his lovers were well aware, it had not been working out. Of course, audience-wise the band was a howling success. It would be a while before that changed – no matter how much the insolent music press jeered (bless them) about 'the Ax effect'. But Jordan Preston wasn't happy. He didn't like being Mr Dictator's bandmaster; there had been tearing rows, and the Chosen were taking *their* break from the circuit back in Taunton.

The Few gave him a little space, politely silent. It's a common tale, the rending and the tearing when a band splits up: but always painful, no matter what the circum-stances.

'Hey, hold on,' said Felice, suddenly. The most shocking feature of Fergal's news had been recounted and then lost in the discussion. 'Slow down! You go up there. You find out if this is a hoax or not, you come back and Ax talks to the PM. I get that, that's okay. But what if the – the baby-impaling is real?'

'Those Ancient Celts,' put in Dora, 'they were definitely on the high end of normal for human sacrifice. I saw a programme.'

'Then we need to know about it,' said Ax. 'But I never heard of our Celtics doing anything worse than horses. I'm hoping *that* part, at least, is just a fairytale.'

Wethamcote was a small, long-time post-industrial town: no railway; population about twenty thousand. A tributary of the Trent, called the Doe, ran through it. There was a lot more information on Ax's chip, none of it significant. It had been trying to reinvent itself as a tourist attraction, with a box-fresh ancient summer festival, when Dissolution and Crisis Conditions had intervened. Allie managed to reach the festival organisers by landline phone and found them strangely, touchingly, normal-sounding. They were thrilled that Fiorinda wanted to visit, short notice not a problem.

Ax and Sage had no difficulty getting themselves summoned by the barmy army. On the evening that Fiorinda and her companions arrived in Wethamcote (after their side-trip to her father's house), the Dictator and his Minister were in a Volunteer Initiative potato diggers' camp outside Tamworth, where they had arranged to meet some old friends. Fergal Kearney was with them. He had not been unwilling; he'd been eager to come along, but he was keeping a low profile. He knew he was on probation.

The next night they had moved across country with a picked squad of barmies and were bivouacked outside Wethamcote. They contacted Fiorinda on the Few's secure mobile network. She reported that, yes, there was supposed to be a hardcore venue nearby, though nobody would admit to knowing exactly where. It was strangers (said the locals): rich post-modern Pagans with private transport, from as far away as Leicester, or even London. Nobody wanted them, but the Wethamcote police refused to take action, and what can you do?

Ramadan had begun. Before dawn on the thirtieth of July, Ax and the other Muslims broke their fast. By the time they'd finished prayers the infidels of various stripe were up and ready to go. They set out to circle the town, moving with precaution, but nothing too paranoid. They did not expect any trouble.

It was very quiet out in the agribusiness. Not a bird. The men hated it. In their early days, the barmy army had napalmed great swathes of green desert monoculture. They'd been persuaded to give up the full frontal assault (forty million people can't live on goat's cheese and nettles), but this territory was still their heart of darkness, haunted by the great dying. 'They came for the tawny owls,' intoned Big Brock, the re-enactment nut, softly, as the men tramped two by two through a stark expanse of last year's maize stalks, 'and I said nothing.'

'Because I'm not a tawny owl,' murmured several voices in response.

'They came for the water voles, and I said nothing,' piped up Jackie Dando, Romany and ex-regular, the wily entrepreneur who kept the group supplied with drugs.

'Because I'm not a water vole,' the sad chorus answered.

'They came for the buttercups,' sighed Brock, one broad hand on the hilt of the naked sword swinging at his side, the other tucked in his rifle sling. 'And I said nothing.'

'Because I'm not a buttercup,' moaned the barmies, mournful and low.

Fergal, walking beside Sage in the middle of the troop,

glanced uneasily at the living skull, clearly wondering if this was *normal*. Oh, you wait, thought Sage. You have no idea. They can keep this going indefinitely.

'Brock.'

'Yeah, Sage?'

'Shut the fuck up.'

From the top of a rise they looked down on a small wood, roughly circular, a red earth track connecting it to one of the little grey lanes that wandered over the plain of the Trent. There was a clearing in the centre, obscured by foliage. Their tech couldn't give them much detail. Wethamcote, with its church towers, couple of tower blocks, suburban housing, lay to the west. A farm and outbuildings stood about a mile away; there was no track between the buildings and the wood.

'The clearing wasn't there six years ago,' said Ax, 'for what that's worth . . . It's a likely candidate; let's get down there.'

Onwards.

'It'll be the horse-sacrifice,' said one barmy to another, 'that's the biggie.'

'You ever seen it done?' asked his partner, in a cautious undertone. They knew what Ax thought about blood-daubed Pagan rituals.

'Er, yeah, as it happens. Down in Kent, last year. Just out of curiosity.'

'That must make a fuck of a mess, disembowelling a live horse to death.'

'You bet. Don't worry, if we find an active venue there'll be no doubt.'

Ax was in the lead, watching the silent fields, feeling the mood of the barmies, sorely missing Sage's physical presence at his side, but they couldn't both nursemaid the Irishman . . . He should have known that the smack meant trouble. But he had reached for that crutch himself, when he was hard-pressed, and he hadn't had the heart to blame the guy. Shit, if I lose David Sale, what then? He could see himself getting more and more embroiled with Westminster, whatever the outcome of this trip – inevitable, hateful progression. The choices that he'd made were piling up, forcing him down an ever-narrower path, which he had foreseen, but foresight doesn't help; it always feels worse when it happens. I will have to quit the band, he thought. Jordan's right, this isn't fair. Finally, I have to quit . . . I have to admit my life as a musician is over.

It felt like death. It felt like something unforgivable—

They had reached the wood. The men fanned out, muttering about enchanted, sentient trees, trained to attack like mine-carrying dolphins. Cyborg birdies with cameras in their eyes, Wiccan spiderwebs wired to the police station (obviously the police in town were raving Pagans, or they'd have closed the hardcore down). The jokes were many, but there was an edge to them. Ax kept his rifle on his back; so did Sage. The lads got into comfort mode as soon as they entered the trees. 'Please,' said Ax, resignedly, 'Don't, I repeat, *do not* open fire on any squirrels, badgers, or bluetits—'

'N-not unless they shoot first, right Ax?'

'It's not going to happen.'

Their tech said there was nothing warm and big in the vicinity besides themselves. The trees were thick and in full leaf. The lads moved through them, invisible and commendably silent. Everyone reached the bare, beaten earth of the clearing more or less together. It was about forty metres across. There was a close-woven wattle fence around it, as if holding back the trees. On one side, incongruously, stood a prefabricated hut, looking like a festival ground toilet block. Most of the centre space was taken up by a gaping, smooth-walled pit, which had been dug out to a startling depth. In the middle of the pit stood two dark trunks of carved wood, like totem poles. Lashed to the top of each of these was the remains of a human body: a young man and a young woman. They seemed to have been naked. You couldn't tell much more about them, because of the way the bodies had been ripped apart.

There was a butcher-shop smell of old blood, mingled with other scents less insistent: an earthy, heavy incense, piss and sweat, grease and fear.

'Fuckin' hell,' said Jackie, 'how's that for a smoking gun?'

'*Shit*,' gasped another lad, more painfully impressed. 'What, h-how'd they *do that*?'

'Looks like . . . some kind of large wild animal?'

'Well, thanks, Sage,' wailed the young man. 'That's really fuckin' helpful!'

'Sorry. Okay, let's have a closer look.'

Aoxomoxoa swung himself over the rim, dropped lightly and walked around looking up at the grisly remains, touching nothing. 'Dead a day or so, I think. Fuck. It's definitely claws and teeth. *Big* teeth. Must have been dogs or something. Fucking big dogs. One skull crushed, front to back, not much face left. The other, er, missing.'

'Is someone recording?' asked Ax.

'Yeah, Ax.'

'Good. Make it thorough, disturb nothing. Sage, will you get out of that, *now*.'

Chris, the lad with the cam, walked about. Brock unrolled a climbing rope and anchored it around his waist, because even Aoxomoxoa might find the slick walls of that pit a challenge. Fergal Kearney came to join Ax. The others were hanging back, surprisingly devoid of the ghoulish curiosity you'd expect from such a bunch of ruffians and hard men.

'We should get the fuck away from here,' whispered Fergal. '*Away*, right now.' The words sounded panicky. The look he turned on Ax was of grim, vindicated satisfaction.

*

Fiorinda and her party were staying at the Rose and Crown, a fine old inn on Wethamcote's market square. She had the call from her Triumvirate partners about nine o'clock in the morning on the thirtieth. She was at breakfast. She went off to her bedroom to talk to them. When she came down she told the others that the sacrifice venue was found, and they must lay off the topic. Nothing more.

She lived with her special knowledge through the day's programme of bonfire building by the river, folkdancing in the square, lunch in the mediaeval church (where the Christians were broadmindedly serving Lammas bread and ale), and a live set on stage at the public park, where the bored teenagers were gathered. Wethamcote was poorly served for tv reception, as for all kinds of telecoms, but the celebrity guests had put up big screens and donated Rock-Reich recorded footage of this summer's big outdoor gigs: gifts that had gone down very well. As she walked to and fro through the garlanded streets people kept coming up, old and young, all dress codes, wanting to tell her how wonderful it was that *Fiorinda* was here. The security crew fielded a graveyard full of posies. The Adjuvants, big-hearted permanent infants, didn't seem to mind.

It was five in the afternoon before she escaped. Roxane, who'd been having a nap, had returned to the fray: Chip and Verlaine were tireless. She left them all playing bar billiards and getting into a discussion with some local anoraks – about exactly when Lammas *ought* to be cele-brated on the modern calendar. Upstairs in her pleasant room, with the wonky floor, the pretty view, the dead tv peering from its perch, she sat on the side of the bed, head in her hands.

Maybe this is it.

Fiorinda believed that her magic had come to her not from her grandmother (whose powers were very small), but from her father, the ageing megastar who had taken her, like a piece of fruit, and made her pregnant with his child . . . She didn't have a shred of proof. Rufus O'Niall had a reputation for bearing a grudge, and people in the music biz feared him, the way big stars are often feared. No one had ever accused him of being an evil magician. But Fiorinda knew. *She knew because she knew.* For a long time now (a long time in the history of this new world), she had been living in dread of the day when something like this would happen. Something serious, not stupid fortune-telling, or herbal medicine, or nature worship: and she would have to reveal herself, and then Rufus would be able to get hold of her again.

She had defeated him at least once since the Reich began, and nobody knew anything about that secret battle – except maybe Sage, who would never tell. But Rufus O'Niall doesn't give up, he never forgets an injury, that's what everybody says. She had been waiting ever since for him to try again, and *she knew* that magic was the key. As long as she suppressed the magic, she was safe – and England was safe – from the vindictive bastard who would not forgive her; who would punish everyone who'd helped her to make a life for herself.

And that's so many people.

Two days ago she'd visited Rufus's manor house and found nothing there, not even memories. She'd been extremely relieved – though she'd refused to admit it to Sage, she'd been terrified by Fergal's story. But now this. Human sacrifice, and something in her lovers' voices, this morning . . . Something they weren't telling her, about the way the victims had been killed. This could be it, and it doesn't have to have anything to do with Rufus O'Niall. *Magic exists*, wherever it came from. Whether it was always here or whether it has somehow been created, or given power it never had before, by our disasters . . .

She sat on the edge of the bed for what felt like a long time, her thoughts going round and round, fists tightly knotted and pressed against her temples. Then, moving briskly, she got up and changed out of her garden-party frock into more practical clothes, tied her hair in a scarf and slung her tapestry rucksack on her shoulders. She slipped a note under the door of the room that Rox was sharing with Verlaine (for old sakes' sake, though everyone knew it was Chip and Ver who were the item these days). GONE FISHING, SEE YOU IN THE MORNING. She had a word with the security crew in the van, which was parked behind the pub. A few minutes later she was hailing a cycle taxi. She had the taxi drop her at a roofless former shopping mall on the edge of town, where there was some theatre and dance going on, and set off on foot. She knew the way. Ax and Sage had told her where the hardcore venue was.

It took her about an hour to reach the grove.

Where the red track entered the trees she stood in the lonely silence, gathering her resolve. On the edge of the marching potato rows a few wildflowers had survived. There's Rest Harrow, the creeping herb with small dark leaves and dusty pink sickle-shaped flowers, that colonises the margins . . . 'I don't like pink,' she murmured – but she bent and picked a sprig, because the flower reminded her of Sage, and Ax, and the night they had serenaded her with her own music.

She walked into the clearing, twisting the stem between her fingers, and moved around, looking at the ornaments on the wicker walls. Animal skulls. Clay pots full of grease. Lumps of stone and bone. Painted symbols . . . At last she went to kneel on the rim of the pit and stared at the bodies. Something in her rose to greet the horror with the same acceptance, the same relief that she had felt on other occasions. Massacre Night. The withered body of a raped and murdered child. *Yes! These things happen. This is the truth about the world, let it be seen, let everyone know* . . . But she fought it down and went on staring at the pitiful sight until her eyes brimmed and her vision blurred.

She wiped her eyes and stood up. The sprig of Rest Harrow, with Fiorinda's salt tears clinging to it, dropped into the pit.

The toilet block, a little generator in a concrete hutch . . . well, how civilised.

Better not stay too long. This is an evil place.

It was twilight by the time she found the strip of trees where the barmies were camped. She'd been afraid she'd have to call them again and ask for more directions, and feel an idiot. But no, a sentry came looming out of the leaf-dapple shadows, a big sturdy woman-warrior (the barmy army had a few of those). An enamel pin on her teeshirt, a circlet of moorland rushes, said she'd been at Yap Moss, the last battle of the Islamic Campaign. She seemed reluctant to let Fiorinda by.

'Hi. Er, was there a password?'

'Oh, Fiorinda,' said the woman-warrior, very earnestly, 'I'm fucking glad you're here. This is bad shit. *Dogs can't jump that high.*'

Unpremeditated, Fiorinda pushed the rifle aside and hugged her.

'Don't be daft.'

The barmies were gathered in the middle of the trees, a bunch of ragamuffin men, looking grim and scared, sitting around in an irregular circle. She knew most of them, by sight at least. They were veterans from Ax and Sage's Yorkshire guerrilla band. They all stood up when Fiorinda appeared, some of them clutching their weapons.

'I'm sorry,' she said, going over to her boyfriends. 'I had to see for myself.'

'It's okay,' said Ax. 'Understood.'

They hugged her briefly, first Ax and then Sage. Everybody sat down. Sage's arm stayed around her – an unusual public display of affection, but she wasn't complaining. 'What's happening? Any new developments?'

'Well, the farmer's co-operating,' said Ax. 'He says he's

allowed the place to be used as a venue for a couple of years. He gets paid handsomely, anonymous packets of notes, and he stays away from that wood, especially around the big dates. He knew about the pit. He thought it was for the horse sacrifice. He swears he had no idea about the other. He says the cars arrive late at night. They park in a layby; they leave before dawn. That's all we've got out of him so far, except he confirms the opinion of our specialists—' A few of the barmies cringed at this, like puppies who have been nipped and cuffed by father wolf. 'He expects them back tomorrow night.'

'They'll be doing a triad,' offered big Brock, very subdued. 'They like to do three sacrifices over a feast like Lammas, an' keep the bodies displayed if they can get away with it, ter hallow the ground. But I've never heard of . . . anything the fuck like that.'

'I wish to tell you, Fiorinda,' growled Fergal Kearney, 'that this is no fockin' *natural religion*. This is foul invention. The only meaning it has is for hurrying on the dark, which some bastard fellers think a fine plan—'

'Yeah,' Ax cut him off. 'Right.' He looked at the sky, reached in his pocket for cigarettes and took one out; but didn't light it. Last *sawm* he'd given up all drugs for the entire month. He didn't see himself managing that this year. 'Okay, we're not talking to the local coppers for obvious reasons, but we've arranged for reinforcements. We've brought in the West Mid armed response squad, and sent for more barmies.'

'The farmer and his family are under guard now,' said Sage, 'in case they were thinking of giving anyone a call. We can't be sure we haven't been spotted and frightened them off, but if the ritualists come back, we're going to be ready. We'll let them gather, switch on the big lights and move in.'

'Like a night club raid,' said Fiorinda. 'Hey, is human sacrifice the new cocaine?'

Her levity did not go down well with the men. Someone whispered, '*It wasn't dogs.*'

Another voice added, in a hollow tone, 'We were shit scared before we got near.'

'An' that's not like us, Fiorinda.'

'There was an aura.'

'Fuckin' Pagans. They use dark forces.'

This remark earned angry glares. The guerrilla band included an eclectic mixture of faiths. You can believe in the old religion without being a barbaric neo-primitive.

'Oh come off it,' said Fiorinda. 'Pagans, Anabaptists, what's the difference? What we have is some sad bastards whose idea of fun is to watch human beings get ripped apart. There's nothing weird in that, unfortunately. It's normal, horrible human behaviour.'

The barmies looked hurt. 'I don't believe in magic,' announced Zip Crimson, the incongruously sharp-style hippy kid who was one of the babies of this gang, hardly older than Fiorinda. 'It's neo-mediaeval fascist shite, an' I hate the stuff. But that's not to say it doesn't happen.'

'I'm not arguing with you. All I'm saying is, not this time. Hey, I've seen the bodies. I know it looks bizarre. I don't know what the hell is going on, any more than you do. But trust me, there'll be a natural explanation. It wasn't *werewolves.*'

'Thank you, Fiorinda,' said Ax, while the barmies laughed and shuffled about in shamefaced relief. 'I'm glad we can dismiss that option.' He put the cigarette he'd been rolling between his fingers back into the pack, saved by the realisation that he was starving. 'Now, can we eat? The sun is finally over the yard arm.'

All the men had waited so they could eat with Ax. A vegetable stew, which had been cooking in an ATP haybox stove, was served. The barmies, including Ax and Sage, ate with mechanical fervour, like good soldiers – and Fiorinda did the same, because it would please the lads. They drank water (which the barmies carried with them. None of them would touch agribusiness ground-water), apart from the Irishman, who had his ration of red wine. Fiorinda's saltbox was carefully passed around. She noticed that even Fergal, who had hardly tasted his stew, made sure he got hold of it. As he dipped his fingers their eyes met across the shadows. He put the salt on his tongue and nodded fractionally, and then quickly looked away.

It was late before the Triumvirate escaped to the captains' bender, a bigger version of the regular bivouacs, set further into the trees. Sage and Ax shucked their rifles. Sage took off the mask and lit an ATP globe on the groundsheet floor. They sat crosslegged around the glow, silent for a moment in the sheer relief of getting off stage.

'How d'you know it wasn't werewolves, Fiorinda?' said Sage. 'Are you quite sure?'

'Of course it wasn't. Don't be stupid.' She untied her scarf and hid behind her hair. She knew she was getting that look, the one that says *I am fifty years old, and you are making me tired*. 'I know. I shouldn't be here. No girlfriends on manoeuvres.'

Sage had not wanted Fiorinda to come on this trip at all. She had insisted, and he knew why – but he had not been able to explain the situation to Ax, and had been forced to appear (undeservedly for once) a male chauvinist pig.

'Ignore him,' said Ax, 'I want you here, even if he doesn't. You were right to come. You were brilliant with the lads.'

'Tell me one thing,' said Fiorinda, 'd-do you know, were they alive? I mean, when they got torn up?'

'Brock thinks they'll have been garotted first,' said Sage, gently. 'Or doped, at least. You can't have an unwilling sacrifice; it spoils the whole effect.'

'Oh yes,' she said, 'that's true. I'd forgotten. I suppose that's something.'

Sage put his arms around her and hugged her tight.

'Stupid brat, you *terrify* me. Why d'you have to go there alone, what did you have to look at that for—?'

'I just had to see—'

'I don't think we've frightened them off,' said Ax, off on his own tangent. 'I think this is a blank space on the map, far away from the rest of their lives, where they have no connections and feel safe from any interference. Even if they know that Fiorinda suddenly decided to visit Wethamcote, they won't have put two and two together. They're too arrogant. They'll be back, and we're going to bust them.'

'How many people do you think are involved?'

'Not a huge number.' Ax took out his cigarettes, offered them to Sage, who shook his head, lit one and pulled on it fervently. 'We think thirty to forty, max, from the traces in the grove, far as we've analysed the footage Chris took. Which accords with the farmer . . . He reckons there are around ten or twelve private cars; he thinks it's mostly the same cars every time, and a couple of horseboxes. That's why he thought of the horse sacrifice. He admits he's sneaked down to the layby to have a look, but his mind's a blank when it comes to number-plates.'

Fiorinda smiled. 'Whereas, obviously, the horseboxes were for the werewolves.'

'Yeah.'

The roof and walls of the bender were layers of fine mesh, stretched over a frame of plastic alloy rods and heaped with woodland debris: leaves, earth, twigs, moss. A little green caterpillar came swaying down on an invisible thread into the light of the globe. Fiorinda caught it on her finger and returned it to the roof.

'What about David Sale?'

Sage shook his head.

'I can't reach him,' said Ax.

'Oh, God.'

As Ceremonial Head of State, Ax was supposed to have

direct access to the Prime Minister at all times. He had not made much use of this facility. He'd preferred to keep things official. But there'd been occasions, over the last few months, when David had been mysteriously unavailable. His office had covered him; the Cabinet Office had covered for him. The Triumvirate had known there was something going on – and they had colluded with the cover-up, because it suited them. Ax had assumed the PM was over-indulging his rockstar taste for smack, on these little episodes: and that's the price you pay, the downside of tearing up the drug laws. Less crime and corruption, more vulnerable people going off the rails—

'I can't get hold of him, and I daren't go on trying to track him down, because I'll make it obvious—'

'You think he's on his way here?'

'That would be one reason why he doesn't feel like answering his phone.'

'We don't know for sure he's involved,' Sage reminded them, 'We don't *know* he's even into hardcore.'

'Oh, he'll be here,' said Ax. 'This is a set-up.' He stared bitterly at the glowing end of his cigarette. 'I can believe David Sale is into Celtic blood sacrifice. I believed it the moment Fergal told us. He's a Countercultural groupie, looking for adventure; he always was. He's the one who let Paul Javert invent that fucking Think Tank . . . But human sacrifice? No . . . I don't believe that. He's not a monster. I think he's been set up, but he's going to be here, and we can't reach him to warn him off. We have to bust these bastards, can't do anything else. We have to bust them hard and I can see where it's heading. And the Celtic thing will explode too. We're in over our heads. Fuck.'

'We've been in over our heads since Massacre Night, Ax.'

Ax shrugged. 'Yeah, thanks. That helps a lot. The only thing I can't figure is whoever, or whatever agency, arranged this – exactly what did they expect me to do?

Who sent Fergal to us, and why? What way are they trying to make me jump?'

'Unless Fergal's genuine,' suggested Fiorinda, hopefully. 'That would be the simple explanation: and the people who sent him are friends.'

'Hmm.'

The barmies were very quiet: an occasional murmur, a rustle of movement.

'What about the town?' asked Sage, after a while. 'Any suspicious characters, Fee?'

One of their fears, before they came up here, was that they would find a gathering of inappropriately qualified media folk, circling like vultures around this obscure arts fest, already onto the big story. 'There was nobody when I arrived,' said Fiorinda. 'There's an arts and music biz circus arriving now, chasing after me. I'm sorry, Ax.'

'No problem. If things go down the way I think they might, tomorrow night, a news embargo's going to be the least of our worries.'

They talked about tomorrow night, what might happen and how to deal with it, until there was nothing more to be said. Then they took off their boots and lay down together, on a heap of green bracken where Sage and Ax's sleeping bags were unrolled, Ax in the middle as most in need of comfort.

'Don't cry baby,' said Fiorinda, hugging him. 'At least it's not werewolves.'

'Yeah,' said Ax, kissing her and burying his face in her beautiful soft hair, 'but you could be wrong. The way things are going, nothing would surprise me.'

Sage got up again to put out the lamp. He kissed Fiorinda's nose, sighed resignedly, and lay down again beside Ax, his arm around them both.

I *will* talk to you, she thought. I promise. As soon as this is over—

Dawn came too soon. Fiorinda and Sage, left alone in

the nest, woke to hear their lover's voice reciting, somewhere close by, the words that cannot be translated but
may be interpreted—

> I take refuge with the Lord of the Daybreak,
> from the evil of what he has created . . .

Later, at a more reasonable hour, Fiorinda got an escort
back to the edge of town.

Preparations for the nightclub raid came together through
the next day. More barmies arrived from the anti-terrorist
action. The police contingent turned up in two lumbering methane-burning hippy vans, disguised as a pair of
traveller clans. Crowd control and night tech was set up.
Before dusk everything was in place, and there were close
to a hundred armed men (including a few women, as the
saying goes) waiting undercover, ready to move into their
final positions after dark.

The hours slowly passed. At quarter past eleven, Sage –
deep in the grove, part of the silent cordon surrounding
the clearing – heard an owl hoot her question. The male
partner answered from the other side of the wood. Woo,
woo. Tawny owls. Brock should be happy. The desert is
coming back to life . . . but oh, at what a price. He kept
thinking of Fiorinda, walking alone across the haunted
fields, this girl who is more stubborn than God, and seeing
in his mind's eye those carcasses, the sheered planes of
flesh, the thick ropes of blood, the major bones sliced
clean through. *What the fuck did that?*

Fiorinda says there's nothing weird going on.

Would she lie to me? Would she lie to *Ax*? Why would
she lie . . . ?

Beside him, Fergal Kearney shifted uneasily. He had the
toughness of a hard-drinking man. He was coping well
with field conditions, amazingly well, considering his state
of health. But the rifle he'd been given tonight – for the

look of the thing, since everyone else was armed – seemed to bother him. He kept fidgeting with it.

'You want me to take that for a while? They're heavy buggers if you're not used—'

'Tell the truth,' whispered Fergal hoarsely, 'I'm wonderin' how I'd make out if it came to a fight. It's not the first time I've had a gun in me hands. I wouldn't want yez to think that. But . . . I've niver killed a man.'

If it came to a firefight, Fergal would keep his sheet clean. They hadn't given him live ammunition. There's too much that doesn't add up about our Irish 'defector'.

'It's not going to happen. Nobody's going to get killed.'

'How's yer boy? I niver asked after him yet.'

'Marlon?' Sage shrugged. 'He's okay.'

'Marlon Williams, isn't it? I remember I met him onc'st. Lovely boy. Now that must be a very hard thing, not to have the naming of yer own son.'

'I can live with it. Knock it off, Fergal. Continue in that line, an' you'll annoy me.'

'Jaysus, there I go. I've a big mouth, God help me. I didn't mean to offend.'

The glimmering skull was wearing an eye-wrap that gave it the look, in the ash-grey shadow of the night, of some solemn allegorical figure – blind justice? It offered Fergal a crooked grin. 'You're right, it is a hard thing. Now *shush*.'

Softly, in the distance, they heard the murmur of an approaching car.

The car stopped in the layby and two people got out, a man and a woman; the driver stayed inside. They seemed to be checking for signs of danger, but they were confident and didn't investigate very thoroughly. They looked around, with flashlights, and then got back into the car. The rest of the cars arrived an hour later. Barmy signals had detected the use of a radiophone, but hadn't been able to eavesdrop. These people were not amateurs. They got out of the cars and gathered together. About twelve-thirty they set off up the track, dressed for a glitzy night out, carrying coolboxes, swinging flashlights, the women stumbling on high heels. Most of them were wearing masks, strange animal muzzles and horned things glowing in the dark; a few had naked faces. There were murmurs, and occasional sharp bursts of laughter; but mainly they were silent. Where the track entered the grove a small group detached itself and barred the way. The guests were scrutinised, one by one, and briefly questioned: a formality. No digital masks were removed; no one was refused entry.

Sage had been dividing his attention, with the ease of long practise, between several scenes: the dark wood around him, the live feed from the concealed night cameras. A few minutes after the congregation started entering the clearing he spoke softly to Brock, who was next to him on the other side from Fergal.

'Hey, Brock, look after Fergal for me, will you? Got something to do.'

There was a queue outside the changing room. People already sky-clad mingled with those who were still dressed. Grease tubs hanging on the wattle walls had been lit; the women's dresses glowed with colour in the trails of smoky light. Evening jackets, glossy leather. Sage watched from just outside the fence. As expected, the crowd belonged to the green revolution's fashionable camp-following, rather than the Counterculture itself, which made sense. There were hippy extremists who would go for human sacrifice, but they would never commit personal transport hypocrisy to get to the venue.

A horned man went around with a horse-skull full of something dark, marking masked and unmasked faces on the brow. A scatter of conversation rose, and fell, and rose again. Time to move. Sage stripped off the wrap and stowed it, switched the living skull to a conventional, charnel version, grabbed the top of the wattle fence and vaulted over. Ax was with the police and not available for much consultation, but it didn't matter. They'd agreed on what to do if the worst should come to the worst. Which it had. The night camera at the entrance ritual had left no room for doubt. David Sale was here.

A bare-faced woman saw him as he landed. She beamed, eyes like pinwheels. Not much danger of being spotted as a stranger. He would bet most of the punters preferred to be well out of their heads for the business part of the evening, even if they were convinced human sacrifice was the acme of green cool. He hunched his shoulders and stayed near the tallest people, just in case, and watched the line going into the toilet block.

'Ax,' he murmured, touching his wrist. 'Got him. He's inside. Now.'

An explosion of floodlights, a wail of sirens. Loudhailer voices: *This is the police.*

Everyone panicking, trying to leave, finding a wall of bodies and weapons in their way—

Sage shouldered through the naked people who'd rushed for the toilet block and were now scrambling out of it, clutching their clothes. The last of them he shoved out as he pushed his way in. By the light of a dim fluorescent tube he saw stacks of lockers, a row of basins, a row of cubicles, strewn clothes and shoes. In the doorway of the last cubicle, two half-clothed men crouched over the naked body of a third, trying to get him dressed, against his feeble resistance. The man on the floor was wearing a bull's head mask. A white-face clown and a demon of some kind stared up at Sage in desperate consternation.

'Get out of here,' said Sage.

They left.

He shut the door (quite a riot going on out there), restored his own mask to its usual setting, squatted down, switched off the bull's head at the patient's wrist-controller and administered a vicious dose of straighten-up. David

Sale opened his eyes; his face crumpled like a protesting child, then he jerked convulsively into a sitting position, eyes popping, his back against the toilet.

'S-Sage!'

'Yeah. *Sage*. And look, he's got real arms and legs. Want my autograph?'

The Prime Minister clasped the sting on his neck, looking terrified.

'What have you done to me?'

'Don't panic, it's just straighten-up. I haven't hurt you. Yet.'

'No, no. You don't understand. I must be naked. I can't be here. This isn't happening.'

'Shut up drivelling, put the mask back on and get dressed.'

The nightclub raid noises peaked and died down. A barmy signals voice in Sage's ear was telling him the bad possibilities (armed resistance, serious casualties) that had been avoided; the alarming discoveries (sophisticated weapons, mysterious high-tech devices) that were being made. Finally the door opened a crack. Two barmies looked in: Jackie Dando and Chris Page.

'How's it going?' said Sage, looking over his shoulder.

'S'all over,' said Jackie chirpily, full of it as usual, and trying hard to get a good peek at the bull-headed geezer. The barmies didn't know who was getting rescued, but they knew he mustn't be recognised. 'No trouble, just a bunch of naked hoorays, frowing up and crying for their lawyers. We're minding their socks and knickers for them, Ax's orders. No one gets past us, right?'

'That's right. Wait outside. Be with you in a minute.'

'Okay Sage.'

David Sale had dressed himself. He stood by the basins and took off his mask so he could smooth his hair. Sage had to work hard to control the impulse to put his *autograph* on the bastard's slack, terrified face.

'The mask stays on. Please. And please keep your mouth shut.'

The clearing was full of the aftermath of disaster, sights and sounds all too familiar, sobbing people with blankets round their shoulders, armed police, armed hippies. But thank God, this time, no more blood . . . The Prime Minister and his escort kept out of the light. They went through a fresh gap in the wattle fence and into the wood. There was a truck waiting halfway down the track. Sage got in the back with David Sale, Chris and Jackie in the front with the driver. Off we go.

An hour or so later, the sacrificial bodies had been retrieved, bagged and taken away. The barmy army reinforcements and the police were down in the lane, dealing with the night's haul and waiting for extra transport. Sage, in a filthy mood, let it be said, had just called to report that all was well (relatively speaking), and the bull-headed man was in safe lodging, no problems. An armed policewoman was sorting and packing left-behind clothes and personal effects, by the toilet block. Other than that, Ax and the Yorkshire lads, and Fergal Kearney, had the clearing to themselves.

Two new victims had been found, tied up and gagged, in a van that had come along after the cars. From the few questions they'd answered so far, apparently they were street kids – a class that survived, in Ax's England, in spite of the Volunteer Initiative. They knew nothing. Some of the congregation had been making unsolicited disclosures (babbling like lunatics), but they'd been the ignorant ones. The organisers were keeping quiet. The horseboxes, which had turned up as predicted, were empty.

There was no sign of anything that could have been used to do the killing.

The half-moon of the holy month looked down, wan and dim in contrast with the violent beams of a floodlight hung up on a branch. The barmies stared into the pit.

'Maybe they tear 'em up somewhere else,' suggested someone. 'An' bring them here and strap them on them totem poles already like that.'

'Nah, can't be. What about those kids what was going to be offered up tonight?'

'What do they offer them up for? What's supposed to happen? The end of the world?'

'Zip, you are an innocent. You and Fergal both. There's no *reason* for it. They do the sicko stuff because they fuckin' like it.'

'Anyway, Sage got a good shufti, and he said . . . Is Sage coming back?'

'Dunno,' said Ax. 'Maybe. Look, I'm gonna get down there and see what I can find.'

'I don't think the forensic types have finished, Ax,' said Brock, doubtfully.

Ax gave him a pitying glance. 'Call yourself a hippy? Okay, I'll get permission.' He walked over to the toilet block and asked the policewoman.

'I'm sure that would be all right, Mr Preston,' she said, round-eyed. 'Er, certainly.'

'Good. If it turns out it's a problem, it's my responsibility.' The tackle that had been used to retrieve the bodies had been dismantled. 'Hey, someone give me a ladder. My name's not Aoxomoxoa, you know.'

The barmies started one of their interminable arguments, as to whether werewolves require a full moon, or is that vampires, and what about the silver bullets. Ax descended a nylon ladder into the pit. It was more unpleasant to be down there than he had realised: like being inside a hollowed, rotten tooth. The air smelled foul; the ground was soft underfoot, and already churned up by many bootprints. Those 'forensic types' were going to have their work cut out . . . The totem poles loomed above him, seeming twice their actual height. He couldn't make anything of the carving, the light was too confusing.

He started walking round the walls, treading over the place where Fiorinda's sprig of Rest Harrow had been crushed into the mud . . . Fuck. He'd seen other hardcore 'pit-temples', but they were nothing like this size. He imagined the organisation, the hired machinery, the work-men, my God; the blank spaces on the map of England where sores like this can fester. Crisis conditions. Always another disaster, and it always seems totally unexpected; but it's not, it's the same disaster, *things fall apart*—

The thought of the interview he had to face in the morning was like a lead weight on his soul.

'I don't like this,' muttered Fergal, up above. 'Why's he down there?'

'That's Ax,' said Brock, proudly. 'He's not afraid of any fucking thing. You shoulda been with him in Yorkshire—'

'Hey. There's a metal panel here, with a skim of clay plastered over it! Shit, there are *sliding doors* in the walls of the pit! It's like an Eygptian tomb, hidden mechanisms. Hey, this is it. This is how! You must be able to lock or open these doors from a distance, radio-controlled, but it's . . . switched off, or something. I think I can shift it—'

Something made a sound: a hollow, guttural cough.

Even Ax Preston fails to think out of the box some-times. He'd forced one of the sliding panels, found a black space behind it and gone to fetch his torch, which he'd left by the totem poles. It had not crossed his mind that the tunnel might be occupied. He heard that sound and froze, knowing it instantly, on a level older than conscious thought. Instinctively he moved to get his back against a wall. Mistake. Now the ladder was on the other side of the pit. Ax's rifle was up above, where he'd dumped it before climbing down. He didn't even have a pocket knife.

The tigers trotted out on big, soft feet. There were two of them, one larger than the other. In the moonlight they looked huge. They looked as if they could jump out of the pit itself. The barmies stared down, jaws dropping. The only one of them who had a weapon in his hands and a clear shot at the beasts was Brock, and he was paralysed. The tigers were probably hungry. They wasted no time. Both animals, beautiful, calculating eyes fixed on Ax, crouched fluidly, poised to leap.

'Oh, Jaysus fockin' God!' Fergal Kearney's own rifle was on his back; he didn't bother with it. He grabbed the gun that Brock appeared incapable of using and fired a rattling burst into the pit, eyes tight shut, raking wildly to and fro.

Sage had come into the clearing just in time to see this happen.

He crossed the remaining space very quickly, unslinging his own rifle. The pit now held two very big, dead tigers, and Ax, looking stunned but apparently unhurt.

'What the fuck's going on?'

'Oh, God,' Brock had dropped to his knees, covering his face. 'Oh, God help me!'

'It was tigers,' whispered Zip, awed, 'it was *tigers*. We never thought of tigers.'

The policewoman stood by her pile of binbags with her mouth open.

'They were going for Ax!' yelled another witness, excitedly. 'They were going for Ax, Sage, an' he couldn't get out, an Fergal grabbed Brock's rifle, an' shot 'em!'

'Those were *Bengal Tigers*,' moaned poor Brock. 'There isn't a hundred of them left alive in the world. I woulda done it. *I woulda done it*, only give me another second—'

'Make that ninety-eight,' said Ax, climbing out. 'Thanks, Fergal. Good shooting.'

Sage said, 'Are you going to tell me *why* you were in the pit with two fuckin' tigers?'

'I have no excuse,' said Ax. 'I was being unbelievably stupid. I'm sorry. You can beat me up later.' Shoulder to shoulder, they turned to Fergal Kearney. The Irishman was sitting on the ground, the rifle discarded, holding his head and shaking.

'*Oh Jaysus*,' he was muttering. '*Jaysus.*'

'Are you okay, Fergal?'

'Just help me up, Sage, me darling,' Sage helped him up. Fergal clung to tall Sage, almost a dead weight. 'Ah, God, I don't know what's wrong wi' me, it was a wee shock, I'll be over it. That was fockin' loud. That's, that's somethen I never just done before—'

'You did good,' said Sage, intensely. He had taken off his mask. 'I owe you one.'

The barmies crowded round, jabbering with shock and adrenalin and relief. They congratulated the Irishman; they told him he was a natural marksman, but he'd made a fuck of a mess of his tiger skin rugs, that's one thing you'll have to learn, Ferg, you don't want to use an automatic rifle on anything you plan to have for décor after. They talked of measuring the beasts, nose to tail, bet they're record-breakers. But no one wanted to get back into the pit, so they declared everything should be left as it was.

Police officers and barmy squaddies had come running into the clearing, brandishing weapons. They had to be told what had happened. Ax's unbelievable stupidity at once became a deed of valour, but at least Fergal got top honours. The tigers were hauled out and found to be wearing radio control shock collars, which probably explained how they'd been trained and handled, but wouldn't have done anything for Ax. Ax tried to comfort Brock, who was a shattered heap, a situation not improved by his tactless mates telling him that the man-eaters would probably've had to be put down anyhow.

And now we'd better find this Irishman a drink.

'Why didn't you use your own rifle, Fergal?' asked Sage as everyone headed for the lane, carrying the bags of clothes and the last of the ambush equipment.

Fergal grinned sheepishly. 'Oh, I knew I woulda been

firing blanks. If I was in your shoes, I would not've given meself live ammunition tonight, either.'

Sage had taken the PM across country to the M1, where he'd spent the night under barmy army guard at a run-down Travelodge. The debriefing happened at nine the next morning by the roadside. Fiorinda had come from Wethamcote in her van, and sent her driver and his mate off to get some breakfast from the Services. Ax and Sage had been to Coventry and back since Ax's adventure in the tiger pit. They'd returned in an unmarked, dark and dignified private car; Richard Kent, the barmy army's chief of staff, was with them.

Fiorinda stayed in her van. The Prime Minister arrived in a barmy army truck. He looked tired-out by his short journey. He wasn't wearing his mask.

Mr Dictator and his Minister talked to David in the car. Sage sat in the back, unmasked. Ax sat in the front with the Prime Minister; who started off in a blustering mood. He protested that he'd been kidnapped, that the police had overreacted, that the barmy army should never have been involved; the whole operation had been outrageous, unsanctioned, illegal—

Ax said he didn't think he'd overreacted. They hadn't known what to expect after seeing those bodies. They'd had to be prepared for any level of response, and as for the numbers, it's standard procedure. Superior force will minimise violence in circumstances like that, crowd con-trol. If you can trust your men.

And I can trust mine, he added, without any bluster at all.

David took this in, and changed his tune.

'Is this interview being recorded?'

'No,' said Sage.

'There would be no advantage to anyone,' said Ax, 'in preserving this conversation.'

They spent an hour with him, this haggard, unshaven, sixtyish bloke in his dishevelled evening casuals. It was not meant to be an interrogation, but he talked. He said he'd known he was taking a risk. Yes, he knew that digital masks are transparent to infra-red. He wasn't an idiot! (Like hell, they thought . . .) But it was an issue of trust. He had believed he was with people he could trust. He'd had no intention of giving the Celtics political support. He had no sympathy with their anti-recovery, neo-feudal rhetoric. His involvement in the rites had been personal, a pilgrimage, a sincere religious impulse.

He'd *had no idea* what was going to happen at Spitalls Farm (where the Wethamcote grove was located). He'd known nothing until he saw the bodies; no one had told him; he had not been warned. He'd thought he was hallucinating. He'd been off his head, a waking nightmare. You surely don't believe I would condone—?

Once, Sage had to leave the car and take a walk up and down. But he came back, and talked the business-like compassion that had to be talked, along with Ax. The man must not be humiliated. He must come out of this feeling good about his rescuers, or it was all for nothing. They told him that they were going to try and save him.

'You're here now,' Ax explained, 'because I called you to the scene of the horrific discovery. You gave your full support to the barmy army and police operation. You're going to be driven back to London by Richard Kent. Richard'll stay with you for the next few days, and besides reacting like a statesman to the hell that's going to break loose, you're going to tell him everything. Every detail. Please. We need to how this happened, and just how much we have to hide.'

'Ax, why are you doing this?' David asked, tears of gratitude, relief and afterburn in his eyes. 'You could throw me to the wolves.'

'I don't want to throw you to the wolves. I want you to lead the government for me.'

There was another ground-shifting pause.

'You can come back from this, David,' said Ax. 'We've been together a long time. We can go on working together, get the country through this bad patch and reach the future we both believe in. Well, we'll let you go now. You must be exhausted. Call me when you've had some sleep and we'll talk it all over properly.'

David nodded, wiping his eyes. His hands were shaking. 'Is Fiorinda here? Could I . . . could I have a word with her?'

Sage and Ax looked at each other in the rearview mirror. No. We have to do this. She doesn't.

'She's listening,' said Ax, 'but she'd rather not talk to you just now.'

They got out of the car. Richard, who'd been waiting by the truck, came over. They spoke to him briefly. It was another hot day, the sun bright in a blue sky over the flood-damaged landscape. They watched the dark car drive off and walked down to Fiorinda's van. As soon as he was inside the back, out of sight, Sage exploded like a coiled spring released – and nearly put his fist through a window, managing at the last minute to punch the upholstery instead.

'*Shit!* I do not want to be a fucking grown-up. Ever. I want go back to being the giant toddler, *right now!*'

Ax had collapsed on one of the back seats. He held out his arms.

'One condition. I go back to being your mum.'

'*Deal.*'

'Idiots,' said Fiorinda. 'If people knew what goes on . . . Sometimes I'm embarrassed to be in a relationship with you two.' She burrowed between them like a little cat, her nose tucked into the hollow between Sage's collar bones, Ax's chin digging into her shoulder. She'd spent the night

163

doing street-parties and bonfires, acting relaxed and imagining horrors, which had not come to pass, but she'd heard about Ax and the tigers.

God! This life.

But soon Ax freed himself. He stared out of the window. The heart of the country. Not far from here, on Bosworth Field, England's long and ruinous mediaeval civil war had ended. He remembered the vows that he had made, at the beginning of all this. That he would keep the peace. That he would hold this country together, and keep faith with the future, *by any means necessary*. That he understood what it would cost him, and he accepted the deal—

Except, of course, I didn't understand.

'You remember that coup we were worried about? The next blood-fest change of government, and how would we survive? You've just witnessed it. That's what happened last night. A paramilitary takeover, by me.'

'Without bloodshed,' offered Sage. 'And you didn't have any choice.'

Ax ignored him. 'The fuck of the thing is, we might not even preserve the last illusion of legitimate government, because I don't know if I can save David. There are so many gaping holes, and I can't keep a news embargo going for long enough to stop them all. Fuck. I wonder exactly *how many* people there are, including whatever bastards set this up, and Fergal's mates, and David's friends of the hardcore persuasion, and God knows who else, who know just where the PM was last night?'

'There are always people who know the truth,' said Fiorinda. 'It never makes any difference. We'll pitch our version so the public will prefer to believe it, and get it out first, and that's all you ever need. If you're in power.'

Ax's expression became even more desolate, if possible. 'Thanks a lot.'

'Don't thank me.' She stood up and took him in her

arms, his weary head against her breast. 'Thank inexorable fate. It's not your fault, Ax. I know it's not your fault. Sssh. It won't be so bad, it was inevitable, you'll feel okay about it soon.'

'Oh, I'm okay now. I just wish I was dead, that's all.'

The people of Wethamcote had celebrated the wedding of the Sun God and his flower bride with street parties and bonfires and dancing in the square, throwing bouquets, cheering while burning wheels were sent rolling down the streets into the river. Now summer's consummation was over for another year. The town centre was empty, silent and bedraggled. Fiorinda slipped into the Rose and Crown by the back door and was waylaid by the landlady, who was looking very anxious.

'Oh, Fiorinda, there you are, thank goodness. I'm afraid I have a bit of an emergency.'

Oh God. What now?

What now was an industrial-sized sink full of posies, cluttering up the pub's kitchen on this very busy morning. 'I *have no idea* what to do with all your lovely flowers!'

'Is there a hospital that might like to have them? The crew could deliver.'

'I don't know, dear. It's a bank holiday, and besides, the phones aren't working.'

A bank holiday. Bless! Fiorinda, who disliked cut flowers intensely, was tempted to suggest the compost heap, but she controlled herself. Punter feelings must not be wounded. 'Okay, I'll see if I can get hold of a plastic bath. Will any shops be open?'

Mine hostess exclaimed that of course, she could have Carrie (kitchen help) put the flowers in a guest bathroom! She thanked her guest for this brilliant notion and bustled off. Fiorinda stood gathering her wits. The washing-up in the other sink looked very fucking inviting. Gimme a pair of rubber gloves. Let me come and work here, for this nice fat lady, live and all found. I could meet my funky boy-friends in the bar, after I've done up the breakfast tables, and we could dream of being rockstars. It would be heaven.

But no. It isn't going to happen.

I'm going to live and die playing fucked-up Stone Age Royalty.

She turned and found herself looking through the open door of the kitchen straight at Joe Muldur, bright-eyed, bushy-tailed NME journalist.

'Hey, Fiorinda,' said Joe, 'what's up?'

'Fuel starvation,' said Fiorinda. 'Two million clueless people – but I'm lying, it's really far more – insanely determined to be new-age nomads. Empty supermarket shelves. Plunging literacy rates.' She tucked her hand through his arm. 'But you don't want to hear about that, and I'm tired of it. Let's get a drink and talk about wheels on fire.'

The public bar of the Rose and Crown was like a rock-festival morning after, full of music journalists and other hepcats who had caught up with Fiorinda, bog-eyed after the night's fun, drinking on hangovers and eating fried breakfasts. No one was phased by the lack of telecoms. They wouldn't find out there was anything more going on unless they tried to leave and found the town was circled by roadblocks, or until Ax decided to lift the news embargo. Or unless local knowledge prevailed, because the locals always find out: but they'd have to shout pretty loud to get heard in here.

She stood at the bar with Joe, chatting merrily and letting her compadres know, by glances across the crowd, that the debriefing had gone well. So far so good. When Joe took off to find his partner, photographer Jeff Scully, she went and joined the Adjuvants, who were sitting with a West End theatre director who had heard the call and become a passionate Few ally. He wanted to tell Fiorinda what a cunning little vixen she was, stealing the Ancient

British (I'm sorry, I mean Celtic) Tendency's turf from under them.

'But politics apart, this is a *wonderful place*! Wild! These people are Ax's children, living the life. Were you at the Ponds? My God, spectacular, terrific use of the moon and water, I must talk to that team, and all that fire around . . . One could do something terrific, cast of thousands, raw, Brechtian—'

'You're booked,' said Fiorinda, automatically. 'Don't steal anyone, come out here. The rural hinterland needs you. They've been on their own too long—'

Carrie brought Fiorinda's tinned tomatoes and fried slice (there was nothing else left).

'I saved you a sausage,' said Chip nobly, putting it on her plate.

But we survived, she thought. The disaster movie goes on getting worse, but *we won*. Again. It began to feel good.

'Hey, where did you get to the other night, you naughty stop-out?'

'I think she knows a bank whereon the wild thyme blows,' decided Verlaine, grinning. 'And she met there with Oberon and Robin Goodfellow—'

'You know, Sage would make a *great* Puck!'

'Don't fancy Bottom's chances much—'

Tim the theatre director luckily had been distracted by a passing acquaintance.

'*Knock it off*,' muttered Fiorinda, 'keep it down. Have you no sense?'

'And did you know,' said Tim, returning to them, 'we're completely *isolated* this morning? Like a J. B. Priestley. No phones, no radio, no tv, no explanation—'

'I find it exquisitely nostalgic,' boomed Roxane, coming over to join them with hir personal taste in breakfast food: a large Bloody Mary. S/he raised hir glass, with a grave nod, to Fiorinda. 'Where were you, Tim, the morning after Ivan/Lara struck?'

The director took the question seriously and launched into fond reminiscence. Fiorinda decided she'd better take the Adjuvants for some fresh air. They appeared to have been drinking since dawn, and they were getting out of hand.

It was dead quiet outdoors. Shops were shuttered, nobody was about. A little red car sat alone in the middle of the carpark by the statue of Queen Victoria, with a defunct firework lying on the roof.

'So *tell* us, beautiful Fiorinda,' demanded Chip, 'we can be indiscreet as we like out here. What's the story, morning glory? Tell us the gory details!'

A mud-spattered old jeep came rattling into the square and pulled up by the church. Joe Muldur jumped out, with Jeff Scully close behind. 'Hey!' cried Joe, leaping over to them. 'Weird spooky things are going on! We went for a drive, see if we could get into network coverage, and ran into a roadblock. There's been a huge Celtic Hardcore bust, out in the agribusiness. The barmy army was involved, and hundreds of armed police. The naked nutters have been caught red-handed eating babies, boiling innocent aliens, decimating the endangered contents of some deviant's private zoo! Apparently a breeding pair of *Bengal Tigers* got killed and eaten!'

'*Hell* to pay,' Jeff broke in, 'when the Great Green English Public hears about that!'

'The Celtics are going to be sooo embarrassed!'

'Oh,' said Jeff, taking in their expressions and belatedly realising who he was talking to. 'Duh. This is not news. Of course it isn't. Oh, dumb. This is why you were here.'

Fiorinda's eyes did that beautiful and scary thing they can do, where the pupils shoot out wide, and then zip back almost to vanishing point, so you seem to be looking at two frosted grey stones. 'Press conference,' she said. 'My room, at the pub. Now.'

*

The Spitalls Farm affair was the biggest scandal since Dissolution. A network of high society hardcore-ritualists was laid bare, and three other sites of human sacrifice were discovered. Cabinet Ministers tumbled. Prominent members of the Green Second Chamber resigned. The English Celtics (formerly the Ancient British) fell over themselves repudiating this horrific distortion of their religious rites, and declaring their passionate loyalty to Ax. The major Islamic radio station called on Mr Preston to take over, direct rule. Ax said that wouldn't be necessary, he had every faith in the elected government. David Sale took advice, and made a clean breast of his Celtic flirtation, but his involvement at Spitall's Farm never reached the public record. Those who knew didn't talk, and whatever agency had set up the human sacrifice entrapment, they never emerged. The Prime Minister and Mr Dictator both came out of it all very well, and the fate of the tigers was buried on inside pages.

One day at the end of August Sage and Fiorinda met on a station platform somwhere – logistically – between Milton Keynes National Bowl and Cardiff Stadium, where they had been playing with the Heads and with DARK, respectively. They were on their way to Brixton for a stolen night with their lover, who was still embroiled in the scandal and unable to make any of his festival gigs. Fuel-starvation timetabling meant there were hours before the next train to London, so they booked themselves into the hotel next door.

Their arrival was marred by Sage having a pointless argument with the snotty receptionist, who took offence because they weren't planning to spend the night. 'I'm afraid this isn't *Tokyo*, Mr Aoxomoxoa . . .' But who cares. They got a room, with a bed in it. There were strange stains on the ceiling; the windows were rimmed with black mould, the candlewick bedspread was raggedy, the minibar empty. They made love, at length and blissfully, and lay together in the afterglow, Sage propped on the pillows, Fiorinda sprawled lax-limbed as a sleeping kitten across his chest, her cheek resting on his forearm, his crippled right hand warm in hers. He would hold hands now, almost without flinching, even when stone-cold sober. Fiorinda had *trained* him.

'I hope Ax is in a better mood when we get to Brixton.'

'He will be,' said Sage, placidly. 'We're almost there. I think we've pulled it off. In a week or two David will have forgotten his neck ever needed saving, and Ax's secret identity as the warlord of Albion will retire into deep cover.'

'But it won't be the same. We've crossed some kind of Rubicon. Poor Ax, he must be the only person in England who's surprised at how things turned out.'

'He's not surprised. He just keeps *doing these things to himself*, and always forgets how much it's going to hurt. He has to forget, or he'd run away screaming.'

The phone implant figures under the skin of Sage's wrist (it doesn't tick) moved time along, gently. It was the first time they'd been really private since July.

'Do you still think I should tell him about my magic?' The last month had been a crash course in the issues involved.

'If you don't tell him, and someone else finds out that Fiorinda is a witch, that's political dynamite. Do you want to do that to him?'

She sat up. So did he. They faced each other, naked: Aoxomoxoa and his brat.

'I don't want anyone to know. I don't want to be a monster, Sage.'

'Don't be ridiculous. You're not a monster.'

'Oh no? Watch this.' She got down from the bed and sat on the floor in front of the minibar, thought for a moment and then touched the door. Before you could take a breath,

Fiorinda's hand was *through* the coated metal. There was a poisonous, molten smell, an implosion of heat. The front of the fridge had collapsed inwards, bubbling and hissing, and folded itself into the wilting trays, like the innards of a Dali clock. 'Fuck me,' said Sage. 'How are we going to explain *that* at reception?'

'Maybe we should throw it out of the window.'

She was very still for a few moments. Then she reached out and touched the wreckage: a shock. He thought her fingers would be burnt to the bone. But no. The fridge was intact again, as if nothing had happened. She looked up at him, this fragile naked girl, a tumble of red curls down her back, all the blood driven out of her face, sweat standing in clear drops on her forehead—

'Are you going to throw up?'

'No.' She swallowed. 'I don't think so. Give me a moment.'

'Have, er, have you done anything like that before?'

'No. I just knew I could. I've been thinking about it. Mental experiments. Me, Einstein. Destroying something feels like nothing. Just a rush, a *horrible* rush. Putting it back the way it was felt like . . . like climbing a towerblock with a car on my back.'

'That would figure. You're hauling something back through the entropy barrier.'

Fiorinda grabbed her head, as if she was afraid it was about to fly apart. 'Oh, fuck off. You are so fucking un-sympathetic whenever I'm in trouble. I don't need a physics lesson, thanks. Do you understand what I'm telling you?'

'That breaking something is easier than fixing it? I knew that.'

'I'm telling you that whatever anyone else tells you about magic, the real stuff, *the hard stuff*, is deadly danger-ous and fundamentally hateful, and I don't want to have anything to do with it ever, ever, ever.'

'Hmm. But no one was making real magic at Spitall's Farm.'

She looked him in the eye. 'Not so far as I could tell.'

'No one except Fiorinda?'

Her eyes filled with tears. 'Please don't. And now you don't want to touch me. I don't blame you, either. I'm a monster.'

He jumped off the bed, picked her up and carried her back there; wrapped her in the raggedy candlewick and the damp-smelling blankets and rocked her in his arms. Hush, hush, baby. Sssh, little darling, everything is okay, everything will be all right—

'If ever you find out about anyone making magic like mine . . . If anything like that *ever* happens, anywhere in England, then you can tell Ax about me straight away. You won't have to. I'll tell him myself, instantly, if he needs to know—'

'I'm not going to make you do anything. Hush. There's just one thing.'

'What?'

'Back in July . . . What made you decide to visit your father's house?'

She cuddled closer. 'Huh? What's that got to do with anything? That was just me trying to face my stupid past and put it behind me. Sage, do you think you and I are responsible for things like Spitall's Farm? Not Ax, never my Ax, he only wanted to save the world. We were the ones who said *everything's allowed*.'

'Nah. Stupid brat. Hideous atrocities happen all the time, world over, without our help . . . Hey,' he unwrapped her enough so he could stroke the pure curve of her cheek with his lopsided claw; bless her, she didn't seem to mind. 'Break the mood. We're in bed together, did you notice? Isn't that nice. Want some more?'

They made love again, and accidentally fell asleep: woke just in time to fling on their clothes and rush pell-mell through pouring rain into the station, where the London train was stuffed, their reserved seats long gone, every corridor packed. They found a space sitting on the floor between two carriages, where they were politely ignored, wrapped in the anonymity of Stone Age Fame. Fiorinda slept with her head on Sage's knees. He thought of limousines, and private jets . . . Fuck 'em.

What would happen if you tried to pull a stunt like that with the hotel fridge, using ATP, cell-metabolism energy? You'd be dead before you started.

My darling Fee, there's more to this. You are lying through your teeth, and I wish I knew why. But though I would love to investigate your magic, and match it with things we are finding out on the Zen Self Quest, I think perhaps you're right. We should deal with this on a need-to-know basis. Silence is the best protection, as long as it works.

Irresistibly, two images flashed together in his mind: the dismembered bodies on those totem poles and the bizarrely riven, fused and carbonised metal. He felt there was a deep kinship. The same ripping apart of all that's holy? Then Fiorinda's right: magic is bad shit . . . Well, that's depressing, but alas, we still might need the stuff, my brat.

But we got away with it this time. Let's hope our luck holds out.

He tipped his head back against the rattling panel behind him, thinking of ancient rolling stock, and no parts. The Shropshire situation with the Celtics: not good. They're back in the fold, but they still want to take over, and that can't be allowed . . . Rain dashed against the dark glass. The English huddled together, steaming, sharing the cosiness of adversity. What if this is it? What if we never escape from the disaster movie, or the insane responsibilities? If this is our life, the three of us? I'm not complaining.

*

In late September, when the Spitall's Farm affair had eased off and the Festival season was over, the Triumvirate went down to Taunton to do the joint interview that Fiorinda had offered Joe Muldur and Jeff Scully, in return for their silence at a crucial moment – a gig that would grow, and complexify, until it became a treasured monument to the whole atmosphere, the whole *Zeitgeist* of Ax's England when it was new.

The day before they left, Fiorinda visited the National Gallery. She wanted to look at 'She Feeds And Clothes Her Demons' again. The virtual portrait (one of several copies of the original that lived in Birmingham) was still on display. As she threaded through the crowds she was startled to see Fergal Kearney in front of the very picture she'd come to see. She wondered what he was doing in the gallery. It even crossed her mind that he might have followed her in, and then snuck ahead, to meet her 'by accident'. Fergal's shy devotion was not very demanding. He seemed to *avoid* Fiorinda, and barely spoke to her in company. She hesitated; made up her mind and went over.

They stood together studying the girl in the picture, that weary goblin's nursemaid with her inadequate bag of treats. Fergal knew she was there. After a few moments he turned and looked at her. Fiorinda looked back, wondering if she imagined the knowledge, and the grave sympathy, she read in the depths of his sea-green eyes.

'Well, Fergal,' she said, 'so now you know some of our secrets.'

'Aye.'

She could have been referring to the truth about David Sale at Spitall's Farm. She could have been referring to many things. 'What do you intend to do about it?'

Naturally enough, for a man with teeth like that and a half-rotted liver, Fergal had awful bad breath, and he knew it. He covered his mouth, cleared his throat and edged away, embarrassed to have her so close, but she didn't flinch.

'I intend to guard yer secrets with me life, Fiorinda.'

'Thank you,' she said. 'Good. I need people I can trust.'
She walked away.

Bridge House

Outside the Castle Museum in the centre of Taunton there stands a block of granite with a bronze sword in it, buried halfway to the hilt. It features, as Chosen Few buffs will know, in an early video, the one they made for 'Glass Island'. Bridge House, our post-modern Camelot, stands about a mile away. It's a solid, bourgeois, nineteenth-century dwelling in a fashionably dishevelled garden (Milly is the gardener) that was once drummer Milly Kettle's childhood home. The double garage that was the Chosen Few's first rehearsal space is there. A wisteria vine obscures the stone slab above the front door, plastered into place by Ax and Jordan Preston, with the inscription from the ruined city of Fatepur Sikri, *The prophet Jesu says: this world is a bridge, make no house upon it.*

In September of the year after his inauguration, straight after the very low-key celebration of his anniversary, Ax went down to Taunton, cancelling all public engagements, and spent several weeks at Bridge House with his band and his Triumvirate partners, his cat Elsie, and a ten-month-old baby, Ax's nephew, Albi. Visitors came and went. Much of what happened was broadcast live on the English Terrestrial Channel 7 (Cult TV). The whole event became *Bridge House*, a fabulous collaborative work that stands as a landmark in the career of every artist involved; and they were many.

Before we enter that deceptively simple, deeply complex edifice of words and music, sound and vision, time and stillness, inspired impro, let's take a moment to wonder why. Why did Ax do this, and how did he get the brainy bruiser and our boho princess to agree? It's no secret that Ax's Triumvirate partners and his band are not close friends. Why the outside publishing deal? Why didn't The Insanitude label publish this? Why is Fiorinda called 'Miss Brown'? What happened to George Merrick and the domestic robot? Why did our beloved leader drop everything and spend six weeks *at play*, while the country reeled in shock after the Spitall's Farm affair? There are many questions, there are many answers; there is a richness of speculation.

What do we see? First and foremost, we see a great deal of the original Chosen Few playing together in that basement studio, with the addition of fifteen-year-old Maya, a cracking young guitarist ('Tot' Torquil Preston, who comes between Maya and Shane, the Chosen Few's bassist, is at Bristol uni, is not musical, and never gets involved). We see what a tight little band they are, and how obsessively they love making music, Ska and Metal: their roots. We hear them reminiscing about how it was: the Preston brothers growing up on a sink estate, seeing hardly another non-white face except for the Chinese family in the chip shop. Milly Kettle, the leafy suburban girl who met Jordan at college, joined the band, fell in love with big brother and crossed over to the wrong side of the tracks . . . (But now she's back again, and they're all living the leafy suburban life.) We meet Ax's mother, Sunni, a Christian refugee from the Sudan: the woman who gave Ax his centre, and his will to do good. We meet Dan Preston, whose probable antecedents run the whole gamut of the port of Bristol, the likeable ne'er-do-well who gave Ax his edge. We hear the brothers and their sister talk, immigrant hearts, about loving this landscape, this piece of earth where they were born, not made; and about being green. Light green, lazy green (by the standards of today). Car driving, tobacco-smoking, lovers of gadgets, lovers of toys, lovers of tech . . . Ax is not a moderate revolutionary, anyone who thinks that makes a *big* mistake. But he's not a puritan. No way.

What does it all mean?

The effect of Bridge House is cumulative. There are no speeches, no statements. Celtic blood sacrifice is not discussed. The renewed threat of utter chaos, after the disasters in Italy that October, barely rates a mention. But there is a purpose. What we are offered is a glimpse of a compromised and *possible* Utopia, the future as Ax has dreamed it. A life of recreation. Of making art, with people you both love and hate (often equally, and at the same time). Expect no revelations, no soap-opera heated dialogue. Expect openness . . .

Down-dressing Milly Kettle, with her no-nonsense haircut and her gardener's hands, sits in the conservatory answering interview questions while the baby clambers around. Sunlight falls on her. 'I was Ax's girfriend for six years,' she says. 'I loved him, I didn't understand him. We had great sex, we had some good conversations. I·knew he wasn't faithful to me. I put up with it: you know, rockstars. I thought that was it, I thought that was all he had to give. Captain Sensible . . . Then when it was all over I saw him with Fiorinda. He was a totally different person.' How did you feel about that? asks the unseen interviewer, a barely heard murmur. 'Gutted,' says Milly. The wriggling baby suddenly seems too much for her. The interviewer's hands come into shot. It's Ax. He takes his nephew in his arms. He has no child; Fiorinda can't have children. The man and woman look at each other in silence for a long, complicated moment.

This is art, of course. But art is life. Life is performance.

In Dissolution England the Triumvirate and their friends are the Few we have Chosen. They are our Shaman. They take the hallucinatory poison, the wrecking-ball violence of these times, and transform it for us. *Bridge House* is the algorithm of that transformation, a work of art, a set of instructions, a metaphysical packed lunch: survival rations for a journey into the dark.

The Glass Island video. Twenty-one-year-old Ax pulls the sword from the stone, Shane and Jordan and Milly hauling on him like a tug-of-war team. It becomes his guitar. The granite block leaps into the air. The Chosen Few turn into cartoon figures and try to flee, but it splats them . . . Ax is our champion, but he can't die for us. Self-sacrifice is not an option for this messiah; he has to live. He has to keep his personal freedom, paradoxically intact, or his project is doomed and we all know it. Can our big brother have it all? Read the music, watch the movie, get your head into this immersion. Come, and see.

from the Introduction to *Ax At The Bridge*, Dian Buckley,
Orionbooks 20XX

FIVE

Lithium

The day began with a dreary hour or two of admin, getting nowhere because everyone's still on fuel-starvation holiday, moving on to a session in the Zen Self tent, wired up to the brain machines, which lasted until after dark. No joy there, either. He tramped across the site, through snow falling soft and insistent on the dregs of the frozen slush that had been hanging around since Christmas. It was pretty, but immediately made him think of what the thaw would be like. Fucking insane neo-mediaeval crap, this whole Rivermead concept. The van was cold and empty. He had to remind himself he'd warned his band, warned everyone, to leave him the fuck alone. Snow was falling like death on the other side of the obsidian windows. He sat in the kitchen, staring at the mirror door, switching the mask on and off, thinking, what am I doing with my life? What do people see in that face? It has a weird symmetry. It has too much mouth. It has fine lines spraying from the corners of its eyes, and the pores are like cinder pits.

Shoulda stayed in purdah. I *liked* my purdah.

Fiorinda arrived about eight. He had to let her in; he'd locked the box. She pulled off her tam-o'-shanter and her coat, shaking snow from her hair. 'About time. It's *twelve degrees below* out there. What a winter. Is this global warming? Is this because the Gulf Stream switched itself off, or turned upside down, whatever it did?'

'It's just snow.' He headed back to his room.

She came after him, cheerfully. She was wearing the red and gold Elizabeth dress that he loved, which touched him, but couldn't lift his mood. 'Rupert gave me a card for you. Shall I open it?' Rupert the White Van Man of Reading Arena was veteran caterer to the Few and friends: provider of many a corn pattie and cognac-soused breakfast, when Fiorinda and the Heads were Dissolution Summer stay-behinds. She opened the envelope. 'Oooh. I'm afraid it's got a number on it.'

'Bastard.'

He'd been tinkering with the *Unmasked* immersions that were still not working because he never had enough time. He closed it all down and lay on the bed.

'There's a present, too. But you can't have it, because you called him a bastard.'

They got under the quilt together, because it was *fucking* cold, and he couldn't ATP-prime the heating, something wrong with it. Holding her sweet body, his cock wearily half-erect, he wanted to ask, *where's Ax?*, but he was too proud. Another winter of Dissolution and nothing changes, my darling girl and I are among the preterite, with our ruined careers and our love that might have been, and the man we both adore who is too busy saving the world.

Bang, bang.

'I wonder who that could be,' said Fiorinda, and darted out of the bed.

Ax came back with her, snow on his sleek hair and his old leather coat.

'Glad you could make it.'

'Yeah, well. I decided to pop down, birthday boy. I needn't stay if it puts you out.'

Sage turned his face to the wall. 'You can laugh. You'll be playing guitar when you're ninety. I'll be an arthritic ex-ballerina by the time I'm thirty-five.'

Ax sat on the bed. 'Sage, I am not taking that. Fuck's

sake, try to hang on. I'll be with you on the downhill slope to the grave in another six weeks. If I was to start recounting some of the charming things you used to say about me, in the long ago—'

'*Don't!*' shouted Fiorinda. 'Have some *sense*, both of you!'

'Sorry,' Sage rolled over on his back. 'Truly sorry. Rockstar tantrum. I'm despicable.'

Ax leaned down and kissed him. 'Grow old along with me,' he said, entirely without mockery. 'There'll still be good times.' He looked at Fiorinda. 'Does he get his present?'

'He's been really horrible.'

'Yeah, but on the other hand he can't help it, an' I can't be fucked to take it back to the shop. It'd be embarrassing. I'm supposed to have money to burn, and the woman's a major artist. Brace yourself, big cat. You have to look in a mirror.'

They made him strip off his sweaters and stood him in front of the bathroom mirror in his slick black dungarees and shabby teeshirt. The present was a platinum and diamond torque. It lay at the base of his throat, warm from Ax's body, stunningly beautiful.

'I *love* it. My God, how much did this set us back?'

'Dirt cheap,' said Ax guiltily, 'think of all those defunct catalytic convertors. Anyway, Fiorinda bought it.'

Fiorinda was their banker. Her earnings were unencumbered, apart from the sizeable tranche that went into the Volunteer Initiative. Everything Ax earned was swallowed instantly; he was chronically short of disposable income. Sage had to support a major share of the Heads organisation, that sprawling feudal circus, aside from contributing to the Reich and Mary's maintenance (Marlon's trust fund was safely inaccessible).

'Bend down,' said Fiorinda. She unclasped the torque and wrapped it round his brow. 'Mask.' The living skull flickered into existence, adjusted itself and reappeared, its sombre beauty crowned with a circlet of coldly gleaming, diamond-fired metal.

'Now *that*'s what a fallen angel ought to look like.'

The skull mugged, 'Aw, shucks,' and vanished again. He kissed them each in turn, and this moved into a complex, dynamic, three-person snog.

'I know what we should do,'said Fiorinda, breaking out of it. 'We should feed him half Rupert's cake, to get his blood-sugar up, and go out and play in the snow.'

'Huh?'

'C'mon Sage,' said Ax. 'We can fuck later. Snowball fight. It'll make you feel young.'

They ate the apple cake, drank scalding real coffee with vodka chasers, and went out to play in the snow. Not a staybehind was stirring under the dim, suffused blanket of the winter's night sky. They found a bank and made angels, they fought with snowballs until their gloves were soaked and their hands hurt, and came to rest, Ax rolling a spliff on his lap on the lid of his smokes tin, by the White Van. They'd been hoping to get something hot, but Rupert had shut up shop and was not responding.

'Hey, look,' said Fiorinda, passing the spliff. 'There are lights in the Blue Lagoon.'

'That's weird,' said Ax, 'on a night like this. Let's go and check it out.'

He followed them, not suspecting a thing, while they examined the snow and remarked on the number of footprints, quite a crowd, what on earth's going on? They went in round the back, into the backstage bar known as Bartoli's Hideout, through the curtains of marquee membrane, and *Shazzah!* The tent was laid out for cabaret and full of people, colour, lights. He realised he'd been betrayed, spun round and found George and Bill and Peter, his brother Heads, his own *band* had appeared, barring the way, arms folded, grinning like idiots.

Practically everyone he knew in the world waited nervously. Fuck, what can you do?

'Okay, okay. Thank you very much. Let's party. Just don't make a habit of it.'

The entertainment at Sage's thirtieth birthday party, MC'd by Roxane Smith, hir old bones swathed in a fantastical fake-sable cloak, was a phenomenal sampler of Dissolution Music, including a couple of ancient veteran outfits of god-like status. The Few themselves didn't feature (leaving it to the professionals), but in one of the pauses Fergal Kearney, without leaving his place at a table of demi-gods, took up his harp. Fergal had moved into Fiorinda's mother's house, a very successful arrangement. Fiorinda's gran liked him, and he kept the old witch in order with surprising tact. His friends worried about his medical condition, but so far he hadn't needed any treatment crisis-England couldn't provide. His health seemed better than it had been when he arrived.

The techies at the desk quickly gave him a sound cone. The whole tent fell into silence. The Irishman, burnt-out as he was, could command an audience. He gave them three beautiful instrumentals and then decided to embark on 'Who Knocks', the hideous domestic violence song Sage had recorded years ago, in another lifetime. The ravaged voice was still compelling. Everyone held their breath.

Sage stalked through the crowd to where Fergal was sitting. He listened to the end and then moved in: too close, a coiled spring, scary even without the mask. 'You're an insolent bastard, Fergal.'

'I was just thinking,' said Fergal, grinning up at him, gap-toothed, sure of his bardic rights. 'Ye've come a long way since ye wrote that, Aoxomoxoa. A fine long way.'

'You're right,' said Sage, grinning back, blue eyes bright as the diamonds: grabbed Fergal's ginger head and planted a kiss.

Ax Preston and the Chosen took the stage for a set adorned with the most trashy, sentimental buddy-songs ever recorded. Sage armed himself with canapés and attacked, the band ducking and diving, Mr Dictator looking absurdly young, playing up a storm, all of them laughing like maniacs. Fiorinda cheered and stomped with the rest.

He is made of crystal, she thought; everyone can see what's going on inside. Yet no one knows him completely. Not even Ax, not even me.

The crime of witchcraft returned to the statute books that winter, which Ax didn't like at all. As he said, there was no evidence that what had happened at Spitall's Farm was a crime of 'magic' *per se*, and witchcraft laws are notoriously open to abuse. But he had to make concessions to restore public confidence, and this was one of them. Most of the other fall-out was positive. The Celtics were back on board, anxious to be part of Ax's régime. David Sale came off the smack. There was a cleaning of the Augean Stables that had a welcome effect throughout the Westminster administration. Ax's reluctant coup was even, arguably, a great artistic success, since it led to the making of *Bridge House* . . . He did not even have to quit his musical career. The Chosen became Jordan's band, but Ax became an associate, a collaborator, a guest star; the way Fiorinda worked with DARK.

Fiorinda saw the new culture taking form, distilled by Ax Preston's personal alchemy from the slavery and excess of rock and roll. Children would grow up with Ax's manifesto, schools would teach the message. Make music, have fun, tend the garden. Above all, be good to each other: because that's the only way we're going to get through . . . It would be fake, it would be flawed, it would be mostly lip-service: but it would be a damn sight better than what might have been. She felt bad when the

Witchcraft Bill was passed. She was now *lying to Ax*, about something potentially very damaging, and she could not tell herself otherwise. But she didn't waste time worrying about it. She had the Volunteer Initiative to run, and she was working on a new album (which would become *Yellow Girl*). She had her tiger and her wolf, and the Few.

She was busy and happy . . . She believed she was very happy.

Alain de Corlay, the radical rockstar who played the French version of Ax's role, had fallen out *very badly* with Sage over the fixed pitons affair (a cross-channel offensive against rock-climbing purists, organised by Sage out of sheer devilment). But peace had broken out. Alain, although disgusted at the oxymoronic, *untenable* Countercultural Bourgeoisie that the Few had become, wanted Ax for an ally. He was also very intrigued by the Zen Self Project. In February he came over. The Triumvirate went out to eat with him at a restaurant they'd never heard of, but that Alain believed to be not without merit. Fiorinda wore the trouser suit that she'd had made – by George Merrick's tailor, the perfect master responsible for the *Unmasked* outfits – for 'Miss Brown, Mister Blue and Mister Red,' their big hit single from *Bridge House*. It was a beautiful suit, dove grey, exquisitely cut and extremely sexy. But Fiorinda missed her skirts. Maybe that was it. Or it was the interminable length of the meal; or Sage and Alain, babbling on about the *dérèglement de tous les senses*, and how total abandonment of the body to the assault of futuristic, magical science would bring about . . . Would bring about what? Precisely? Fiorinda was very impatient with that kind of gibberish.

Something went wrong, anyway. In the middle of the night Sage woke to hear her crying, and for a moment *he could not find her*. She was gone from his arms, a desolate and terrified ghost . . . He put on the light and she was crouched on the pillows, in her satin nightdress, sobbing. 'Darling, what is it? Sssh, hush, it's okay, I'm here—'

'I lost my baby. My little baby. Oh dear, oh dear. Oh—' She stared at him, eyes open but blinded by the nightmare. 'Oh *Sage*, where is Ax? He's *gone*, and my baby's gone too, and I can't find him. It's my fault, I know it is. I did the wrong—'

'Ax is right here beside me, where would he be? Hey, Ax, *wake up*. Bad dream.'

Between them they coaxed her back under the covers. She did not appear to wake, but she seemed to escape from her grief and terror, and to believe that she was safe at home; and Ax was not lost . . . When she was sleeping quietly they slipped out of bed, found dressing gowns and went to the kitchen. Ax sat at the table and took out a cigarette. Sage looked for the Ndogs, chose a popper and pressed it to his neck.

'What's that?'

'Potassium. I'd forgotten to take it.'

Ax shook his head and grinned. 'Why don't you just eat a banana?'

Eating a banana would not address the rate at which use of the neural-aligner snapshot drained the system of vital elements. It couldn't be helped. He was Olwen's best labrat; he couldn't make the gaps between rides wide enough, but he wasn't going to get into that. He knew he could convince Ax in five minutes that what he was doing was okay. He was saving his reasoned arguments for when Fiorinda needed to be pacified.

'Not so easy to come by, these days. What d'you think? Is there anything we can do?'

The room was bright and kitchen-white; it was electric light in here, not ATP. They looked at each other, baffled, saddened. Fiorinda had been sterilised without her consent when she was thirteen, after she'd given birth to her father's child, the little boy who had died when he was three months old. They knew she longed for a baby. But she refused to consider going to the whitecoats, to see if the sterilisation could be reversed.

'I don't care if she never has a kid,' said Ax. 'Well, okay, I'm lying. I'd give a lot to see her with my baby in her arms. Or yours, big cat.' But Sage had Marlon. 'But what I want is Fiorinda. She nearly died, the first time. Did you know that?'

'Yeah.' Sage poked at the jumble of poppers in the incense box, absently sorting out a few gentle downers. 'I knew that. But she was a child then. It would be different.'

'I think she doesn't want to go to the doctors because . . . It's a fuck of a thing to get into, fertility treatment. Leave aside the, er, moral dilemma. Even with full access to the miracles of modern medicine you can give yourself years of pain and grief, and end up with nothing. Talk to Felice.'

'Are we *sure* it's the baby thing that's bothering her? What else happened tonight? She was wearing the suit. You know, that suit pisses her off. She says it makes her feel post-career. She's not *Fiorinda* any more, she's some boring grown-up.'

'I love her in the suit. Makes me so horny. She's the most erotic thing I've ever seen.'

'Me too.' They grinned at each other. 'But I'll *burn* it, if it gives her nightmares . . . I was talking about the Zen Self too much. It could have been that?'

'Dunno. Fuck, we're going to have to tell her she's doing this.'

'Hmm . . . I don't know. I don't want to make a big deal over a couple of broken nights.'

'See how we think in the morning.'

Sage came and sat down, pulled his chair close and put his arm round Ax's shoulders. Ax leaned back against him (the oxytocin thrill of physical contact, that lingers for months or years), reached for a lighter and sparked up.

'You ever thought of giving up tobacco, Ax? You know, there're other ways to get high.'

'Knock it off,' said Mr Dictator, firmly.

Dian had sent them her book, an early copy. Congratulations were in order, and they better be tactfully phrased, the media babe is *proud* of this one. Here's the sword in the stone, on the front. Ax sighed, leafing the pages, shaking his head. 'Strange woman. Pop-journalists live on a planet all of their own.'

'As rebel-icons it is our fate to become corpses in the mouths of the bourgeoisie.'

'Don't fucking start . . . I hope she never finds out about the crass actuality of Fiorinda's horsetrading.'

'Nah, water off a duck's back. She'd spin it to make herself look good. Never pity them, Ax.' They looked at the pictures, already touching and nostalgic as old family photos. 'Are you *sure* you want a kid?' Sage yawned. 'You know, I remember from Marlon, they can wake up howling fifteen times a night, and do it for months.'

'I'm sure. But not if it's going to fuck her up like this—'

'So this is what you do,' said Fiorinda, coldly. She was standing in the doorway, hollow-eyed and tousled. 'You get together late at night and discuss loopy Fiorinda. What's the matter? You yearn for fatherhood? You want to trade me in for a fully working model?' The two men stared at her, guilty as charged.

Don't answer. There is *no* correct answer.

'What happened?' she asked.

'You had a nightmare,' said Ax, cautiously.

'Oh, I see. Have I been having nightmares often?'

'Er, one or two,' Sage admitted. 'It was me and Alain, wasn't it? We pissed you off.'

Fiorinda gave him a sour smile. 'That's right, change the subject. Full marks for low cunning, let's talk about something else than babies. Okay. Fine . . . You are kidding yourselves. There's nowhere further to go than here. There's nothing *beyond*. What happens after the total derangement is that you settle down and become an institution.'

'Please forgive us,' said Ax. 'We won't do it again.'

'Whatever it was. We are tactless oafs, but we love you.'

'Oh shit, okay. I'm being horrible. Come back to bed. I love you too.'

She had no more nightmares, that they knew about, but she was starting to remind them of the damaged teenager they had known. A couple of weeks later Ax was alone in the Brixton flat one evening, reading a stack of government papers and wondering where his girlfriend had got to. Sage was down in Reading, occupied with the Zen Self. At last Fiorinda called to say she wasn't coming home. He asked her where she was. She said she was out, and it transpired that she meant out with someone else, yeah, and why not? She would not be home before morning, so don't wait up and don't bother to call me again because I'm switching my phone off now.

He settled to his work again, feeling lonely and shaken. There'd been a time, during Pigsty's monster hippy régime, when Ax and Fiorinda had both played away relentlessly, and in the most hurtful way possible. So, not new bad news. But where is all of this coming from? What's happening to my darling?

Half an hour later Sage arrived, big and bouncy, growling about the fucking trains.

'Where's Fee?'

'Out.'

'Oh,' said Sage, surprised. 'Back soon?'

'No.' Ax kept his eyes on the document he was reading. 'She's at the 69, with that Chinese drummer. Not sure of the name. Very pretty young guy. She won't be home.'

'*What?*'

'You heard.'

'Ax, I don't get this. She knew I was coming. She asked me to come up tonight.'

'Welcome to my world.'

'Shit. What's *wrong*? What the fuck is wrong?'

'Don't know. Could be that she's nineteen, wild and free, whereas you are turning into an unavailable neuroscience nerd and I am a fucking bureaucrat.'

Ax went on reading. Sage sat on the opposite couch, chewing the surviving joint of his right thumb and staring at the gas flames. Silence reigned.

At last Sage bounced to his feet. 'Ah, this is no good. Leave that. Get your coat, c'mon, you can drive me somewhere.'

Ax found himself being guided, swiftly and surely (curiously, Sage was a good navigator when not behind the wheel) towards the south-west motorways.

'Sage, what is this? I am *not* driving you to Cornwall.'

'No, no. Devon will do fine.'

Ah well. What's the point of being a rockstar dictator if you can't burn up some private transport hypocrisy records once in a while. They reached Croyde at two in the morning; parked the car. Sage led the way through the chill and breezy, sea-scented night, the sparkling moonlight, to a café with a weatherboard upper storey, and started chucking gravel at a window. Shortly a woman's body appeared there rosily in lamplight, generous naked breasts broad moon-apples eyeing them. She opened the window.

'Oh, hi, Sage.'

'Hi, Mel. Keys, keys!'

'Just a minute.'

She vanished, came back and chucked a bunch of keys into Sage's cupped palms.

The keys opened a cavernous workshop on the beach, smelling of wax and solvents; white dust hung in the air. They suited up, took a couple of boards and headed for the water. Before the first plunge Ax was ready to rebel, but once he was in it the sea was thrilling, warmer than the air, full of tremendous life. The waves came in beautiful sets, creaming straight as if drawn by a ruler, not big, but big enough. There was no rivalry, no competition, not tonight: it was pure joy. When they'd had enough they sat on the beach, insulated by good suits and warmed by all that energy. The moon was fabulous.

Ax sifted cold silky sand through his fingers. 'Maybe we're not quite over the hill yet.'

'Nyah, this proves nothing. My dad's over seventy and he still surfs.'

'Your dad is *over seventy*?'

'Yeah. He's seventy-five.'

'He doesn't look it!' Sage's dad was five foot eight or so, olive skin, silver-dusted jet-black hair: you could see he'd been the spit of Marlon Williams when he was a kid.

'Mm,' agreed Sage gloomily. 'He doesn't, does he? People will be taking him for my younger brother in a year or two.'

Ax grinned at the sea. 'Fancy a fuck?'

Sage glanced at him sidelong, looked at the sky and laughed, glittering with mischief. 'Shit. I was planning to jump on you.'

'Go ahead.'

'Nah. Too late. It wouldn't be the same. Well. There's a mattress in the loft.'

The mattress was very seedy. The icy dark air wrapped them round. They lay together afterwards, intertwined, unwilling to move, while the cold crept over their sweated skin, and breathing slowed—

'D'you think we're taking this too seriously?' whispered Ax.

'No baby, I don't . . . I never would have believed I'd end up in bed with a bloke, but you're the love of my life. You and Fiorinda, both. *Nothing* else matters. Nothing.'

'I meant, the way she's behaving. As if she's really fucked off with us—'

'Oh. Hahaha . . . Well, no. I think you're right. We have to stop being boring.'

'But you're the love of my life too. You and Fiorinda. Nothing else matters.'

'All we have to do is remember that.'

They pulled a disreputable rug over themselves, slept for an hour or two and zoomed back to London in the morning light, making a steady hundred and forty klicks around the potholes and the surface breaks. Sage, curled up in the passenger seat, opened an eye once and mumbled plaintively, do you have to drive so fast?

'Yeah.'

She was home. She came out into the stairwell as they let themselves in down below.

'Well,' said Sage, 'did you fuck your pretty Chinese kid?'

They stood looking up: eyes shining, purely delighted to see her back safe. Her heart turned over. She realised she had *no idea* why she had been trying to hurt them.

'Yes I did,' she said, in a small voice. 'But I don't know why. I'm an idiot.'

They bounded up the stairs and hugged her. 'I don't mind if you want to fuck other people,' said Sage. 'Well, I do, but that's my business. As long as you come home—'

'You missed a *great* night out,' Ax told her, between kisses. 'Stick with us, sweetheart. We're not dead yet. We'll show you a good time.'

And the shadow passed, as if it had never happened.

In March Kevin Verlaine had a bad snapshot trip. This was a first. The rest of them had taken a hammering, in spite of the most careful mood-control and pre-medication. The afterburn from a painful vision was horrendous, even though you lost the actual memory within minutes. (In a way, Ax had been lucky to get away with purely physical symptoms.) Only Ver had escaped. The others had teased him about the purity of his life; but now no longer. He was so distressed he had to spend the night in one of the Zen Self labs, deep inside the eau-de-Nil dome. Sage sat up with him (Ver couldn't bear to have anyone else around) wearing the living skull mask which, for some reason, the patient found comforting. Hour on hour, listening to the kid's incoherent despair, and telling him, over and over, *There's no new bad news. Whatever you saw, it isn't anything that wasn't there before. The world is the same as it was yesterday. You lived with it then, you can live with it now . . .*

By morning Sage was exhausted, but Verlaine was calm again. They ate breakfast together, alone, because the patient was still fragile – yoghurt and fresh bread, Welsh honey and the weak malted ale (disgusting watery stout) that was the current Staybehind breakfast beverage of choice.

'Sage,' said Verlaine, 'does Ax know about the *Flowers for Algernon* scenario?'

Flowers for Algernon was the nethead term for a terrifying possible hazard of keeping one of the pre-Crisis brain implant chips in your head too long. Yes, Ax knew about it. No, he would not consider getting rid of the thing. He needed his chip. Sage felt a prickle of unease . . . Verlaine had cut his long hair recently, not short enough to be an annoying *imitation* of his idol, but getting there. Silky brown curls clustered around his head. He looked innocent as a child.

'Yeah. He knows. Tell me about it. Fucker thinks he's the exception to every rule. What put that into your head?'

'There was something about it in my vision. I don't think his chip had failed, that wasn't what gave me the horrors, but it made me think—'

This was another first. It was nearly twenty hours since Kevin Verlaine had taken the neural aligner and made his brief, elliptical voyage to the state of all states. He wasn't supposed to remember *anything* by this time; and it didn't matter. According to received wisdom, snapshot visions were a side-effect: noise, not signal. They were not glimpses of the *actual* future (if there is such a thing); or past, or present. You wake up remembering your lover's deathbed, with circumstantial details that may or may not be 'accurate'. This tells you nothing. No one here gets out alive, we knew that already—

'Oh really—?' Sage began, in the most casual tone possible. Fuck. If only Verlaine was still hooked up; this we have to see, it could mean anything, it could mean nothing, but I have to know what is going on inside that curly head, *right now*—

At that moment something came into the cell, filling every angle of the walls, every atom in the air. A limitless sweetness, an intensity, a perfume, a sound, a delicious taste . . . Synasthesia. Sage and Verlaine grinned at each other, involuntarily. The world is terrible, full of hideous cruelty – and yet when we have approached *the whole* of all that is, its penumbra falls on us as this ravishing delight.

That's the Zen Self. That's what keeps people addicted to the quest.

The visitation passed. 'Shall we log that?' asked Verlaine.

'Yeah. How d'you feel now?'

'Oh, better.'

'D'you remember what you were just saying?'

'No. What was I saying?'

'I can't remember either,' Sage lied. 'Come on, let's check you out.'

He gave the kid a thorough neuro and physical debrief, and found nothing untoward. Verlaine headed back to London. Sage returned to the van, accessed Serendip and they went over Verlaine's trip together. It turned out that the young Adjuvant had been given a double dose of snapshot. Olwen had discovered that the capsules were going walkabout, so she'd changed the system; the new delivery method had been subverted by human error. It was recorded on the video. Oh, fuck. Well, thank God he took no harm, and we'd better keep him on the bench for a while.

Olwen was intrigued by Sage's report that Verlaine had apparently 'remembered' something from his trip, after twenty hours. But she was not convinced. By then Verlaine no longer remembered remembering anything, and his scans showed no confirmation. It could have been a telepathy artefact (they happened all the time, a useless irritation to the experimenters). Sage could have been worrying about Ax's chip himself.

Consciousness and memory are worse than DNA, said the guru. We have to be very, very careful not to be fooled by contamination. And no, Sage, *you will not* up your own dosage. It isn't worth it, it's not the answer. We're making progress. Just be patient.

Fiorinda went to the Benelux with DARK, travelling by sea because the Channel tunnels, in poor repair since the Deconstruction Tour, had finally been closed down. They toured with a set mainly from *Yellow Girl*, and the new DARK album *Safo*; and had an interesting time, dodging riots and living on their wits. When they came back, the Few were celebrating. *Unmasked*, the first album to escape from gulag Europe (legitimately, through a mathematically-proven virus-free Swedish transcript) had scarfed up five Grammys. The band had known about this, but they'd just had official confirmation, via the Internet Commissioners; plus a disc of the award ceremony — which Sage and George had converted, after a lot of hassle, to a format that would run on Crisis Europe hardware.

It was the end of April. The new Rivermead building was finished. They went down for a preview, before the

Mayday opening ceremony. Fiorinda the no-fixed-abode brat had a home of her own at last: a suite of rooms on the upper floor of the complex. The main room – called the *solar* – was huge, with vast rectilinear windows (justified as solar-collectors, really there because Topsy the architect was a closet sixties fan). The party settled there, after a tour of the premises, to watch the Grammy show on Fiorinda's neo-mediaeval pewter framed wall screen.

The Heads were playing it down. They were a sensitive bunch of laddish idiots. Grammys, pah. Hardly an award at all. It means nothing.

'It's the Apocalypse Now awards,' growled Sage. 'Fucking masters of the universe. First they machine-gun you, then they give you a Bandaid.'

'I thought you were on their side,' said Ax. 'Don't I remember you saying the Internet Commission had every right to take us out and shoot us after Ivan/Lara?'

'That was before I knew they were going to make their sanctions permanent.'

'Fucking typical,' complained Bill. 'First time 'e ever lets us make a mass-market record, and he has to wait until we're stuck in the gulag with our assets frozen.'

Aoxomoxoa's fans in England must have greeted the revelation of 'Unmasked' much as the crowd at Newport greeted Bob Dylan with his electric guitar—

The Few and friends cheered and jeered. Oh, my, Sage. *Bob Dylan!* How're we going to keep him down on the farm now—?

Silver and Pearl Wing, leaders of the rugrat-pack, were in Fiorinda's neo-mediaeval bedroom. They sat on a roll of leftover matting, sharing a spliff.

'When you look in a mirror,' said Silver, 'do you feel as if that person is you?'

'No. Because it's a reflection.' Pearl liked to cut the crap.

'Think about it. Does the face you see, what other

people see, match the person you think you are inside? It doesn't. Your natural image of yourself doesn't have a face.'

'I don't know what you're talking about.'

'Oh, nothing.' Silver paused to take a thoughtful draw, the spliff clamped elegantly between her fourth and fifth fingers. 'Just something Sage was saying to me.' Beside them on the floor lay a package of mottled bark-paper. They were planting a charm, which they intended to retrieve when it was loaded with psycho-sexual power, and use for business purposes. 'We'll put it under the matting, in the middle. Fiorinda sleeps in the middle, and female sex energy is stronger.'

'How do you know?'

'Mum says so. Don't you ever listen, cloth ears? Male sex energy is piddling.'

'How do you know Fiorinda sleeps in the middle?'

'Easy. Just watch them. She's always in the middle.'

'But how will we know where the middle of the bed's going to be? It isn't here yet.'

'Feng Shui.'

Ruby and Jet, Anne-Marie's little boys, the three-year-old and the five-year-old, wandered around the big room, tugging at hippy wall hangings; clambering on strange, artistic furniture. Smelly Hugh, AM's villainous-looking but gentle partner, nursed Safire, the new Wing baby, while AM herself gave a magical-herbalist consultation to the Powerbabes. Felice was pregnant at last, after years of sorrow. Poor Rob! He had longed to be a family man, but Dora and Cherry had been adamant that Felice, senior Babe, had to have the first child. He was ecstatic now, glowing like a pregnant girl himself . . . Roxane presided, on one of the Roman cross-framed chairs, built of oak timber from the great storm. If Ax is a shameless socialist, s/he mused, and Sage is passionately conservative, that leaves Fiorinda to lead the party of Gladstone. Is Fiorinda a Liberal? That doesn't sound right . . . Then s/he smiled at hir mistake. Of course. Our young queen, compassionate nihilist, is above politics, and served with equal love by Her Majesty's government and Her Majesty's loyal opposition.

Long may the coalition endure.

I hate rush matting, thought Fiorinda. It hurts your feet, and food gets stuck in it. Thank God I'll never actually have to *live* here. Is it ridiculous to feel nostalgic for a sign that says AUTOMATIC DOOR NOT WORKING? For the smell of carpet glue? She saw the Few and Friends as courtiers, gathered round the neo-mediaeval triple throne, and a wave of bitter malaise swept over her, coming from nowhere, but instantly justified. *This is not my world!* Fergal Kearney, sitting over the other side of the room with Doug Hutton, the security chief, was watching her with puzzled sympathy . . . She rearranged her face. Look happy: that's your job. Stone Age Royalty.

'Tell us what's going on with the Zen Self, Sage,' suggested Cherry, tickling Safire's little chin. 'Like when you told us about quantum cryptography that time.'

'Yeah,' agreed Felice, 'That was cool. Alice was the bad guy.'

'What is consciousness?' suggested Rob, trying to sound scientific.

The weird science cabal – Dilip and the Heads, Chip and Ver – winked at each other.

'Ah . . . How long is a piece of string? Consciousness is different things to different people. It depends on the situation. It depends what you're trying to measure. It's not a very useful concept—'

'Okay, he doesn't know the answer,' said Ax, grinning. 'Better try another question.'

'Every moment of perception has its global brain state: perceptions, recall, emotions, sensations, all bound together. Your sense of your self is formed by a crucial collection of these brain states, stored in memory. It's a blurred template, just enough for us to get by. But all those global states are also real objects in information-space, also known as the sum of all possible states, and there the record is perfect. Achieving the Zen Self, which means gaining unlimited access to the state of all states, would incidentally include the entire complex, past present and future, of the information-states that make you, you. What we're doing at the moment is rewiring our brains to take the weight. If you dope your firing patterns right, under certain conditions, you move into phase with information-space for a very short time. Every time you repeat the experiment there's a lasting physical effect, tiny but real. Your brain gets nearer to being able to process its own total awareness.'

'And that would be the Zen Self?' suggested Dora.

'Er, no. Zen Self, stable fusion, is another huge scale-up. But achieving the first level awareness might trigger the second step. That's what we hope will happen.'

'So what do we get out of this?' asked Ax. 'Time travel? Boosted psychic powers?'

Sage smiled with wondrous sweetness, and so did the other labrats: a strange effect. Peter Stannen, who had now learned to live without the veil, looked particularly beatific.

'Zen Self is an end in itself. If you were doing it, you'd understand. But trust me, Ax, there'll be results. One day, my lord, you will tax the stuff.'

'You get visions of the future,' said Allie. 'I saw about that on Channel Seven.'

'Nah. Popular misconception.' (AX MUST GET THAT CHIP FIXED!)

Allie looked bemused. 'But I thought the drug, snap-shot, gave you visions?'

'Information-space is sort of an eleven-dimensional kaleidoscope,' explained Verlaine helpfully. 'Or, um, it might be sixteen. Are we on eleven or sixteen currently,

Sage? There's no way of knowing that what you see under snap is, uh, real, or just an aspect.'

'Of course it's all real, really,' murmured Chip. 'And nothing is real, too—'

'Snapshot's a nickname,' said the boss. 'The drug's a neural aligner. "Snapshot" is what the scanner does. In case something falls off the edge while you're out-of-body, like vision or motor control or whatever, Olwen's scanner has a *rescue me* snapshot of your last normal state, so she can re-install—'

He realised, a little too far into this cheery description of routine brain death, that some of his friends, including his girlfriend, were now staring in fascinated horror.

Hmm. Maybe I better back-pedal.

'It's never happened.'

'You LIAR!' shouted Fiorinda, jumping up. 'You *bastard*!' She stormed out.

'You'd better go after her, Sage,' said Allie, 'and by the way, if you've been risking your life and faculties like that, and not telling her, you *are* a bastard.'

Sage went after Fiorinda. Ax looked at the weird scientists. 'Has it ever happened?'

'Not seriously,' said Dilip, caught between two awesome fires.

'We're talking milliseconds,' said George. 'No danger. An' Olwen's in charge.'

'Like hell,' said Ax. It was well known that Sage could wrap Olwen Devi round his crooked little finger. He pulled the Les Paul, which he'd brought with him on this auspicious day, into his lap, and plucked a couple of softly zinging chords.

'Information-space, mm. It's a concept. Pity that stuff does not agree with me.'

Fiorinda was sitting on the plinth of the dead-motors sculpture at the main entrance. She looked up as Sage joined her. She wasn't angry. 'Don't worry, I know I can't stop you. I wouldn't try.' He sat beside her. 'When we first met, you were like Einstein in a hamster cage. I remember thinking, after I'd talked to you a couple of times, fuck, no wonder he has to sedate himself with alcohol. He'd go bonkers in this biz, otherwise.'

'I felt much the same about you, my brat.'

'Huh. Very funny.'

This tired-eyed, secretive girl is almost singlehandedly directing the drop-out hordes operation, an economy of three million. People, not currency. When the media folk want to know what's her role in the Triumvirate she says, *I'm the girl. I do the housework, of course*. Some household.

'I wish I could stop you from dismissing what you do. What's the VI budget at the moment? You got a rough estimate?'

'I never think of it like that. Think about the money and you're lost, that's old, money doesn't work any more, we have other currencies. I think of it as a shape,' said Fiorinda. 'A three-dimensional, no, a four-dimensional puzzle, because everything has fit inside the envelope and everything has to keep moving . . . Okay, I admit. It's a fascinating hobby. But I do it for Ax, because I love him. It isn't what I want.'

'Fiorinda, what's wrong? Tell me what's wrong. I know you're not happy.'

The light of spring was so beautiful. Beyond the tented town, a mist of colour moved like smoke through the budding trees on the other side of the river. She turned to him. No words, just a look, a sad gaze in which both of them were drowning—

'Excuse me.'

Pearl Wing had appeared, and was staring at them. Silver and Pearl were both, in principle, pretty children, with soft, pale brown hair and Chinese black eyes, but temperament came shining through. Pearl stood four-square, arms folded, glowering like a bulldog puppy in a smocked dress.

'Can I ask you something about your sex life?'

'Go ahead,' said Fiorinda, 'if you feel lucky, punk. Try it.'

Pearl skipped a step backwards. 'Who sleeps in the middle?'

'Hahaha. Usually I do,' said Sage. 'Now clear off.'

Mary Williams announced she was sending Marlon to boarding school, and Sage was *over my dead body* . . . Mary got her way, but Marlon was allowed to visit Brixton. He developed a huge crush on his dad's girlfriend: dropping her name all over the place, as he cut a swathe through the young scene at the Insanitude. *My sort of step-mother, you know, Fiorinda* . . . Sage hadn't been allowed to have his son on a visit since Marlon was four. The improvement in relations with his ex was a profound relief; ironic that it should come when his miraculous new happiness was running into trouble.

Fiorinda is unhappy; Ax is burying himself in his work.

Or should that be, Ax is burying himself in his work; Fiorinda is unhappy?

And Sage is conflicted, seeing both sides.

One day he met Fergal Kearney in the Mall. Sage was coming away from a meeting in Whitehall. Fergal had been at the San. He was heading for St James's Park, to feed the ducks. They strolled through the park together. Sage had been wanting to talk to the Irishman. The Celtic problem was in resurgence (if it had ever gone away), and a problem was developing between the London barmies and the Kilburn Celtic street-gangs. The 'Celtics' were not necessarily Celtic Nations-origin, but a native Irishman would be a big asset in the peace talks.

Fergal had a lot of status with the barmies as well. He'd been formally inducted into the barmy army after Spitall's Farm, with the proper militarised hippy ceremony – something Ax and Sage had missed, owing to their having been imposed on the army from above, by President Pig, rather than joining up.

They discussed Fergal's possible role.

'How are you keeping? You're looking better.'

'Fer a man with cirrhosis and a cancer fighting over his bones,' said Fergal, 'I'm in terrific shape.' He heaved a sigh. 'A fine fockin' defector I've turned out to be. I'm a crock, Sage, me darling. Some days, I'm jest incapable of rising from me bed.'

'You don't have to get up in the morning to help me with this.'

'Well, other days I'm not so bad. The ould witch is dosing me.' He gave Sage his gap-toothed grin. 'Okay, I'm yer man. I jest hope I don't say the wrong thing, and have yez punching me lights out over the conference table. That wud be unfortunate.'

Sage laughed and shook his head. 'I don't do that anymore.'

'Aye. I was fergetting,' agreed Fergal regretfully. 'Those days are gone.'

They sat on a bench by the water. Ax's England passed by, ignoring the Minister for Gigs and his companion. Fergal took out a greasy paper bag and began to throw crusts, judiciously favouring the little brown mallard ducks.

'And when you've sorted the Kilburn Celtics,' remarked Sage, staring at the scuffling waterbirds, 'you can get rid of Benny Prem for me.'

Sage and Fiorinda would have been very happy if Benny Preminder had left with the ratflight after Spitall's Farm. Alas, he was still around. Fergal shook his head.

'On that, I don't know what to say to ye. Yer Liaison

Secretary has a slimy little way about him, right enough – though I think I've niver seen him but on the telly. But there must be something in him, or Ax wouldn't keep him on. Ax doesn't do a thing without a reason, an' it won't be that Benny has any secret hold over him, will it?'

Prem, Sage thought, was like the obnoxious favourite at the court of some rock and roll megastar: the guy everybody hates and you can't figure it, until you realise he's the man supplying the star with drugs. Not in this case, of course: but it's like an addiction. Benny is the one that got away, the one person who has *never* succumbed to the Ax effect. And we can't have that, can we? Oh, no no, no.

He sighed. 'Benny's been with us since the beginning. I think Ax feels we owe him something. But he's dangerous. Could be dangerous. I've a strong feeling he has contacts with the ritual magic persuasion. They still exist, you know.'

'Aye. Like rats in the house. We fockin' ought to have cleared them out, when we had the chancst. But it's a wee bit difficult to see how, with non-violent methods.'

He won't listen to me, Sage was thinking. Over Benny Prem or anything else. When did he stop listening . . . ? Is it Ax who has changed? Or is it me, am I making excuses for my own feelings? All I know is that *she's unhappy*, and that's not in the contract. Being the Minister for Gigs, being the third party in the threesome . . . It was okay, because I love him. But what if Fiorinda is unhappy? What then?

Fergal cleared his throat, venting a whiff of carrion breath sauced with red wine. Sage realised he'd been silent for too long. The Irishman was looking at him uneasily. 'No offence, but if ye're lairy about Mr Preminder, is it not Ax ye should be talking to?'

'Yeah,' said Sage, 'you're right. Why didn't I think of that?'

He didn't talk to Ax. He was afraid of where that conversation might lead.

In July they went to Tyller Pystri, the first time they'd managed to get back to their spiritual home all year. On the second night Sage was working late in his studio: a small, damp room that held some relics of a cottage parlour, in the chinks of the hardware. Ax and Fiorinda were sleeping upstairs. Fiorinda was having nightmares again, and they'd fallen into the habit of sharing the burden. One night on, one night off.

He sat at his desk, glad of a chance to work undisturbed, but feeling depressed. Why are we sleeping apart? It's not right, especially not *here* . . . When did things get to the point where immersion-writing is something I do in my spare time? A south-west gale was roaring through the Chy gorge. He was distantly aware of it, through the code and the background noise of his thoughts. It was a warm spell in a poor summer, but wild.

Something came into the room behind him. Menace and dread. He spun around, stripping off the eyewrap. Fiorinda stood there, naked. She came up to him, a savage grin splitting her face, and leapt astride his thighs. Her nails bit into his shoulders. 'Fuck me,' she said. 'Come on, fuck me, fuck me. Pretend I'm six years old. I'm your little girl, fuck me—' One look into her eyes, and he knew he wasn't going to talk her down.

He came out of the chair holding her and carried her into the living-room. He didn't think she was strictly conscious, but when he reached for the Ndogs box she recognised that. She exploded, fighting like a wild cat, clawing at his face. Okay, no drugs . . . One of her dresses lay by the door to the stairs, the storm-cloud indigo. He pulled it over her head, pulled her arms through the sleeves, added a Guernsey from the back of the kitchen door, grabbed his keys and hauled her, struggling, out into the night. He hardly knew what he was doing, just knew he had to *get her out of this*. He got her into the Volvo, pushed her down, strapped her in . . . Zoom round to the other side of the car. Drive.

Out of the gates, *can't see a thing*, ah, lights, fucking retro handicraft, you have to *switch them on*, that's better. He was on the track to the sea before he realised it hadn't occurred to him to go and wake Ax. *Shit*, what if Ax is lying in a pool of blood? Oh, *fuck*. No blood on her. My God, what am I thinking? Ax is fine, she's in one of her night terrors, I have to calm her down, that's all.

They never took the car beyond the house. The track was in a terrible state, but too bad. This is an emergency.

As I was walking through Grosvenor Square,

he sang softly,

Not a nip to the winter but a chill to the air
From the other direction, she was calling my eye—

Could be an illusion, but I might as well try. The first time I saw you, my darling, that cold night in Amsterdam, I said to myself, she is my soul, and it was no illusion. Not often in your life you get to be so right as I was when I decided, come what may, I would never leave your side. What's wrong with you, baby? This has been going on too long. We won't set the quacks on you, but we have to *talk about it*. He kept on singing, clutching the wheel of Ax's precious car in his ugly, untrustworthy hands, eyes glued to the potholes. A thin, small voice started to join him, from a long way off.

She wore scarlet begonias, tucked into her curls,
I knew right away she was not like other girls—

'Where are we going?'
'To the sea.'
'But it's the middle of the night.'
'Best time. Let's finish "Scarlet Begonias".'

He kept on singing, up the hill and across the cliff-top pasture, a mile and a half of inchworm, painful driving. She didn't speak again, but she sang with him, their golden oldies, things they'd taught each other when she was fourteen. The path down the cliff had suffered over the last year. It was beyond a joke; he kept an iron grip on her arm, but the cove was just what he wanted: a moon-curve of white sand swept clean by the gale, glimmering under the cloudy, starlit sky. He stripped off, stripped her of the Guernsey and her dress, and ran with her into the boiling, buffeting water. Fiorinda started to laugh, breasting the tumult and leaping like a dolphin. The change was so immediate it shocked him, but *trust me*, said the ocean, and he did, but he didn't let her out of his reach.

She jumped into his arms, wet hair, arms and legs, slippery as melting ice.

'Had enough?'

'Yes!'

They plunged out into the air again, and now the south-west wind didn't feel cold. Fiorinda wrung salt water from her hair. Sage dragged a plank of driftwood into a shelter of windbreak boulders and they sat there, cuddled close, a nest of clothes around them. 'Now,' he said. 'Tell me about it. This time *you must*. Do you remember coming down to me tonight?'

'I remember being in the car, and you were singing. What happened?'

'You were sleepwalking. Tell me about the nightmare. Will you tell me?'

'No.' She grabbed his crippled right hand, holding onto it hard. 'Oh, well, yes. It won't sound like much. I had a bad dream . . . Then I thought I woke up and someone was fucking me, a horrible fucking that I had to bear because I had no right to refuse.'

'Shit. Is that the nightmare? Is *that* what you haven't been telling us?'

'I don't know. Maybe. I forget. I'm being raped by someone I can't refuse, so that's not rape . . . and I can't open my eyes. Then I manage to open my eyes, and the man who's fucking me is you, or Ax, but I know it's really my father. And then I wake up.'

'Your *father*?'

'If it's you, it's not so bad. I can say, fuck off you sad bastard that's ridiculous, you can't fool me. But if it's Ax, that's awful, because *it could be true*. I try not to believe it, but Ax is getting so different. He could be turning into m-my father . . . and that's . . . I think that's what all this is about. M-my father is trying to m-make me hate Ax.'

'What? Fiorinda, slow down. Your *father*? You mean Rufus O'Niall?'

She looked up. The babbling girl-child vanished, as if a wave had gone over her. Fiorinda came back to herself, and her invincible defences rose, shutting him out. My God. *What is going on?*

'Oh,' she said. 'I don't mean literally, Sage. I mean, that's what my nightmares are about. It's classic, isn't it? My father fucked me, and now that I'm grown up it all comes back, all the suppressed memories. I have to get rid of him . . . I have to get him out of my head. *Then* I can go to the doctors and we'll see if I can get pregnant, but it won't matter if I can't because maybe we can adopt a baby, and I'll be free and we'll be happy.'

Now she was crying, the tears spilling down her face. He pulled the Guernsey round her shoulders and held her close. 'You should have told us, Fiorinda. Darling little Fiorinda, trust me. One day he *will* be gone. One day, you'll look for that black hole of an obsession and it just won't be there. You'll know that you could see him coming, and you wouldn't even bother to cross the street.'

'You mean Mary,' said Fiorinda softly.

He sighed. 'Yeah. I mean Mary . . . I mean, I understand. I always did.'

They moved apart, and sat side by side. Fiorinda hung her head, hiding behind a tangle of salt-wet curls, and drew in the sand with her finger. 'It's true I was obsessed with him. Even right up to Dissolution Summer. He filled my mind. But you're wrong, Sage. That's over. I'm *ages* past that stage. I just want to be rid of him and . . . somehow I can't be.'

'When we first met,' said Sage, 'I knew what had happened to you . . . I used to be afraid I'd remind you of your father, because I'm so fucking big, and you're like a child in my arms. I thought you could never possibly want me. It used to make me desperate.'

'Sage. Idiot. It never crossed my mind. Sometimes I think you're me in another skin, which can be weird, but I *never* thought you were my father . . . Oh. Is that why you wouldn't fuck me when I offered, that time?'

'Hm. As I recall, it wasn't a very appealing offer.'

'Hahaha. Nobody talks to Aoxomoxoa like that! You said you weren't so hard up you had to jump my scrawny little underage bones, and I was so mortified.'

He smiled, between rueful and tender. 'Well, I lied.'

'I was *so fucked-up*, when you met me. I didn't know it, but I was like spoiled meat.'

'Yeah, I knew. And I was scared, Fiorinda. I didn't dare to touch you, because I knew how fragile and hurt you were, and I'm a coward. I was afraid I'd break something, the way I always do . . . It was Ax who took on that job.'

The wind and the sea roared. The beach had an unearthly luminescence as their eyes grew accustomed to the night. 'You gave me unconditional love,' she said, 'when no one had ever loved me before. It's something I can't ever repay.' She climbed into his arms and looked up with starry eyes and a sweet and joyful smile. 'My Sage, my darling. You are so good to me. Hey, did I ever tell you, I'm madly in love with you?'

Fucking-with-intent to cut Ax out would seem the

greater crime, but holding her naked in his arms, feeling nothing but tenderness, he knew he'd never been in worse danger.

'C'mon. Into the sea again. One rush, and then home.'

On the way back they stopped at the waterfall pool to rinse off. He carried her in under the holly trees (ouch, ouch ouch) and doused them both in the churning pot, unbelievably much colder than the sea, which the Chy had pummelled for itself in a dark rocky dell. It was magical, but his hands were starting to act up. When they were dressed he offered her the keys. Fiorinda could drive, though she rarely wanted to. She refused, laughing, oh no, I'm the girl, *you* drive. He was too proud to explain. He tackled the lumpy descent to Tyller Pystri with extreme caution, Fiorinda beside him in his old Guernsey and her rustling skirts, singing under her breath and smiling angelically.

'What's up with you, brat?'

'Nothing. I'm very, very happy and I love you very much.'

'Nyah—' He switched on the skull, rotting flesh and lively maggots version. Fiorinda yelped, and . . . the Volvo swerved. Crunch. They both jumped out to look. Oh, shit. The left headlamp had collided with a corner of jutting rock.

'I was driving,' said Fiorinda.

'Don't be *stupid*. I was driving.'

They stared at each other, for too long.

'I shouldn't have been driving,' said Sage. 'My hands are fucked.'

Silently they got back into the car. Fiorinda nursed it onwards, through the gates and onto the hardstanding under the twin beech trees. There was a light in the living-room.

'Let me tell him,' said Fiorinda. 'It was my fault. My pathetic nightmare.'

Ax didn't make a fuss about the car. The three of them spent the rest of the night together in Sage's bed. But things were not good. In the morning Fiorinda remembered some of what she'd said on the beach, and was very frightened. She decided she would walk to the garage shop to see if they had any chocolate. Leave them alone together: it was the only trick she knew.

When Fiorinda had left Ax came into the studio and sat in a tattered armchair that had been there since the cottage was a holiday let.

'So, tell me what really happened?'

Sage tried to tell him.

'What d'you mean, she *frightened* you?'

'What I say. She was completely out of it, like *not herself*, literally, when she came downstairs. It was horrible. And you slept through this?'

'I slept through it,' said Ax, 'fuck, look who's talking. You should have woken me.'

'I'm sorry about that, I don't know how that happened. Could we keep to the point? I took her to the beach because . . . well, to break the mood, and then she started talking about her father. Listen to me, Ax. She said things, really strange things, that, if I took them a certain way, I would be very scared—'

'You're telling me Fiorinda's going nuts?'

'No . . . I mean, I don't know what to think. We know what happened to her. We know things like that have a way of surfacing years later. That's what she says herself, and it could be true, but I'm afraid there's something else, something worse—'

'What are you on about? She's been under hellish stress for years, and now it seems like every woman friend we have is either pregnant or dandling a baby. It must be fucking awful for her, and it brings back the hell she went through when she was thirteen. What more do you need? We knew she was vulnerable, we knew what we were taking on. We can help her through. But you're not helping by getting melodramatic in the middle of the night, taking her *skinny dipping*, for fuck's sake—'

'Crashing your car.'

Ax shrugged contemptuously. 'Oh, forget that. I knew you'd dent it sometime.'

'We're too old for her,' said Sage, abandoning the idea of a serious discussion. 'I expect that's why I got the father stuff. She wants a boyfriend her own age and she doesn't know how to tell us. Come to think of it, nothing more likely.'

'Bastard,' said Ax. 'You know so fucking well how to wind me up. You always did.'

'I could say the same of you.'

'You should have woken me.'

'I wish I had.' Sage left the desk, came to Ax's chair and kissed him fiercely. 'Let's go next door.' They moved next door, to the bed: the sexual heat between them strong as ever, while trust and faith begin to founder; isn't it always the way.

August passed. Reading Weekend came, with Fiorinda and DARK headlining on Saturday night. The crowd in the arena was huge, in defiance of Travel Restrictions Hell, and there were record numbers at the big screen sites. DARK's set, climaxing with a glorious rendition of 'Chocobo', Fiorinda's brilliant dancetrack from *Friction*, was the live music event of the year. The Dictator and his Minister missed the whole thing. They'd taken oxy again and were in Bartoli's Hideout, getting drunk and discussing the ever-fascinating topic, *did (does) Fiorinda fuck Charm Dudley?* How blessed it is to have someone you can talk to about a lover's fears. 'No, no no. Yeah, they used to roll-around fight. But there wasn't anything sexual in it. I *saw* those fights—'

'You say that because you're kidding yourself, Sage—'

The big screen above the bar was running instant replay: Fiorinda and Charm duetting on 'San Antonio Rose': Fiorinda in her silver and white cowgirl dress and the red boots, looking so wonderful, playing so tight with Charm, *do they or don't they?*

Fiorinda and DARK walked into the Hideout and took in the scene. The dyke rockers and Harry Child, DARK's new bassist (replacing Tom Okopie, who had been killed by a British Resistance landmine, in Boat People summer) closed up around their singer and walked straight out again. Sage and Ax, locked into each other, stealing kisses, holding hands, deep in their twisted obsession, didn't even notice.

'Jaysus,' said Fergal Kearney, who was propping up the bar with a few of the Few. 'Why the fock do they do it? It's no wonder she's mad. That stuff eats yer brain.'

'They do it,' said Dilip sadly, 'because if they don't do oxy occasionally they'll forget what's supposed to be going on, and they'll be at each other's throats.'

'And break her heart,' said Rob.

Fiorinda came back alone later, and teased her boyfriends the drug fiends into some semblance of normal behaviour; and things were okay again, after that, for a while.

She dreamed that the Few were visiting a bathhouse. There were glistening tiles, turquoise pools, mirrors, drifts of white steam; everyone was naked. She knew it was a dream, because this was something they had never done together. She was sashaying around with her tiger and her wolf on either arm, having a fine time. But why do I keep looking at myself? Why don't I look at my friends, some of whom I have never seen naked? Surely I'd be interested. Why don't I look at Sage and Ax? They are glorious. Am I not proud of them? She had no choice. Something behind her eyes wanted to dwell on these breasts, this small waist, this bum, these slim thighs, and Fiorinda must comply, she must stare into every reflecting surface . . . She woke, sweating, sitting bolt upright: but she did not scream. She'd trained herself not to scream.

Sage and Ax were fast asleep. Where are we? It's Brixton.

Huddled there, arms wrapped around her knees, she imagined telling them that she was being attacked by a psychic monster. But if this was really Rufus O'Niall invading her dreams, why did it feel as if it came from inside herself? From the mistakes that she had made, from the stupid choices of a fucked-up, worthless little girl. And what good would it do for Ax and Sage to know, if this was a magical attack? It takes magic to fight magic . . . She would tell them nothing. She would fight her own battle.

Sage was dead to the world, a warm rock. She slipped out of bed, round to Ax's side, and crept in beside him. *Little cat*, he murmured, and they moved together, into the way they used to hold each other, falling asleep, before the threesome began.

Oh Ax, my darling Ax. I can't be losing you.

Ax was making lists again, like the lists he used to make in Dissolution Summer, except now the project was not *how to take over*. Been there. Done that.

Restore mixed arable farming
Recruit more hedgeschool teachers
Recruit competent drop-outs to the 'Nation of Shop-keepers' project
Convince Boat People recruits to above that they won't be stoned to death, they'll be accepted in isolated rural communities
Build a lot more solar and wind power plants. Quickly
Keep the CCM united. Which means keeping the Celtics on board

But try not to compromise too far on greenfield campsites
Street-fighting
Measles vaccination
The anti-science riots

The Celtics must be sweet-talked along, because the unity of the CCM is vital. The power plants were also desperately important, and a million other things. The big lies and the petty ruthless shortcuts accumulate, but it's all necessary. Shit. No wonder his Triumvirate partners were pissed off. But the modern world was still falling apart, and Ax had to use the power fate had handed to him, he had no choice. Even if it meant pushing for *okay, fuckit, draconian legislation*. He had a stand-up fight with Fiorinda over the Call-Up Bill. She said, what happened to fostering lifestyle choices? What happened to, 'Utopian revolutions turn rotten in about six weeks, because you can't impose the rules of the Good State by force—?'

He said this isn't about Utopia, and she said, *yeah, I spotted that*. He said you have to do drastic things in desperate situations. He was only applying the good lessons of the Volunteer Initiative on a bigger scale and it was a temporary, emergency measure—

'What is temporary about this?' she yelled. 'This is not *temporary*! We are not going to get to the other side, Ax. There is no other side!'

They were alone in the living-room of the Brixton flat. Sage hated these fights, he usually managed to be elsewhere. Ax walked away, as far as the terrace windows: the Brixton back gardens in grey autumn, planted with vegetables, urban field strips.

'You knew this was what I wanted, from the beginning. I can't quit.'

'You told me you never wanted to run the country. You said that was bullshit.'

She cries in the night, and he goes on doing exactly what

makes her unhappy. It doesn't make sense . . . But he was doomed. He would work himself to death at this impossible job, and make her hate him, because it was better than facing the pain.

What happened to the sweet love you and I had?

'Oh Ax,' she said. 'My darling Ax. The house always wins.'

Fiorinda sat up late by the old gas stove, wrapped in her gold and brown shawl, with Elsie curled on her lap. There wasn't much heat in the flames, the pressure was too low: but the sight of them was comforting.

She was trying to read, but she couldn't concentrate.

There on its stand on the bookcase is the Sweet Track Jade, just returned from an exhibition: the jadeite axe, ancient symbol of civilisation in England, which the Few had given to their beloved leader on the night of his inauguration. There is the *Times* cartoon of Mr Dictator, with Sage and Fiorinda as big cat and little cat, that they'd decided they liked, and bought the original. The take-off of a famous Hockney picture: Sage and Ax drinking sherry on the terrace, the cat walking on the wall, Fiorinda just a glimpse of party frock. 'Mr Preston, Mr Pender, and Elsie'.

Here is our life, hollow and empty. Here am I, trapped in the official story.

About one in the morning Sage came in. The Heads had had a gig in Camden, something about promoting country life. She hadn't been tempted to attend. She heard him ambling up the stairs, into the landing bathroom, where he pisses gallons, singing that he has a brand new combine harvester, *and I'll give you the key*. He came into the room, stumbling only a little, and shed his coat. He was wearing brown corduroy trousers tied under the knee with string, a white shirt without a collar and a red handkerchief tied around his throat. He looked stunningly beautiful, slightly ridiculous, and *very* smashed.

'Ax not back yet?'

This was the night of the Call-Up Debate, an emergency session to push the new legislation through. Ax was at the House of Commons, giving David Sale his support.

'Nah.'

'D'you know what's going on?'

She shrugged. 'I suppose David and Ax are getting their own way. There'll be very few Members actually *in* the House, because nobody does that anymore, but they'll move their mouths a lot, the cameras will angle it to look like a crowd, and there'll be a thrilling hard-won victory around two a.m. I think that was the plan. Check the Parliament Channel and find out.'

'Can't be tossed.'

He descended to the floor beside her in the old Aoxomoxoa style, something between collapsing and folding up like a telescope. 'You've been pouring horrible, horrible quantities of alcohol down your neck, haven't you?'

''Fraid so.'

'Shit. I really needed someone to talk to tonight.'

'You can talk to me.' He lifted her onto his lap (Elsie snarled and fled). 'I'm here now. I will listen. I jus' won't remember in the morning, an' then you can tell me again.'

She wrapped her shawl around them both. 'Sage, I can't live like this.'

'Now, tha's a shame, because I was just thinking . . .' His soft mouth traced her hairline, his arms tightened in the warm hold that would never fail, 'I would happily spend the rest of my days like this here. There could be minor improvements, we could both be naked and my cock inside, but this is very fine.'

'Idiot.'

When Ax got in he found them like that, fast asleep in the pearly glow of a single ATP lamp. He sat on the opposite couch, took out a cigarette and smoked it, watching the lovers, thinking: you'd have to have a heart of stone to want to come between them.

Stones in his heart.

Sage opened his eyes. 'Well? Did you win, you and David?'

'Yeah. Let's go to bed.'

Two days after the Call-Up debate Dan Preston had a massive heart attack. No warning. Ax's father had hardly been near a doctor in his life. In better times maybe he'd have lived; or maybe not, who can tell. As it was, he was dead before they got him to a functioning cardiac unit. He was fifty-eight.

After the funeral Sage had to go to Edinburgh on a trade mission. The Scots were interested in developing bi-location devices. (Strange the way the futuristic developments keep going while a civilisation falls apart; but perhaps that's how it always happens.) Fiorinda went to London and took over Ax's diary as well her own, so Ax could stay in Taunton with his mother. Sage and Fiorinda kept in touch using the new, commercial model of the bi-location phone. Fiorinda had never tried faceting before. It sounded like modern drugs, but Sage persuaded her. They knew they'd better stay off sex, but one thing led to another and they couldn't resist. He thought he was making love with her naked soul.

Sage returned to Brixton after a little Stone Age Royalty diplomacy on the back of the trade mission. He and Fiorinda didn't say a word to each other about what was going on between them. There was nothing to be said, nothing to be done; and Ax must never know. They talked to Ax by normal means, and he said he was fine. He was glad he'd been getting on better with his dad over the past year or so, and Dan had never wanted to get old, so as sudden deaths go it was okay. And his mother was bearing up.

The night he came back from Taunton the three of them had terrific sex, the best sex they'd had in months. After Fiorinda was asleep Ax and Sage sat up together, drinking single malt and discussing the Edinburgh trip. (They couldn't have had this conversation with Fiorinda: she went ballistic at any mention of politics at the moment.) A decade or so down the line those canny Scots might be drawing up a new Act of Union, the way things are heading. Wales isn't going to object. Basically, the Welsh don't give a bugger for national government. Most of them don't care if the talking shop is in Tokyo, as long as it's not in Cardiff . . . And so what. It wouldn't be the worst thing that could happen.

'We'll be long gone by then,' said Ax. 'The Reich will be history.'

'The modern world will be back in place,' suggested Sage. 'We'll be rockstars again.'

'Mm.' Ax looked into his glass. 'You know that Romanian gig? The Danube dams?'

Since before his inauguration there'd been endless invitations from the Continent, from people who wanted Ax to break up fights, speak at conferences; even to tour with the Chosen. He'd declined them all. The Dacian greens were the latest. They wanted Ax to arbitrate with their government, and others, over their plans to free the great river.

'Yeah?'

'I'm going to accept. I've been thinking for a while that I ought to get out there, see what's going on. I'll be back by Christmas. It's a good opportunity.'

When he'd convinced his Triumvirate partners, Ax went to Reading to see Olwen Devi. Sage had insisted that he have his chip checked out before he left the country, and Olwen was going to do it. She decided to give him a full medical while she was at it (she didn't think this would be a problem with his London GP). Ax, like his father, was the *never had a day's illness in my life* type, and he didn't like the idea. But he submitted with good grace.

The report was good. The heart was fine; last you a century. The respiratory system likewise, though Olwen seemed less pleased about that. It always annoys people when a tobacco smoker doesn't show any sign of suffering from it. Everything was fine, except for the chip. She said he ought to get rid of it. That was a shock. It hadn't been serviced for years and he'd known it needed fixing (no alarming symptoms, but he knew). He hadn't been expecting anything so final. The idea of living without his other mind, his library, his internal security, was a hard blow.

'We'll have to see about that when I get back.'

They were debriefing in an office in the Rivermead health centre. Rain stormed at the small square windows in Topsy's thick metal-and-mulch walls: looks like we'll be inaugurating the new flood refuge soon. Olwen looked at him compassionately. She wore the Zen Self mainframe as a jewel on her finger. She understood.

'I want to do it now, Ax.'

'I have to go to Romania in two weeks. This is not the moment for brain surgery.'

She might have asked what was so all-fired crucial about the Romanian trip, but she did not. She knew from the look in Mr Preston's eye she would get nowhere.

'All right. We'll do it as soon as you get back. Hm. I will give you a facet of Serendip. She'll look after the implant, and that will be fine for a few weeks. No longer!'

'But I wanted to use it on my trip. Could we talk about that?'

'We could talk about that.'

He went up to Yorkshire to see Sayyid Mohammad Zaid, his mentor in the Faith. They talked at length, alone and with Mohammad's family; and with other vital English

Islamists. They spoke of the Islamic Community's duty *to be* the presence of God's mercy and compassion on earth: a spiritual hegemony, far greater than material power. Ax extracted a firm acknowledgment that the plan to make England into an Islamic State was indefinitely on hold, which was a result he'd been working towards for a while. These goodwill agreements might fall apart the moment your back is turned, but they mean something. He stayed three days, and came away feeling his burden lighter. If I've fucked up everything else, he thought (too weary and deadened for prayer, thinking only of the state of the country), that's one good choice I made. From Bradford he went to Easton Friars to see Richard Kent, the barmy army's chief of staff, then a circuit of the big staybehind camps and urbans, talking to hippy councillors and green gangstas. So many people wanted a piece of Ax.

He even managed to make it (alone) to the monthly Liasion meeting with Benny Prem. Poor Benny, sitting behind his enormous desk in his big empty office: it's like visiting some cranky old lady. Benny was in a huff, feeling slighted as usual. He wanted to know if there'd be a meeting while Ax was gone. Ax said Fiorinda might be forced to cancel, as she would be very busy, but he'd remind the Minister.

Benny said, sulkily, 'Does Sage always do what you tell him?'

'When he feels like it,' said Ax, ignoring the insolence.

I will even miss *you*, he thought, as he took his leave. Absurd as that might be.

He'd kept Benny on out of pragmatism, though he knew his partners didn't believe it. But sometimes he looked at the guy and saw himself: the mixed-race boy made good, overcompensating, always hungry for the certainties that he can't have . . . He hoped he could persuade Sage to look after him. It would be a kindness (not that Benny could appreciate kindness, poor bastard); and it would be wise.

When Ax was gone Benny took out his dossier and made the ritual entry.

Ax is leaving the country.

He was getting impatient. It was months since he had reported that the fruit was ripe; he still didn't know who his patron was, and nothing had changed except that Triumvirate had gone from strength to strength. But he had faith. He was *sure* something would happen now.

Fiorinda had been very surprised to discover that everybody, including Sage, took it for granted that *she* would be Ax's deputy. But she had accepted her fate. They'd had the briefing, the meetings with the suits and the Ceremonial Head of State staff. There was one more thing, a conversation he didn't want to have at home. He came to find her one day when he knew she'd be working late in the Office at the San, and waited, chatting with anyone who offered, until everyone else had gone, even Allie.

It was twilight outside. 'Lot of memories in this view,' he said, staring out through the Balcony doors. Gold gleamed on the Victoria Monument; the Japanese banners at the Insanitude Gates caught the light from the lanterns that hung there, but Central London was in deep shadow. He could remember when that darkness had seemed very strange and ominous. Not anymore.

'Yes,' said Fiorinda.

He walked around, looking at the noticeboards. These noticeboards in the Office, corkboard ruthlessly knocked up on the gaudy, shabby walls, were sacred. The old ones, the full ones, were never dismantled. They were framed and sealed. Allie sold scanned copies of them as Few merchandising; you could see the attraction. Here's the whole history of the strange days of our rule, inscribed in old jokes and Post-its, withered memos, photos and newspaper cuttings. Like a folk museum, touching and sad.

Fiorinda watched him, looking puzzled, as he came up to her desk.

'D'you recall the day we sat around those tables and I told you all I was going to demand the repeal of the death penalty, or I would quit? It's hard to believe, isn't it?'

'It was another world.'

'Yeah . . . People are making such a fuss about this Romanian trip. Makes me wish I'd made a habit of going to conferences. Maybe the Chosen should do a foreign tour, the lazy bastards, and I could tag along, pretend I'm still a rockstar.'

She nodded.

He sat beside her, looking at the ring she had given him, turning the rust-red bevel so the inscription caught the light. *This too will pass.* 'We never had a romance, do you remember? We just climbed into bed together and that was it. No fireworks.'

'I remember plenty of fireworks.'

'Maybe, later. But I like to remember the way it started—' He'd better shut up. He was getting maudlin, going to ruin everything. 'I want to give you something.' He showed her the bi-loc. It was the clunky early version, but not the standard prototype. 'Okay, this is a tricky kind of satellite phone. It works through my chip. It's the one we used to hack out of the quarantine. I want you to have it, so you can always reach me.'

'But you're not going outside Europe.'

'No, but . . . Telecoms go down, phones get lost, terrestrial networks crash. I can't lose my chip, and you won't lose this. You don't need to know anything technical, it's like a normal bi-loc to use.' He closed her hands over the handset. 'Call me if you really need me. But be careful, we don't want aggravation with the Internet Commisioners. Don't tell anyone that you have it. Not even Sage. He, well, he'd be happier not knowing I've given you contraband to look after.'

'Okay.'

She tucked the phone in her bag. They stood up, and hugged each other. The veil between them was very thin. He knew that he had only to say the word, one plea for mercy, and she would pity him. She would be his little cat again. But he had vowed to himself that he would not say that word, and he wasn't going to break down now.

'I'll miss you very much,' she whispered.

'Me too,' said Ax. 'I'll miss you. You'll look after Elsie for me, won't you?'

'Yes. I'll look after Elsie.'

Two days before Ax was due to leave Fiorinda and Sage went down to Cornwall by train. Ax had things to do; he followed them in the Volvo the next morning. The visit to the cottage was a last-minute *tour de force*, but they'd all wanted to do it. It was November, and the floods were out. The Somerset Levels looked like melted tundra, the once and future landscape of meres and marshes and hilltop towns clearly discernable. He stopped at Wheddon Down in the rain to recharge, bought a sack of damp birch logs for the price of a cup of coffee and heard that the Tamar was threatening to break its banks. But when he reached the river it looked okay. He talked to the Flood Watch, one more patient conversation with the English, and crossed over the Guinevere Bridge one more time.

On Bodmin Moor he stopped the car. He wondered about Sage's wolves, and thought he would get out and listen for them, but he didn't. He wiped his eyes, and drove on.

He had been daunted, almost *frightened*, at the thought of this last night. But it was okay. They stacked Ax's birch logs in the hearth to dry, they did the usual Tyller Pystri

224

things; they talked about Ax's trip. It seemed to Ax there was a painful silence behind every word they spoke, but if they felt the same, they made no sign. At midnight they banked the fire. Sage and Ax went out in the dark and rain to take a piss, a little ritual. They'd always liked pissing together. And so to bed.

He didn't sleep. In the morning he packed the car. Fiorinda was driving back with him, to see him off. Sage was staying at the cottage. Ax couldn't remember how this arrangement had been made, but it was settled. Separate goodbyes. He walked out to look at the Chy, and then went into the studio. Sage was sitting there staring into space. He jumped up when Ax came in. The words won't come. The last chance to break the silence is here: and then it's gone, and the words didn't come. They hugged.

'Stay off the smack, okay?'

Ax had been an occasional user, back at the beginning of all this. Sage the ex-junkie had hassled him into giving up.

'Is that all you can think of to say?'

'It was a joke. Uh, poor taste. I meant, look after yourself.' Sage thought, if he had been Ax he'd've had an itemised list, covering every insane reckless thing Ax might think of doing, and he'd extract a promise for every one. Don't take drugs from strangers. Don't jump in pits with tigers. Don't march on Moscow, don't . . . Don't take on the world, fuck's sake, it's bigger than you.

'I just want you to come back safe.'

'You . . . same.'

'I'm not going anywhere,' said Sage.

Ax nearly said, forgetting he'd wanted separate goodbyes, *at least you could have come to Dover* . . . But he didn't. Fiorinda was waiting outside. She and Ax got into the car. Sage came down the track, loping beside them through the rain to open the gates; and this is the last moment. The little Chy roaring, the leaves on the oak trees tattered gold, Sage in the rear view mirror, bluest eyes, there, he's gone.

The ferry (a massive old thing, rattling empty) left Dover at six in the evening after several hours' delay. Fiorinda was long gone. He'd told her he didn't want her to wait around. The rest of the Dacian expedition had settled in the saloon, getting stuck into some hard drinking. They were picking up a chartered flight to Bucharest in Paris. Ax stood by the rail in the stern, guitar-case over his shoulder, and watched the cold, grey water churning away.

I don't blame you, brother, he thought. I *do not* blame you.

When had he realised he had to go? After that night at Tyller Pystri in July? Or before that, or later? It seemed to him now that he'd always known that he was living on borrowed time. You can't give a guy like Sage limited access to the love of his life and expect him to accept the idea, sit there like a dog with a biscuit on his nose. Not indefinitely. This is *Aoxomoxoa*, for fuck's sake. And you can't go on watching the girl you love tear herself apart . . . They would never have left me, they would have been loyal. He set his teeth at the thought of their *loyalty*, letting Ax tag along, all three of them knowing the real situation. Fuck that. I had to leave. No more nightmares now. She'll be happy. She'll get the injection reversed, she'll have his baby. Oh, God, have I really kissed her for the last time? Really never hold my darling again?

The pain in his heart—

He'd left his bag indoors, but he'd brought the jade axe out on deck with him. He took it from inside his coat. The Sweet Track Jade, dropped or laid as a sacrifice by the causewayed road from Taunton to Glastonbury, more than five thousand years ago. A slim, unpolished, leaf-shaped blade of blue-green stone, perfectly crafted, beautiful to hold. What a rare thing to own: my badge of office. One last good look. A swing from the shoulder. There, it's gone. He didn't see the splash. Will an arm clothed in white samite rise, to hand his sacrifice back to him, to restore his loss? Nah, no arm clothed in white samite. Nothing.

He watched the water for a while, fists in his pockets, the wind and rain whipping his hair, then he went back into the warm saloon. So that's that.

SIX

One Of The Three

Ax was in Romania, and having a wild time of it from what they could make out (communcation wasn't easy). The Heads were in residence in Travellers' Meadow, after a break in which they'd been attending to their separate lives. They were hoping to discuss a new album, if their boss could ever find the time. On a cold Sunday morning, George and Bill sat at the kitchen table, browsing sections of the *Staybehind Clarion* and drinking tea with condensed milk, and whisky chasers. No fresh milk. Reading Site dairy cows were having trouble with the wrong kind of grass. Peter lay on one of the astronaut couches, thinking about his latest kaleidoscope. Making strange kaleidoscopes was his secret vice.

Fiorinda walked in, barefoot and tousled, wearing an ancient blue cashmere sweater, the ravelled hem a couple of inches above her knees. Morning Fio, mm um. As she boiled a kettle and stretched for mugs the fine wool moved, beautifully revealing, over the slender, rounded body beneath, making you realise how very chaste those party frocks are. (Fiorinda turns cartwheels on stage, all you get to see is more frills.) She left, giving them a sleepy smile. George drew a breath and quietly, slowly, exhaled.

'He'd kill yer,' said Bill, without looking up.

'Not even in jest, Bill Trevor,' said George sternly. 'I'd rather top me'self than do anything to harm that little girl.

Nah . . . I just feel like her dad, jealous of the boyfriend. Not,' he added, hurriedly, 'her particular dad, mind you.'

'It'll wear off,' Peter consoled them. 'She's here all the time. You'll get used to it.'

George and Bill looked at each other. Yes. It's true. Peter Stannen is an alien lifeform.

'I hope I die first,' said Bill.

Fiorinda had to get back to London. Sage walked her to the station, spent an hour at Rainsfords-the-gym at the Oracle; dropped in on the Boat People's welfare office for five minutes and was embroiled there for another hour in Town vs Counterculture issues. When he escaped he headed for the North Bank. The river was quiet and full, the sky was clad in decent grey. Before Dissolution there'd been classy riverside residences here. Now it was a pocket wilderness, frequented only by the kids. He sat on the verandah of a rotting summerhouse, overlooking a misted clearing that had once been someone's lawn. He needed to think.

When the three of them were first lovers they used to play a game: what does it take for the most brilliant sex in the universe?

One big cat, one little cat, one animal-tamer
One stud, one babe, one chameleon
Two musicians and an artist (not sure I liked that one)
One white boy, one coloured boy, one yellow girl
One Muslim, one Methodist (lapsed), one Pagan (VERY
    lapsed).

How about this? Two cyborgs and a witch.

The cyborg issue was not a problem. ATP, weird neuroscience, the brain implant, that was all fine, covered by Ax's personal prestige. Fiorinda as a witch would be different. The public, Countercultural or otherwise, would not like it. They'd feel that Ax had lied to them. There were soundbites from his anti-ritualist speeches, at the time of Spitall's Farm and later on, that would come back on him. (Our magic belongs to the future, not the past. Hi-tech is the magic that works . . .) The Celtics, fucking hypocrites, would make trouble. And some people would be genuinely afraid . . . Yet Mr Dictator was going to have to know, and then decide whether to tell the truth or risk exposure.

Ax's absence was a reality check. Sage waited for Fiorinda to speak, and maybe she waited for him: but they would keep silent. Stolen moments, heartbreak kisses, Ax comes back and we carry on as before. Why make the pain worse for ourselves by spilling the beans? But something else had emerged, something that had been on Sage's mind for a while; except it had been lost in the fog of relationship-grief. He remembered that night at Tyller Pystri in July with alarming clarity now: exactly how Fiorinda had behaved, and the things she'd said, un-guarded and still in the grip of her nightmare. He knew, though she didn't wake up screaming anymore, that she was still having those bad dreams.

I think we're under attack, and I think Ax has to be told. But if I'm right, what the fuck do we do? If Fiorinda can't protect herself—

If *she*'s helpless, where does that leave the rest of us?

The situation in Bucharest sounded exhilarating. There was ice and snow. Packs of feral dogs roamed the streets. The official CCM of the Danube Countries was at war with its factions. The Gaia-wants-us-to-commit-suicide party was at war with everyone, and oh yeah, the suits were also involved. Mr Dictator said it was hectic, and he didn't know if he would be home for Christmas. He sounded energised and focused: Ax restored, Ax in his element.

He'll come back, and we'll sort the magic problem. The way we always do.

Oh God, if there was a way to make Fiorinda my own that wasn't so tainted . . . I could take her from him now, I know I could. But how could we forgive ourselves?

Two dead leaves drifted down through the dim November air. He watched them fall, his mind filling up with blank stillness, with sadness. There was a tiny sound beside him, a little sigh. He looked round. A small girl had materialised and was sitting there with her pale brown head bent and fists thrust in the pockets of a homespun woollen frock.

'What're you up to, Silver?'

'Oh, nothing. I'm just sitting.'

No peace for the Minister. The Wing children stick like burrs, but Catechism sometimes shakes them off. He picked up one of the fallen leaves. It reminded him of Fiorinda. Sunburst yellow is her colour; not green, that's wrong.

'Okay, what tree's this from?'

'Er . . . beech. I mean oak. What were you thinking about?'

'None 'er your business. Field maple. Oak are the long crinkly ones, remember? Now tell me why they fall off.'

'Because they're decide-uous and they decide leaves in winter isn't cost effective.'

'Fair enough. Describe me the mechanism.'

Silver glowered. 'It's done by horseshoes. Why do you know all this stuff, Sage? You're not a herb-medicine doctor. Who told you?'

'Ooh, I dunno. I think my mum must have told me, a long, long time ago.'

'How do you know it's still true?'

'Good point.'

The child stared at him intently. 'What did your mum look like? Was she nice to you?'

Something rapped against the crumbling woodwork.

They looked up. Pearl was sitting astride a branch, bare legs and feet dangling, wonderfully camouflaged by dirt, grinning like a juvenile post-human gargoyle. 'I stalked you! I stalked you!'

'Fuck off!' yelled Silver. 'You little creep. I found him, he's *mine*.'

'That's enough,' said Sage, with menace. '*Go away*, both of you. Get lost.'

The girls went, in fear and trembling. A couple more years, he thought, and that won't work. The over-thirties will be killed and eaten. A chime in his ear.

'Sage?'

'Hi, Fee. What's wrong?'

Not very loverlike, but Fiorinda *never* calls just to hear the sound of your voice—

'Sage, the axe is gone. The Sweet Track Jade. I suddenly noticed. It's gone.'

'Huh? William must have moved it.' William was their cleaning person in Brixton.

'I've asked him and he says no. I've searched. It's not here. It's *gone*.'

'Okay. If it worries you, I'll come up.'

'I won't be in. I'm going to see Gran and Fergal . . . Could you meet me there?'

He reached the house in Neasden about six. When Fergal had moved in, Fiorinda had decided to close most of the place up. Security-shuttered windows stared from the gloom, over the tall laurel hedge. She let him in to the basement where Gran and Fergal lived, in a cosy rat's nest (Gran did not get on with cleaning persons) stuffed with furniture from the empty rooms up above. In the old lady's bed-sitting room Fergal was cooking supper, cabbage and bacon and potatoes, on an old gas stove squeezed in beside a mahogany Victorian dining table; refreshing himself with draughts from a pint glass of red wine. Gran sat up in bed, wrapped in frowsty shawls, swigging home-made elderberry liqueur and indulging in flirtatious banter with her keeper.

Sage kept up his share of banter through the meal, and the old lady glowed: she loved male company. Fiorinda sat silent, eating nothing, tracing kitchen knife marks on the mahogany with her fingertip. Her grandmother seemed unconcerned by this sullen behaviour. Fergal kept casting wistful, worried glances, but he didn't comment.

They left after the first rubber of whist. Fiorinda closed the garden gate and took an ATP torch from her bag (London suburbs were very poorly lit nowadays). She looked up, her eyes so shadowed in the pearly light that he felt a cold presentiment, a jolt of impending doom.

'That house chokes me. The moment I step inside, I feel as if someone's shoving concrete down my throat. I don't know how Fergal stands it.'

'He seems to get on with her okay.'

'Oh, it's not Gran. It's the place. I should come and see them more often, but I *can't.*'

They went back to Brixton. The Sweet Track Jade could not be found. They couldn't remember when they'd last seen it. Neither of them had spent any time at the flat since Ax left. They'd been living in the van, except for a couple of nights in Battersea, at the Heads' converted warehouse. Sage tried to reassure her. The axe would turn up. Ax would know where it was; they could ask him next phone call. But they were both strangely shaken. The Jade was a potent symbol. After his beloved Gibson Les Paul (which of course had gone to Romania), it was Ax's most precious possession.

'I don't like it that we can't talk to him,' said Fiorinda. There were no private phone connections to Bucharest. Ax had to call *them*, and his calls came through to a landline phone in the Office at the San. That was the way Ax had set it up, and they hadn't noticed anything strange about the arrangement. They hadn't been paying attention, because . . . because . . . They drank wine, smoked spliff, had incandescent sex: went to bed and had more. Later, Sage woke and found her sitting up, hands pressed to her forehead. Her skin, when he touched her, was clammy with sweat.

'Fiorinda?'

'Oh God, shit. Shit, shit . . . I think I was my mother in that dream.'

She returned to herself. 'It's nothing, Sage. Just a stupid dream, caused by me having to visit my gran. I don't want to talk about it, let's go back to sleep.' She slipped her arms round him and snuggled down, tugging him with her. 'Mm, I love waking up in bed with you, you're so big and warm . . . Is Ax asleep? I want to be in the middle.'

'He's in Bucharest, sweetheart.'

He knew she didn't get back to sleep, and neither did he.

Constrained by the lack of privacy, they didn't ask Ax about the Jade. It did not turn up. Fiorinda stayed in London; Sage went back to the van. Suddenly they didn't want to be together. Working as Ax's deputy in his office downstairs at Brixton, Fiorinda kept coming back to the briefing notes he'd left. He'd been very thorough. Contingency plans for everything. She looked around, and chills went up her spine. This looks like a dead person's room. This room has been *cleared*. The office looked like its normal self; Ax was always neat. The knowledge was in Fiorinda.

A week passed. On Saturday it was the Full Moon dance night at the Blue Lagoon. Fiorinda went down by train. The Staybehinds were settling into their fifth winter of principled squalor, unafraid. Things would be tight, but Fiorinda would help them out with drop-out hordes rations (date-expired cakes, apricot jam, tinned mackerel) and if all else fails, you can make alcohol out of practically anything. There's plenty of calories in alcohol. There were no outsiders this month, just Fiorinda and Sage and the

Heads. Fiorinda wore the red and gold 'Elizabeth' dress. She and Sage left early, around midnight. Fiorinda realised she didn't want to go back to the van, so they walked up to Rivermead, to the official residence where she never resided: hand in hand, harmonising softly with each other, *darling save the last dance for me* . . .

The sky was overcast, the moon invisible. The scent of cold woodsmoke, the faint faecal stench from the campground reminded Sage of Wharfedale, and a barmy army bender that he had shared with Ax Preston, four years and a thousand lifetimes ago. At the foot of the grassy bank below the dead cars sculpture they stopped and he began to kiss her. She helped his clumsy, urgent hands to open her coat; to unfasten the fascinating hooks and eyes in the front of the stiff bodice and find her breasts. She was thinking that the way she felt, *sparkless*, not aroused at all, would have been okay for Ax. Ax didn't mind if you were a bit out of tune for sex. But Sage never wanted anything but bona fide celestial music—

'You're thinking about Ax.'

'Yes.'

They parted and sat down a few feet away from each other on the ground. Fiorinda was shaking. She desperately didn't want to have this conversation. But here it was.

'Fee. Do you love me best? Do you love me more than you love him?'

'I loved you first, only I didn't know it. I love him with all my heart, but I've never felt about Ax the way I feel about you.'

'Then you have to come away with me. We can't do this. This is impossible. We have to leave, jump ship, before he gets back. I can't lie to Ax. I can't do it anymore.'

'He's not coming back, Sage. That's why he took the Jade. I don't know what he's going to do, but he's not coming back. Fucking Romania in November, fucking *Danube dams*, was it likely? We accepted it, we said yes, yes, fine, fine, because *we wanted him to go*. We thought it would be a break from pretending, a nice little holiday for us. He left because he knew we were cheating on him.'

'*Cheating* on him? Huh? How do you—'

'You know we were.'

'He wouldn't leave us like that, saying nothing. He wouldn't just walk out—'

'Yes he would. It's exactly what Ax would do. Do the necessary thing, cost what it costs, and sort the details later. He decided to get out of our way.'

'Oh, God. You're right.'

'I know I'm right.'

Sage gasped in agony, the recent past suddenly, hideously, irevocably present to him: Ax coming into the studio at Tyller Pystri that morning, looking so alone, so lost. Oh God, and his father died two months ago. He made nothing of it, so neither did we. We ignored him. Clear and sharp, how callously they'd betrayed that beautiful guy, *who has given his life for us, time and again*; how they'd thought, we'll have our secret life, and it will be okay because he'll never know . . . As if Ax wouldn't know that they had stopped loving him. He covered his face.

'Oh *Ax*. Shit, I can hardly bear to look at you.'

Fiorinda looked at him, unflinching. 'Yeah,' she said, 'you and me, we're just fuck-buddies. It's Ax you love, I knew that. You'd better get out of here. Go after him.'

She stood up. Sage stood too, and grabbed her. They clung to each other, bone-hard. This is it, he knew. Now, this moment, our only chance. Drive the van to Southampton Water, get a ride across to France, find a plane that's going back to the real world. We'll live in Alaska, up in the mountains, cabin in the forest, it's a big place, Alaska. We could lose ourselves, never hear about Ax's England again. The big crazy Englishman and his beautiful wife; I've dreamed of that. We could be happy. Just have to be sure we never speak his name.

'You have to come with me. He *knows*. This is what he wanted, for us to quit.'

'No!' she sobbed, pulling away. 'I won't leave Ax. I won't ever, *ever* leave him.'

He wouldn't let go. He kissed her, eyes and cheeks and hair, forcing his tongue between her teeth, mastering her body, overwhelmed by his own strength, by sheer despair. Fiorinda fought back, struggling, terrified, knowing she hadn't a chance—

He backed off, staring at her. She pulled her dress and her coat together. 'That's interesting,' she said, clipped and cold. 'I never thought I could be afraid of you.'

'What have you to be afraid of?' said Sage. 'You could fry me to a cinder in a moment.' And where is Ax? Where is Ax to say *fuck, what is this? This is a nightmare. Who started this conversation? Stop this, you lunatics* . . . Fiorinda crouched on the grass, her face on her knees. Sage knelt beside her, head bowed.

Silence.

'What can we do?' she whispered. 'Tell me, please?'

'We can go back to the way we were,' said Sage at last. 'You and Ax will be lovers, and I will be your best friend. It worked. All we lose is the sex, and that's no loss. I'm not fit to be your lover. I knew I wasn't.'

'But what shall we tell him?'

'That I tried to rape you? That I can never touch you again? On an open line?'

'Sage, *don't* . . . We could write to him. We could send a letter by courier. But oh, what if someone else read it? You can't be sure what happens to a letter.'

'We can't tell him,' said Sage. 'Ax is flying dambuster raids in decrepit pre-Cold War bombers, with half-trained eco-warrior pilots, and I don't have to be there to know he's taking insane risks with his life. We can't tell him about this.'

'We have to wait until he comes back,' whispered Fiorinda.

'Yes,' said Sage, clutching at straws. 'We'll tell him, as best we can, on that open line, that we love him, and we need him, and he should come home soon as he can.'

'When he comes back we'll tell him we aren't lovers anymore, and it will be all right.'

'Now I'm going to the van.'

They both stood up. Fiorinda, biting her lip, said, 'Sage, don't take it all on yourself. It was me too, never doubt that. I was in it with you, all the way.'

Cruel to be kind. He steeled himself to hold her one last time, because from now on friends can hug Fiorinda, but not me; but she looked so forlorn. 'It will be okay, baby. It will be all right.' And now let go. Walk away and leave her crying. Go on, do it. You knew from the start it would come to this, in the end.

Fiorinda walked into Rivermead, past the hippy watchmen in their self-elected livery of red and blue, who had been idling around the forecourt and probably heard and seen most of that. So it goes. No secrets from my household guards. Stone Age Fame.

This brand new mediaeval bedroom that feels so ominous, as if it holds ghosts.

She felt relieved, shattered but relieved, as if something rotten had burst open. The bed was not made up; no one had known she would sleep here. She took a quilt from one of the carved oak chests and lay under it, on the lumpy, scratchy, embroidered bedspread. We won't fuck, and we'll work hard. Ax will come home, and everything will be okay.

She was in shock. The pain didn't start until later.

Ax did not get back for Christmas. Since all was well at home, he decided to stay on in Romania after the dambusting for a fact-finding tour; and then go straight to the Flood Countries Conference in Amsterdam, in January. The Amsterdam Conference had started life as a meeting for alt.techies from the countries that were threatened by rising tides and coastal storms. It had grown in the planning. It was going to be a major event, the first truly Pan-European gathering of Countercultural leaders and luminaries, journalists and activists and academics since the Crisis began. A few years ago national governments would have been uniting to suppress the anarchists with maximum force. Today that had all changed. The eco-warriors were still feared, but they had to be treated with respect. They might be the only people who had any solutions.

Sage and Fiorinda were trapped. They had no plan but the one they'd formed, half-drunk and in shock, after the Blue Lagoon that night. Unjustly, irrationally, they felt abandoned. They desperately needed him and where was Ax? Too busy saving the world. *You go for it*, they told him, on the open line. We miss you like hell, but we can run the show for a while longer. Obviously you should be there. You do what you have to do.

Ax's entourage came home. The Netherlands government had not been happy about having Mr Preston at the Conference with the status of England's Ceremonial Head of State; and that suited Ax fine. He would be travelling as a private citizen from now on. Christmas and New Year went by. There were a few reminders (street-fighting, rural terrorism) of how near they were to the edge, and to what extent the stability they'd achieved rested on the personality of one man. Then the Conference began, and all was well. It was like the Islamic Campaign, watching Ax on the news.

The Flood Countries Conference had caught the public imagination, and was inspiring feats of broadcasting that had not been attempted since Ivan/Lara. Ironically, it was no easier to get hold of Ax in person than it had been when he was in Romania, but his friends could follow his conference-floor triumphs on radio and video, and sometimes on live tv. It was as if someone had opened a window in a stuffy room. They'd been locked in on themselves for so long. Now something was happening in Amsterdam, in the Tropenmuseum and the Lyceum, that revived the charged and thrilling atmosphere of Dissolution Summer. Do we make through it to techno-green Utopia? Or do we fling ourselves into the dark? It seemed as if these questions were really being decided.

The Few and friends gathered at the Insanitude to watch Ax dominating the Data Qaurantine debate: arguing fiercely for restored global connectivity and against the isolationists; roundly condemning irresponsible attempts to break out of jail. It was scary for those who knew that Ax himself had hacked the quarantine, and that there were people in his live audience in Amsterdam who also knew this. But he got away with it. He had the Conference eating out of his hand. Of course.

Before Ax had left on his trip, the Few had been fearing the worst. No one in the English media would have dreamed of breaking ranks on the situation, but it had been common knowledge in the inner circles that the Triumvirate was in trouble. Now their friends saw Sage and Fiorinda obviously unhappy, but obviously loyal to Ax: and they hoped for the best. But they were wrong. Amsterdam was just a respite.

After the Data Quarantine debate Sage took the train back to Reading, alone. He'd tried staying in Brixton, sleeping in the music room; it didn't work. It hurt them both too much. Their friends must have noticed that Sage and Fiorinda weren't living together, but so far no one had been tactless enough to comment. George and Bill and Peter were in Battersea. Olwen Devi was not on site; she was in Cardiff. He spent some hours alone in the van, brooding in shame and misery. At four in the morning he went to the Zen Self dome and let himself in to the scanner lab. He knew that Serendip was aware of him, but she wasn't going to start treating him like a burglar.

He thought of Ax as he prepared himself. Blood test, just for the sake of interest. He grinned sourly at the hormone profile that appeared on the screen. Yeah. About what he thought. You can't use snapshot as a crystal ball. But if you give it the right type of brain state to work on, you might get a result . . . The beautiful guitar-man has an amazing ability to do the right thing, the thing that will work, putting everything else aside.

Why can't I do that? Why am I such a fuck-up?

He had noticed over the years that Fiorinda sometimes knew what was going to happen before it happened – without apparently knowing that she knew it. It wasn't a big effect. Only a closet trainspotter, nitpicking obsessive, passionately interested in the babe's every word, would have clocked it. Blindsight . . . He had been sure for a long time that Fiorinda's magic *must be somehow akin* to the goal of the Zen Self quest. But she's terrified of her own power, and it could be she has good reason. She can't be involved in this . . . The implications are weird. We thought it was all or nothing. But if Fiorinda can know things, and if Verlaine remembered his trip, then I can—

The drug entered him. Intravenous is slower, he waited—

A moment later he was back in the lab, wide-eyed, heart pounding, bathed in sweat.

'Well,' he said, aloud, when he could speak. 'That's . . . quite an answer.'

When Olwen Devi came back the next day he argued his case (telling her nothing of the vision he'd seen). He was so convincing that she let him take the same massive dose again, under controlled conditions. The results were thrilling. It was the solution to a long impasse – and, as so often happens, devastatingly simple. But Sage was on his own, taking the adventure where no one could follow him.

Each of the other labrats tried the new approach; and each of them in turn received a stark, imperious warning. Go no further, or you will destroy yourself.

They had reached the final engagement. There was only one champion now.

In another enclave of Ax's England a very different feeling was stirring. Mr Dictator will be back this time, but he has found a new role, on a larger stage. Of course he will complete his five-year term: but it is time to start thinking the unthinkable. Who's next? Who will be our next funky Countercultural President? A post which has become – as everyone knows, though Ax has carefully preserved the forms of democracy – the centre of all power and policy in England?

A group of interested parties met in Benny Preminder's office. They were an eclectic collection. Four of them were genuine, gamey-smelling hippies in full neo-mediaeval drag. Two were middle-aged Countercultural superstars, though not great friends of Ax Preston, from the Green Second Chamber. The other five were 'suits' – up-and-coming mainstream government types, who had realised that the *other* Counterculture was much broader and stronger-rooted than the rockstar version. Techno-green Utopia can't compete with the ancient folkways. Benny quietly presided over this radical Think Tank, and those fuckers at the Insanitude would have been surprised at how he relished the irony.

What about the Minister for Gigs? Wouldn't he be Ax's natural heir?

We ought to know if he wants the job, because he'd be a very popular choice.

Murmurs of assent, and respect. Benny did not go along with the current fashion for 'discovering' Aoxomoxoa as an intellectual and an arts-science genius. Please. This is still the fellow who brought 'The Diarrhoea Song' to *Top*

Of The Pops. But he understood that these people lacked an insider's perspective.

'I don't think we need worry,' he remarked, smiling discreetly. 'Sage is a very clever guy, of course, but he's not a political animal, and he just won't turn on the juice in a political situation. We can discount him.'

'What about Fiorinda?' proposed one of the hippies, a splendid Amazon, her features etched from brow to chin in spirals of indigo.

They liked the idea of Fiorinda. Or what about Ax's nephew, Albion Preston? An infant prince, a regency? That could be attractive, but the country isn't ready for hereditary rule, not yet . . . Fiorinda then. Benny's expert knowledge was invoked once more. He said he thought Fiorinda was a distinct possibility. The little lady is a realist. If we can assure her that this is not a *hostile* takeover, she might well come on board.

They went on trying out ideas: always with the cautious proviso that Ax steps down of his own free will . . . Benny smiled to himself, and said little. It was early days. These people didn't trust each other yet. None of them had noticed, or if they'd noticed, they hadn't commented, that he had left an empty chair at the head of table.

They'd find out what that meant, in good time.

He felt like someone who has been watching a stage magician, or a trick artist. Nothing seems to be happening. Vague passes in the air, random brushstrokes. Then suddenly, from nowhere, the picture emerges. You see that every move was planned, that nothing was left to chance, and you can't believe you didn't get it—

Oh, it's so easy, with these rockstars. Just set them up, and watch them fall.

The weather turned very cold. Old people died in unheated rooms; a few recalcitrant beggars froze to death. Fiorinda, struggling to keep her 'demons' warm and fed, was grateful for a drop in the number of new drop-outs. She'd hated the whole idea of the Call-Up, but the delightful prospect of being organised into forced labour (real soon now . . .) seemed to keep borderline cases at home. In Amsterdam the green nazis were saying, on the strength of two hard winters, that it was *Die Eiszeit*. Europe would die by ice, not by floodwaters. And let Gaia's will be done. The Conference was running well beyond schedule, and Ax had decided to stay until the end.

Since everything was fine at home.

Oh yes, Ax. Everything's fine . . . How could he be two hundred miles away, and so totally out of reach? She dreaded those phone calls: still on an open line. The Netherlands authorities reserved the right to censor the Conference delegates mail, and eavesdrop on all telecoms, but Mr Preston could have fixed something. Obviously he didn't want to. He didn't want to talk to Fiorinda and Sage. But that was okay. They didn't want to talk to him either. They longed for his return, and dreaded it.

On Mr Dictator's birthday the Insanitude management held a mediaeval banquet. It was supposed to be in the Quadrangle, but the tent was too big, so they had to move it to Horse Guards Parade. There were too many vegetarians to justify roasting an ox, the splendid pavilion was made of something other than painted canvas and the flaming torches were fake, but the ambience was very authentic. Freezing mediaeval draughts. Jongleurs and troubadours working the crowd. Armed guards in fantastical red and blue livery. The cross-tables were packed with Insanitude staff and their families, notable Boat People, Volunteer Initiative stalwarts, exemplary crewpersons. The Few and friends sat in state at a High Table on a red and blue swathed dais, but descended from thence in fine chivalric spirit to serve the dinners.

There was an interminable award ceremony, with countless prizes for Best This and Most Promising That. Trust

Allie, the prizes were good and the winners were popular. The Admin Queen knows how to keep people pulling together. David Sale, as special guest, made a jolly speech about his career as a wannabe radical rockstar (he did not mention heroin, or Celtic blood sacrifice). Fiorinda responded, with a couple of jokes and a little wild-cat grin. She did not mention how depressing she found the company of those liveried guards, with their far-from-mediaeval weapons on open display. While she was speaking Sage and the Heads turned up, all of them skull-masked, and took possession of one end of the dais table. She couldn't help noticing that Sage was *extremely* smashed.

She sat down again, between Rob and Dilip, and tried to pay attention to the conversation. Rob and Felice had a five-month-old baby girl with them, Ferdelice: sleeping like a little angel, unbelievably beautiful. Cherry was at home with Dora, who was three weeks off her due time, and getting pangs that might be real. Allie told the story of when she'd been birth-companion to her sister. Allie would probably never have a child herself, she wasn't the type, but she loved her twin niece and nephew, totally bonded to them . . . Chip, in drunken cameraderie, announced he was feeling broody. Fiorinda kept an eye on the end of the table. Fergal was there, sitting next to Bill. That was good. He wouldn't be afraid to pitch in if there was trouble with the boss. Nor think any worse of Sage for it, alas. Hard-drinking men understand each other.

She noticed that Fergal was watching Sage with a strange, fascinated kind of attention; then she realised why, and felt sick.

'Scuse me folks.'

The tent-kitchen was a crowded, shadowy cave: charcoals glowing, ATP slow-cookers hissing. The Insanitude management, cooks-for-the-night, were serving out dishes of frumenty and junket, marzipan sculptures and a kind of jam-porridge, onto a row of big trays. 'Not yet, Fiorinda!' they shouted. 'Give us a few more minutes!' The leaders of the rugrat pack were under a table, running a game of Blackjack. She'd known they'd be out here, getting warm and nicking treats.

'Silver. No, not you, Pearl, *Silver*, out of there. I want you to do something for me.'

'What is it?' said Silver. 'I'm busy . . . Hit me, banker.'

'I want you to bring Sage to me.'

'Oh, yay!' Silver grabbed her takings, shot out of the casino and bounced to her feet.

'Don't tell him, bring him. *Lead him to me by the hand.* Seriously. I'll be in the cloakroom. Can you do that?'

The kid's face fell at Fiorinda's tone. But she nodded, and darted off.

One end of the kitchen had been partitioned off to make a cloakroom. Fiorinda went in there, dismissed the person who had been minding the coats, and waited. It was very cold. ATP patches glowed dimly on the dark walls. A surplus of coats, no room for them on the racks, lay on a trestle table, like a heap of dead animals.

Silver appeared, leading Sage by the hand.

'Thanks. You're a good kid. You can go now.'

The skull mask turned towards her voice. 'Hi, Fee. What's the problem?'

The little girl had gone. He stood, uncertain, towering in the dim light. She watched him wonder what the fuck to do next for a few moments, then let him off the hook.

'Can you see anything?'

'Er . . . no. Not really.'

'Oh my God, *Sage.*'

'Sssh, hey, it's okay—' He stepped forward and located the edge of the table, the gestures of his masked hands so casual you wouldn't have known anything was wrong. He's a genius at stage-survival in altered states. From the table to the coat-minder's chair. He folded himself down and

246

took off the mask. 'It's nothing. A little bleeding behind the retinas. I'll be fine tomorrow, promise.'

No one had told her. *Sage had not told her* what he was doing. But she knew all about it. The fucking media folk couldn't get enough of the Zen Self project: the thrilling story of how Aoxomoxoa was trying to kill himself with weird drugs, in the name of science, had equal billing with Ax in Amsterdam.

'If that's true,' she said, trying to keep her voice under control, 'why are you here doing the I'm-so-hard-I-can-saw-my-own-head-off? Why aren't you lying in a darkened room with a cold compress over your eyes? Don't tell me Olwen know you're doing this, because I don't believe it—'

He was wearing the blue-dyed leathers he'd worn to be Mister Blue, and a dark red shirt. He'd let his hair grow out since November. Someone had dressed it for him in yellow Celtic corn-rows (she imagined Zen Self groupies). Unshaven beard glinted silver-gilt along his jaw . . . Shambolic, rail-thin, oversized male megababe: the fucked-up rockstar, oh, he really looks the part. But where's my Sage, who would never fail me?

'Uh, didn't mean to piss you off. I just thought . . . I should make an appearance.'

Three Heads came into the cloakroom, unmasked, looking guilty. They were followed by Dilip, Chip and Verlaine. The weird science cabal clustered around their leader.

'You're a fucking idiot,' said George to the boss. 'I *told* you. I'm very sorry, Fiorinda.'

'You'd better take him home.'

Rob and Fergal, Felice and Allie appeared, pushing through the partition with a waft of kitchen warmth and noise. Felice was holding the baby in her quilted carrier. Roxane, Anne-Marie and Smelly Hugh were close behind them.

'What's going on?' said Rob. 'Is this a private bust-up, or can we all play?'

'Nothing,' said Sage, 'is going on. I made a . . . hm. Did something I shouldn't. I'm sorry, er, Fee. Really sorry. I'll call you in the. In the—'

'Morning,' supplied Fiorinda, shaking in fury and terror. 'Sage, what did I ever do to you? *I don't deserve to be this frightened!*'

'Nah, don't be frightened . . . Little glitches. It happens. Fine tomorrow.'

'Bastard. When did you last inject heroin?'

'Huh? Um, I dunno. Ten, no, shit, eleven, no, fuck, nearly thirteen. I think, nearly thirteen years ago—'

'Too good to last,' said Fiorinda bitterly.

'This is beyond a joke,' said Rob. 'You have to cool it. We need you, Sage. Are you out of your mind? You have to lay off the Zen Self shit, at least until Ax gets back.'

Now the battle lines were drawn. It was a stupid venue for a fight, but this one had been brewing for weeks, and once they'd started they couldn't stop. Voices were raised, harsh things were said. The weird scientists quit the scene, taking Sage with them. The others gathered around the trestle table, in silent dismay. The Few had never been divided before. They had been closer than brothers and sisters, closer than a rock and roll band, united against the world.

Fiorinda sat on the coat-minder's chair. Felice handed the baby (who was still sleeping, the little angel) to Rob and put her arm round Fio's shoulders.

'Sweetheart, can you tell us what's gone wrong between you two?'

Any of the weird scientists would have thought that was an irrelevant question. To everybody left in the cloakroom it was crystal clear that Sage, the ex-junkie, had taken to drugs because he'd bust up with Fiorinda.

'I don't want to talk about it. We'll be all right when Ax comes home.'

'We have to tell Ax,' said Rob. 'Right now. Enough is enough.'

'I heard that it's murder trying to record the new album with him,' said Dora. 'And that's from the crew. God, if *Heads crewpeople* are telling tales, it must be bad—'

'Ax knows,' said Fiorinda, 'he's not on another planet. He knows about the Zen Self. What are you going to tell him? That Sage is doing weird drugs? For fuck's sake. I'll talk to Sage. He'll tell me why he's doing this. Sage wouldn't do this to me for no reason.'

'Oh yes he fucking would,' snapped Allie. 'He's *poison* to you, Fio. He always was.'

Fiorinda didn't react. She just shrugged, and shook her head.

David Sale came through from the kitchen and stood there in his suitish dinner jacket. 'Is there anything I can do to help?'

The Triumvirate had hated David Sale after the Spitall's Farm affair. But when you've hauled someone back from the brink, and covered up for him, and forgiven his sins: and you were being cynical and pragmatic, but the person believes you sincerely care about him, it turns out there's the basis for a genuine relationship.

'No,' said Fiorinda, standing up. 'Thanks David, but no. C'mon, folks. We're on. We have to serve the mediaeval pudding course.'

Two days later Sage was at the Office, perfectly lucid, eyesight fine, doing early work on the Festival Season line-ups with a very frosty Allie Marlowe. Rob and Allie and the Babes still wanted to tell Ax he had to come home at once, but Fiorinda said no. She said she'd talked to Sage, and he wouldn't do anything so stupid again; and Ax would be home really soon, anyway.

She had talked to Sage. He'd come to Brixton to try and

explain. They'd stayed up all night: saying terrible things, renewing their hopeless vows, pleading with each other for some solution that didn't exist. Snapshot abuse hadn't been a big topic. They pulled themselves together, and did a video-postcard to send to Ax, something the censors wouldn't deface. They made a big effort, because they were afraid he might have heard some kind of rumours. We're fine, we're happy, the Rock and Roll Reich is doing great, don't you worry about a thing. *Ain't misbehaving, saving it all* Love you.

At least Fiorinda wasn't having nightmares anymore. They'd stopped.

In the scanner lab, deep inside the geodesic dome, Olwen's ace neuronaut lay on the recovery couch. She sat beside him, watching his still face. What visions do you see? she wondered. She knew he was suffering. But he never gave reports . . . She'd dismissed the medical team. They wouldn't be needed. Sage's vital signs were fine, considering what he'd just put himself through. She could give him the calcium and potassium herself.

From the first trial, almost from the first time she'd set eyes on the tall young man in the eerie and beautiful mask, she had known that he would be her star. His visual acuity was part of it (he can see the colours of the stars). And his digital art. Perhaps even, paradoxically, the hippocampal damage of traumatic childhood illness. He had outstripped the others, even young Verlaine, long before his breakthrough over the dosage. He had taken wild risks, and she'd been happy to let him. They were two obsessives together, determined to go all the way.

Now she was afraid she'd become complicit in a work of self-destruction.

He opened his eyes and gazed at the misty-green angled planes of the ceiling.

'How do you feel?'

'I'm good.'

'Keep your head still.'

She checked his eyes. No retinal bleeding this time. No problems on the screens. She unhooked him and sat down again, taking his crippled right hand in both her own.

'Sage, I have to talk to you. You are getting ahead of my technology. You have to let me catch up. My scanner cannot model what's happening in your brain anymore, when you are in phase. Serendip doesn't have the capacity. You realise what that means? If you lose something when you are out-of-body, I won't be able to reinstall. You could lose your sight. You could lose your motor control, your power of speech, your proprioception, *permanently*. It could happen tomorrow.'

'I know,' he said, turning his tranquil blue gaze towards her. 'I understand. I've worked without a wire before. Used to do it all the time.'

'I was willing to help you. But I don't think you're doing this for the Zen Self now. I think you're doing it because you are very unhappy, and my darling, that is not right. I will not help you to kill yourself.'

'You're wrong,' said Sage. He sat up, swung his legs over the side of the bed and reached for his shirt. 'It's true, I'd sooner dance the night away with my wild best friends. But since I can't do that, never no more . . .' He grinned at her, very sweetly. 'Some drugs you only take when you're desperate. It doesn't make the experience less amazing. I'm not suicidal, an' if I was, I wouldn't do it this way. I wouldn't bring the Zen Self into disrepute. Trust me. I know what I'm doing.'

'You have to slow down.'

'I have to speed up.'

She went with him to the lab-exit. Two of her team-mates joined her, Zen Selfers in red and green, to watch him walk away. They had all taken snapshot in their time; or that drug's predecessors. They knew the allure. There comes a point when you are told, by some grim physical warning, that you have gone as far as you have the capacity to go . . . and then all you can do is serve the ones who will venture on, always a little further. It was a fine day in very early spring, a clear sky: light without heat. Reading Arena, seen through the frame of the exit, had the intensity of the penumbra, the usual after-shock of an experiment: every blade of grass distinct, every passing face a Rembrandt portrait.

'Do you think he will kill himself?' asked one of the Selfers.

'No,' said Olwen, 'I don't. But I think Ax has lost his Minister. And God knows I love that great boy, but for all of us, that may be the greater disaster.'

'But Ax is coming home, isn't he?'

Olwen touched the ring on her finger, the many-faceted golden-white stone that was the Zen Self's mainframe computer. 'Maybe.'

The Flood Countries Conference was over, at long last. They knew Ax had had a triumph; they didn't know when or how he was coming home. Finally, a message came from the Conference Gofers' Office. Mr Preston has snagged a ride on a private plane with some Welsh mediafolk. He would be flying into Cardiff, no reception committee please: he planned to make his own way to London. He'd be in contact with everyone soon. This was very puzzling. They told themselves it was a Crisis Conditions fuck-up, crossed wires, and all would be explained when Ax got to England.

Not long now. . . Not much longer.

Sage sat by the river, where the bank was wide, near the Caversham Bridge. His eyes were open, but he saw nothing of the riverside. Fiorinda was moving away from him through a crowd of people in evening dress, her silver curls threaded with a few whimsical strands of copper red.

Still walking like she's got oilwells in her backyard, same as she did when she was fourteen years old. Ax was there, in white tie and tails. He saw them meet, he saw Ax's flashing smile, unchanged . . . Where is that cathedral-roofed hall, with the tall, light-filled windows? Why such a wrenching pang of joy; and how much more of this can my heart stand? He imagined the great muscle full of hairline fractures, stress on stress. One day it will just shatter into bloody flinders—

George was sitting beside him (how long's he been there?).

'Hi, boss.'

'Hi . . . George, what would you say was the prettiest blossom tree, this time of year?'

'I reckon that would be the wild cherry.'

'Yeah. I believe you're right.'

Sage relapsed into silence. George considered the former giant toddler genius with very mixed emotions. You had to respect the way Sage was keeping going. Doing what he was doing with the Zen Self, and still pulling his weight as Ax's Minister: and all on no drugs whatsoever, except for the snap, not a lot to eat, no proper sleep; and no sex. Not that the sex would be an issue, the amount of snap the boss was pumping into himself. But though they were still loyal, none of the Heads could forgive the way Sage was treating Fiorinda. They would never have believed it of him.

Partly, George blamed Ax. You can't fucking treat the boss like that, no matter what he did. Tell him that you love him, and then walk off and leave him. He's the sweetest-natured bloke that ever breathed, but he's not the most steady character; you have to know that, and you have to accept it.

Townies and staybehinds strolled by; oars stroked the water. Silver and Pearl, with their little brother Ruby, had got themselves a skiff and were flailing around in mid-stream, a danger to the traffic. 'Those Wing kids,' said George. 'They are a liability. I ought to warn you, by the way . . . Smelly told me he and Ammy are planning to ask you to take Silver off their hands.'

'Hnh?'

'Well, she's got her periods. She's coming up on eleven or twelve. They're thinking, they couldn't do much better than see her set up as junior wife to the Minister for Gigs. 'Long as Fiorinda approves, of course.'

'*What?*'

Ha. That fetched him out of Neverland. But George's satisfaction was shortlived; the boss looked so utterly horrified, so *desolate*.

'Oh God, this is it. This is the world Fiorinda saw, and we wouldn't believe her.'

'Now don't take on. It's just hippy nonsense. I'm not proposin' you accept the offer.'

'Oh, fuck, George. This situation gets worse and worse. *I want out of it.*'

George sighed. He stood up and reached out a hand to pull tall Sage to his feet.

'Don't we all. C'm on. Let's get to London. And thank God Ax is back.'

Ax was in England, but none of the Few had yet spoken to him, not even his Triumvirate partners. Apparently he'd spent the night in Taunton (according to a garbled message, from the Welsh media-folk with the plane), and he would be at the Insanitude today. But he still wasn't answering his phone, and they hadn't been able to get through to Bridge House, either. Allie had left messages, to no avail. Fiorinda came to the Office from a Volunteer Initiative hospital shift. The room was empty except for the Few, who were standing in a huddle beside those schoolroom tables. 'Don't come near me,' she said cheerfully, feeling so uncertain (oh, what will I say to him?). 'I'm harmless, but I stink of disinfectant. We have a typhus outbreak in Central London, fucking hell.'

For a moment she saw Ax in the middle of the group, but he had changed. His body had thickened, shoulders bulked; his hair was cut short. There was something odd about the way he was standing. The figure turned, and it was Jordan Preston.

'Where's Ax?' she said.

Sage shook his head.

'He isn't here,' said Dilip.

'He isn't back,' said Allie, tight-lipped. 'We didn't understand the messages.'

'He's gone to America,' said Jordan. 'He sent a scrambled video, with that Welsh tv crew. They hand-delivered it to us. We decrypted it last night. D'you want to see?'

No intro, straight to Ax on the screen. He was in a room that looked like an open-plan office, with worn, grey, utilitarian carpet and ranks of windows, that had been turned into a dosshouse. He sat on the floor, smoking a cigarette, his guitar-case and a backpack beside him, a paper cup serving as an ashtray. He looked very like himself, which was a shock, as if the months should have changed him, his hair in sleek wings, the carnelian ring on his finger, eyes that smiled, but didn't quite face the camera. Figures crossed in the background, out of focus. 'Hi,' said Ax. 'I'll make this short. I've been offered a meeting with the Internet Commissioners. It means I have to go to the States, undercover. I have to leave at once. I'm afraid I can't pass this up. If we don't shift that fucking quarantine soon, the breach could become permanent. I'm not sure when I'll be back, depends how it goes. Anyway, I'm glad everything's okay. I know you'll be fine, and, well, remember you're volunteers, you're always free to quit, and thanks for everything. Sorry about the cloak and dagger stuff.'

Someone off screen said, 'Hey, Ax—'

He said, 'Yeah, in a moment.

'Sorry this is so rushed. I'll be in touch when I can.'

Something on the recording triggered a wallpaper effect. Briefly, Ax's face was in every cell of the fly-eye wall, smiling and turning away. Then he was gone.

'Fucking typical,' said Jordan. 'It's what we always wanted. Why now? What the fuck's he playing at? Why just him, and not the band?'

Between Fiorinda and Sage there passed a long, strange look. Yes. Good morning heartbreak, come in, sit down. This empty world is ours. He's really gone.

'Well,' said Fiorinda, with a glance around, gathering the Few, 'Ax has gone to America. Good for him. It's about time the Rock and Roll Reich had a US tour. We'll just have to hold the fort for a while longer.'

The punters were given a cover story about further important travels, and they accepted that. The Floods Countries Conference had put them in an international mood. They wanted Ax back, but they liked the idea of him out there conquering the world. David Sale was thrilled. Like Jordan, he had a reflex reaction to the letters USA. The Few and friends were shattered. Ax had been away for nearly six months. How could he not come home? How could they go on managing without him?

Jordan stayed in London, not at the Brixton flat, but at the Snake Eyes house on the Lambeth Road. He was a lost soul. When he tried to get himself sorted in a gangsta pub, the South London Yardies turned him over to the barmy army for correction.

Fergal brought him to Battersea Reach, where Sage had been in residence since Ax failed to turn up, taking time off from the Zen Self for essential Triumvirate business.

'If you plan to stay in this town,' Sage told him, 'you have to get yourself a street map. There are places I wouldn't go without an invite, an' I've been living here off an' on for years. Also, if you really need a firearm, fuck, there are easier ways—'

Jordan said he knew about Sage and firearms. Everyone knew about Aoxomoxoa's exploits on the Islamic Campaign. Fucking war hero. You think that makes you—

'That?' said Sage, starting to get irritated. 'That wasn't a war. One shopping mall bomb in Leeds took out worse casualties than most of our pitched battles. I've been in videos with more risk to life and limb.'

'Yeah. But Yap Moss was different.'

Sage remembered arriving at Easton Friars with Ax, after the battle. We handed the French girl over to barmy army intelligence, and then we were told the casualties. Nearly five hundred dead, on that stretch of winter moorland, and that was when the army was just guessing about the Islamists . . . He remembered telling himself, this is where I stop being human, by any terms I used to know.

Don't envy me, he thought. Don't you dare *envy me*, where I am now and how I got here. I'll take a lot from Ax's brother, but I won't take that.

'You're right. Yap Moss was different. That's why that's where it stopped.'

He pushed back from his desk, tugged open a drawer and took out an automatic pistol, checked the clip and held it out. 'Go on, take it. Go and blow someone away in an alley, find out what it feels like. Go ahead. But don't come back to Ax afterwards.'

'Ax isn't coming back,' said Jordan, furiously. 'He's quit. He's left us all stranded, you and Fiorinda know why, and no one knows what the fuck's going to happen now.'

In the background, Fergal sighed.

Jordan glared, Sage stared; it was Sage who gave way.

Jordan's an idiot, but he's wise enough to see what it

might mean, for him and his family, if our little knife-edge Utopia starts to break up—

'Nothing's going to happen. Ax will come home, everything will be fine. I'm sorry. Take the gun. Learn how to use it. You're right, you should do that. Just in case.'

Jordan shook his head. He looked strangely satisfied, as if all he'd wanted was to see that gesture: the gun pulled out, some acknowledgement of the way things really were, the other face of Ax's England.

'I changed my mind. Milly wouldn't have one in the house.'

'Tell her I say so.'

'Ax fucking hates those things, I know he does. I reckon I'll leave the rock and roll gangster stuff to you, white boy. It's more your style.'

Jordan left. At a glance from the living skull, Fergal stayed.

Sage removed the clip, shoved clip and automatic back into the drawer and gazed around at the clutter of his room. All this life, dry and dead, like a carapace, like an exoskeleton ready to be shed. Must think about Taunton. Can Bridge House be made safe? Milly will not like armed protection. Not at all. I will get my head in my hands. Maybe not tell her. Be discreet.

'Was it about the rat-catching?' prompted Fergal.

He wondered how long he'd been silent.

People were dying of typhus in Central London, the first notable outbreak of disease in the capital (by some miracle) since the cholera in Boat People summer. The London barmies were busy decimating rodents with glee and megadeath efficiency: something someone should have thought of long ago.

'No . . . something else. Fergal, you come from West Cork, don't you?'

'Aye,' said Fergal, 'Skibbereen. I haven't been there in a while.'

'That's where Rufus O'Niall lives, isn't it?'

'In Cork? Aye. In his bran' new ancestral castle, on his fockin' private island.'

'You had any personal dealing with him? I mean, in recent years?'

The Irishman's sea-green eyes studied Sage, with reserve. 'I've niver been back to Cork in recent years, an' I don't move in them circles. He was a Belfast lad when I knew him. I wouldn't say personally, even then. I hear he's still an ill feller to cross.'

'So they say. What happens to people who cross Rufus? Exactly?'

'Oh,' said Fergal, getting to his feet, now definitely uneasy, 'ye'll prob'ly know all me stories. He's that sort of feller, that's all.' He cleared his throat, 'I'll be on me way, an' leave yez to the computer work.'

Sage looked up and the room was empty. Who was here just now? Oh yeah, Fergal. Fergal, and Jordan Preston. Something about a gun. He checked the drawer, automatic still there. Who took out the clip? Was that me? *Shit*. He pressed the heels of his hands into his eyes and slowly, doggedly, recreated the last ten, fifteen minutes. He was used to the aphasia now, intermittent fault, he could work around it. Stone-cold-sober blanks in business hours were something else: with the authority I have, the responsibility, *oh shit*. But he wasn't going to stop. He groped for a pack of Anandas, struggled to take out a cigarette and failed. I will forget her name. And I cannot tell her why. The blood thrummed in his veins, *oh Fiorinda* . . .

But he wasn't going to stop.

A late Easter. April well begun, and it's only the fifth Sunday of Lent. Roxane Smith, in hir role as post-gendered Christian (otherness was the theme for this Lenten season) gave the homily at the evening service at St Martin's in the Fields. S/he was very surprised to see

Aoxomoxoa standing in the shadows at the back. He returned with hir in hir taxi to the rooms s/he now occupied, in a service block on Queen Anne Street. S/he lit the stove in hir living room – the central heating was minimal – and opened a bottle of wine. Sage, fists buried in the pockets of his leather jacket, sat in an armchair, gazing round at the book-lined room: the awards, the netsuke, a few good prints, a few cheap gewgaws that meant much. His natural face had been his face during the Triumvirate era, and s/he realised s/he'd been missing the mask. It's a strange and very beautiful thing.

'Well, Lord Jim. What can I do you for?'

'Oh? When did I stop being Mikhail Lvovich?'

Years ago, in the lost world, Roxane had made a game of calling Aoxomoxoa after various high-culture fictional characters. The next time their paths crossed, s/he would *know* that Sage's 'satiable curiosity ('The Elephant's Child', Rudyard Kipling) had forced him to track down the reference. And s/he would smile. It was a good joke on the king of the lads. Mikhail Lvovich Astrov was a character in a Chekov play. Tree-hugging conservative, daydreamer doomed to slave at the grindstone, takes his vodka without bread, indulges in a pointless flirtation with another man's wife. (But that last was unintentional comment: Sage had been Mikhail Lvovich since Dissolution Summer.)

'I don't know,' s/he said, pouring wine. 'You tell me.'

'Put me out of my misery. What did Lord Jim do?'

'He's someone in a Conrad story. He jumped ship in the midst of a disaster, convinced he had a right to do so, leaving a crowd of hapless punters, as he thought, to drown.'

'Uh-huh.' Sage nodded. There was a lengthy silence.

'I need to ask you something. It's about the Zen Self project.'

Roxane sat in the opposite armchair, and sipped hir wine. 'If you must.'

'Okay, so, I'll try to be brief. You'll have heard about the visions, where you might think we can get previews of the future, but in fact we don't.'

'Yes. I saw a television programme about that quite recently.'

'You see, the time you spend in phase with information-space is infinitesimal. You bring back a whole story, and it's bullshit. Emotional truth, that's what we say. We can tell when someone's reached phase from the physical record, but it is impossible to tell whether you visited the future, the present or the past. There's no difference; there's a difference but it's very complex, so complex it's invisible. You have visited *the whole*, and every point is interconnected, over and over, with every other point. You may assume you, so to speak, visited the future if you come back remembering something about your son grown up, but you could be wrong. Are you following this?'

Roxane shook hir head.

'It doesn't matter. This is not the question. Anyway, that's how it was. Then I had the idea, because of something that happened to Ver, that if you took a lot more snapshot you could stay in phase longer, deeper. More would stick and it would speed things up. Nobody believed me, because the science says it shouldn't work, but it does. I'm the only one who's done it. No one else is nuts enough.' Ghosts of tiny muscle-movement braided and flickered across the planes of virtual bone: the skull is grinning ruefully.

'Yes, I heard about that.'

'You see I asked a question, back in February, which is something else that's not supposed to work, but it did. I visited a very revealing moment . . . Snapshot goes for the jugular, if it gets a chance. You may have heard that. You must be calm when you take it because if you're full of

adrenalin and corticosteroids, stressed is the term, you'll
see stuff that matches. I did that, and I got my answer, but
now I'm not sure.'

A pause that lasted, longer and longer.

'Can you tell Fiorinda about this?' Rox asked gently.

'If I could tell Fiorinda, do you think I would be here?'

'So you're going to tell me?'

'No. Okay, now here's the issue where I need advice. I
want to achieve the Zen Self for myself. I don't know if
this makes sense to you, but once you've seen that you
could be complete, once you've seen it's *possible* to be
complete, it's a goal that's irresistible.'

Roxane nodded. 'Yes. You came to the right place. I
understand.'

'Huh? Oh, you mean your surgery? I never thought of
that. Well, good, maybe you do understand. So there're
two reasons for me to achieve the Zen Self. One is that
it's something I must do, or things will turn out very
badly. For my Fiorinda, and my Ax, and, fuck, *generally*.
The other is my own salvation. So why do I do it? This is
the problem. This is very fucking important, Ax, sorry, I
mean Rox. If I choose the wrong motive then I won't
achieve the Zen Self, it's as simple as that. I know I
won't, because I will falter, I will fall, unless I'm absolutely
certain.' The skull laughed silently, in breathtaking detail:
the naked minutiae of a human expression. 'You tell me.
Should I be thinking selfish, or stupid?'

'I don't know what to say.'

There was another long silence.

'The details are useless. Like a memory that you cling to,
and it was never really like that, you know what I mean . . .
But not the significance. That's real. When your firing
pattern is in phase with information-space you're *there*,
wherever you landed, and it's *from the brain state* of there
that your mind constructs the visions. Emotional truth.
So I can't be wrong. I can be wrong in every detail, but I

can't be wrong in what I know. I'm not trying to change the future. You can't change the future, and it's changing all the time anyway: that's simultaneity. It's a paradox. Eleven-dimensional kaleidescope, like Ver said. But if I don't choose right, it will be disastrous. Yeah, it's confusing. Tell me.'

'I'm afraid I don't see how I can help.'

The skull grinned at hir, not very pleasantly this time.

'You know, you saved my life once. You remember the Africa Tour? "Mba Kyere", I am passed over? Mary had told me she was getting married, and her bloke would adopt Marlon and I would never see him again. Bullshit, but I believed it. I was trying to kill myself. Not smack, alcohol, much more efficient. George said to me, you know, if you die now, Roxane Smith's gonna to write your obituary. Kept me alive.'

Who'd be a critic.

'I am glad to have been of service. There are few rockstars I'd rather keep alive.'

'Hahaha. All I want is an answer. Just say what you think.'

I genuinely didn't understand the question, s/he thought. But s/he was moved to pity, and by the memory of what Sage had been to them, through this long dangerous journey. S/he remembered Massacre Night, blood seeping from the mask. Pigsty's goons had to rough him up: it didn't bother him at all, he was thinking only of how to protect us. Sage dead calm and rock-steady, from the moment the shit hit the fan. He was our tower of strength.

'Do what seems right to you, Sage. We've trusted you all this time. Trust yourself.'

The skull looked amused, and then cast down. 'Is that it?' he said. 'Oh fuck. That's a challenge. Okay. Thanks.' Silence again. S/he realised Sage was not aware of these silences, which were curiously *infectious*. The two of them

263

might have gone on sitting for hours in this anonymous room laden with mementoes.

At last he shifted in the chair and said anxiously, 'I hope . . . It wasn't because you fell out with Chip and Ver over the Zen Self that you left Notting Hill—?'

Roxane set hir wine glass down on the small Afghan table at hir elbow and folded hir elegant, aged hands around one knee. 'No, Sage,' s/he said with dignity, chin up. 'I found myself *de trop*. The boys would never have banished me; I withdrew.'

'Oh. Right.' A little crooked smile of fellow-feeling.

'It doesn't matter. My relationship with Kevin was always based more on love than on sex, and the love is still there.'

'Well, I think I'll go now.'

S/he went with him to the door of the room. 'Sage . . . When I feel the need to call on supernatural power, I get on my knees – which is not so easy as it used to be – and I perform an arcane invocation that begins, *Our father in heaven* . . . As you say, every detail may be fucked up; the significance is not. I have been young, I am now old, and I have never found, or heard of, any tech fix or psychoactive drug that bettered my results.'

The skull looked at hir, almost as blank as a Hallowe'en mask. S/he was suddenly very disconcerted. Has Aoxomoxoa really visited eternity? Does he know the truth about what lies there? *Know* it, beyond argument, beyond faith? Don't tell me, s/he thought. Please, let me cling to my illusions. But Sage was on another tack.

'Did the punters drown?'

S/he shook hir head. 'They didn't. But I'm afraid it didn't do Lord Jim a lot of good.'

'Figures.' S/he offered hir hand. He took it and bowed over it, the mask vanishing so that it was his natural hand s/he held; and his natural face that smiled at hir, as he went out the door. Roxane was left wondering if the whole strange, unconversation s/he'd just had with the Few's mad scientist might possibly be under the seal of the confessional.

Perhaps it was.

As soon as they knew what had happened to Ax, Fiorinda went north for a meeting with DARK. She had to tell them they'd have to do without her, from now until don't know when. It was very hard. She hadn't known it would be hard; she'd thought this was the least of her worries: but she was giving up her life. This is how Ax felt, she thought. At least she wasn't taking DARK's lead guitarist. Drums, bass, keyboards, two guitars, and everyone could sing if pushed. Charm said, yeah, and we'll change our knickers frequently, bossyboots. Fuck off, this is *my* band: but what's this in the tiny polecat eyes of the dyke-rock empress? Could it be sympathy? They did a last gig, live at the lambtonworm headquarters in Middlesborough-on-Tees, and she left for London.

Ax had disappeared off the face of the earth. There was no mention of his 'undercover meeting' on the quarantined satellite link the Internet Commissioners used for essential communication, and they couldn't ask about it, because they had no way of knowing who was in on the secret. Don't make waves. They might not hear from him for weeks, or months. Sage might be dead by then.

The weird science cabal couldn't help her. The Heads, *Sage's band*, had given up on him. The others, Dilip and Chip and Ver, were still in thrall to the fucking quest. They thought what Sage was doing was insane, and incredibly dangerous, but they admired him madly and they would do nothing to stop him even if they could. They were as bad as the punters. At Reading Mayday concert the Heads did an *Unmasked* set, and the mosh roared *Zen Self Zen Self Go For It Sage!* as if they thought he'd invented a new way of juggling with chainsaws. Fiorinda, watching with the others because she had not been able to bear to stay away, saw how the dancing had been reduced to what he could manage (muscle weakness), and her world darkened. She had already seen Aoxomoxoa on stage for the last time. Gone. Never no more.

She went to talk to Olwen, feeling scared because she was afraid of Olwen Devi. The meeting turned out to be tough in a different way from what she'd expected. Fiorinda had friends she loved that she had also fucked, but she had never fucked anyone *for love* except Ax and Sage. She'd thought other people were the same, and she hadn't realised how Olwen felt. It was awful. Olwen didn't say a word of reproach, but they both knew it was all Fiorinda's fault for not being content with one boyfriend.

But Olwen was helpless too, and that was Fiorinda's last card.

It was hateful, pathetic.

The position she was in made her blood boil in impotent fury.

They had stopped seeing each other because it was such hell, but she stayed at Rivermead where she could at least be near him, and hear about him. She managed what work she could, and David and Allie were very good about it. When she heard Sage had gone to visit Mary and to see Marlon at his boarding school she knew it was over, because he wouldn't be doing that except to say goodbye. But he came back, and apparently the Zen Selfers were still talking weeks or months. Sage was weaker, so they had to space the sessions out, and he couldn't take so much of the drug. So there was still hope. Months! May, June, July? Ax could be home.

A few days after she started hoping again, it was all over the campground that Sage had been 'out' – that is, brain-dead – for nearly six minutes. His brain hadn't suffered because they'd been supercooling him and pumping him with oxygen, but his heart had started bleeding and given them a big scare. It had been touch and go. Now Olwen Devi had refused to give him any more life support, so he was leaving. He would go to the Zen Self parent company in North Wales. They regarded Olwen as a renegade, but they knew about Sage and they were willing to help him, as long as he understood the terms. With them, there was no way back. Win or lose, once you pass through the gates of Caer Siddi you don't come out again.

One night in the last week of May, Fiorinda sat at her piano in the big upper room with the windows facing west. There was a fire burning in the enamelled metal fireplace, but the room felt cold. She'd been sitting there for a long while, not playing, just looking at nothing. Occasionally she'd rub her arms She was wearing the red and blue printed chiffon that she'd worn when they went to Tyller Pystri, the night they asked her if they could both be her lovers. Elsie the cat was curled up asleep in front of the fire. Someone knocked at the door. She went to open it and there was Sage. She had known he would come to her. She'd been afraid, but he didn't look as if he was dying. He was leaning against the door frame with the collapsible look he got when very drunk, and Sage-very-drunk was someone she had known and loved, God knows, since the very beginning. She stood back and let him walk in.

'Remind me,' she said. 'Where are we in the rules? Am I allowed to touch you?'

'You're a vicious brat.' He walked over to the hearth, moving with the stringless-puppet uncoordinated grace of Sage-very-drunk, and sat in one of the cross-framed chairs. 'Come and sit on my knee.' It was only then that she noticed he wasn't wearing the mask. She had not seen his natural face since the time he came round to Brixton, after the mediaeval banquet. Oh yes, the night we cried. His hair was shorn again, and she was glad of that. He looked like himself, only very thin and very tired.

She came and sat on his knee. His arms closed warmly around her. She pulled open his shirt and burrowed her face against him, inhaling the scent of his skin.

He kissed her hair. 'Oh, Fiorinda . . . I'm leaving.'

'I spotted that.' She sat up. 'Nothing would get you into a room alone with me except *oh, Fiorinda I'm leaving*. I know all about it. Olwen Devi won't give you life support any more, so you're going to Caer Siddi, to achieve the Zen Self or die in the attempt. Oh *God*,' she wailed, hammering at his chest with her fists, 'do you ever listen to yourself? What's *Zen* about it? Where is the *don't cling! don't strive!* in what you are doing to yourself? How can you reach something called "the Zen Self" by force, by hustling?'

'It's not like that.'

'What is it like then, *bastard*?'

'Fee, please don't talk to me like that tonight. *Please.*'

'What, you think I ought to be nice to you because after tonight we'll never see each other again? You're off to kill yourself, and I ought not to waste our last precious moments yelling? For fuck's sake!'

'I am not going to kill myself.'

'Like hell.'

'This is something I have to do, Fiorinda.'

She freed herself, though it was terrible to leave his arms, and stood in front of him, shivering hard, but *still fighting*. 'You're doing this to punish yourself, because we cheated on Ax and we can't ever be lovers any more. Is that fair, Sage? Do you really think that's fair to me, or fair to Ax? Or, or, fuck, to England? I still love you, you know. Are you telling me that without sex there's nothing left between us?'

'I will love you till I die.'

'Great. So when's that? Next Wednesday?' Her knees giving way, she knelt, shivering, and stared into the flames. 'No, I'm wrong. This is because of my magic. You think

268

you'll have magical powers. Shit, how can you want the filthy stuff?'

'It might be different, coming to it the Zen Self way.'

She turned and stared at him in contempt and disbelief.

Sage got down beside her, moving carefully into one of his giant pixie poses. He was so calm. 'I want to be complete,' he said. 'I don't think this is anything like your magic, Fiorinda. Though I think, I suspect, that you may have made your magic like it. Zen Self is like when you are for a moment very happy, and you truly forgive and understand the whole terrible world, including yourself and everything you've ever done. It's like getting back to that state where everything is right, via the tech, and making it physical reality. Everything in your whole life fits, it's coherent, and you are *there* in all of it. There's nothing you're afraid of. There's nothing you have to forget, or cut out, or hide, or deny. That's what I want. I have seen it, and I cannot turn back.'

'So join a fucking monastery.'

'Too slow.'

She remembered sitting with him by the river, one day in another Maytime, and he had told her that he wanted to go into the desert to find himself. We never listen when the people we love are saying the most vital things. 'You could wait till Ax comes home. I love you, Sage. I'm not totally surprised you're doing this. It's always been in you, you've always wanted *everything*. But please wait. Just wait.'

'I can't. It's now or never.'

'What did Mary say?'

'Oh, I didn't tell her. I meant to, but . . . it wouldn't work. But it was okay. I'll never know how to behave to someone I injured so shamefully, but it was better. Almost like two normal divorced parents, discussing the kid with decent forbearance.'

'What d'you tell Marlon?'

'Something like the truth. He . . . he was scared. I've

always told him too much. I don't remember all of it. I get blanks, you know. I tried to leave him smiling.'

Fiorinda looked down. Tears fell on her hands.

'I made a new Will. George knows, he'll tell you about stuff like that.' (If he's left me Tyller Pystri, she thought, I'm going to kill him.) 'I've told Ruthie to look after the cottage until Marlon decides what he wants to do with it. But you and Ax can go there any time, if you want. My desk's sorted, I mean, my Minister for Gigs desk. Allie very nobly helped me with that, though she hates my guts. She loves you, Fee.'

'I know.'

He took her hand. 'Now listen, my brat. You have the Few, and David, and you have Fergal, who will look after the barmies down here. You have a tough job, but there are people you can trust. You don't *need* me, Fiorinda. You are much stronger than I am.'

'What shall I tell Ax?'

'Tell him that I love him. Tell him I didn't have any choice. Tell him I'm sorry.'

And the seconds ticked away, and the minutes ticked away, soundlessly. This crippled hand, holding mine. It will be gone. He will never touch me again. She could not conceive of what it would be like, on the other side.

'Just stay with me here, for a few days—'

'I can't. George is going to drive me to Caer Siddi in the morning. He hates my guts too, but . . . I'm still the boss, an' rock and roll feudalism's good for something. I, um, I need to get there soon. I need medical support, pretty constantly. Caer Siddi's one of the few places, if not the only place—'

'In the morning!'

'Yeah. I'm sorry, I thought you knew. We'll be leaving early. Don't get up to see me off. Please don't do that. This is our goodbye. Well, that's about it. I'd better go.'

They stood up together. He was very pale, under the

wheaten gold of Ndogs sunscreen. His blue eyes had that inward, covert concentration they get when he's so smashed walking across a room is a feat of acrobatics. So this is it.

'Stay with me tonight. Stay here with me, just once, what harm would it—'

He shook his head, ruefully. 'I wouldn't be any use to you, babe.'

Fiorinda gasped and recoiled, and her stricken face broke him. He stumbled and half fell, to his knees, clinging to her, sobbing, 'Oh God, *Fiorinda*. I'm sorry, I'm sorry. Oh please Fee, I love you, don't send me away like this, please don't be like this, please—'

She crouched over him, holding him, rocking him, stroking her fingers through the warm lamb's fleece. 'All right, all right, I won't be horrible. Don't cry, don't cry. Always love me, and it will be all right. Darling Sage, it's okay. I don't mind if you have to do this, I don't care about anything, as long as you always love me—'

'I'll always love you.' He stood up, wiped his eyes and bent and kissed her, the soft pressure of his lips, his hands on her shoulders. 'My brat. Goodnight.'

She went into the mediaeval bedroom, in which the three of them had slept together only once. He is still here. I have hours and hours left. The hours passed, the light began to grow around the curtains at her windows. Before it was fully light she got up, washed her face and left the building. She hurried across the arena and the camp-ground. The morning was cool and fair, the tented town-ship very quiet. She came to Travellers' Meadow, and the van wasn't there. That preposterous grey space capsule, which had been her home, her rock, her refuge, the centre of her life since Dissolution summer, was gone.

She stared at the bare earth where it had stood, stunned, trying to grasp the size of this task that the two men of

271

destiny had left for her. In Rainsford's-the-gym, just out of curiosity, she had once tried (when they weren't looking) to lift one of those fat weights that Sage and George toss around so casually. What happens? *Nothing* happens. There is no strain, no mighty effort, no terrible costly victory. Absolutely nothing shifts.

I cannot do this, she thought. I can't keep Ax's England going. It's impossible.

Something touched her hand. Silver Wing was standing there, a skinny unbrushed child in a brown smock, her small face pinched with grief, her eyes brimming. Silver didn't say a word, nor did Fiorinda. They hugged each other. He's gone. Our wild best friend, our beautiful lord. He's gone, and nothing's going to bring him back.

> I leant my back against an oak
> Me thought it were a goodly tree
> But first it bent, and then it broke
> And so proved false my love to me

SEVEN

Big In Brazil #2

They were sleeping on rock, in a cave. It was very cold. Ax got out of his sleeping-bag and went to the entrance. We are on the slopes of Mount Elbrus. I am in the ancient world. Far into the distance below, the Caspian basin was on fire. Eco-warriors had set the wells alight, and no one had yet managed to cap the flames. The landscape, under a reddish, Martian dawn, looked like fucking *Mordor*. But the strangeness of it gripped him, and he intensely wanted Sage to see this . . . A stab of pain, a glimpse of what was waiting for him, when he let himself feel his loss. But not now. He spoke aloud, quoting from the *Odyssey*: 'For in my day, I have had many bitter and shattering experiences in war and on the stormy seas—'

A voice behind him joined in, also speaking Homer's Greek.

So let this new disaster come. It only makes one more.

'You know the Odyssey?'

The older of his two minders grinned, his seamed face and the gaps in his teeth reminding Ax of Fergal Kearney. Lalic. 'I'm a Macedonian. Come and have breakfast.'

With Serendip on his chip, a facet of Serendip, that is, Ax could speak and understand any language that hit him. It felt somewhat like demonic possession, but he could handle it. He was afraid it meant he was behaving as if everyone he met belonged to the same tribe: luckily the eco-warriors didn't give a shit for national identity. Murderous factions yes, borders no. This war is everywhere. He'd met Lalic and Markus, the younger minder, in the last days of the dambusting tour. They'd said *come with us*, and here he was, on a pilgrimage. The small plane took off from a boulder field. They flew north, over the flames, with the cinder-grey pans of the Caspian sea floor in the east, a sullen gleam of water in the distance. What's that great wen down there? Oh, fuck, that's *Stalingrad*. Volgograd. They landed in marshland. (Lalic and Markus flew by sight, since most of their instruments were bust. They treated their little plane like a motorbike; they'd park it anywhere.) Walking through reeds, they came to a stretch of water, like an arm of the lost sea. There were hippy guys with rifles, who provided a boat. 'What's going on here?' he asked, expecting another apocalyptic environment-damage story.

'Sssh. Wait. She'll come.'

Something very large glided up. He saw an eye. He'd never seen such a big fish. He'd never been near to such a big, living wild thing in his life.

'She is a sturgeon,' said Lalic softly. 'We think she's two hundred years old.'

'Not such good caviar,' said Markus. 'Beluga. But okay when there is nothing else left. This is our reserve, it's what we do: but they are too few to recover; all the sturgeon will go. She is our partner, mascot, wife, you could say. Magic fish.'

The magic fish, which looked to be fifteen, even twenty feet long, had the muzzle and barbels of a bottom feeder. She cruised around, seeming gravely interested.

'The war is already lost,' said Lalic. 'In the west you hear rumours: running out of water, no more fertility in the soil, and you start fighting in the streets. We go on fighting too, with bombs and guns, but we know. We are losing, it is too late, it's finished.'

'You can't say that,' said Ax. 'We're not losing. This isn't the end of a long campaign, we've only just begun. We can turn it round.'

He was thinking of Lalic and Markus, and the magic fish, when he set out for the Floods Conference venue in Amsterdam one January morning, in the different cold of the North Sea coast. The city had reliable mains power, wave power mostly. Good for them. The sky was clear of smoke and the air clean, which made a pleasant change from Bucharest. Or London. He walked by the Singel-gracht, looking at the buildings, taking in the atmosphere: a dark shape swimming up through his mind, like meeting life itself, *life* with eyes looking back at you. He was thinking that none of the mistakes he'd made in England mattered. Spend time with Utopians whose concept of the Good State is that everyone eats meat once a month and we never run out of ammunition (and Lalic was a Doctor of Philosophy once, by the way), and you learn to respect the scale of this task. You make a mistake, you *move on*. Don't waste time on it.

Just as well the distances in Amsterdam were small. Ax hated bicycles, and he couldn't buy a bus pass. He'd had a ridiculous conversation with a young woman at the Metro-station: no I can't sell you a *strippenkart*, Mr Preston, because you're an eco-warrior, but could I have your autograph? At least she'd had the grace to produce *Put Out The Fire*, and the 'Miss Brown' single. New Year's fireworks piled in funeral pyres, a flotilla of drab, icebound houseboats, white-faced coots pattering across the grey ice . . . he almost ran slap into someone standing in his path. It was Arek Wojnar, Polish music publisher and radical computer geek: a stocky bloke with a stubble of dark hair, slightly mad-looking pale blue eyes and a light-the-sky smile.

'Ax! I said to myself, that's the amazing Mr Preston, and

I was right! Striding along, thinking world-changing thoughts. Which hotel are you at?'

'No hotel. I'm dossing in the Tarom building.' The block that had housed the Romanian Airlines office was providing unofficial accommodation for a raft of Eastern Europe hippies who had no money at all.

'Oooh, is *that* where the English are?'

'No, just me. I'm here on my own.'

'I see,' said Arek, looking pleased. 'Travelling light. Good! I was worried for you. You have been spending so much time among the suits.'

Arek was no mean suit himself when it came to wheeling deals and preying on hapless artists. But he reserved the right to be a wild and free idealist in his spare time.

'Yeah, me too.'

By the time they reached the Lyceum, and the gabled, turreted Tropen Institut, the winter pavement was awash with dreadlocked outlaws, sober hippies, adventurous suits. They met Alain de Corlay, and moved through the day in an enclave of techno-greens-with-music-biz-connections. Debates, seminars, posters: how much new bad news can you take? The conference was far bigger than had been planned; much of the programme had been moved to university halls, but the museum remained the centre, its tropical dioramas making a very fitting backdrop. These jewel islands that are drowning; this colourful Southern poverty, choking on its own shit. This showcase of human diversity which has become a relentless casualty list . . . On bilingual placards Ax read the Netherlanders' core interpretation of what goes on, the same from Aleppo to the Philippines, *in times of trouble, the people will cling together and support each other*. My bus pass would seem to be an exception, he thought. But it's a good sentiment.

In the afternoon there was an angry debate in the glass-roofed Light Hall, which was the main museum venue.

The topic in the programme quickly became irrelevant; it was a slanging match between the techno-greens and the pan-European Celtics. The media people had turned out in force, and it was heartbreaking to see their pleasure and relief. *Aha! A binary opposition! Now we get it! Hold the front page!* But what can you do? At the end Ax had to duck out to escape being mobbed – the classic rockstar experience, which he'd never had before in his life. He was outraged, and even a little frightened. He'd been living in a hothouse where there wasn't a media person, or a punter, who would say *boo* to Mr Preston. Back at the Tarom (having spent a while in a stockroom full of Javanese puppets and carved totem sticks, guarded by some kindly Tropen staff), he found Arek and Alain and a bunch of other techno-greens, making themselves at home. 'Ah, here he is,' said Alain, maliciously. 'The man of the moment. It was those fucking dams, Ax. You are feared!'

'I didn't do anything. I was just holding the coats.'

'Of course! You didn't do anything. Nothing is going on in the Danube countries but a lot of running around, gang shootings and knife fights. Along comes Mr Preston and, so quietly, so gently, tells the suits, now let's be reasonable, this is going to happen, let's see if we can have it happen in a controlled way. And . . . KABOOM!'

'Come off it, Alain, you can't call me violent. I am getting stigmatised as the moderate around here, just because I don't like bloodbaths—'

'Our US correspondent is looking for you, Ax,' said someone in Alain's party.

General laughter.

'Yeah,' said Ax, accepting a paper cup of coffee from Alain at the hot drinks station. 'Anyone here from the English Counterculture and speaks English? I caught that.'

Alain's eyes narrowed. 'Oh yes. What's this, Mr Phrasebook? I have been wondering all day. When did you learn to speak French like a human being?'

'He was speaking Polish earlier,' said Arek, acutely. 'I think it's his chip.'

'Nah, evening classes.' However, the truth would be more annoying, and even in this empty world, annoying M. de Corlay remains a worthwhile project. 'Oh, okay, it's Serendip. I have a facet of Serendip on my chip, that's who's doing the ST. And it feels bizarre,' he added, unaugmented, 'so I'm going *au naturel* for the evening, if you don't mind. English or nothing,' A feeling like gentle claws withdrawing their grip.

'Nom d'un nom,' said Alain. 'Possessed by the machine. Ax, what are you doing to us? You realise how the Celtics, those savages, how they'll *love* this?'

'Nyah, you're just jealous.'

They went out to a big mass-market bar on the Leidesplein and argued about techno-greenery until Alain decided he had better things to do. Arek stayed with Ax, eyeing up the non-revolutionary pre-clubbers through a haze of cannabis smoke and complaining of the dullness of life in Cracow, where Countercultural violence and Crisis panic had never really taken off – just endless bitching about the Quarantine.

The music loop in the bar featured the dancemix of the Heads' current single, 'Heart On My Sleeve'. Also Fiorinda's 'Chocobo'. They came round incessantly.

'How familiar it is, how Polish, this pointless faction-ism. Did you know, Ax, I am a Celt! The Ancient Celts were everywhere, a truly European *phenomenon*, I know I must not say race. My eyes are typically Celtic! I can be on both sides of the bloodbath! But who would have thought Western Europe would be the first to go? It's unreal.'

'Anyone who looked at a population density map, that's who,' said Ax.

'Huh? You think it's that simple?'

'I think when the shit hits the fan, suddenly things get

very simple, and that's the worst fucking shit of all. The challenge is to keep things complicated.'

Here comes 'Heart On My Sleeve' again. Arek propped his chin on his hand and gazed at Ax, soulfully. 'How did you do it, Ax? I have been trying to get Sage into bed for years and years. He has just laughed at me. Held me off with one hand, you know—'

Ouch, ouch, ouch. Ax shrugged. 'Try getting him killed a few times. Wreck his career, steal his girl, make him into a murderer. Worked for me.'

'Oh dear, don't tell me you two have fallen out. My perfect couple!'

Ax would have to find the right tone for answering questions about his lovers.

'Nah. Nothing's wrong. We're fine.'

Arek shook his head. 'It's the girl. You should ditch the girl. She had made trouble between you, of course she has. Women always make trouble—'

'You know,' said Ax, 'Sage is right. The gay nation stinks. Bunch of shit-for-brains self-centred misogynist wannabes. I fucking hate 'em.'

'Okay, okay! I step off the holy ground! But my God, you must not part with Sage. He is your Charioteer. Your hero-companion, your guide in battle. That's very Celtic!'

'Arek, I wouldn't mind just *not hearing* the word Celtic for a few hours.'

Someone came up. It was the US Correspondent. She wanted to introduce herself, which, at this juncture, Ax found extremely welcome.

Arek grinned and winked. 'Now I'll go and find some other conversation for a while. You want to come along to the darkroom at De Olifant later, Ax? It might be fun, huh?'

The US Correspondent was a futuristic-Utopian who'd often been around in the chatrooms, before Ivan/Lara.

She'd usually been dressed (so to speak) as the Addams Family butler. He tried not to look taken aback. He'd had 'Lurch' down as a female teenager, shy and bold, full of naïve enthusiasms, which appeared to be right. He hadn't envisaged her weighing in at sixteen stone (or thereabouts; and she wasn't tall), with a sparse thatch of straw hair, a slab-of-whey face and tiny eyes almost devoid of brows or lashes. He offered her a cigarette. She looked at the pack with alarm and said earnestly, 'I think it's *great*, the way you're the eco-warrior king of England, and, but, but you smoke cigarettes and you take drugs and you drive a sports car. That's so cool.'

Americans won't say 'Dictator'. They just won't buy it. It pissed Ax off no end to be associated with the departed royals, but he knew there was no use arguing.

'It's not a sports car. Let me buy you a drink, then.'

'Oh no. No! I'll buy. It's wonderful to meet you, er, Ax—'

They chatted. Her real name (sorry, her original name) was Kathryn Adams. She was a journalist, kind of, by profession. She came from Maryland, and she was a designer baby. She had been born a trisomy, a Down's Syndrome. 'My parents had the learning difficulties fixed, but they didn't give me the cosmetic therapy because they're Christians, and now I'm grown, I don't want it. I like being, you know, invisible.'

Invisible wasn't the term Ax would have used, but he soon understood what she meant. Lurch is a smart cookie, and nobody to look at her would ever guess it. What a decision to take. Ax did not think of himself as vain, but he couldn't imagine it. (After talking to her for a very few minutes, he didn't doubt that doing without the cosmetic changes was voluntary. She smelled of serious money.) She had to get back to her hotel. He went to find Arek, who had got himself totally smashed, and hauled him out of a fracas with some Belgian hippies – something to do with the European Flag, and the good name of the Blessed Virgin Mary.

I can do this, thought Ax. In Bucharest he'd been an automaton, performing 'Ax Preston' routines (the suits, the mob, the Deconstruction scenario); and feeling nothing. He'd been afraid of Amsterdam, where there'd be people he knew. But he was okay. Walking on knives, but he was fine. He was good.

Next morning at the Tropen, Alain found Ax eating his breakfast, alone at a table in the museum café. He came over and sat down, bright-eyed and malign.

'So, you left the Milky Bar Kid home alone. Was that wise, my friend?'

Ax ate his black rice pudding. Shards of soft, fresh coconut on top, fucking ace. What it is to be off the offshore island. 'Why wouldn't it be wise?'

The little Breton put his head on one side, his eyes snapping with *schadenfreude* (or whatever is the French for that). 'Hm . . . I should tell you, when I was in Reading last, I said to Sage if he and Fiorinda needed a place to run, they could come to me.'

'Oh yeah?' said Ax, unmoved. 'What did he say?'

'He didn't say anything. He hit me. With force. Then he picked me off the floor and we went on with our conversation as if nothing had happened.'

'We drop the subject,' said Ax, grinning.

'Of course. You trust him, that's your business. Not another word.'

The days passed. The European Crisis opened up before him. So much bad news, but as Ax kept saying, this is not the end of the world. This is a wake-up call, amplified by panic. Accelerated change . . . There were scuffles between technos and Celtics that led to conference-goers being banned from every decent club round the Rembrandtsplein. There was a live album recorded at the Paradiso, with Ax playing guitar in a Floods Conference supergroup: a very mixed bag. The Van Gogh Museum was stormed by art-for-a-cause locals (street theatre, no damage to a major tourist attraction). Ax managed to avoid seeing much of the English contingent, or the rest of the British nations, by the simple expedient of becoming the spokesperson for the techno-greens, a role that everybody seemed to think belonged to him anyway.

He felt like a visitor from another planet, because no one knew what was going on in his head. No one knew that in his heart he had quit the job that made him famous. Maybe his secret freedom made it easier for him to take on the Conference: he knew he was doing well. The quarantine debate went like a dream, and yeah, he was aware that the US correspondent was in the audience . . . Alain jeered at Ax's 'tendresse' for the Ugly American (and his general sucking-up to Uncle Sam), but Ax ignored him. The kid was interesting, whoever she was; and he liked her.

One freezing night, alone for a change, he met a music-biz delegate from Dublin who told him that Feargal Kearney, who'd vanished from the Irish scene about two years ago, was rumoured to be dead, died in a rehab clinic on the wrong side of the Quarantine. Ax was guilty of not liking Fergal much. When someone 'accidentally' shafts you, *every time you talk to him*, then on some level he's hostile, even if he did save your life. But he didn't contradict the story – just in case Fergal really had faked his own demise. They'd never got to the bottom of how their defector had acquired the David Sale evidence. It was always possible that he'd left serious enemies behind him in Ireland.

Another day he went with Arek to the Stopera, to see one of the stranger signs of these times. In the underpass between the Town Hall and the Musiektheater, the Amsterdammers kept an exhibit showing Netherlands sea-levels. There was a woman standing by the plaque representing 'Normal Amsterdam', the basic sea-level of Europe. She was swathed in grey, she wore a wreath of dead flowers and birds, her face was blurred: she was about three metres tall.

'Can you see her?' asked Arek.

'Yeah.'

'What do you think? Is it a hoax? Another art-for-a-cause stunt? A trick of the light?'

'No,' said Ax. 'I could be wrong, but no.'

No one knew what she meant. The grey lady had simply appeared. She had become the Conference mascot, but no one had claimed responsibility. She was insubstantial, but unlike a traditional ghost she turned up on photographic film and other recording media. Ax thought of the unpleasant apparition he and Sage had once met in Yorkshire. This was broad daylight but the feeling was the same: a compelling presence, a bending of reality.

'She's crying for us,' suggested Arek, sentimentally. 'She is Gaia, weeping for us.'

'More likely she's crying for herself. I don't know that she's, er, on our side.'

'But why now? Ax, what is happening to this stupid world? An economic crash and *pouf*, there are ghosts in the streets. I don't think I like it.'

Ax shrugged. 'You don't have any problem with the Blessed Virgin Mary.'

They turned and made their way through the grey lady's small, permanent crowd. So far people just came and looked. Maybe if she stayed she would become a shrine. 'Ach, you're right,' said Arek. 'But the spiritual should be spiritual. Visions are supposed to be in the heart. This is wrong, it feels dangerous. You keep telling me our crisis is a normal adjustment, Ax, but this is not normal. Serious laws are being broken!'

'It has to happen occasionally. A new model will come along.'

But as he strode through the Conference, making it work because that was automatic, the pain that he had put aside, the tears that he'd promised himself, began to overwhelm him. Every time he made one of those bland, open-line phone calls he could not stop himself from hoping that Fiorinda would cut through the pretence, damn the eavesdroppers, and beg him to come home. Every time he returned to the Tarom dormitory late at night he imagined that Sage would be there, a dearly familiar tall shadow rising from one of the scruffy armchairs in the unlit lobby, *hi rockstar, just thought I'd drop by* . . .

But they would not come to him.

They were pretending they didn't know there was anything wrong. *They were lying,* he could hear it in their voices. He forgot that he'd walked away so the lovers could be happy; all he knew was his burning pain. The video-birthday-card (which reached him in the first week of March) destroyed him. Fiorinda and Sage in the music room in Brixton, singing 'Ain't Misbehavin' . . .' So beautiful together. If he could have reached them, he'd have killed them both with his bare hands. He was in company, he had to look pleased. Late that night he went up to the Tarom roof (the only privacy available). The Rijksmuseum was strung with fairylights; there were people skating in the dark. He smashed the disc, ground it under his heel, and then crawled around picking up the fragments, because this was all he had left of his darlings, and cried, and cried, and cried.

The Conference finally came to an end. The grey lady might remain until deep waters drowned her, but the cheap hotels were emptying, the hippy caravanserai were being dismantled. All the coverage was retrospective now. What do you think, Mr Preston? Who came out on on top, the Celtics or the technos? Where's the next round going to be held? What has the Conference achieved? Where are we going? At six o'clock one morning, in the rain, Ax sat looking up at the house where Rene Déscartes had once stayed, hiding from the world. *Everyone in this town except me is thinking about business* . . . But Ax had no philosophy to fill his empty head. Throwing the Sweet Track Jade into the sea had been a childish gesture. He knew he had to go back to England and make it official. He had to resign, and then what?

He had no plans.

I'm over, he thought. I'm *finished*, and this is how it feels.

Later he met Lurch for breakfast in the Ekeko café at the Tropen. The US Correspondent was staying at the Amstel InterContinental, a fact she had touchingly tried to keep from her impoverished European pals. The Light Hall was being prepared for a new exhibition. They took a nostalgic stroll through the dioramas, this entrancing giant dollshouse so haunted by the great dying: the rainforests, the corals, the eroded soils. The dancing, the funerary rites: everything must go. She asked him about Sage and Fiorinda. Everyone did that. It was natural. Those two were the hot couple of the hour.

'They have a pact not to write about the relationship, don't they? How does that work? I mean, all musicians write love songs. Is it legally binding?'

'I don't know how it works. I don't write lyrics, I'm out of it.'

'What about "Heart On My Sleeve"? How can Fiorinda think that isn't about sex?'

'It's the relationship that's off-limits, sex is okay. Or it could be,' added Ax, who found this topic galling as well as miserable, 'she thought it was about someone else.'

'Where did you think you were heading, setting up the Rock and Roll Reich?'

'Lurch, to tell the truth, a lot of things happened by chance.'

'But you did have a ground plan?'

'Are you recording this? I suppose you are, since you record everything. Look, why don't you give me a list of the questions, and we'll work something out.'

Takes one to know one. He had spotted on the second day that she had an eyesocket gizmo of some kind. 'I'm sorry,' she said, crestfallen. 'I should have asked.'

'Well, it's customary. But don't worry about it, I don't mind.'

So Ax talked – about the Rock and Roll Reich, and the poisoned world, and the music, how rock and roll is about *expressing yourself*, and it's the only way to go, the only kind of Utopia that will work, and luckily people need to be good to each other, it's as natural to us as greed and murder – arguably more natural, by a small but vital margin, or we wouldn't be here . . . They settled finally in the Yemen exhibit, a peaceful little upper room with dark red velour couches around the walls. Ax turned the ring on his right hand, wondering if this inteview would ever be published. He didn't see how. 'No, I don't expect the Reich to last for a thousand years. An idea doesn't have to be a lasting success to be worthwhile. Nature is profligate, a lot of wonderful things are ephemeral, and that's the way it will always be.'

He was thinking of the love affair. The American girl nodded respectfully.

'What will you do with this? I thought you weren't allowed to re-import any kind of digital device once you've taken it out of quarantine. Won't your gizmo be spotted at immigration and destroyed, with all your records?'

'Not if I declare it. I plan to do that, and have the recording bonded until it can be cleared for downloading. It won't lose value . . . There's just one other thing. Why did Sage write a track about Watergate? That's so weird.'

He sighed. Okay, forget the liferaft-earth spiel. Aox-omoxoa is *much* sexier. Tell me. 'It's a beach.'

'Oh. In what sense? Uh, what kind of a "beach"?'

'It's a beach with sand, not an ancient political scandal. A surfing beach in Cornwall.'

She nodded, with the look journalists get when they know you are winding them up. Moving on. 'Where are the other Musketeers this morning?'

'The other Musketeers?'

'Arek and Alain,' explained Lurch, with a shy grin.

'Oh yeah.' Ax smiled at her. 'Then I suppose I'll have to call you D'Artagnan.'

She blushed with pleasure, and looked sweet – a triumph of the human spirit. She's a good kid, and when you get to know her you can see it, no matter if she's, er, not conventionally attractive. He'd had to put some effort into protecting Lurch from the ribald cruelty of the techno-greens (both male and female). But he hadn't had to make a big deal of it, even with those who most hated and despised the USA. People liked her.

'The other Musketeers are coming down from this,' he said. 'They have things to do, places to go. They are packing.'

Lurch drew a deep breath. She gazed at him so nervously and solemnly that for a frightful moment he thought he was going to have to deal with a sexual proposal. The US Correspondent wants me to take her virginity (no question she's a virgin). Oh, great.

'Ax, would you come to America? I mean, to the USA?'

He grinned. 'Yeah, I'd probably come to America. If anybody asked me.'

'I'm asking. I'm, um, the truth is I'm here for the Internet Commission. I'm empowered to ask you to come back with me and talk about ending the data quarantine. Under cover, but they want to meet you in person. You're the one they trust.'

Ax was thrown into turmoil. His sense of destiny was rekindled. He had *seen* that Kathryn Adams was worth cultivating, and here was his reward. But the dazzling offer, paradoxically, cruelly, made him want to get back to England. If his lovers were missing him, in spite of everything . . . then he would go straight home, and the Internet Commissioners could wait. He couldn't bring himself to call Sage or Fiorinda direct, though the paranoid security had been relaxed and he could have done that. He called David Sale instead. He didn't mention the data quarantine (he didn't trust the connection that far). He said he'd been asked to intervene in something, and it meant a few more weeks away.

He was still going to quit. But this wasn't the moment to announce his resignation.

No problem, said David. You have a *wonderful* deputy. You carry on with the great work! He wanted to know how Ax felt about Sage and the Zen Self. 'He's been getting some amazing results, but he's pushing himself very hard. I expect you know about it—'

'Mmm, yeah,' said Ax. He had not been paying attention to the Zen Self bulletins. 'So, my Triumvirate partners are getting on fine without me?'

A slight delay. A guilty tone, when David answered.

'Oh yes . . . Er, I supposed you've talked to them? About this other trip?'

'Of course I have,' Ax lied. 'They want me to go for it.'

So that was how it was. Ax is out of the picture, everyone knows he's been dumped. Ax can carry on being good will ambassador for as long as he likes, nobody needs him.

He deleted Serendip. He would declare his chip, but he wasn't going to risk trying to take *her* through US immigration. She was probably a state secret, and a Welsh state secret at that. Goodbye gentle claws in my brain. I'm sorry it wasn't a closer relationship: some people can be friends with a computer, some can't . . . From now on it would be the wrong kind of pidgin Spanish, and the wrong kind of English. He arranged some cloak and dagger stuff to cover his exit, and made the video that would travel back to England.

It had to be short because he was about to break down in tears.

He waited a week in Seattle, confined – no, *asked to stay* – in his hotel room, for security reasons, in case he was recognised in the street. He thought this was ludicrous until he checked his home entertainment and discovered the scads of Rock and Roll Reich sites, cartoons, fanpages, interviews – all pure fiction, none of them admitting this even in the smallest print. Oh well, better to be talked about than not talked about. He channel-surfed, honed his openness to unexpected difficulties and off-the-wall opinions, and played guitar to pass the time. From one of his windows he could see into a vacant lot, where two north-west coast native persons had set up house with a mattress and some sodden cardboard. They drummed and sang, on and off, through the drenching spring nights. Just like Brixton, really.

There was a new, exclusive interview with Sage in one of the online glossies. The splash had Fiorinda in a pink party frock, with a wreath of roses (sloppy: she detests pink and she hates cut flowers) gazing up passionately into the eye-spaces of the living skull: a tempting yet decorous opening superimposed—

SAGE ON FIORINDA

When they first met, she was fourteen years old
She's the wildest, rawest talent in the Rock and Roll Reich
Her boyfriend is the post-human, post-Muslim,
post-modern king of England . . .
What does Aoxomoxoa really, really think?

He decided he didn't need to find out.

When the meeting came it was a damp squib. He sat in a spartan office with half a dozen funky leisurewear types, five men, one woman, and they spent an hour saying nothing. Lurch, who was also present, was deeply, deeply mortified. She asked him to please stick around, more will come of this, give it a chance. Ax had no idea what to do with himself. He had no money. He didn't care. He lay on his bed in the hotel room, feeling no desire for food, alcohol or any other drug, a million miles away from prayer, without a thought of God, gazing at the Les Paul, which stood in a corner in its case.

On the third day of this themeless meditation the phone rang. He picked up the handset (antique, ivory-coloured, to go with the Art Deco theme of the room). 'Hi?' He thought it would be Fiorinda.

'Hi . . .' A male voice, a long pause. 'Are you Ax Preston?'

'Yeah.'

'Uh, heard you were in town. D'you want a gig?'

Thus began the unofficial, low-down, Ax Preston US Tour. He played in the back rooms of bars, in small venues; in the private homes of US musicians. When transport wasn't provided he travelled by train and bus. He didn't want a car, and even here, in the heart of empire, air travel was not for normal people any more. He met famous names, he played the Blues where the Blues were born. He slept in cheap rooms and unbelievably fancy rooms, and walked around semi-tropical towns at night when he couldn't sleep, talking to anyone who offered. He felt like Johnny B. Goode. He knew that to many of the people he met, punters, promoters and musicians equally, he was a curiosity (the post-Muslim, post-modern king of England). But to others he was a pretty good guitarist, which was all he wanted to be. And the fingers still worked, though it seemed to him he couldn't remember the last time he had really played.

Something drained out of him. Some kind of demon.

He knew for the first time how utterly, insanely burnt-out he had been before he left England. He knew that his task as Dictator was over, but that he would return to the struggle, in some way. He had lost everything, and he was happy.

He was in this mood when he got the call summoning him to Washington, DC. It turned out Lurch was a genuine fairy godmother. Ax was going to meet the President. She came to DC herself, and they had a rendezvous at the Franklin Delano Roosevelt Memorial Park: FDR looking vulnerable and chipper in his wheel-chair by the gift shop, handsome walls of dark red granite, water features. There was a soup kitchen line of poor people, executed in bronze (strange notion). I HATE WAR, said the writing on the wall. THERE IS NO-THING TO FEAR BUT FEAR ITSELF. Lurch was *exalted*, and jittery. They took the lunch she'd brought to a quiet spot by the water. He understood (he'd been oblivious in Amsterdam) that he was a figure of noble romance to this redoubtable girl, which made him feel partly guilty and partly wryly amused. On the other hand, she was nervous as a mother hen about the impression he would make on Mr Big.

'Don't wear your *it's the ecology* teeshirt.'

'I was thinking of wearing my Deep Throat suit.'

'Huh?' said Lurch, looking seriously alarmed.

'Watergate,' said Ax. 'Sorry.'

'Oh. You can see the building you know, it's on the bus tour. Ax, Fred's truly smart, but he has to have a handle to pick things up by, and he thinks you're in charge—'

Ax laughed. 'Whereas you know I'm not. It's okay, I'm used to that problem.'

Two majestic, angular herons flew over, low and strong like cruising missiles. The grey squirrels and the sparrows chattered in a wealth of green. One of the squirrels came over and peered at them enquiringly. Ax broke off the crust of his sandwich.

'Hey, you mustn't feed them.'

'Why not?'

'It creates an artificial food chain.'

Well, God forbid the great American nation should *create an artificial food chain*.

He shook his head. Controlled hilarity at America, part of his cure. 'You people—'

Lurch gazed at him with reverence. He knew why their rendezvous was at this location. She didn't need to tell him that Roosevelt was her hero; or that she saw Ax bearing the greatest American's banner into the future that shaped so darkly, not only for Europe but for all the world. 'I know you'll do it right.'

Ax met the President at seven a.m. in a room with a tasteful repro version of the Insanitude's décor; but stunningly *clean*. It wasn't the top venue, but at least it was in the West Wing. It was like meeting the most sacred icon of someone else's religion. You're not a believer, but you're affected by the aura. Mr Eiffrich talked about the quarantine (though it was not, he pointed out, strictly his baby). He talked about the need for it, and the reasons why the goalposts for restored connectivity had been moved. Yeah, several times . . . Ax didn't get the feeling anything was shifting. He got the feeling that the leader of the free world didn't know what the fuck to do with the funky green Ceremonial Head of State of a former world-class country, that's totally gone to the dogs—

The party moved on to a buffet breakfast. Ax and the President stood side by side, having scrambled eggs spooned for them. You could get caviar, genuine Russian, with your eggs. Ax declined the luxury. Got any boiled babies?

He kept his tongue behind his teeth. No Lennonisms.

'I can't get over your accent,' said Mr Eiffrich.

Ax was tired of hearing that persons of colour were supposed to speak the same piccaninny who's-in-the-house argot, wherever in the world they were brought up. He was equally tired of hearing that idiotic circumlocution *persons of colour* . . . He had noticed he was the only non-white on the eating side of the napery this morning.

'Put me in the front room, turn out the light, you wouldn't know if I was black or white.'

'Hm. I was expecting Estuary English, because you all seem to speak that way now, with some Caribbean, usually it's Jamaica. But I can't get your mix at all.'

'It's West Country,' said Ax. 'With Manchester-Mersey-side. The whole music biz is affected by that, it's historical. Some US English, from tv culture. But there'll be Jamaica in there, a little. And my mother's from the Sudan.'

'Oh? North or South?' They moved on along the table.

'North. But she's a Christian.'

An acute glance. 'How'd she take your conversion?'

'My mum takes everything well, Mr Eiffrich.'

'Call me Fred. C'mon, let's eat. Let's talk. Tell me about the Amsterdam gig. My niece, she records everything and sees nothing, you know what I mean?'

The freshness of the morning had gone before Ax left the White House. He drifted at random over green lawns and came to rest at the feet of yet another eighteenth-century celeb. A minor deity. The crowds vanish in the vastness of the sacred places, I'm in the ancient world again. He remembered his first meeting with Mohammad, at the end of the Islamic campaign. The recognition, the feeling of rightness. His encounter with Mr Eiffrich had been nothing like that . . . but it had been a good con-versation, good business. The task could be passed on to others, and Ax could start planning his return trip.

It appeared, amazingly enough, that it was Ax Preston's England that had been snarling up global connectivity (something he would have to spin, in Europe!). Not the raging civil disorder and social collapse on the Continent, oh no. It was the rockstar with the hippy army, taking over Buckingham Palace. And here's me thinking we were the ones that looked sensible and reassuring. There you go, no accounting for taste: and now the President has met Ax, and decided he's an okay sort of guy (the Ax effect again, weird how it hardly ever fails). The President of the USA may be only a titular monarch these days, kind of a Fujiwara, feudal Japan situation, with the great lords of commerce calling the shots. But he has friends in high places, there's reverence for his traditional standing . . . and that's how things work. Person to person, it always comes back to that. A smile, the look in someone's eye, an exchange of pheromones, and everything shifts.

He sat on the plinth of the statue, thinking about his lovers. He'd been thinking of them a great deal while his mind was on its journey to recovery. He felt terrible about the way he'd left them, how bewildered they must have been, how abandoned they must have felt. He'd been ready to go back and tell them he was sorry, even before Lurch's phonecall. Now that would be his next task. They were made for each other and I can't stand in their way. Yeah, tough to accept, but what the fuck was all the rage and despair about? If they will let me, I'll be their best friend. He saw himself accepting the role that Sage, noble soul, had accepted once, and been prepared to bear for a lifetime. If my big cat could do that, then I can.

And it would be cool (balm for his pride) if he could say, oh yeah, and the data quarantine is fixed. Which he should know before he left, and he was confident.

Ready to leave, he took a look at his minor deity. The statue was of John Paul Jones, the Revolutionary War hero. Great tactician, always in trouble, ended up as rear-admiral to Catherine the Great, of all things, dishonourable discharge, died in France . . . The story was instantly in his mind, presumably from his chip. He'd long ceased worrying about the difference between chip memories and 'real' memories. Another populist hero who outlived his glory days. Greetings, compadre . . . But I will not go to the bad. I can't be their lover, but I will love my darlings, which is the important thing, and no one can take it away. I will make something positive of the rest of my life, I swear it.

Surrender? I have not yet begun to fight.

He returned to the Four Seasons and told the friendly desk staff he'd been to see Mr Eiffrich. They thought that was pretty funny, and told him again about how England is that place where it rains all the time. In his room, using his pay-as-you-go phone, he called Lurch, discreetly let her know the good news, and said no, he didn't want company tonight. Alone but no longer alone, Fiorinda and Sage restored to him, he slept for hours.

Later he went out (in a downpour) to eat at a tapas bar, DC style, booths and islands all majestic polished wood; a little stage at the back. When he was eating the waitress came and ducked down by his table. 'Excuse me, Mr Preston, would you play for us?' Heads turned. The bar staff and manager grinned hopefully. DC has heard about Ax Preston, the guitar-man from England. They may not know why he's famous, but they've heard he will do this sort of thing, and it sounds like a desirable freebie.

'Yeah, okay. You'll have to provide the guitar.'

So he played, sitting on a stool with an acoustic guitar, the pick-up plugged into a little amp. In the USA, at the kind of venues Ax had played, he'd had to get used to stepping over cables again. He checked out the crowd and decided there were none too many Ax Preston or Chosen fans. He was a free agent; they didn't have a clue what to expect. He gave them Willie Nelson, *blue eyes crying in the rain* . . .

Goodbye, my blue-eyes, and goodbye my darling girl. I love you both, I know it's over; and I'm coming home.

*

The next day Lurch came to see him at the hotel. She told him he had another gig at the White House: a musical entertainment. The President would be honoured if Ax would play at a reception. It would be in a couple of weeks' time, and she knew he wanted to get home, but he really ought to do this. There'd be other meetings on the data quarantine that he'd need to be part of, anyhow.

Ax felt, irrationally, somewhat demoted. Put in his place.

'I don't suppose you'd care to arrange for my assets to be unfrozen, if I'm staying? I think the Chosen do have *some* US earnings piled up in bond.'

'You don't need to worry about expenses. I'm embarrassed you ever thought that.'

Lurch (aka Kathryn Adams) was used to the kind of money where you never, ever have to think about it. She had the rockstar-toddler mentality on the subject (though she'd be hurt if you told her so). Ax's behaviour, walking out of the hotel in Seattle and going on the road, had been mystical and strange to her. It hadn't crossed her mind that he simply wanted to be in charge of where his next sandwich was coming from. So we start to get to know each other, and there are jarring moments, but she's still a very good kid, this fairy godmother of mine. And the leader of the free world is her Uncle Fred.

'Okay, let's look at the line-up.'

She hadn't expected the question, but she located the information and showed it to him on her very cool virtual-screen palm-top. The line-up for this musical entertainment at the White House put Ax on stage with a notorious outfit of blood-daubed-Celtic wannabes who openly supported Europe's green nazis, and a bunch of African-American Islamic hate-merchants whose rants advocated graphic slash and burn tactics against Females, Christians, Homosexuals, Asians, Koreans, and so forth. Both bands were respectable corporate-earning names. They have no idea what they're talking about, they're just trying to make a buck, all in fun and free speech, and Ax would be a fool to take offence.

He sighed. He could see someone had tried hard to put together a themed package.

'Sorry, Lurch. I can't do this.'

He explained why not. He made her understand he was serious. I don't have to play if I don't like the set-up. I've never been that kind of rockstar, don't plan to start. Thanks, but no. Lurch *blanched*. He would not have thought her whey face could turn any whiter, but it did. She argued her case, becoming agitated. The person who put this together didn't understand. I do, I tried, but what the President, uh, or people round him see is, they'll see you *being awkward*. Please Ax. You can do this. You have to do it.

Sorry, said Ax. Credibility issue, for my position at home. Surely the White House can understand a credibility issue?

Ah, well, he was thinking, watching her shocked face, so that's the way things are, and that nice civilised patrician gent I was talking to was really Pigsty Liver.

She left, saying she'd get back to him.

Ax, crestfallen and exasperated, supposed he could say goodbye to the quarantine deal. He wondered if his life was actually in danger (she had been so flustered), but decided not. Things aren't that bad. Fred isn't Caligula, he's just an emperor whose favour is easily lost; and if Ax no longer had a patron in this town, that was okay. He had a contingency plan.

In the morning he took the Metro to Dupont Circle, bought himself coffee and a muffin and went to sit in the park. People walked briskly; a class of teenagers were doing drill-exercises; sparrows flirted and chirruped and hunted scraps. The central fountain featured a *ronde* of undraped forms, male and female: sleek, pallid stone bodies. Two white guys, clad in running shorts and singlets, were sitting on the rim of the bowl talking quietly. Could one of them be my man? He wondered if he'd been stupid about the gig, but decided he'd been right to say no as an opening gambit; see what Lurch comes back with. He put the problem aside and thought about getting home. On Lurch's VIP ticket he would have flown into Shannon by private jet (no flights to England, but he could have handled the rest of the journey). Getting out of the USA otherwise, when he had little money, wasn't supposed to be here, had a chip in his head and came from a contaminated country, was not going to be straightforward. But he was working on it.

I like to be in charge of my next sandwich.

The sparrows caught his attention. What a strange city it is, where nobody feeds the birds. He wanted to crumble some of his blueberry muffin for them, but respect for Lurch's feelings restrained him. I'd hate to create an artificial food chain . . . One of the little birds came closer, without the bait. She hopped to within inches of his foot and looked up. He saw in extraordinary clarity the blonde stripe above her shining dark eye, the soft pelt of smoky brown feathers. She reminded him of Fiorinda, this little bird, and he had a wistful thought that she might come to his hand. He could almost feel the tiny claws, digging into him—

Oh

He recognised the penumbra of something untoward happening in his brain, and the next instant there was Fiorinda, her living ghost: Fiorinda, in her storm-cloud indigo and the orange fluffy cardigan, one arm across her breast, the bi-loc set in a white-knuckled grip against the side of her head. His heart *leapt*. Oh God, she has remembered. My telecoms-allergic babe finally realised *why the fuck* I gave her that thing. She looked as if she'd been crying.

'Ax!'

'Fiorinda, my baby. What's the matter? What's happened, sweetheart?'

'It's Sage—'

'What's the matter? Have you two fallen out?'

'Ax, you have to come home. Sage has gone. Olwen wouldn't give him life support any more. You don't know because we didn't tell you, he wouldn't let us, but he was taking far too much snapshot, in the Zen Self experiments. He said he couldn't stop, it was something he had to do, and now he's gone to Caer Siddi.'

The moment he saw her, the moment he heard her voice, the world turned upside down and righted itself, and he was *there*, in the world he thought he'd lost, loving her and Sage, grasping that they were in trouble and he'd have to sort it out—

'You two haven't been getting on then, I take it. And the stupid bugger wouldn't let you tell me . . . Fiorinda, don't cry, it'll be okay. Just explain to me what went wrong.'

She shook her head, her trouble only darker. 'N-not at this distance, Ax . . . You don't understand, he's *gone*. He was, I think he was dying when he left Rivermead. No one who goes to Caer Siddi ever comes out again. He's never coming back. *Sage is gone*. Things are okay here but not too good. Fergal's taken command of the London barmies, apparently Sage told him to do that, but I'm not sure, what do you think?'

'I'm on my way. I'll be with you soon as I can. Fiorinda, *don't worry*. It won't be as bad as you're making out. I'll talk to Sage, I'll go and haul him out—'

'Oh.' She looked around. 'You're outside. Can people see me? Do I look weird?'

'Yeah, they can see you, like a ghost. They won't worry. It doesn't—'

'Shit. I'd better break the connection, this is contraband.

299

Please, please come home as quickly as you can. I love you.'

She had vanished before he realised that he could have touched her.

He was on his feet. He sat back on the bench and reached for his cooling paper cup of coffee. His eyes were fixed on the Art Deco fountain; his mind was racing. I must go home, I must get back there. They've had a bust-up about the Zen Self, and Fiorinda's alone: but there's something else. Something I ought to know. *I can feel it.* Ideas started to click together in his mind, hints he'd dismissed, disregarded inferences, a cascade that he couldn't stop: straws in the wind, random objects out of place that reveal the direction of a great secret mass of moving air—

'Oh my God!' he gasped, starting to his feet again, his whole body thrilling with fight-and-flight. '*My God*, Sage! What have you done?'

If desperation had been enough he would have dived through the ether, halfway around the world, and snatched her out of danger, as if from a burning building . . . A youngish, good-looking Hispanic bloke, in worn-down funky leisurewear, was coming towards him. 'Mr Preston? Hi, I'm João. You waiting for me?'

It was his underground ticket home.

The man offered his hand. In the split second before he took the hand Ax remembered that this was no longer a gesture between negotiating strangers in the USA. Yesterday morning the President clapped Ax around the shoulders and squeezed his arm, getting physical without a qualm; but he didn't shake hands. They don't wear gloves, that would be the wrong message, but they don't touch skin to sweaty skin on the first date. Bio-terrorism's a real danger. He remembered, but he took the hand because it was too late, and everything went black.

*

Where am I? He was lying on his side on a hard, dusty surface. He thought it was wood, floorboards or planks. He was handcuffed, blindfold; he couldn't hear anything. When he moved, he found the cuffs were locked to a wall. Further inventory: he was wearing teeshirt and underpants, he had some bruising he'd rather not think about, a sore face, the taste of old blood in his mouth, but no serious physical pain. *Where am I now? I've been moved. I was somewhere different, they have moved me.* A blurred impression of the past few days began to surface. He lay still, deathly afraid, *Oh, Fiorinda . . .* Okay, it could be worse. *I could be naked, could be still gagged, could have been hurt much worse. This isn't too bad. This is not an absolutely hopeless fix. Objective one, calm yourself. Be open and ready for whatever chance comes.*

At last, footsteps. Someone ripped off the blindfold.

It was the bloke from Dupont Circle, with some others: two deeply tanned white guys, one with grey bristle hair, the other much younger. Two stocky, dark-skinned guys, alike as brothers; a tall, thin man black as tar. They all had handguns. The older white guy was clutching his and looking trigger-happy. The others less so, guns in reserve.

'What's going on? What's happening?'

'You've been kidnapped, Ax. You'd better co-operate, or we'll hurt you.'

He sat up, cuffed to the wall, and tried to look around the room without appearing to do so. The bed had no mattress, just dusty planks. No window was in his line of sight, and neither was the door. A sink in a corner. Bare dingy-brown walls. It could be a very cheap, shabby and dirty hotel room. He couldn't hear traffic.

'So, what is it you want?' He gave them a rueful smile. 'Contrary to the sound of the thing, I don't have easy access to large sums of money, but—'

'It's not for money!' shouted the old white guy, the gun

shaking in his hand. 'We're not interested in your fucking money!'

'Hey, we *do* want money!' countered one of the two stocky guys, in a hurry, as if fearing Whitey would wreck the deal.

'Yeah, but this isn't *about* money!' repeated the older bloke, furiously. He sprang forward and gave Ax a smack in the face with the side of the gun that knocked his head back, ringing, stinging. 'This is about the blow!'

'I don't have any cocaine, either. Not on me.'

'I mean the MARKET! This is about what *you did*, you bastard. And you're going to fucking UNDO, or you will never see the light of day again!'

'This is not personal,' said the man from Dupont Circle. He put his arm around Ax's shoulders and leaned in close. 'I want you to know, Ax, I am your biggest fan. I admire very much the Rock and Roll Reich. Fiorinda, the Power-babes, the Reading Festival, I am there. Be good to each other, I believe that. But you have to help us. You do not know what you did. I know you will help us when you understand.'

The white guy started ranting again. The others joined in, saying things that were slightly more coherent, no less lunatic. They were in the drug business, or they had been, until the market crashed. They believed that their careers had been wrecked by the legalisation of recreationals in Europe – and, above all, by the synthesis of artificial cocaine. They held Ax Preston responsible. He was the man who had ruined their lives. What they expected him to do about it was unclear. He was a hostage—

That seemed to be it.

Deathly afraid, he lived for days in that room, chained to the wall, taken twice a day, handcuffed and blindfold, to a toilet: talking whenever they would let him, trying to romance them, trying to find out where he was, hoping he would get to speak with someone rational. He got nowhere.

It dawned on him that there was no one rational, no one in charge. He was dealing with an amputated limb, a flailing poisonous tentacle no longer connected to any organised body. He could not call Fiorinda; the b-loc link was one way. But it was okay. She would realise something had gone wrong and she would call him again. All he had to do was stay alive and she would send in the cavalry. Unless . . . Unless the the nightmare scenario he'd envisaged, just before this disaster, was real, and it had intervened.

The kidnappers were volatile, but not violent. Not even older Whitey, apart from the tantrums; which grew less. They didn't hurt him anymore, though he knew it was in them: especially in João. After a few days they let him do without the blindfold, except for the toilet trips. They gave him food, rice and beans, and water from the sink. João kept saying he would borrow a guitar so that Ax would feel at home. Ax Preston, he always has his guitar. Like Jimi Hendrix.

One day (the tenth day since he'd woken up cuffed) the six of them came in with another man. The newcomer wore a suit of white overalls, like a house-painter; he was carrying a rigid metal briefcase.

Ax's heart stood still.

'Hey,' he said, 'what do you want me to do? I didn't cause a global recession, and I can't disinvent synthetic blow, fuck's sake, can't put the genie back in the bottle—'

'Ax, we have to prove that we've got you,' said João, reasonably. 'This is a *good* thing, be calm, don't worry. When we have proved that we really have Ax Preston, then we can have the ransom paid, and everything will be fine. We are not bad people, Ax.'

'Take a photograph,' he whispered, his lips scarcely able to move.

'That's fucking stupid,' said one of the stocky pair (only 'João' had a name, so far). 'Don't be *stupid*, Ax. Any picture can be faked. What would a photograph prove?'

'Blood sample. Tissue sample.'

They already had his ring, the ring Fiorinda had given him, along with everything else he'd been carrying. They had plenty of ID.

'We could cut off your hands,' said João. 'But we will only take something that you don't need, that losing it will not make you less of a man, but more.'

The man in the painter's overalls set his briefcase on the floor and opened it, with the stoic expression of someone who knows he should be in a better job. Ax couldn't see into the case, but he could see the man donning a pair of slick medical gloves. He watched, rigid with fear, as older Whitey and João confabulated over a needle and a syringe, works that had been travelling loose in Whitey's denim jacket pocket. Is this a clean needle, are you sure? It doesn't *look* very clean. Oh fuck.

'Don't put me out,' he said, urgently. '*Don't put me out.* I have to be conscious!'

He struggled furiously, things having reached the point where there was nothing to be gained by staying calm. They got him strapped down, face down, on his bed of boards. Okay, okay, I'll keep still. Don't knock me out!

But they did.

When he woke again he was still lying in the dirty room. His wrists were cuffed in front of him, but not fastened to the wall. He put both hands to his head and found a crusted and sticky dressing where they'd shaved away a patch of his hair and cut open his skull. If that gets infected, I am fucked. He could not remember his own name, but he could feel it, like something he could touch through a veil, through water . . . All kinds of knowledge were immanent in him. He knew that the engine was working just the same as it had been before, but the syncromesh was gone. *If that gets infected I am fucked* . . . The person who could put that thought together knew everything, but like an amputated limb, a lost arm of the sea. He tried to get up and fell off the bed. Right arm and leg (or maybe left arm and leg, same side, anyway) were not responding. He tried to crawl and found that the limbs that felt paralysed moved, more or less, but he couldn't think about it or everything went haywire. He remembered effects like this from, whoooh, long time ago, long time ago. When the chip was first put in.

Says the amputated limb, the lost arm of the sea.

He crawled in the direction of the daylight, the place where he'd always known the window must be. He pushed himself up the wall, with great difficulty, and touched glass. He was looking out of a window after all this time (not a fuck of a clue how long, at this moment). Aha. Beard. Touch his chin. The beard is grown way past where it was, it is soft and sparse. I don't grow much beard, but what there is is strong enough for a daily shave, annoyingly. I will not grow a beard. He remembered promising Fiorinda that.

Says the amputated limb, the lost arm of the sea.

He could not make sense of what he saw. He noticed for the first time that he couldn't make sense of *anything* he saw. Not his own hand in front of his face. Light and shadow, greyscale; other than that, scrambled pixels. *I cannot do this.* He turned and let himself slide down again with his eyes closed, tears burning his eyelids. Oh fuck, oh Fiorinda, I can't get there, *what's happening to you?*

He sat for a long time in the same position, in the sweltering damp heat of the dirty room. Nobody came. Every few hours, or maybe every few minutes, he had no way of telling, he opened his eyes and tried again. The need to shit will come. Where will I shit, where will I piss if they don't take me to the toilet? I'll choose a corner. I can handle getting the pants down and up, cuffed. I think I can do that. There's water in the sink. Live on water, for a long time. Someone will come. I'll think of a way to beat this. I will. He opened his eyes and tried again . . . He opened his eyes and tried again, and had the strangest sensation of the whole input being *there*, but unavailable. The animal can see perfectly. Ax can't.

Now this is what Sage warned me about. The brain becomes parasitical on the chip, routing everything through there, so if the chip goes you are fucked: and I *wouldn't listen*, because I couldn't consider giving up my special stuff. Poor Sage, he must have been scared to death. What an arrogant stupid wanker I am.

He opened his eyes and tried again, he opened his eyes and tried again, not knowing whether he would lose everything that had been left to him, but giving thanks to God for what he had. I have Sage, I have Fiorinda, I can think of them. God is merciful.

He thought of them. The faces were not clear, but he could feel them, filling his heart.

It could have been days later: he opened his eyes and tried again, and the dirty room took shape. God is good. God is great. It looked different. Could be a different room, for all he knew. He listened, am I deaf? There was not a sound. He pushed himself up the wall and looked out of the window again. The dirty room was on the first floor of a breeze-block building in a row of similar buildings. It seemed to be on the edge of a town. The street below was broken up, and trailed away into red stones and earth. He could see derelict industrial things beside a broad, nearly-dry riverbed. On the other side of the nearly-dry river, the green rafted towers of the trees began. They go up forever. They go on and on. Where the fuck am I?

It took him many weeks to come back from losing his chip. The neurological effects were terrifying, but most of them passed quite quickly. Psychological withdrawal was, in ways, much worse: the shakes; disorientation, inability to concentrate, inability to eat, or even to swallow – and a fathomless, engulfing despair that wouldn't give up. He had lost England, he had lost the Qur'an. He had lost his mind and become an animal like these animals his captors. It was like being in Hell, because there was no escape. The cartel took care of him; they wouldn't let him die. He would wake to find one or other of them spooning sugar-water into his mouth.

They brought him fresh clothes; they brought a slab of foam and a sheet for the boards of his bed. They cleaned the dirty room a little; they fetched in some furniture. João brought the promised guitar, and an amplifier so they could have a real concert. There was no power in this building but apparently there were others nearby that were still hooked up; the kidnappers ran a cable to Ax's room. João told Ax he should try to play the guitar. He must try to get better.

When he came back to himself, he discovered they still had the chip. João carried it around in a dog-eared Jiffy bag. The cartel would sit looking at this Jiffy bag, in Ax's room, arguing and getting nowhere, bewildered by the task of sending it anywhere. They were afraid they would be traced by their DNA on the package. It had them (especially Martín, old Whitey with the hair-trigger emotions) crying in frustration. How could they send something to England? An unreal place. Buckingham Palace Road, London. Beyond imagining. Ax had fallen into the hands of the unculture. They were grown-up toddlers. They had no idea how to follow through, how to make a project work.

He tried to convince them to send it to Kathryn Adams in Washington (he had no qualms about making that suggestion; they knew about his US sponsor. They knew everything). But they wouldn't. They weren't taking that kind of risk. Eventually it vanished. He supposed they'd sent it somewhere, but they wouldn't tell him anything.

He sat in the corner of his bed, cuffed to the wall again except for the toilet trips, trying to calculate the time that had passed while he was incapable. Three months? At least three months since he had been kidnapped . . . He must get to England at once. Fiorinda was in trouble. The terrible urgency coursed through him, scouring his blood: there was nothing he could do.

He thought of how his lovers had pleaded with him to be more careful, Sage saying, *Some nutter's going to walk up to you and shoot you in the head, Ax. Have mercy on me, take some precautions.* But Ax wouldn't listen, because Ax Preston mustn't go that way. No bodyguards, no armoured limousines, no razor-wired VIP lounge, *fuck* that. So he had carried on impressing the punters with his attitude, and his darlings had let him behave like an idiot, because they'd known he could hardly stand the life his choices had forced him into. They'd let him try to stay human. They didn't know about the petty little kick he'd got out of walking modestly among the common people, with his secret all-areas pass, knowing that at any moment (even here in the USA) he could get treated completely differently. Such balm for all those years of being not famous. He thought of that sneaking thrill now, with deep and cruel shame.

So this is where I end up, this is how I pay.

I knew I would have to pay.

The dirty room was in a ghost town. When he'd first woken up cuffed he had held off from screaming for help, because he was Ax Preston and he wanted to rescue himself. If he hadn't been killed straight away by trigger-happy Martín, it would have done him no good. No one lived around here. When his hearing had recovered he sat and listened to the silence for hours on end (a branch falls, a bird cries, something four-legged trots along the ghost town street). He knew that the emptiness went on for miles and miles. He would hear the cartel's battered RV drive up; or the rust-bucket Ford that belonged to Martín, jolting over potholes. He would hear them coming from a long way off, and he would hear them leave, the noise slowly dying away.

Martín and João were Brazilian. The others were US, except for Orfeo, the black man, who was a Cuban. But Ax didn't think this could be Brazil; he couldn't see how they could have transported him so far. *I was taken on a long road journey, I think . . . I think I'm in Mexico, or, what comes next?* He could not remember the names of any Central American countries. His thoughts crawled around the gaping hole where the chip had been, like lost souls. *It's more than three months. But now I'm stronger. Now I can get started. Escape. Befriend them, romance them, get the cuffs off.*

There's a road, I can follow the road.

His right arm and leg weren't good. Getting better, but not very fucking good.

He was rarely left alone. Most often at least two of them sat in the dirty room with him, night and day, and the others would be in the RV. They swopped around. Someone, (João?) was wise enough not to let any one develop a special relationship with the prisoner. It was no burden to them, apparently, to spend their whole time hanging out in this dump. They had nothing better to do. He kept a count of days on the wall. When they spotted it (the marks were fingernail-faint) there was a long discussion, and they decided to let him continue. But all the days were the same. He improved his Spanish, and learned to speak some Portuguese.

From an early stage he had tried to reach his lovers by telepathy. Not as crazy as it sounded . . . the Zen Selfers took telepathy for granted. They routinely came across what they called 'telepathy artefacts', different people's thoughts bleeding into each other, in the course of their experiments. Ax had been amazed to hear about this, but they weren't impressed. It's a bust, Sage had told him. The signal-to-noise problem's ludicrous, and what's wrong with a phone implant? In this endless silence, and since thoughts of them filled his heart, he hoped the signal-to-noise problem should be less.

Nothing clearer than a feeling ever came back to him, except once.

One day, one hot, damp silent afternoon, maybe around the seven months mark, he was alone. He was sitting with his eyes closed, enjoying the rare pleasure, when he heard Sage's voice saying softly and distinctly, like the start of the first track of *Unmasked*, 'Hi, Ax.'

He opened his eyes and there was Sage, sitting cross-legged at the other end of the bed. He was unmasked, tanned. He was wearing white drawstring trousers and nothing else. Bare feet. His hair had grown out of its crop and was combed into cornrows. He was very thin. He smiled without speaking: and suddenly Ax was at Yap Moss, absolutely *there*, on the winter moorland, with Sage there too, wearing the living skull mask. They were about to say goodbye, it might be forever, and plunge into the battle: and even now, knowing all the loving that would come after, it seemed a good way to part. No hugs, no tears, no last minute avowals: just I say, 'Transmission Mast—' which is where we'll regroup if we survive. He says 'See you there,' – and we swing away from each other, into the mêlée . . . The moorland faded. Ax was back in the dirty room. Sage was still sitting there, like a b-loc living ghost, his blue eyes and his beautiful mouth between solemn and smiling. But his face began to break up, pixel by pixel: a trick he used to do with the mask, that Ax had never liked because he was afraid the process wouldn't stop, it would go on until not only the mask had vanished, but the face under it. Which is exactly what happened now, until Sage wasn't there anymore.

For a long time Ax sat gazing at the empty space, feeling the white light of absence.

He didn't know what he had seen, a ghost or a vision or a figment of his imagination. He only knew that Sage was gone out of this world, and he must mourn his friend and lover as dead. But Fiorinda was still alive, in her desperate trouble. He knew that, equally surely. He thought they often passed each other, in the hot nights when he couldn't sleep, like prisoners walking in opposite circles in an exercise yard.

Fiorinda in her dark world, and I in mine.

There were no seasons. Sometimes the rain fell in pounding silver rods for days, but there was no pattern to it. Rain or no rain, the dull heat continued unbroken. The cartel had more discipline than Ax had given them credit for, and they kept it up for an incredible length of time. They didn't know how to get hold of a ransom, but they knew how to handle a hostage. No one was ever alone with Ax; Ax was rarely left alone. Ax had no idea where he was, and he was never given access to any clues. Sometimes the guards brought music or videos to the room for entertainment, but never a radio. He gathered from their squabbles that João allowed no careless talk: no one outside the group knew about the prisoner. The routine of keeping Ax cuffed to the wall, except when he was taken to the toilet, was *never* relaxed. But discipline finally broke down over the guitar – which had been lying in a corner, forgotten, since they realised their brain-damaged hostage couldn't begin to play it. João became convinced that Ax had recovered. He would be able to play, if he wasn't handcuffed to the wall. There was a huge discussion, which ended with an agreement that Ax's conditions should be changed a little.

Ax kept out of it and didn't mention that his right hand motor control was still shit.

The RV turned up with a stranger on board. Ax was very scared when he saw this man arrive. He immediately associated a stranger with the freelance brain surgeon. It didn't help that the guy was dressed in grubby white overalls. But no, all this one did was tear up some grimy vinyl, pound out a hole in the concrete floor with a chisel and mallet and set a thick metal hasp in there, in cement.

Ax was left alone with the handyman for a good ten minutes. He knew it couldn't be an accident. He could see exactly where this was going, but if there's no chance, you take anything, so he talked to the guy anyway. The stranger – thickset, coffee-skinned, wedge-shaped Indio features – kept his eyes, behind plastic goggles, on his job. *You are not like them*, said Ax. *You are normal, you come from the normal world, from sane people. Help me. Tell someone.*

No response. Maybe one shifty glance, quickly quenched—

The cartel came in and sat there watching the cement dry. Baz, the younger white bloke, combed his stringy blond hair with his fingers and complained the whole thing had been unnecessary. Ax could have played with one hand chained to the wall. João made smalltalk with the handyman and tried to engage Ax in a staring match; which Ax declined. Then João and the stranger went out. Felipe and Simon, the stocky brothers, unlocked Ax from the wall and took him to the window, a gun in his back. The Indio, with his toolbox and half a bag of cement in one hand, was taking a wad of notes from João. It looked like a lot of money, but Ax didn't even know the currency so he couldn't tell. The man turned to get into the RV. João took out his gun, shot the handyman in the back of the head and stood there, while the shot echoed, looking up at Ax.

See what you made me do.

João came back indoors and offered Ax, still loose from the wall, a cigarette.

'Just so you could play guitar, Ax. Just so you could play again.'

'You were going to do it anyway,' Ax shrugged indifference.

One of the more unpleasant things was that he knew he had been raped, in the time he didn't remember clearly, right back at the beginning. He had a strong feeling it had been João, the major Ax Preston fan, and only João. He couldn't be sure. He could never be sure it wouldn't happen again. In a situation like this you had to accept that things could get much worse, at any moment. Live with it.

João laughed, sat down again and started a fake conversation with his pals.

And if you think that's the first death I've had on my conscience, thought Ax, you haven't been paying much attention to your favourite sensational soap-opera, bastard.

Now Ax could be shackled at the ankles and locked to the floor with his hands free and play that guitar. He said he was tired, he would try it out tomorrow. João accepted the little show of resistance. He was clearly feeling pleased with himself.

Night fell. Ax listened to the cartel arguing about how to get rid of the corpse, his eyes fixed on the darkness, his shoulder against the wall. Hopeless urgency. He was a useless soldier, guarding a door that he could not guard, that was thousands of miles away.

He dreamed that he was with his friends. They were in the blasted ruin of a stone-walled cottage, in the village in Yorkshire where Sage had been captured once in the Islamic Campaign. There was a war going on again in England, and they were on the front line. It was good. He had forgotten about his friends. He'd forgotten that he loved them, and how much they'd been through together; but here they all were, dirty, cheerful, very much themselves: Rob and the Babes, Allie and Dilip, Chip and Ver

313

and Rox, the Heads . . . Allie and Rox were loading a stack of antique rifles that looked like something from the Wild West. Sage was jiving around, cheerful and serene, distributing the rifles, making sure everyone was in cover, singing a rude ska song, *Put wood on the fire, Jackie, Good wood on the fire Jackie*, a tune the lads used to like, but Jackie Dando wasn't here, only the Few . . . When Sage got to Felice he kissed her deep and long (Ah, we all knew about *that* piece of chemistry, and we knew neither of them would do anything about it, it would only cause trouble). But Rob smiled benignly. Nothing could break this mood, this lightness . . . It came to Ax that the reason they were so happy was that they knew they were going to die, and probably within the hour. They would die together, die trying . . . But *oh God, where's Fiorinda?*

He woke soaked in sweat, full of dread, his heart pounding.

I have to get back to England, *right now* . . .

The dirty room came back into focus; the terrible urgency seeped away. It was afternoon. Martín and Orfeo were playing a game of cards, with a coolbox of beers at hand. Martín saw that he was awake and came over with a bowl and a spoon.

'You must eat something, Ax. You'll get sick, you'll die.'

He had stopped eating, a sudden and involuntary failure. He'd been trying to play the guitar, and it had opened old wounds. Orfeo the Cuban folded his lean height down beside the bed (shadow of my Sage rises in memory) and took Ax's hand. Ouch. The sores on his wrists were worse again because the cuffs only went on at night. His ankles were giving him hell, also. 'We're your friends, Ax. We don't want you to get sick and we don't want João to hurt you. Come on, you know we don't want to hurt you.'

He couldn't stop the tears.

'If you're my friends, then for God's sake, *let me go—*'

The black man and the white look shook their heads sadly. The cartel would never let him go. They'd given up hope of the ransom. They were keeping Ax out of inertia, like a troublesome pet; but in the end they would kill him, and it would be better so. What else could happen? He imagined himself returning to England after endless years. Sage dead, Fiorinda's agony over, everything that meant anything to us forgotten, what would I do, how would that be life?

Martín's cellphone chimed. He listened, looked significantly at Orfeo, and the two men left the room. Ax heard the Ford start up and rumble away.

He reached over and picked up the guitar.

He couldn't play very well. But he could play. *For in my day, I have had many bitter and shattering experiences in war and on the stormy seas* . . . Where's that from? It's from the *Odyssey*. What if my chip library comes back? What if I have copied stuff, back-up in the grey cells, that I put there without knowing I was doing it? He leaned his head against the wall, his fingers falling into stillness. Ah, there's no pain like hope.

What's that? What's that sound?

He could hear someone playing a guitar. Someone out there in the ghost town or the jungle was playing an electric guitar—

Martín and Orfeo fooled him by coming back from wherever they'd gone on foot. They came up to the room and looked at him, and the guitar he'd hurriedly set aside.

'What was that you were playing?'

'Oh, nothing much.'

'Play it again. I liked that.'

So he played again, casually picking out the tune he had heard.

I'm lonesome since I crossed the hill, and over plain and
    valley—

315

'A strange rhythm,' said Orfeo, who liked to think he was informed about music. 'Where is that from, Ax? West Africa? Mali?'

'Nah,' said Ax. 'Somewhere much weirder than that.'

Felipe and Simon arrived in the RV, bringing cooked rice with tuna flakes. Ax ate, willingly and with appetite, which pleased everyone. Orfeo tested Ax's teeth (a little obsession of his) and insisted Ax eat the lime that had been squeezed over his rice, chewing the skin and pulp. You will thank me, he said, genuinely kind.

Martín wanted them to hear that curious tune. So Ax played 'The Girl I Left Behind Me' for them, but differently this time. Returning power coursed through him; he felt utterly unafraid. The certainty of destiny. The four kidnappers sat there transfixed. 'My God,' said Orfeo, when Ax stopped to rest his hand. 'My God, this is really Ax Preston.'

A day passed, two days passed. Ax didn't do anything, he didn't say anything. He felt as if he was holding his breath. Very early in the tropical morning, on the third day from the afternoon when he had heard that other guitar, Felipe and Simon were sitting with him, and Baz, the younger white guy. They all heard the sound of a helicopter, circling overhead. The cartel representatives hurried down to the street. Ax was left alone, shackled to the wall, listening to the sound effects. A strange vehicle drove up. Then the kidnappers talked with some other people, in Spanish. Suddenly there was gunfire . . . and all hell broke loose. Helicopters. Something heavy (it sounded like an APC) roaring up the washed-out road. Felipe and Simon screaming at each other, having fled back inside the house. More fire, thunder of booted feet, voices shouting in New World Spanish and American English. Men and women in uniform filled the doorway of the dirty room. 'My God,' said the man first through the door. 'My God, this incredible. You were given up for dead, Mr Preston, months ago. This is unbelievable!'

'I'm glad somebody believed,' said Ax.

They freed him from the cuffs. They helped him upright and wrapped him in a blanket (Ax thought of Massacre Night; of the clearing at Spitall's Farm), and took him outside. There were an amazing number of soldiers milling around, American and Mexican. The officer in charge said they'd found the ghost town house a week ago, and come up with the guitar ploy to signal that help was near. Their information had been that Ax was in imminent danger of execution. They'd been monitoring the warm body count in the house, so they'd known it was safe to open fire as soon as those three men came running out . . . The doctor who dressed Ax's sores was a young black bloke with humorous eyes, who appraised Ax's bearded face and said, 'You don't look much like him.'

'Who?'

'Axl Rose. I'm into classic hard rock.'

'Yeah. Sorry. Not a single tattoo. How many of them did you get?'

'We killed three here. We'll get the others, don't worry.'

He was sitting in the back of the APC, dressed in camouflage fatigues, sipping a cup of US armed services bouillion, when the girl who had believed in him arrived. She'd been kept back, out of the firing line. He'd known it *couldn't* be Fiorinda, unless she'd forgotten everything she ever knew about playing guitar. But he'd hoped.

One look at Lurch's face, and he knew the news was not good.

'Hi,' she said. She was holding the Les Paul, in its case. 'I've, um, been carrying this around since you've been gone.' She gave it to him, sat down, took out a pack of cigarettes and gave him those too. 'I'm so glad.'

'So am I,' said Ax. 'Thank you, Kathryn. I owe you. Mightily. Now tell me about Fiorinda. What's been happening in England? I'll need to talk to David Sale—'

'No . . .' The Ugly American wet her lips. 'David Sale's dead.'

'David is *dead*? David Sale is *dead*?' he repeated, stunned.

'Ax, there's no easy way to tell you . . . It's a different world. Things have changed so much. I don't know where to start.'

EIGHT
The Night Belongs To Fiorinda

Fiorinda put the bi-loc phone back in its hiding place in that never-furnished spare room, which had been partially colonised by Sage's stuff, and remained a complete dump. *Sage.* Ghosts of him . . . She was hiding the phone from herself as much as anything. If she had it in sight she'd be calling Ax every five minutes, and she mustn't do that. In the kitchen Elsie was playing don't-step-on-the-floor, mad-eyed little cat perched on the fridge psyching herself up for the suicidal, really insane bit where she leaps for the hood over the cooking hob. Claw marks scoured in plastic showed the frantic record of failure. 'Don't do it,' said Fiorinda. 'Life is still worth living.' She sat at the table, in afternoon sunlight, her hands pressed over her eyes to hold the memory of that grey, cool morning.

The day Sage had left, as soon as it was too late, everything had become clear to her. The nightmares had come from her father; how could she have doubted it? He'd been trying to break up the Triumvirate, and Fiorinda, FOOL, IDIOT, had played right into the bastard's hands. One of those drowning moments when your blood turns to ice-water: if she had only told them . . . If she had told them? What could they have done? A terrified little voice deep inside said there was no defence against her father's power. But that was learned helplessness (hope to God—) and she had remembered the phone now. She had talked to Ax. She wished she had touched him, but no, better not. I don't want bi-loc, I want him *here*. I'll touch him when he's here.

Oh, my Ax. My darling. Sage is gone, there's a monster stalking me, but we love each other again and at this minute *I'm happy*. George said he'd delivered Sage to Caer Siddi without further medical emergencies (and she trusted George not to lie to her about that). So there's hope. Ax will come home; we'll fetch him out. Ax is right, the Heads and I are fucking idiots about Sage. He's got us hypnotised, we're like hypnotised rabbits. Yes master, of course master, of course it's right for you to drag your own brain down your nose with a fishhook . . . *Why* did I let him go?

Shit, why don't I go up there and get him back myself? What a coup!

She knew she was kidding herself. But you have to refuse to believe the worst while it's staring you in the face if you're going to achieve anything at all. That's Ax Preston's philosophy, and we can learn from it, we realists. Elsie jumped: flailed, scrabbling, and fell. No pots on the stove, so not really spectacular. 'Stupid cat,' said Fiorinda; picked her up and carried her, kissing and cuddling, into the living room, where she sat down with her own phone and called Fergal Kearney. Now I will get a grip. For a start, I will find out what's happening with the London barmies. There's something *odd* about this idea that Fergal 'takes over'. The barmy army doesn't work like that, I'm sure it doesn't.

She worked for several hours in Ax's office downstairs: visiting meetings, typing memos, reading reports; tracking the maze of surplus-trading whereby the Volunteer Initiative scraped the barrels of pre-Crisis overproduction. Okay as long as she was locked into the system, lonely and heartsick whenever she raised her head . . . I'll commute to the Insanitude in future, she thought, or Whitehall if I have to. Working here isn't good for morale. At seven in the evening the entryphone chimed. She remembered she'd asked Fergal to come round. She answered, and there he was in a window on her desktop screen.

'Good evening, Fiorinda,' he said gravely, 'will you let me in?'

'Of course.'

They went up to the living-room and talked, and opened some wine. Fiorinda had been sexually active (or acted upon) since she was twelve years old. She had no illusions about the male heterosexual mind, so the unease she felt didn't bother her. His thoughts are probably roaming, he can't help it; he's okay. Strangely enough (or not so strange), she'd never been alone like this with Fergal before. It was mutual. Fergal was shy of female company; Fiorinda was afraid that he'd say something about her father. Having someone around who (maybe) knew Rufus O'Niall's secret made her feel more secure, but she didn't want to talk about it. She hadn't expected him to stay long, but he appeared in no hurry to leave. They were both non-eaters, not interested in food, so they opened more wine and went on chatting.

Next thing Fiorinda knew, she was in bed and Sage was fucking her. A moment at the wellspring, the wingspan sweep of his shoulders, his taper waist, the beautiful muscles of his bum . . . but no. *This is not Sage.* She was in the nightmare, the worst nightmare. She fought out of it and lay there shuddering. No one to call, no comfort. The evening wouldn't come back to her. Damn. I must've got drunk. She couldn't remember what she'd said to Fergal, or what he'd said; the whole conversation was gone. Fuck. I'm an idiot. Something moved heavily beside her in the dark. A body turning over, a disgusting waft of carrion breath. Oh, shit, thought Fiorinda. Shit! What the fuck possessed me—?

Fergal put the bedside light on and there he was,

propped on one elbow, his coarse-grained face and aging, geezer's body, rusty mat of hair around his nipples, slackened flesh over middle-aged muscle, red tan stops at the throat and the rest is cheesy-white. Then he laughed, and all thought of dealing with this daft, embarrassing situation ended.

For a moment Sage was there: a perfect simulacrum, except for the malevolence.

Fiorinda shot out of bed and grabbed her kimono.

'*Who are you?*'

Sage was gone. Fergal sat up, legs over the side of the bed. He had an erection, but his sea-green eyes were blank, bewildered. He looked like an old man in hospital. 'I'm dead.'

'*What?*'

'Oh Jaysus, I'm dead, can't someone kill me?'

'Of course I won't kill you. I don't kill people. What the fuck's going on?'

'Augh! This can't be right. Why the bluidy hell can't someone do something?'

His eyes came into focus. For a moment someone she had never met before was staring at her, out of such naked fathomless fear and agony it caught her breath—

The entryphone light on the wall by the bed was winking.

Fergal leaned towards it and listened. 'Aye,' he said, 'come up.'

She ran into the living-room. This is going to be bad, I'm an idiot, *why* am I here alone? Because we are wild and free, citizens of Utopia. Because I'm supposed to be safe, Brixton is my . . . The door opened. Three big, Celtic-style barmy army types came in. Oh yes, she thought, I remember. Fergal took over. One of the men grabbed her. She didn't struggle or scream. If I'm to die, I'd die before I could be reached. If not, I don't want this public, not until I *think*. The other two started going through the room.

'What are you looking for?' she asked, calmly.

'Something they can use,' said Fergal Kearney, coming out of the bedroom, and she noticed that the brogue had gone out of his voice. He was dressed. He sat at the back of the big open room, turning a chair to face the scene that Fiorinda and the three men made: very relaxed, one leg crossed over the other. She didn't understand, and then she did, because one of the barmies had found Elsie.

Poor Elsie, she's not half as tough as she makes out. She was scared out of her mind, so cowed she didn't even spit until the men began to hurt her. Then she spat and clawed and bit and yowled and struggled, but it didn't do her any good. Fiorinda yelled, 'STOP IT!' and 'LEAVE HER ALONE YOU BASTARDS! WHAT DO YOU WANT?' But they weren't going to stop, whatever Fiorinda surrendered. This wasn't that kind of torture. There was only one way to stop what was happening.

The agonised little body went limp.

The two men put Elsie down on the rug, tried her eyes and shook her a bit.

'The cat's dead, Rufus,' said one of them, doubtfully.

Fergal laughed. (No. That's not Fergal Kearney. It never was.) A rumble of soft thunder. A body that belies its occupant. Behind him on the wall Mr Preston and Mr Pender were taking sherry, in a clear, cool, dispassionate light . . . She was conscious of the grip on her arms as something that was happening far away, but acutely, immediately conscious of each breath she took. The sound of air taken in, the expansion of her lungs. The cat's little mad presence trotting around the flat, insistent lap-seeking missile. She loves Ax best. She loves him with all her tiny heart. But Sage and I, we can be useful occasionally. We know where the food is, we'll watch when she shows off.

'What do you want?'

'I want you.'

She stared at him, fighting her thoughts into order, fighting terror and bewilderment: seeing the long masquerade, stunned and yet not surprised. *The first time I met Fergal Kearney, I felt sick to death . . . But Fergal saved Ax's life! Oh, he didn't want Ax dead. That would have been too easy and too quick, he wanted to* destroy *Ax. That's what this has been about. He's not going to kill me either. He doesn't have to rape me, he can take me any time, he just did it. No, he's not going to kill me. He wants more than that.*

The smile that Fergal's face was wearing sat uneasily in the facial muscles of a difficult, diffident loser of a dead artist. 'This is nothing,' he said. 'This is just so you know where we are at. If you're wise, you'll tell no one. Think about your options.'

She was released. The four men walked out, shutting the door behind them.

She listened, and counted them out of the front door. Then she ran to the spare bedroom, unearthed the bi-loc, ran with it into the unused bathroom adjoining and smashed it on the terrazzo floor. *Oh God, if he'd known I had this: a piece of weird tech* slaved to Ax's chip *. . . Oh God, what use he could have made of it.* Trembling, she swept up the bits and dumped them in the plastic and metals bin. *One problem dealt with.*

She went back to Elsie. The men had put all the lights on; the room seemed very bright. She dimmed them – and remembered that the fake Fergal had been able to light the ATP lamp by the bed, which shouldn't have been possible without the treatment. *The only thing I know is that I don't know if he has any limits. Oh, shit. Think, think, think . . .*

'Elsie,' she whispered, 'you can come out now, sweetheart.'

The tortoiseshell cat stirred, curling herself up as best

she could. She licked one of her paws and looked up at Fiorinda, bewildered.

'Now, darling,' said Fiorinda, stroking the little warm head, 'listen to me. I'm not completely helpless. In a way I've been preparing myself for this for, ooh, a long time. Long time. In a way, I always knew it would come. There are things that I can do, or at least things I can try. I've been incredibly stupid. Well, I don't know, maybe not so stupid . . . Anyway, I'm on the case now. I think I can hold things together. I think I can hold the pass until my Ax comes home. But I can't protect *you*, Elsie, my darling. I can't let this happen again; and it would.'

Her heart stood still, her gaze poised in darkness. *I can't protect Ax's little cat.*

'So you have to go to sleep now. Curl up and go to sleep. You know Ax loves you. And I love you, and even Sage loves you, though he pretends not. I've seen him stroke you. I've caught him *talking* to you, before now. So you go quietly to sleep, little one, thinking about how we love you. Go to sleep, go to sleep.'

She carried on stroking and murmuring until she was sure that Elsie was really dead this time. Then she packed up, swiftly and resolutely, and headed for Rivermead, just as the dawn was breaking. The new building, the fixed abode she'd never wanted, already consigned to sorrow and disaster, was the place where she would fight her battle. Not on holy ground. She took the body with her because it was no time to go digging holes in the Brixton garden; and otherwise someone might find a dead Elsie in the trash and think that was *very* weird.

The day after Fiorinda moved to Rivermead, David Sale called her with urgent news from the Internet Commission. Mr Preston has disappeared. The quarantine talks had gone very well indeed, but then Ax had vanished. Everything possible was being done to trace him. They agreed to keep it to themselves for now. 'We don't know,' said Fiorinda – who knew Ax had been alive and fine, and on his way home, the morning before, but could not tell David this. 'I don't think he counts as missing yet. It could be he's ducked under their radar because he wanted to. He may have his own agenda.'

Ax didn't come home. She could not call him: she had smashed the bi-loc. She slept uneasily, and woke, and wandered her shadowy rooms. She was not alone. There were plenty of people in the building, but no one else slept in her suite. She had been dreaming of her early childhood. She found a tall dim mirror, framed in metal, and stood looking into it, still in the atmosphere of the dream, still held by scraps of memory she had not known she possessed. Who is this woman in the mirror, this sallow, worn-down redhead with the flinching shoulders and look of dumb endurance? That's my mother. What a dog's life she must have led, long ago, between him and Carly. How English, how familiar. The horrors that hide behind closed doors, in suburban streets . . . Fiorinda's Aunt Carly, the procuress, had told Fiorinda the child that her mother had mortally offended the music biz. She'd been cast out, and that was how she'd become a bitter, reclusive has-been. Fiorinda had looked for traces of this ancient scandal when she was grown – and found none. There had been no upset. Suzy Slater had just dropped out and vanished, for no visible reason, after her break up with Rufus O'Niall.

It was because you knew, she thought. It was because of what he did to you. You tried to keep me out of it, but you knew that one day he would come back for me and there'd be nothing you could do. No wonder you were the way you were.

'Mum?' She touched the glass.

I never had a mother before.

Once upon a time there were two sisters. Suzy the journalist had an affair with a big rockstar and got pregnant by him. Little sister, whose career consisted of wanting to be around celebrities, was incredibly jealous. They had a mum who claimed she was a witch. Suzy didn't believe in that stuff, but Carly had inherited her mother's 'psychic powers'. She spotted Rufus O'Niall as a magic-maker, and she let him know it. So then Rufus started fucking them both, enjoying this very piquant situation. It was Rufus, Carly and Suzy, and Suzy's baby, until Rufus was tired of the rows and left for fresh pastures. But he didn't forget he had a daughter. In due course he sent Carly to the cold house of Fiorinda's childhood, the year when Fiorinda's mum was ill in hospital. And Carly took the girl to be seduced by her father

A child, three years old, peeping in through a bedroom door, sees something that she doesn't understand. When you're three you don't understand it's *weird*, only that Mummy's crying. They're hurting Mummy and Mummy can't stop them. MUMMY'S NO USE. You have to get to hate Mummy because how else could you bear it, seeing her so helpless? You grow up from being three to being eleven, and you're a hard little piece: gullible, selfish, greedy. You're easy meat when Carly arrives on Rufus's mission, looking so glamorous. You don't have the slightest idea, and when Mum finds out what's going on, she says nothing because she dares not. She's afraid, so afraid.

The story ends happily, with the little girl running away and making a life for herself . . . But the happy ending didn't work. Fiorinda had tried to make a life for herself, but all she'd achieved was to bring ruin on the people she loved.

He's going to destroy England, because of me, and I don't know how to stop him.

*

There had been a leap in the traffic on the Internet Commissioners' satellite link with GCHQ. The media folk were onto it, and they'd become less docile without Ax around. Somehow, suddenly, there was a buzz of rumour. Allie and Fiorinda and David had to go public before worse damage ensued. Yes, Ax has been in America. He bust the data quarantine deadlock in undercover talks. Yes, it's true we can't trace him just now, and that the US authorities believe he may have been kidnapped. But there's every reason to hope he's alive and well.

As soon as we have further information we'll let you know.

On a warm June evening, while this news was spreading through the country to shock and disbelief, Fergal Kearney came to Rivermead. Fergal had taken to going about with an entourage. Three big barmy army squaddies (unfamiliar faces, but who knows all the London barmies?) were always with him. Nobody liked this. It was a point of honour with the Few that except on public occasions they walked unprotected in the crowd. But no one said anything, because Ferg was a well-loved figure who had a lot of credit. He'd come to see Fiorinda, nothing odd about that. He went to her rooms, with his friends.

She was alone up there. She had too much on her mind for casual company.

Dusk filled the wide windows of the solar. The sky was overcast; elven glimmers of ATP light marked the tented town. She opened the door for her visitors, walked away from them and stood looking out: Fiorinda with her hair brushed and burnished, wearing an antique violet satin sheath dress that left her arms bare, and narrow dark blue trousers. There was a fire in the grate, in spite of the warmth of the night, and the air was scented by big planters of living flowers. Fergal's men took the rock and roll princess and placed her in one of the cross-framed Roman chairs. They set another chair, an oversized, hieratic wheelback, opposite. Fergal went to stand beside this throne, his eyes dull, his gap-toothed mouth hanging open.

The timbers of the cross-framed chair sprang back into life, just as they had left it. Branches clothed in cold, sodden grey bark swept up and engulfed the girl's body, bearing down thickly on her arms and across her breast. Grey twigs tangled into her hair and tugged backwards, holding her head like a bridle so her face was lifted, chin up.

Something like smoke came out of Fergal's mouth, trailed to the floor and grew. Then a big man with chestnut skin and the curling, shining black hair of a Restoration monarch sat in the wheelback chair. He wore a dark purple mantle with golden gleams in it and fringes of gold, over fashionable evening casuals, Italian sandals on his feet.

He was not young, but still flamboyantly goodlooking.

'I knew,' said Fiorinda, her stretched throat moving, her eyes forced to gaze at him, 'that if I stuck around here long enough, eventually you would turn up.'

'Did you want me to turn up?'

'Oh yes . . . Rufus, I have an offer for you.'

He laughed. 'Really? Make me your offer.'

'I will be your consort. I will be everything you want me to be.'

'Everything I want?' he murmured. 'What a promise.'

'Only you have to leave Ax and Sage, and all of Ax's friends, alone.'

'Hm.'

'Forever.'

'Now, Fiorinda. I don't sign contracts that say *forever*.'

'I think you do. I think you've signed one already; why not another? Come on, don't balderdash me. Say yes, why piss around? You know you're going to.'

He laughed again, soft thunder. 'My bossy little girl. You haven't changed!'

'Well,' she said, 'think about it.'

Rufus raised an eyebrow, incredulous. 'I should *think* about it?'

'Listen. You don't just want me, you want the Rock and Roll Reich. I know you do. You want it partly to get back at Ax, but you really *want* it too. Ireland's still living in the modern world, and you don't like that. Ax's England as your private fief would suit you down to the ground. You took your time putting this together. You were the one who set David up with the human sacrifice ring, and then brought us the evidence so we'd have to do something about it, and Ax would be forced to take power in a way he never wanted. You sent me those bad dreams, because you knew I'd be stubborn and I wouldn't tell them what was happening, and it would make big trouble between me and my boyfriends. You've been very patient. Why rush it now? Sage is gone. Ax isn't coming back either. They're finished. You know that, and I know that. The people need time to get used to the idea. What you should do is you should *court* me. You court me, you win me over. Gradual change, we both have our credibility intact. Do we have a deal?'

The three squaddies were looking nowhere, doing nothing. Fergal Kearney, the dead man, stood unoccupied, like a strange, awkward polychrome sculpture. Rufus sat and smiled, not at all displeased at having his own plans explained to him by his little girl.

'Let me see.' He rose, a haze like smoke around him, crossed the floor and leaned over her, appreciation gleaming in his eyes, the thick shining curls of his hair seeming to touch her shoulders. He stroked his lower lip, weighing it up. His hands were manicured, the oval nails stained, not varnished, a deep blood-red.

'If you try to run away I will not come after you. I will stay here like a fox in a chicken-run. You don't want that. If you tell anyone what I am, I will know it and I will kill

330

them *instantly*, man woman or child. They will be where Fergal is. Do you know where he is? He is not dead, he's in Hell. A real, physical scientific Hell, Fiorinda. It doesn't matter that his body will die eventually, he will still be there. Do you understand? I can make eternal torment a reality.'

She nodded, as far as the bridle would let her. 'Okay, got that.'

'If you leave your body, at any time: the same. I will put your friends in Hell.'

'Leave my—?' said Fiorinda, and then, 'Oh.'

Rufus chuckled. 'Yes. You understand. But you know so little . . . *You have no idea*, my child, my only true child. Don't you want me to teach you? Aren't you even curious?'

She stared back at him, unafraid. 'There isn't anything special about what you can do. Magic is just power. You have the power. I know that. The rest is verbiage.'

'Ah! You still have your thorns. My briar rose.'

He stooped, as if he would kiss her.

'You'll take me when we seal our bargain,' she said. 'Not before.'

Rufus laughed, stepped back and bowed. 'So be it. I consent. I will wait.'

He returned to the wheelback chair and sat for a while watching her. Then the living ghost vanished. Fergal came back to life; the squaddies returned from their blank patch. The men left. When they were gone, the Roman chair reverted to its normal state. Fiorinda dropped to the floor, arms huddled round her knees.

Well, that didn't go too badly.

When she could walk without her legs giving way she went for a prowl around the building. She thought what had happened must have had an effect: she'd find people crying, hiding under their beds. No one had noticed anything untoward.

331

Everything okay? Yeah. G'night, Fiorinda. They liked seeing her around at night.

Back in her rooms, she crouched by the dying fire. My father has sold his soul to the devil (I don't believe in the devil, but it describes the situation). I don't know the extent of his weaponry, I don't know how I can stop him in the end . . . But one step at a time. *One step at a time*, that's the only way. He likes to listen to me talking bullshit. I have real power over him, power he chooses to give me, but it's still real. Have to see how long I can spin that out. He's old; there might be something there. And I'll think of something, it will come to me. Oh, *fucking hell*. I can't protect forty million people!

But I can try.

Fiorinda ran the Few ragged through the dreadful length of that summer. She never stopped. She spoke to the nation officially (such of the nation as could reach a Big Screen or a working tv) only once, making a firm plea for calm; but she spoke to the Counterculture and the crowds at the free Crisis Management gigs incessantly – schmoozing every front row, trailing around every campground, as if bent on telling the people of England *one by one*: that Sage would achieve the Zen Self, and return in triumph, and Ax would come home with the end of data quarantine in his pocket; and meantime, business as usual. Utopia on a liferaft, stick together against the dark. We'll do this for Ax. He trusts us to keep on track . . . The bricks-and-mortar media folk had finally started noticing that the Celtic Movement was actually the majority in the English Counterculture. Fiorinda didn't let that story go unchallenged, she insisted that the Celtics were also Ax's people, but she puzzled her friends by ignoring the resurgence of things like illegal ritual sacrifice. They began to wonder at some of her behaviour.

The nonstop Festival Season ended. The anniversary of Ax's inauguration passed.

Sayyid Mohammad Zayid, Ax's sponsor in the Faith and the leader of English Islam, came to London on a delicate mission. He and Allie met Fiorinda in the small office she was using at the Insanitude. It was October the fifteenth. There had been no news of Ax since he had disappeared in May. Mohammad and Allie had to tell Fiorinda that her relationship with the Irishman, Fergal Kearney, was causing scandal. He'd become her most trusted advisor, and people didn't like it. The Islamics, especially the young men who were Ax's most passionate supporters, believed that Fergal was influencing Fiorinda so that she favoured the Celtics whenever there was trouble. (There'd been many outbreaks of street-fighting between 'Celtic' and 'techno' gangs in the past few months, in spite of all Fiorinda's efforts to keep the peace.)

Fiorinda in person, spruce in her dove-grey trouser suit, an indigo shirt and a crimson string tie, bearing her terrible grief with grace and pride, defeated them. They tried to talk to her, but she was a stone wall. She would not take their advice.

Mohammad Zayid believed that Aoxomoxoa's love for his friend's wife – in his mind he called Fiorinda Ax's wife, he was too old to change his habits – should have remained chaste. He was sure Sage had been right to repent, and dedicate himself to the great scientific project which was also a spiritual quest. But he attached no blame to Fiorinda. This wise and courageous young woman, protector of the poor, with a strange but innocent light in the back of her grey eyes, is never to blame.

'Aye, well, we'll leave that . . . But you should be thinking of another address to the nation. It's five months now, lass. The troops need your encouragement.'

'There's nothing new to say,' said Fiorinda. 'We hang on, *keeping the Celtics on board*, until Ax comes home. End of story. I don't want to say it too often. I'll get tired of repeating myself. I'll sound insincere.'

Mohammad, the strongly built, badger-bearded York-shireman in his good, subdued tailoring, was looking older, and very weary. He had loved Ax like a son.

'I know it's hard, Fiorinda. I'm not asking you to give up hope. But—'

'Did you do anything about getting a new kitten?' asked Allie, helplessly.

Ax's cat had disappeared when Fiorinda moved to Rivermead. It's the way cats behave, but Fiorinda had loved Elsie, and she must be so lonely—

Fiorinda rolled her eyes. 'Oh, for fuck's sake, Allie . . . er, sorry, Mohammad—'

The three of them went along together to the Office. A much-travelled Jiffy bag had turned up that the postroom thought the Few should look at. There was still masses of this kind of stuff: the fanmail of Ax's disappearence. At first they'd opened it all personally. Now they let the postroom and the police filter everything; the loss of that chore had been another small death. Fiorinda sat down by Fergal Kearney, substitute bodyguard. Mohammad, with a curious glance and a reserved nod for the Irishman, took the place on her other side.

The inner circle was united again, their quarrel over the Zen Self forgotten. Everyone who had been with Ax on Massacre Night was here today, except for Peter Stannen. He was at Caer Siddi in North Wales. The Heads believed that Sage was still alive. They were obstinately trying to get in contact with him, to tell him what had happened.

'This could be a live one,' said Chip, 'if you go by the stamps.'

The others set their teeth, glancing at him with hatred. But the boy can't help it.

'Oh Chip,' sighed Fiorinda. 'Don't do that to us. Please.'

'It's been through quarantine,' said the techie who'd brought up the packet. 'It passed straight through at port of entry and ended up in our normal mailbag. We've given

334

it the usual tests, and then some. It's harmless: I mean, you can open it.'

Fiorinda looked at him. He kept his face blank. She put on latex gloves and goggles. The security techs insisted on that, even while they told you a strange packet was perfectly okay. Her tongue felt thick in her mouth; her heart had started thumping. Layers of tape had been stripped away, and the seal loosened. She finished the job, aware that this was ritual. I must, officially, be the first to see—

There was a sheet of folded paper. She glanced at it, and passed it to Mohammad. There was a ring. Everyone knew the ring. There was a small bundle of surgical dressing, stained with old blood and fluid. Fiorinda peeled it open, releasing a faded waft of putrefaction. A silicon wafer lay there, clotted with tissue and tangled with a few long, dark hairs. Fiorinda took off her goggles and stared at it, breathing slow.

'It's his warehouse stack. They've sent us his brain implant.'

Verlaine gave a sob, and stifled it with his fists. No one else made a sound, but the circle of tables rang with shock, and acceptance. Terrible relief.

'Oh God,' whispered Felice, at last. 'Oh, *Ax*—'

'Ah,' breathed Mohammad. He bent his head and murmured in Arabic, a prayer that no one else here could join; a part of Ax's life that none of them had understood.

'He isn't dead,' said Fiorinda, tallow-pale. 'He is not dead.'

'Be Jaysus,' said Fergal Kearney, shaking his head, 'this drawing out the agony is doing no good. Ye might be better off to face it, Fiorinda me darling. Time's up.'

Typical Fergal, crashingly tactless whatever the circumstances. Even at this juncture, the Few winced and looked away. What does she see in him?

'Time is not up,' said Fiorinda, very distinctly. 'This is

not the moment for any sudden changes. That would be crazy.'

Fergal cleared his throat. 'Maybe yez'll change your mind.'

She ignored this. 'I'll have to call David. Allie, we'll need you too.'

The Prime Minister came to the Insanitude at once. Fiorinda and Allie spent the afternoon with him. The packet, the ransom note, the chip and Ax's carnelian ring were taken away for forensics; the news was despatched to the US search operation, via GCHQ. They still had no direct contact with the USA. The connectivity deal was going through, but it had been delayed by Ax's disappearence . . . The kidnappers wanted a global ban on synthetic cocaine, an end to European taxes and regulation on imported recreational drugs (except alcohol and tobacco), and a hefty sum in hard currency. They wanted these terms made public, and publicly accepted, on all major tv channels and news-sites, or his friends would never see Ax Preston alive again.

'If we could offer them the money,' said Fiorinda. 'If we could find the money—'

'We can't do any of the other things,' said Allie. 'But we could try that.'

'I let him go,' said David bleakly. 'I was the last person to speak to him, I was excited and I told him he should go. I had no right. I can never forgive myself.'

They tried to draft a press briefing, but it was beyond them. They decided it could wait until tomorrow. Fiorinda went back to the Brixton flat, refusing to let Allie come with her. She desperately needed to be alone. She knew that David and Allie had been humouring her . . . The ransom note is gibberish. Ax has to be dead. The bad guys cut his head open. He's dead. The flat was immaculate. The night her father had revealed himself she'd tried to clean the patch of cat shit, piss and blood from the rug where Elsie had died. William the cleaning person had done a much better job . . . She knew the aching cleanliness was an expression of William's love and sympathy, but it felt like a morgue. She fetched Ax's old leather coat, which had been sent back from Amsterdam where he'd left it behind, and sat on the couch by the cold gas stove, hugging it. Will they give me back his ring? When can I have his ring? She couldn't cry. She just wanted Ax's ring.

She would have stayed like that all night. But something started to grow in her: a really horrible premonition. Finally her phone rang.

'Hello, Fiorinda.'

'Hello, David. What is it? Is there more news?'

'No. I . . . just . . . wanted to say I'm sorry for everything. He was so good to me. You guys, all so good to me. I should have stopped him. My fault. America. Not safe.'

'*David*, where are you? What are you doing? I'm coming round.'

The phone was dead, but thank God it had been a landline call and she could trace it.

David had started using heroin again. Fiorinda had spotted him, challenged him over it and made him promise to lay off: but she was very scared. She took a taxi to Battersea to pick up George and Bill and the Heads' First Aid kit. Within an hour from the phone call they were at the condo, near Canary Wharf, where the Prime Minister had a bolthole. She'd kept trying to call ahead all the way; no answer. They went straight up. David's Secret Service minder was sitting in the lobby outside the third-floor flat, watching tv. He didn't know anything was wrong; he thought the PM was asleep. He was shocked to find that somehow his own phone had switched itself off, which was why Fiorinda had been getting no response. The door of the flat was locked; no reply from within. Fiorinda was *incandescent*. She insisted they must get inside, at once, right now—

And there he was, the Prime Minister of England, in his style-catalogue furnished hideaway, with his needle and his spoon: dying the rock and roll death.

They should have been able to save him. George and Bill were perfect masters at drugs-related First Aid; he was still breathing, all the signs were of a simple overdose. But it didn't work out. When they got him to hospital the whitecoats discovered massive and irreparable brain damage. Twelve hours later Fiorinda, who was at Battersea waiting for news, got a call to say that David's wife (they were amicably separated), and his grown-up son, had been advised that there was no hope. They'd decided to let David go.

The media of the three neighbour nations called it a tragic accident. Crisis Europe tabloids invented a conspiracy linking the death of the PM to Ax's disappearance, probably masterminded by the ex-Royals. The English, Countercultural and otherwise, took it for granted that David had topped himself due to horrible stress, but they forgave him. He'd had his faults, the old raver, but he'd been much loved. He had a cracking funeral, watched by millions on the big screens of the Countercultural Very Large Array.

Allie put the most hopeful possible spin on the ransom note, and the media folk backed her up as best they could. It was lucky they hadn't briefed the press already the night that David died. They were able to make something of the cruel irony: if only David Sale had lived to know the 'terrific good news'.

Fiorinda understood that her bluff had been called.

Time's up.

Ferg called, Fiorinda. He says you invited him to stay the night. Shall I make up a guest room? Fiorinda's friends were suspicious, but the Rivermead housekeeper had no idea. She wouldn't dream of questioning Fiorinda's behaviour, no matter what, but she thought Fergal Kearney was a good old geezer, a kind uncle, a shoulder for Fiorinda to cry on.

'Yes,' said Fiorinda. 'Any of the rooms on my floor, that would be fine.'

The night was dark. The Rivermead building had no draughts, no sighing woodwork or rattling windowframes, but there was a wind blowing somewhere. The leaves on the oaks at Tyller Pystri are tarnished green and gold. Somewhere, anywhere, three people could lie under a hedge, rain on their faces, without a house or a home, no direction known, don't care. And I loved them both. Lots of people have weird relationships, why shouldn't we? Nobody understood, nobody knew. It was just us, and no one else.

She stood in front of the tall, metal-framed mirror in her cream and green kimono. It was very pretty. Such a fresh green, reaching up from the hem in abstract fronds, into magnolia-petal clouds. Dr Barnardo's, Battersea, long ago . . . Why should I be afraid? Ax loves me, Sage loves me. I love them both. Everything real is good, and *this will work*. Until I think of something. She let the gown fall open and looked at the girl's body, still yellow-brown wherever it had been exposed to the summer's sun. He likes his daughter to be white, gets a kick out of having a white girl-child in bed; but tough. It'll have to do.

This is my body, for the last time.

She went to meet her father.

Olwen Devi was in the Zen Self main space, helping to dismantle one of the more complex neuroscience rides. It was a cold and rainy morning; the rides area was empty except for Zen Selfers. They were making their preparations for departure very quietly, so that when they were ready they could vanish overnight . . . Fiorinda wandered in, wearing her shapeless old rain jacket over the violet satin sheath, and her army boots. She came over and watched, head down, fists buried in her pockets.

'Rats leave sinking ship,' she said. 'Very wise, Welsh rats. Where you going?'

Olwen straightened. 'Yes, we're leaving. I'm sorry, Fio, but we must.'

'No, don't tell me,' said Fiorinda, 'that's right, *don't tell me*. Don't trust me.'

The rock and roll princess had lost weight she could ill afford to lose in the last months. She still looked wonderful on stage, but this morning her sallow, rain-streaked face was haggard and her stubborn jaw looked oversized. Her eyes were sick-animal. She walked away. She had no business in the Zen Self tent. She was just moving about at random, because it eases the pain; and stealing a moment of truth. Got nothing to say to Olwen Devi, but at least don't have to put a face on. Nothing to hide.

'Wait—'

The guru had followed her, and laid a hand on her sleeve. Fiorinda looked at the ring on Olwen's finger. Could Serendip do anything? Nah. She's just a computer, dumb bundle of noughts and ones, however you dress it up.

'What?'

'Fiorinda, removal of an implant, even if it's done crudely, need not be a disaster. Ax was supposed to be away for six weeks. That chip ought to have come out as soon as he got back. It was not in a good state. You may take it from me, if it hadn't been removed, he would be in worse trouble by now.'

Fiorinda nodded, indifferent, and wandered off into the rain.

There was no question of a violent coup after David Sale's death. The remains of the Coalition Cabinet stepped down of their own free will. A cross-party group, drawn mainly from the Green Second Chamber, took over the reins. They invited special representatives from the CCM majority – Celtics, that is – to join them. It was the end of the hybrid system (said the takeover-advertising), and the first genuinely Countercultural Government of England. The Few were not surprised to find that Benny Preminder, their hateful Countercultural Liasion Secretary, was closely involved in these changes. They were dismayed, but they had a contingency plan. The Rock and Roll Reich could work with a hostile government.

Keep up the free gigs: they've become a reassuring ritual. Look after the drop-out hordes. Protect the science base.

Fall back. Adjust. We don't need to be centre stage to keep Ax's vision alive.

Pray that nothing worse happens.

One night in November Rob Nelson woke up in a hotel, on the motorway somewhere outside Northampton. Felice was sleeping in the bed beside him. Dora and Cherry were in the living-room of the suite with the babies, Ferdelice and Mamba, on the fold-down sofabed. Members of the Snake Eyes rhythm section were snoring gently on the sofas and the floor in the main bedroom. Room space was tight: this place was half closed-down. The band had been on stage until after midnight, playing for free in a dance venue that was icy-cold until the sweat started running, and now it was . . . He looked at his watch. *Two a.m.* Shit. Everyone else was dead to the world. He got up, feeling very angry and wishing he'd elected to sleep on the bus. No one comes hammering on my door at 2 a.m., waking my babies. That's out of order! It was Doug Hutton standing there.

'What are you doing here? Were you banging on my door?'

'I'm sorry, Rob,' said the Few's security chief. 'I had to fetch you, not call you.'

'What's wrong with using a mobile phone?'

'I'm not sure. You'd better get dressed. I think it's urgent.'

Wondering who the fuck was hassling him, Rob followed Doug through spooky dark corridors to the barely lit, dilapidated lobby, his breath puffing ahead of him in the cold air. He was amazed to see Fiorinda, huddled by the desk in her old winter coat, her hair wrapped up in a scarf, her pale face bleak and sullen.

'How did *you* get here?' he gasped.

'Doug drove me. What did you think? The common people can't get around much anymore, but I'm a rock and roll princess. I have dazzling privileges. Come on.'

He felt wrong-footed. Fiorinda could still have that effect on him, shades of his old distrust for Ax's arrogant toffee-nosed new girlfriend. Outside the front doors there was a big car waiting. He got into the back, thinking, *there's a reason for this, so I'm not going to shoot my mouth off*, and was amazed again to find Dilip sitting there, silently.

'What's going on?'

'I don't know,' said the mixmaster. 'Trouble of some kind. She's not saying.'

They drove into the countryside, along very dark lanes. Fiorinda was giving Doug directions using a penlight and a road atlas. At last they stopped and pulled off the road into a field-entrance. 'You stay here, Doug,' said Fiorinda. 'You two, with me.'

There was a low, white-painted fence, and beyond it an unlit carpark in the middle of nowhere. Trees loomed over it, the nearly naked branches stirring in a night wind against a pallid, suffused sky. Fiorinda stood looking round, still saying nothing.

'I was nightwatchman,' said Dilip quietly, 'on the late shift. She arrived, with Doug. She said I had to come with her. Not another word. What d'you think's going on?'

'I don't know.'

Nightwatchman meant Dilip'd been in charge at the club for the late shift at the Insanitude, which finished at midnight in winter these days; and it was very quiet. Immix and fx were out of style: too techno. They both looked at Fiorinda, standing there in the dark with her head bowed, shoulders hunched and her arms wrapped around herself. It had crossed both of their minds that she'd actually flipped. It wouldn't be unexpected. She had been behaving strangely since Ax's chip had come home, or maybe even longer. It had shocked everyone when they'd realised she was sleeping with Fergal. Not that they begrudged her any comfort she could find, but it was so *unlikely*, and she must know she was giving serious offence to the Islamics—

'Fio?' said Dilip, cautiously, 'are you okay?'

'This is a Roman site,' said Fiorinda, as if he hadn't spoken. 'Or pre-Roman. There's the remains of a theatre, through the trees. That's where the pit will be.'

Rob had noticed a display board by the fence, traces of laminated surface dimly gleaming. So this was some kind of ancient monument, and a venue for Celtic ritual. His skin crept. Either she's flipped or she's up to something very screwy . . . Then he saw the dark-coloured van, no lights, parked in a corner. A jolt of adrenalin: something rose up from the ground there, bigger than a big dog, blackness visible on darkness.

Fiorinda grabbed his hand. Rob was instantly disarmed. 'It's okay, Fio—'

'We can do this,' she whispered, intensely, '*we can win*, we can all get safe home, but you have to trust me. *Please* . . . Don't either of you move until I tell you.'

She'd grabbed hold of Dilip too. They didn't know what she was talking about. She let go of them and walked towards the van. Something like black smoke moved to and fro as if measuring the threat she posed, as if it was thinking of springing at her throat. Rob thought he saw eyes, and the shine of bared teeth.

Dilip caught his breath. They both started forward.

She turned on them savagely. 'I said *stay put*. Do what you're fucking TOLD!'

So they stayed put while Fiorinda walked slowly up to the dark-coloured van: and then the black smoke thing was gone. The branches of the trees tossed and sighed, like restless, barely contained wild animals.

'Okay,' hissed Fiorinda, 'we're in. Come on. Help me.' They went to join her. She gave Rob a tyre-iron that she had been hiding under her coat. He grasped it with relief. Things began to make sense, some kind of sense. He forced the doors. Muffled shapes shifted and made whimpering sounds inside the cold, naked shell of metal. Fiorinda produced a torch and switched it on.

'Oh *shit*,' breathed Dilip.

'I know what the sacrifice is for, now,' she whispered. 'I know what *bringing on the dark* means. Let's get them free.'

Rob had a pocket-knife, and so did Dilip. Fiorinda had a knife too, but while Rob and Dilip were cutting the kids' bonds and getting the gags out of their mouths she got down again and kept watch, leaving them the torch. The human sacrifice victims were two boys and two girls, white kids; in their mid-teens at a rough guess. They were skinny and draggle-haired, but clean as butcher's meat; and dressed in thin white linen tunics, tied at the waist with gold cord. 'Why did the bastards leave them dumped here?' wondered Rob. 'I don't think they were dumped,' said Dilip. 'They weren't left unattended.'

The kids didn't speak, or even sob, when the gags came off.

'Who did this to you?' asked Rob, gently. 'Who brought you here?'

They just shivered. They were in shock, or drugged, or

scared catatonic . . . The men looked for something to wrap them in, but there was nothing in the van, not even a tarp to hide this horrible freight. They stripped off their coats and covered the children, one coat between two. 'This country—' sighed Rob. 'We've got an epidemic of psychos now . . . is there a light switch in here?'

'I can't see one. We should call the police. Unless Fio already has.'

They heard vehicles approaching, and coming close. Rob got down to join Fio; Dilip stayed with the kids. A big van without lights came into the carpark. It stopped. Someone switched night-filtered headlights on. Dilip thought of the black-smoke creature, which Fiorinda had outfaced. In certain states of consciousness the internal and the external world can change places: the presence of horror can be visible. Rob had a moment to realise that if this *wasn't* the police they were in big trouble—

It *was* the police: Fiorinda had called them. They took over; the rockstars bowed out.

Fiorinda had had an anonymous tip-off from a Celtic informant. She'd called the police and rushed to the place herself, picking up Dilip and Rob on the way. She hadn't told them what was going on because she'd been hoping it wasn't true. When she saw that the van was there, she'd been too shocked and scared to explain right on the spot . . . Sorry, Rob, sorry, Dilip. Didn't mean to freak you out.

'Jaysus fockin' God!' said Fergal, when they were debriefing this incident in the Office. 'An' what if it'd been a fockin' ambush, Fiorinda me love? Whut then? Whut business was it of yez to go after these lost kids?'

'They're friends of Ax Preston's,' said Fiorinda. 'That makes them my business.'

Fergal gave her a fond, gap-toothed grin. 'Aye, well, fair enough. But ye'd be better to stick to yer volunteer work, darling. T'wud be more fitting.'

Dilip and Rob refrained from comment. There were things that Fiorinda's explanation did not explain, but they didn't want to talk about it with Fergal around.

Nobody could talk to Fiorinda, because Fergal was always around. He'd become Fiorinda's official boyfriend over-night; he was lording it over the London barmies; he was getting courted by the new government. The Few were being sidelined, but not Fergal Kearney. They saw the way things were going, but they couldn't believe it. They honestly didn't care about their own loss of status, but the idea of Fergal taking the place of Ax and Sage was *outrageous*. How could Fiorinda let this happen?

Allie finally cornered the elusive princess in the Office at the end of a working day. 'Sorry, Allie, I'm in a hurry,' said Fiorinda breezily. 'I have a gig in Richmond.'

She was still doing lo-key solo spots, though Fergal didn't like it.

This is where she rips my throat out, thought Allie. But it's either now, or I ask her secretary for an appointment, and get told Miss Fiorinda's very busy. My God.

'No, you have to give me five minutes. I need to talk to you about Fergal.'

Fiorinda, poised for flight, seemed to change her mind, or relax her guard. 'Oh yeah? Do tell. I'm betraying Ax? Fuck it, what do you expect me to do? Turn celibate for the rest of my life? That may be your little bolthole, Allie. It's not for me.'

'I wasn't going to say anything about—'

'Hey, maybe you think I should committ suttee, only we'd have to burn me with just the implant and a bit of dirty lint, not having a dead body.'

'NO!' yelled Allie. 'Knock it off, Fiorinda! That's NOT what I think. I think my leader, my ONLY HOPE in a shit situation, has become so infatuated with a deceitful, destructive middle-aged geezer that her *stupid* choice of play-away fun is ONCE MORE going to rip the country apart—'

Oh no. Didn't mean to say that. Didn't mean to say any of that—

Fiorinda said nothing. Her face had gone tallow-pale, her mouth set tight—

'I'm sorry,' said Allie. 'I didn't mean . . . I'm like a rat in a trap. Screaming pitch.'

'Me too,' said Fiorinda. 'We all are. It's stress.'

'About Sage. I didn't mean to say—'

'Shut up, Allie.'

Fiorinda sat down, took out her smokes tin, lit a spliff and handed it over. 'Okay, let's talk about Fergal. I know he deceived us. I know he's a Celtic sympathiser. But I want to keep things going, for Ax, because *he's not dead* . . . and this is the way to do it. I don't know if you ever noticed, but the Counterculture is very male-oriented.'

'Ha!'

'I need a consort. I need to keep the Celtics. He fits the bill. I admit it's not my greatest idea ever. But until I think of something better, you'll have to trust me.'

'It's a marriage of convenience?' said Allie. 'Is that what you're saying?'

One of the doors to the Office opened. Fiorinda's secretary (a new girl, recruited from the Celtic majority) looked in. 'Oh, Aoife,' said Fiorinda casually, 'I was about to buzz you. I'll be along to my room in a moment, thanks.'

The girl left. Allie stared at Fiorinda, round-eyed, open-mouthed.

'I'm glad we've had this talk,' said Fiorinda, meeting the stare. 'Now you can spin this for me. Get the Few, and the staff, to accept what I'm doing, and not rock the boat—'

'My God. Does she *spy* on you? How bad is this? *Tell* me, Fio.'

'I'm getting my share of the deal, Allie. I'm fine.'

Allie nodded. 'You've got to talk to Mohammad,' she said, abruptly. 'You need him on board, or the Islamics are going to explode over you and Fergal.'

'I'll talk to him. You're right. I should have done that. I'll get to it.'

They were silent. 'What a weird conversation,' said Fiorinda at last. 'Do you ever think about the way things used to be, Allie?'

'Sometimes I get a kind of reverse déjà vu. It doesn't seem real.'

'We'll never get back there.'

'No,' The spliff was finished. Unpremeditated, they gripped hands. Allie felt that she'd been dealing with a stranger for weeks, and this was Fiorinda again: but how changed. Like Fio with a deathly illness, hollowed out inside.

'This is our life,' she said, suppressing her shock and pity, 'the only one we've got. I can't stand what you're doing to yourself. But I believe in the Rock and Roll Reich, and I've seen the bloodbath route . . . I'll help you all I can.'

Allie explained the situation to people, discriminating carefully. Fergal Kearney is a necessary evil; we need him because we have to work with the Celtics. Fiorinda isn't blind to his faults, but she respects his differences and he respects hers. This way we're in a position to influence the new régime . . . It reminded her of the way they'd dealt with President Pigsty. And here we are again. Not everyone was satisfied, but it was better than people seeing Fiorinda – as they thought – betray everything the Reich stood for. Fiorinda talked to Mohammad. She couldn't tell from the blunt, reserved way he responded whether he understood too much or too little: but there was an effect. The violence died down, and the respectable Islamic media went quiet about the 'Celtic takeover', although some of the comments about Ax's faithless wife continued.

The Brixton flat was shut up. Fiorinda and her new boyfriend used Fiorinda's mother's house as their *pied à terre* in London. Their home was at Rivermead, the Counterculture's showcase complex. The Few had not been invited there: it had been one of the things they had failed to understand . . . When Allie knew the truth she and the Babes invited themselves, bringing Rob along so he could take Fergal out drinking at the Blue Lagoon. The babies had been left at home. The women got themselves sorted with spliff and wine and settled round the fire, dismissing those terrible chairs and settling on organic hippy beanbags.

'I don't get how anyone can think of God as a human being,' mused Allie, gazing at the smoke that rose from the spliff she was holding. 'It's too much. Fuck. Just *think* of that face. God must be an abstract. The colour purple, you know—'

'You going to smoke that?' said Cherry. 'Or philosophise? Pass it over here.'

'I don't believe in any of that shit,' said Fiorinda. 'Never did.'

She should have known she couldn't keep the Few out of it. She should have known that she'd have to feed them some plausible line. Thank God for Allie . . . The warmth of wine and cannabis flowed through her, loosening her grief. Surreptitiously, she wiped her eyes. Felice moved over and hugged her. 'Hush, baby. You're among friends. You can cry for those sweet guys tonight; we all miss them too.'

'Did they *really*,' wondered Dora, 'serenade you with "Stonecold"?'

'Yes,' said Fiorinda, 'they really did. They serenaded me with my own music, and then they took me to Tyller Pystri, got down on their bended knees and they proposed. It was the most absurd performance I ever heard of.'

The others cackled and rolled their eyes. 'You are a jammy bugger, girl,' said Cherry.

'Both of them, what a jackpot. Hey, I'll take Sage,' offered Felice.

'Yeah. We know,' chorused her fellow Babes.

'I'll take Ax,' decided Allie, judiciously. 'He's *elegant*.'

So here I am, reflected Fiorinda. Where I knew I'd end up from the moment the shit hit the fan. Left behind by the heroes, down among the women. Reduced to the status of a domestic animal – and getting fucked by the bastard who took over because I go with the territory. But I don't care. I will keep the faith. I will bring them all safe home. She closed her eyes and lay back with her head on Felice's cushiony shoulder, thinking of how much she loved her prince, and how proud she was to have known him. She knew Ax was alive and he would come back. Sadly, she was afraid she wasn't going to survive that long. But one moment at a time. Take it one moment at a time.

Rob had been apprehensive about going out with Fergal. But it was okay. The Irishman was the same as he'd always been (if you forget the part when he'd saved Ax's life, and we trusted him). He does the talking. All you have to do is sit there and nod.

Fiorinda had been most afraid for the Heads. She knew she could trust Dilip and Rob to accept that she had a plan, and work with her. The Heads might decide it was their male-animal duty to die in Fiorinda's defence, whether she liked it or not. But she was wrong. George and Bill and Peter had weighed up the situation and resolved that they would do nothing to endanger their adopted princess. They would look at the larger picture, review the options there, and meanwhile carry on trying to get the boss out of Caer Siddi. It was Chip Desmond and Kevin Verlaine who decided they weren't going to take this.

The Notting Hill flat had changed after Roxane left. First they'd lived around the spaces where hir furniture and books had been, then *spaces* had encroached until they'd got rid of everything except the fx generators, the home entertainment, a gel-bed, and the pieces Roxane had found it inconvenient to move. They'd lived in an ever-changing virtual world, nothing real but the floor and walls, and been immensely pleased with themselves – until Fiorinda came round and said it felt like being in a tv studio, and where was her autocue? Which had deflated them slightly.

Deflated wasn't the word for it now.

Idleness and misery had closed over their heads. Their career as global techno stars was on hold. The Rock and Roll Reich made few demands now that Fergal and the Celtics were in the ascendant; the Zen Self project had deserted them. They couldn't hang out at the Insanitude, because more than likely Fergal would be there. They couldn't go and lean on Rox for support because . . . because . . . They had money, for whatever treats this sixth winter of the Crisis would let them buy, but they hadn't the heart for dissipation. There was nothing to do but mourn for Ax and Sage, and sit in their naked rooms watching daytime tv.

One afternoon, like too many other afternoons, Chip lay sprawled on the gel-bed. Verlaine sat crosslegged on top of a sideboard that had belonged to Roxane's grand-mother. The Second Chamber was on the box, and they were jeering at it listlessly. In the curtainless windows Cézanne iterations blanked out a dark December day.

'It's classic,' said Chip. 'First the revolution has its romantic violent phase, that was the Deconstruction Tour. Then comes the struggle to survive. The power structures re-form, and you get a new set of suits identical to the old set. Except totally unaccountable, different buzzwords, and they now have a taste for blood. Fucking horrible.'

'It was never *our* revolution,' said Verlaine. 'We only tried to make it better.'

'Fat chance. The world is too strong. We fought the law, and the law won.'

Fiorinda's appeasement was successful, to an extent. The Volunteer Initiative was still going, and the hedge-schools; and a raft of Ax's emergency measures had survived. But they weren't in the mood to look on the bright side. Were we killed at some point without noticing? Is this Hell?

'I wonder what he's got on her,' sighed Verlaine, gazing wearily at the screen.

But that was no secret. Fiorinda was a hostage: giving Fergal sexual favours and consort status, because he threatened her with bloody civil war in the Counterculture, if not all of England, if she refused to play. A fucking horrible situation, indeed.

'I wish we could get something on *him*,' said Chip. 'Something slow and painful.' Silence for a moment, then he began in a different tone, 'Pippin, what if we could? What if we could *discredit* the bastard? Like we did Pigsty, remember? Find out something that even the Celtics won't take. I don't know what, but I bet he has shit we can stir—'

'No, he doesn't. The suits' Intelligence Services did a job on him, after Spitall's farm, remember: and came up empty. He's just a hardened old rockstar-radical who lied to us about his politics, and got away with it because *radical* can mean totally opposite things.'

'Yeah, but . . . but. That was then. That was in the full flush of the data quarantine. Things are a lot squishier now. I betcha if we hack around a little we can get to stuff that the government spooks couldn't reach. We wouldn't have to have a plan. Just start by finding out anything we can about Fergal Kearney—'

They were desperate for action.

Verlaine got down from the sideboard. 'Merry, I believe

you're right. The young queen is in durance vile; we must rescue her. It's a secret mission. This might be dangerous, and we *must not* get caught. We will be risking our lives.'

A pause for thought.

'Let's go,' said Chip.

Fiorinda had a new double life. She was still acting as Mr Dictator's deputy, and managing the Volunteer Initiative. The Second Chamber Group wanted Fiorinda as Ceremonial Head of State, and Rufus was indifferent to the charity work; he let her carry on with all that. But now, instead of being a rockstar in her spare time, she was Fergal Kearney's girlfriend. When Fergal's friends and close associates gathered in the upper room at Rivermead on the long winter evenings, Fiorinda was their hostess. She saw documents and overheard conversations that made the most hair-raising rumours from the Floods Conference a reality. Often she was able to use her knowledge: tipping off the police (reliable police, people she trusted) over ritualist venues, getting her drop-out agricultural labourers out of the way of trouble, securing food supplies before they could be destroyed by the Gaia-wants-us-to-commit-suicide fanatics. Sometimes, if she had the chance, she intervened directly. Rufus didn't care; he liked to indulge her. Fergal's friends never appeared to put two and two together . . . but that was because the handful of people who formed the inner circle were in on the big secret. They knew that Fergal Kearney was Rufus O'Niall, the megastar magician, occupying another man's body, and they weren't going to tell him his girlfriend was a security risk.

They wouldn't say *boo* to him. He was their secret weapon.

Sometimes she played the piano for them. Sometimes Rufus/Fergal called her to sit by his feet so he could fondle his girl while he dominated the conversation. Most often she sat with some sewing (she was not expected to offer drinks and canapés; there were servants for that), watching and listening. And as she watched him, the rock-lord among his courtiers, Fergal's body hardly disguising the real presence, she began to hope.

Rufus had wanted England for his private fief. He wanted his daughter-bride on the throne beside him in a splendid new-built castle; public ritual sacrifices of the unfit; a subservient populace stripped of the corrupt 'free-doms' and 'civil rights' of modern civilisation. He wanted every imaginable luxury for himself, packaged in the neo-lithic-mediaeval style he preferred; and he wanted an end to the masquerade. He was tired of occupying Fergal Kearney. He wanted to possess England, and possess Fiorinda, in his own shape. He had prepared the ground. He expected the Second Chamber Group to deliver the goods, and Fiorinda saw it dawning on him that the bastards couldn't do it. Thanks to Ax Preston and his stubborn efforts, England's not going to be the magician's neo-mediaeval theme park, not without a messy struggle and Rufus O'Niall doesn't tolerate *messy struggle*.

Benny Preminder had been working for Rufus for years. He'd been the inside man, passing information. Benny must have found out about real magic long ago; it was galling, if she'd cared, to realise how easily the Triumvirate had been fooled. Benny Preminder leads a charmed life, oh yes, and we never guessed. It never crossed my mind . . . But that was over. Rufus had had his revenge, and he'd reclaimed Fiorinda. Now Benny was like the talent scout who has introduced a raw megastar to the corporate backers. The Celtics were telling Rufus he could go global. (Fiorinda could not discover *how* they planned to use Rufus's magic as a weapon: maybe they didn't yet know themselves.) He was very interested. He liked the inter-national Celtics; their goals suited him . . . But on the England deal, he was starting to feel double-crossed.

They can't hold him, she thought. He's a *rockstar*.

She had a triple life. The third life happened between the sheets, and involved a dead man's body with carrion breath. But the less said about that the better.

Every moment an embattled island. I am going to win.

Fiorinda's grandmother, who had known it was Rufus all along, dosed her with potions and ointments intended to restore her fertility, and told her that the Pharoahs of Eygpt always used to marry their daughters. Fiorinda didn't try to make Gran see the enormity of what she was doing. Talking to Gran about morality just made you feel as if you were going nuts. Rufus was unconcerned. He could wait until he was with her in his own body before he made her pregnant . . . She had no idea what he could do. Maybe he could reverse the injection right now if he felt like it. But she was glad she'd held out against Ax and Sage when they'd been trying to get her to go to the whitecoats. At least she need not face that horror; not just yet, anyway.

In the earliest days of spring Fiorinda started to have yet another life. This one happened in a small room tucked away in the North Wing of the Insanitude, called the Fire Room. It involved Fiorinda and a young woman called 'Lurch', in the US, talking to each other in lines of type. She was anxious about this life, because it was part of a network of secret resistance to the Fergal Régime, a situation she'd been trying very hard to avoid. But she loved it. Now there are two people, talking to each other directly, who actively, positively believe Ax Preston is alive.

The winter passed. Rufus kept his bargain and didn't touch Fiorinda's friends. The drop-out hordes, and the country as a whole, suffered some depredations, but April came and the dark ages were not much nearer. The Rock and Roll Reich was standing, but Fiorinda's broad beans weren't doing so well. The trouble with these Rivermead courtyards is that slugs delight in the damp nooks in

Topsy's Barcelona Cathedral walls. They get up very early in the morning, in prime commuting distance from snack heaven.

Fiorinda crept doggedly along the rows of over-wintering beans, plucking slimy bodies with her bare hands, and dumping them in a pot of vinegar. Silver and Pearl were incredibly impressed by this method, but prefered to stick to more civilised means of slaughter. The morning was rain-washed, the sunlight weak and cool, the leaves so green. Bless, thought Fiorinda, a word that came to her often now and she didn't know why. Bless the beans, I suppose. Bless you, beans. Flourish so I can eat you . . . a slight contradiction there, but never mind.

Her troops were getting restive. The Fergal Régime was encroaching and Fiorinda's story that she was keeping the Rock and Roll Reich alive by appeasement was wearing thin. But she was winning. Rufus was getting heartily tired of the masquerade; and Fergal's sick body (she thought) was failing. She wasn't sure whether this last was a good or a bad thing, but she felt it was good. He's going to quit. He will take me with him, of course, but he will leave my friends alive and well, and he will leave England in peace, because he's going to honour his bargain. Not from pity, fuck no, but because he wants a willing sacrifice. That's magic.

'What a slug likes best to eat,' muttered Silver, squatting on one of the mosaic paths, dealing summary justice with a lump of brick, 'is dead slug—'

'Hey, have you filled the beer traps?'

'In a minute,' said Silver. 'I'm making a *cordon sanitaire*.'

'You're making a filthy mess.' Fiorinda raised her head and saw the pert cones of Silver's infant breasts pushing at the fabric of her smock. I will have to say goodbye to my handmaidens, she thought sadly. I'm going to have to forbid them to come near me.

'Where did Pearl get to?'

Silver looked guilty. The courtyard had several exits. One of them led, via a cute little artsy-crafty stair, directly to Fiorinda's rooms. She never let them go up there. Naturally it was from this door that Pearl appeared, quickly hiding something under her cardigan when she found Fiorinda staring at her.

'What's that you've got, Pearl?'

'Nothing.'

'Give.'

Pearl handed over a tired-looking, lumpy packet of mottled green paper. Fiorinda saw at once what it was, and her blood ran cold. '*What's this?*'

'It's a charm,' whimpered Pearl, cowed by the blaze of Fiorinda's eyes. 'Silver hid it under your bed. T-to collect sex energy, for business purposes. *She* made me fetch it.'

'It was ages and ages ago,' pleaded Silver, equally scared. They were utterly forbidden to enter that bedroom now. 'W-when it was Sage and Ax—'

'You stupid little fucks! Fucking idiots! Get out! Get out of here, fuck off, go!'

She ran with the packet to the water-closet toilet on the colonnade, the way that led to the old hospitality benders, where the Wing children lived with their mother; tore it up frantically and dumped it. Whoosh. Sanitation bugs will do the rest . . . Her stomach turned. There was clinging slime on her fingers. Dead slugs.

Oh God. She pitched her face over the bowl and chucked and chucked. Oh God.

Face in her hands, she leaned back against the wall. It won't be much longer now. He'll take me with him, back to his private island. He will try to make me join him in his devil's bargain, and this time Ax and Sage won't be there. I will refuse, I will resist. I will be torn to pieces, and then Rufus will do whatever it is the Celtics want him to do: and there will be no one who can stop him.

I can't help that. I have no answer.

But one step at a time. One step at a time. Deal with what's in front of you. I'm winning this round, but the endgame could be sticky. I have to remember he's only humouring me. The only power I have over him is that I know the way his mind works. I must get the most vulnerable people out of his sight, because this 'bargain' might not hold to the very end. She had despatched all three Heads to Wales to concentrate on their daft mission at Caer Siddi. Rufus had shown no interest in Ax's band; but she'd had Allie fix up a tour of the Highlands for the Chosen, to be safe. That dealt with the Preston brothers and Millie, and Ax's mum to babysit little Albi, and Doug Hutton too. I must get Mary Williams and Marlon sorted . . . Her stomach heaved again; she tipped herself over the bowl and vomited bile and water.

Someone knocked on the door. Fiorinda hauled herself to her feet and opened it.

'Are you okay?' said Anne-Marie Wing. 'The girls came back in a state and—'

'I'm okay.'

Fiorinda crawled back to the toilet, which she didn't feel safe to leave. Anne-Marie came and bent over her.

'Are you pregnant?'

'Fuck, no.'

Anne-Marie took her hand and squeezed it. 'They told me what you found. I know why you were so upset. I know what he's got on you, love,' she whispered, black Chinese eyes shining with tears, Scouse accent abrasive. 'I've always known, becoz I'm one too, you know . . . But no one will ever get it out of us.'

Anne-Marie had minor psychic powers. The law against witchcraft was not Fiorinda's biggest worry, but this was careless talk and she wasn't going to encourage it. 'Dunno what you're talking about,' she mumbled, sticking her head back in the toilet.

*

Chip and Verlaine, moving with extreme caution and covering their traces meticulously, had hit paydirt. They'd traced Fergal to a discreet rehab clinic in Sweden, where he'd stayed after he'd parted from the Playboys. They'd hacked into the records and read about Fergal's drug habits and his medical history. They'd found notes on his liver and his lungs and his lymph nodes, of which they understood not a word; and it didn't look interesting anyway. But they had also found some detailed scans of his brain – which after their Zen Self experience, they could read like print. These scans were rather amazing. There was severe damage to both the hippocampi, vital engines of memory transcription and recall. There was more than damage. It looked as if those two little deep-buried organs had been burnt out with a hot wire.

'He's dead,' said Chip, looking at the evidence. 'He's the living dead.'

'Let's get the Swedish translated. See what the white-coats say.'

The Swedish, when translated, proved equivocal. The brain scans were described as anomalous, no further comment. Fergal Kearney had checked himself out soon after they were taken. No fowarding address, no aftercare appointments. Chip screwed up his face in bemusement. 'If these scans are Fergal Kearney, our man isn't. Someone whose brain looks like this would have *no memory*. He couldn't function.'

'Hm. I wonder who paid his bills? It's a classy joint.'

They couldn't get anywhere on that issue. The Swedish hospital took better care of its financial than its medical records. They sat together on the bare floor of their décor-impoverished environment, pulling faces, trying to figure it out.

Paydirt that makes no sense.

'Someone who gets his memory burnt out of his head, deliberately—'

'Why the fuck would anyone do that?'

On the morning of the Mayday concert, Fiorinda visited Reading Site Boneyard. So few years, but already this corner of a field, sown with wildflowers and decorated with strange hippy memorials, had softened and grown old. Here's Tom Okopie's memorial slab, with his name and his dates and the Greek word ΑΓΑΠΕ . . . Which means love. Tom, who fucked me when I was fourteen and he was eighteen, and some people would think he took advantage, but I didn't. So long, Tom. Freedom to flail. Here's Martina Wyatt, the Countercultural Think Tank's Riot Grrrl, who died on Massacre Night. So long, Marty. She supposed she must add Ax Preston and Sage Pender to the list, sexual partners she would never see or touch again. But I will go on loving them. Whatever Rufus does, the memory of my lovers will protect me, my dead will be with me; and I will know that I won the fight . . .

So I will be okay. Somehow, I will be all right.

She headed back. The arena was filling up as she wandered through it. The punters hadn't stayed away. They have forgotten everything Ax ever tried to tell them, thought Fiorinda. They can't see any difference between what we were doing and the fucking Celtic Régime. It's all the Counterculture, isn't it? It's all green-is-good. Ah well, it just goes to show. People actively prefer the crappy junk food version of anything.

Bless. Little thirteen-year-old boy, bug-eyed, mud to the armpits, must have been sleeping in a binbag out in the rain last night. Bless. Evil-tempered woman that sells tofu salad wraps that taste of ammonia. Bless, naked woman with stupid expression. She reached Rupert the White Van Man's van, *Anansi's Jamaica Kitchen*, and bought a cup of dandelion and chicory 'coffee' with a hefty slug of cognac. Rupert didn't want her to pay, but she pleaded with him and he took her money, letting her feel young again for a moment . . . Rastaman, there's more grey in your dreads than the first day I met you. But your smile is still wonderful. She stood by the van sipping her hot drink, surveying the motley crowd, thinking, bless you Rupert, my good friend.

She had no idea what this 'bless' business meant. She couldn't remember how long she'd been doing it. Most likely it was not achieving anything. But if he can curse, maybe I can bless. It's worth a try.

If there is justice in heaven . . . Unfortunately, all the evidence we have says no.

She saw the band coming towards her and went to join them. DARK had come down from Teesside a week ago. She'd been rehearsing with them. She was hoping she would not fuck up too badly on stage this afternoon. But hey, what if I do? It surely won't be the first time. Though it might be the last.

Not everybody hated the takeover, but enough did to make the atmosphere backstage of Red Stage, which was Main Stage, poisonous. The Second Chamber Group had decided to turn half the Mayday concert into a political rally, with speakers on Main Stage most of the afternoon. Green lords and ladies and their friends were swanning around, very pleased with themselves: many of them simply, naïvely delighted to be *hanging out with the Few*, still the most exclusive social set in the new England. Benny Preminder looked particularly happy. Here he was in the inner sanctum, and not a thing the Few could do.

The original radical rockstars were scattered in separate islands through the throng. Fiorinda sat with DARK – Cafren Free, Fil Slattery, Gauri Mostel, Charm Dudley and Harry Child. Rob Nelson and Dilip Krishnachandran were with Anne-Marie's helpmate, Smelly Hugh, who was recounting a cartoon he'd seen in the Staybehinds' vidzine, *Weal*. 'It's about Fergal,' said Hugh. 'Fucked if I knew what was going on. You know those tigers what he shot? They were a pair, male and female. Big cat and a littler cat, right? Well, in this cartoon, it's like, the tigers are Sage and Fiorinda, and Fergal is protecting them, no, he's protecting Ax, so he kills them.'

'Well bizarre—' said Rob vaguely. Smelly was a gentle soul, but a slow thinker. Explaining *anything* to him would drive you up the wall.

'Yeah, but it's not really Ax. Ax is meant to be *England*, so that makes . . . Er. Either of you two know what leg-iti-mate succession means?'

'It means *bollocks*,' Dilip yelled at him, rattled beyond endurance. 'It's *bollocks*—'

'Oh,' said Hugh, meekly. 'Right . . . I was only asking.'

'Hey, hey,' said Rob, a hand on the mixmaster's arm, 'calm down, DK.'

Chip and Verlaine came into the area. They saw Fergal and walked right up to him, pleased to note that he had several fully tooled-up media persons in close attendance. They had thought hard about what they planned to do. They knew it was on the cards that they would end up getting shot. Or macheted to pieces: some of the weapons on display around the Irishman were not very civilised. But they needed to confront him in public, in a way that didn't involve the others; and where they had a chance of being heard before the minders intervened. Backstage at Mayday was it. They'd convinced themselves this was what Ax would have done: take the direct action, sort the details later.

'Uh, Fergal,' said Chip. 'We want to show you some-thing.'

Verlaine laid a couple of gleaming cells on the plastic table where Fergal was sitting and held up a third so the sunlight caught the colourful image and brought it to life.

'These are copies of scans of your brain, Ferg. Taken in that hospital in Sweden, where you got your natural, organic memory machinery burnt out.'

'We can only think of one reason you'd do that,' said Chip. 'We think you've got a big implant. We think you went all the way, ditched your human self, and it's just a bunch of evil, futuristic anti-Gaia microchips stuck in your brain that's talking to us—'

'Because if you didn't do that you can't be walking around, with scans like this.'

The Adjuvants had scripted this with care, trying to make the language simple but arresting. They spoke loudly and clearly, but with good-humoured calm. They hoped they sounded like Tarantino gangsters, *interesting* gangsters, *not the kind that instantly needed shooting* . . . They had calculated rightly. Nobody pulled a gun. Fergal himself seemed fascinated. By the end of their delivery the whole crowd around Fergal, celebs and minders, liggers and media folk, was silent: attentive and mystified. The music and the muffled noise from the arena surged up, suddenly vivid. In the background Fiorinda was on her feet, white as milk, Charm and Gauri holding her back—

'So we want to ask you to take a new scan, F-fergal,' said Chip, beginning to quake.

'Prove it isn't true,' explained Ver. 'But if you're *not* this person, who are you?'

Fergal stared at them. There was a murmur of astonishment from the onlookers who could see his face. 'Fock—' he whispered. 'Fock—' A slack-jawed old man with sea-green eyes, his voice as thin as a reed. His head began to jerk and nod—

'*Fergal!*' said one of his own men, grabbing his arm. 'Come on. Get you out of—'

Fergal didn't get up. He fell down. He fell from the chair like a suit of clothes folding.

'Heart attack—' said someone in the crowd, urgently.

'Oh God, what's that smell?' cried someone else.

Fergal Kearney lay on the bruised grass, shrinking like a wax model held in the flames, his clothes wetly stained, his face melting from the bones. He lay there, in seconds, dead and putrefied.

Fiorinda had stopped struggling and was standing transfixed. No one was looking at her yet. A bunch of the politicos rushed up to the body, Benny Preminder at the fore, brandishing his dogtags – an absurd gesture, but he didn't look absurd.

'I'll take care of this. I'm Ben Preminder, Counter-cultural Liaison Secretary, this is mine.' He stooped over Fergal, theatrically grave, and stood up again. 'Someone call the police. This man may have died by witchcraft!'

There was a babble of disbelief, a surge of people trying to get a look, or to get away.

'No one leaves!' cried Benny. 'There are suspects who must be questioned!'

'Come on, princess,' muttered Charm Dudley, putting a ferocious lock on her singer's upper arm and hauling. 'We're out of here.'

'What? Why should I—?' gasped Fiorinda, shaking, mulish, resistant.

'For fuck's sake,' hissed Gauri. 'Just don't argue.'

If they could have got her onstage they might have made it. The enemy wouldn't have wanted their own goons grabbing the princess in front of that crowd of punters, and it would have been a brave Thames Valley police chief who authorised the arrest of Fiorinda on Red Stage at Reading Festival Site. But they didn't think fast enough, and Fiorinda was obstinately screaming to the Few and friends that they were to LET THIS HAPPEN! SORT IT LATER! So what support they had was scattered and uncertain. It was DARK against the world, and of course they lost.

The police turned up and took over. Fiorinda was escorted to Rivermead, where she spent the next days in her rooms under armed guard, while Benny marshalled his 'evidence'. Then she was formally arrested and charged with the murder. This would be the first attempt to enforce the new law for a serious offence since the Witchcraft Bill had been passed. No one knew how the case should be handled; they were looking back hundreds of years for precedent.

But Benny thought he could make it stick.

NINE

Love Minus Zero (No Limit)

The Heads came straight back from Caer Siddi, but they
had trouble on the way. They were stopped at the border
on the English side, hassled, kept waiting for hours for
personal transport vouchers; and finally informed there
was a curfew due to Fergal Kearney's death, so they
couldn't travel until the next morning. It took them three
days to reach London. They found the Insanitude crawling
with strange hippies from Fergal's own London barmies,
who said they were looking for evidence of criminal
magic. Allie had called the police, but the police, omin-
ously, had declined to intervene. Of course there was
stacks of evidence, and as for criminal, it depends where
you draw the line. The hippies left eventually, taking
whatever random items had caught their fancy: a set of
bongos, several expensive fx generators; scented candles.

Fiorinda had been taken from Rivermead to a remand
centre, a grisly Victorian building on the outskirts of
Reading. She had been allowed no visitors, and she hadn't
been allowed to speak to a lawyer – on the grounds that
there was as yet no procedure for dealing with someone
who could wield (allegedly) such incalcuable powers. The
Heads managed to get themselves in because the assistant
governor was a Heads fan. She was very confused about
Fiorinda, but she could not resist George Merrick, Bill
Trevor and Peter Stannen, fresh from Caer Siddi, where

her hero Aoxomoxoa was pursuing his incredible journey into inner space.

They were taken to see the celebrity prisoner and met with the heartbreaking sight of the rock and roll brat literally behind bars. At least the screws left them alone, so they had some privacy (maybe). 'It's to protect you,' said Fiorinda, on her side of the bars. 'Iron's supposed to be proof against witchcraft.'

'Does it work?' asked Peter.

Fiorinda shrugged. 'Well, I'm still here. I haven't turned into a bat and flown away.'

'Don't talk like that,' said George. 'We'll get you out, my love. This is ludicrous.'

'Fiorinda,' said Bill, urgently, '*don't* talk like that. Don't be a fucking idiot. Nobody has a sense of humour when you're on the wrong side of the law.'

She smiled. 'Py kefer Myghter Arthur? Ny wor den-vyth an le—'

George answered her, feeling as if someone was squeezing his heart in a vice, 'Whath nyns yw marow; efa vew, hag arta efa dhe.'

This Cornish traditional couplet was the password and countersign of the secret resistance to the Fergal Régime: *Where is Arthur? No one knows, but he lives and he's coming back.*

'Did I pronounce it right? I've been working on my Brythonic intonation.'

'Not bad,' he croaked.

Unfortunately, one of the results of the murder charge was that they were no longer in touch with 'Lurch', the American girl who was convinced that Ax Preston was alive. The Few's secret direct link with the US had been spotted and closed down. There had been no more solid *evidence* that Ax was alive than there'd ever been – just the usual 'leads' that would come to nothing. But they knew how Fiorinda had been clinging to that lifeline.

They would not tell her. It would be needless cruelty.

Things were looking ominous. Fiorinda's personal popularity was immense, but Fergal had died and rotted in minutes, in seconds, before upwards of a hundred witnesses. Millions of people had seen it now, on the Big Screens or in their own homes. As for Chip and Verlaine's story, forget it. The autopsy had been conducted with scrupulous correctness. The inside of that skull had been soup; nothing could be said about strange brain surgery, but there'd certainly been no microchips. Meanwhile Benny was producing witnesses who would recount 'strange rumours' about Fiorinda going back to when she was fourteen, denouncing the Few as traitors who had been getting rich off the Reich (helped by Fiorinda's evil magic), and setting himself up as the defender of Ax's honour. A few brave media folk were holding out, but the rewriting of history was published and broadcast widely. The worst aspect was that the accusation was partly true. No one had talked about it, for obvious reasons, but some of her closest friends had known for a long time that Fiorinda was a witch. She must go on denying it, they must all deny it: but that lie wasn't a good start for the defence case. If they were ever allowed to make one.

They tried to give her a hopeful spin. You're the nation's sweetheart, he won't dare to hurt you. Fuck, there's an *army* of staybehinds and drop-outs who would die before they'd let anything happen . . . Fiorinda walked around her share of the room, arms folded over her breast, head bent. She came up to the bars and stared at them, her eyes flashing in that strange Fiorinda way, pupils flared and then down to pinpoints.

'George. Did Sage trust Alain?'

'He's not dead, Fiorinda,' said George. 'You got no reason to say he's *dead*—'

Eyes like grey stones. 'Did Sage, *who is dead or he would be here*, trust Alain de Corlay? I think Alain's okay, but I know I'm losing track, so help me with this.'

He gave it up. 'Oh, yeah. The boss trusts Alain. They got their differences, but it's surface, er, more or less. It was play-fighting, the way they used to piss around.'

'Good. I want you three to take Marlon and Mary to Alain, in Brittany.'

'Fio, I think we should stay in England,' protested Bill.

'Well, *you think wrong*. Think mediaeval, *idiots*. I have no child. Ax has no child. One of the three had a child. Listen to what you've been telling me. Suddenly Benny is Ax's champion . . . Legitimate succession. Get it? Now convince Mary however you like, but get Marlon out of the *fucking* way, before he's a *dead* legitimate heir.'

She wiped her eyes. 'Oh, and the Chosen can't stay in Scotland, because I'm afraid Benny could reach them there. You'd better get them to Brittany too, and Sunny (Sunny Preston was Ax's mum). If you could send all the Prestons to the US, that would be even better, but I suppose that's a r-remote possibility. And *don't fucking argue* with me.'

George nodded, heartsick. 'Okay, Fio. Anything you say.'

'Clearing the decks,' said Peter. 'In case things get dodgy.'

'Yeah, Cack,' said Fiorinda, anger disarmed, with a very loving look, Peter's old nickname bringing back the ghost of their happy days. 'Just in case.'

She tried to think, she tried to plan, but it was like trying to jump back onto a racing, spinning fairground ride. She had been able to think of getting the Heads out of the country, and Mary and Marlon, the Chosen and Sunny, because those tasks had been on her agenda. She could not form new ideas. She spent her hours sitting on her narrow bed in the remand cell, staring at the opposite bed, which didn't have an occupant. She could not believe that this body was her own again. It didn't feel like her property.

What am I supposed to be doing now? Refuse to admit I'm a witch. Ax's girlfriend can't be a witch. That would be a real fuck-up.

What else?

Nah. Don't think there's anything else.

She recalled the long evenings at Rivermead, and Benny Preminder's secret little smiles of triumph. How he'd enjoyed seeing Fiorinda cut down to size, and how unfair that grass-cuts like that can still hurt when you're in total pain for much bigger reasons. Ax was always nice to Benny. You have to be good to people who hate you, unless you're going to flat-out assassinate them. It's the only answer. But I was rude to him whenever I got the chance . . . Probably that's why he turned against us and let Rufus in. All my life, every time I could do something wicked or stupid, that's what I did.

Every time I had a choice, I chose wrong. It's all my fault.

She wished she could think about Ax and Sage, but the memories wouldn't come. That part of her was dead already. All she could do was wait for Rufus. Every day, every hour, she waited for him to arrive, the way he had come to her at Rivermead. The cell door would open and Benny Preminder – or whoever else the magician chose to ride – would walk in. The screws would leave. A smoke would fall from Benny's mouth and Rufus O'Niall's living ghost would be there.

He didn't have to come that way. He came to her mind instead. She could see him: the big lordly man with the chestnut skin and shining black curls. She could hear his voice, rich and strong and so anciently thrilling, telling her that he had not abandoned her. This was a test. All you have to do is use your magic, Fiorinda. Iron bars can't hold you. I will be waiting for you in Ireland. Come to me, you belong to me . . . Remember when you were a little girl, how you wanted me to love you, and make you my bride?

We will rule the world together . . .

I can't do this. I can't fight anymore. *Please* someone make it stop.

At the end of May Charm and Gauri and Fil visited her in prison. It was the same set-up as the Heads had described in the remand centre: Fiorinda behind bars, in a basement with no natural light. She was very thin in her prison overalls.

'You took your time,' she said.

'We've been inside ourselves,' said Fil, who was sporting a cast on her arm.

'What did you do?'

'Fucking pathetic compared to first degree murder,' said Gauri, two fingers splinted and a limp. 'We got beaten up resisting arrest and they sent us down for that.'

'It was your arrest we were resisting,' said Charm. She had a support collar round her neck, a bad split lip not yet healed and a crop of yellowing bruises. 'Don't you remember?'

'Vaguely. I never had a degree before. Hey, d'you think *by witchcraft* rates an A* ?'

'Triple First,' said Fil. 'Summa cum laude. Defo.'

But tears started in Fiorinda's eyes. 'Why doesn't Allie come to see me?'

'She can't,' said Gauri. 'None of the Few are allowed.'

'Oh. Well, I've had Benny Prem. He asked me why did I hate my common-law husband, and why did I start a riot? I kind of pointed out I didn't start the riot, I tried to stop it, and he kind of hinted maybe I should plea bargain.'

An uncomfortable silence. 'Maybe you should,' said Gauri.

Fiorinda took this on board. 'No. I won't do that. I didn't kill Fergal. I can't tell anyone how he was killed, but it wasn't me. I'm innocent.'

The screws stayed by the doors. They were very upset

about the way *Fiorinda* was being treated, but they wouldn't leave the room. There was a painted line on the floor, which DARK were not to cross, but it wasn't alarmed: this room had nothing electronic in it, on the theory that magic interferes with that kind of stuff. They'd been told they couldn't touch her, or give her anything. The visit struggled on painfully. When time was up, Charm stepped over the line and shoved her hand through the bars, closed in a fist. 'Quick. Here. Take it.'

'What is it?'

It was Ax's carnelian ring.

'No,' she said, pushing the hand away sadly, 'no use. The screws would take it from me, and anyway, I'm not the same person.'

That was the last anyone saw of Fiorinda. They heard she'd been moved, but nobody could find out where. The situation was hardening; it was a case of get out and hope for the best, or stay and end up in the same boat, unable to help her anyway.

Ax was rescued in the middle of July. He had been chained up in that room for a year and two months. He spent a week in hospital, and then flew back to Europe in a gas-guzzler jet plane from the President's fleet: Ax and Lurch and a couple of minders alone in the forward cabin. They came in low over the south-west of England, in a clear blue morning. Ax looked down through the window beside him at a place that looked like Narnia. Such a golden green, such enchantment of light and shadow, it couldn't be real, it could only be a cutscene from a fantasy game. Oh my God, that's Silbury Hill. That's *Avebury*. He was gripped by an emotion that had no problem co-existing with his terrible grief and fear, so it couldn't be joy. But it was something.

He realised that the plane had stopped losing height.

'What's happening?'

Lurch had just woken up. 'I'll find out.'

She had a throat mic. He couldn't make out the murmur of her questions, or hear anything of the replies. Apparently Lurch had some difficulty herself. She left her seat and came back after an agonising five minutes.

'We can't land.'

'We can't land at Heathrow? Well . . . where then? Luton? Southampton?'

'No. We can't land. New update, it wouldn't be safe. It could be disastrous.'

'*Shit.*'

She was saying that if he landed in England it would sign Fiorinda's death warrant. The bastards who had hold of her would be pushed into finishing the job.

'Have we enough fuel to get us to Paris?'

'Just about. We can reach Alain de Corlay now. Do you want to talk to him?'

'Yeah. I'll talk to Alain.'

They landed at Charles de Gaulle. Ax was taken at once to a gravelly urban campsite on the outskirts of Paris, where a fair-sized contingent of the barmy army was ensconced, under the command of one of Richard Kent's staff officers. Richard had stayed in Yorkshire. It must have been staggering for the barmies to see Ax. He didn't feel a thing. He walked round, seeing all these faces bewildered by amazement, so gripped by fear for her that the last year had collapsed into nothing. He talked to people he knew as if he'd last met them a week ago. He knew he was freaking them out, but he couldn't help it.

The tale of what had happened in England beggared belief . . . yet he had seen it. That morning in the park at Dupont Circle, when Fiorinda called him on the b-loc, she'd asked him a question about Fergal Kearney. His mind (chip-driven) had instantly gone into overdrive, assembling a new picture, a whole *gestalt* shift, from clues like that garbled bar-story he'd heard in Amsterdam. He'd *seen* that Fergal was an enemy agent, and he'd even known who had to be running the bastard. He'd known his darling was in terrible danger from a vindictive devil who had already once destroyed her—

Maybe it was just as well he'd known, and been tormented by that vision, all the time he was helpless. Or he'd be gibbering now.

There were more barmies at Alain's family place in Brittany. Ax's band was there too, and his mother, and Marlon Williams and Mary, the Powerbabes, Roxane Smith, the members of DARK, Anne-Marie and Smelly Hugh, and all the kids. Anne-Marie's family had had to leave, because of AM's magic. The Babes, DARK and Rox had got themselves into trouble with Benny's régime defending Fiorinda. The rest of his friends were still in England. The Heads had recently returned there to organise a jailbreak. They were standing by, waiting for the word to go ahead.

From the barmies' camp they went to a hotel, an old brownstone building in the city centre. A council of war had been convened in a big first-floor room with swooping chandeliers, a long polished oval table and windows that overlooked a courtyard where chestnut trees towered. There were barmy army staff officers and netheads, a couple of French government suits, and some significant French Counterculturals including Alain and his muscle-bound girlfriend Tamagotchi. Tam was dressed as a space person, which added a glimmer of rockstar lightness to the proceedings. Sayyid Mohammad Zayid was there too, with an entourage of English Islamic soldiers from Yorkshire. Richard Kent, at Easton Friars, was with them on a video screen.

Until this morning they'd hoped that Ax's return would change everything. Richard had been due to be at the airport, with enough show of force for a military reception; or to protect Ax if things went sour. It was clear now that

Benny had never intended to let Ax land. He had nothing to gain and everything to lose. So they were back to the cat and mouse game that had been going on for weeks: Benny Preminder offering to negotiate and then backing out, using the threat of Fiorinda's death by mob violence to hold off the invasion that he knew was being prepared.

Benny, who had seized the initiative when Fergal Kearney died, had emerged as the spokesperson for the Second Chamber Group, but he might not be the leader. It was thought there was someone else in the background.

They talked about the invasion, which was being financed by Allie Marlowe's ransom fund. The 'Free English Army' had been gathering for months, sneaking over to France in small parties. They had weapons, ammo, sea transport; no air power, but there would be a first wave of parachutists, dropped from borrowed helicopters. There was an organised resistance on the ground, waiting to join them; and popular feeling was substantially on their side. But the Celtics were organised too, and the other nations of the former United Kingdom were neutral at best. They had their ties with the English Celtic populations to consider, and though they acknowledged Ax's claim, they still recognised the Second Chamber Group as England's legal government.

Ax felt himself going into an *Ax Preston* routine, and let it carry him. Implications, details, difficulties . . . Which cities can we count on, what about the regions, what fuel or power sources will we control? *I have been here before*, he kept thinking. The barmies had been ebullient, convinced it would be a walkover now that Ax was back. He knew he had to keep them that way: but the people round this table were not so optimistic, and rightly so. This is not a good situation. This is *not* a walkover. He worked at making everyone believe he was still Ax Preston, and wondered when should he break it to his backers that he didn't give a flying fuck for the Dictatorship?

Not now. Get Fiorinda out of jail first.

When everything had been said he gave them a speech he'd been thinking out on the plane, because he'd known there was a very good chance that he would end up here, in this situation, rather than on the tarmac at Heathrow. Short and positive. It seemed to go down okay. He dealt with a blur of congratulations, people who wanted to press flesh, and went into an adjoining room with Mohammad and Alain and Lurch and Tam.

The room was a quiet salon, decorated in brown and gold. Someone had given him a letter from Fiorinda, written before she was formally arrested and smuggled out. He read it, put it in the inside pocket of his jacket and walked over to a mirror on the wall to hide the tears that were stinging his eyes. *Elsie's dead. My little cat; I won't see her again.* The face in the mirror stared back at him, like an old friend who knew you when; and you don't want to meet him because you don't want to be reminded.

'You look the same as you always did,' said Alain. 'The astonishing Mr Preston. My God. A year chained up in the jungle, and ten days later he's planning the first invasion of England since the Conquest.'

'Better without the beard,' said Ax.

I have been here before. What did Verlaine say, a long time ago? Time is a helix. Time is a kaleidoscope: the pieces remain the same, only the pattern shifts. He remembered sitting in a hotel room with Sage on the night of the Armistice Concert at the end of the Islamic campaign. He had vowed he would never play the hateful game of soldiers again; he would die first – and here I am, back from the dead.

Be careful what you swear to God.

This was the ops room. There was a table spread with desktop hardware, maps, documents, phones, reconnaissance pictures of the disputed territory. They went to it and sat down and entered a different atmosphere: the world of the Floods Conference, where the fate of England was only a part of the much larger Crisis. He wondered how Mohammad came to be so at home here. But there was so much he didn't know.

'We can speak freely,' said Alain. He'd been guarded in the cellphone conversation when Ax was on the plane. 'We are secure as we know how, in here.'

'Okay, let's talk,' said Ax. 'Bring me up to speed.'

'After David died,' began Mohammad, 'and Fergal revealed his true colours, Fiorinda insisted on dealing with the situation her own way. She spoke to me in such terms I had to accept what she was doing. But we weren't going to let it go on. I had George Merrick onto me, and Richard; and Alain here. We had our plans—'

'Fiorinda was keeping the peace,' protested Lurch, with heroine worship in her eyes. '*By any means necessary*. She was saving lives.'

'She was immolating herself for your fucking Utopia, Ax,' said Tamagotchi. 'We were going to stop her. It was crazy.'

'So what held you back?'

'The warning Fiorinda gave me, and the evidence of my own eyes. Your wife was the intimate hostage of a very evil man,' said Mohammad grimly. 'It wasn't going to be easy to get her out of that safely. And there was something else.'

'This would be the secret Celtic problem?'

'Those primitives we were fighting on the streets of Amsterdam have grown fangs, Ax,' said Alain. 'You will find out . . . For now what matters is that the Celtics have been looking for a weapon. They want to reduce the population of Europe, but *drastically*. They have seeded cholera among the drop-outs, they have destroyed food stores, but it's been small stuff. We've lived in fear of a biowarfare attack, but apparently the Celtic leaders have ideological objections. The idea of spreading an engineered plague stinks of "science". It could be they are even restrained by commonsense. They don't want to include themselves in the firesale . . . Last winter we heard – I am speaking for the French Counterculture, for the techno-greens – that the weapon had been found; it was in England, and it was not scientific, it was *magical*. Which of course we had to take seriously. Personally I detest the supernatural, but one cannot deny that the world is getting stranger.'

Ax nodded. The young American looked very puzzled.

'Well then, Fiorinda was passing information to us, very useful information. She could tell us nothing about this magical weapon, but naturally we suspected Fergal was involved. Then Fergal Kearney died, in that spectacular way. Fiorinda was accused of witchcraft and we learned, over here, that Fiorinda's friends were secretly convinced that she *was* a witch. We did not believe that she had murdered Fergal. We took over where those two boys, Chip and Kevin, had left off, and we traced a connection between that Swedish clinic you have heard about and a certain Rufus O'Niall. We put this together with the stories that have been told of Rufus, his strange escapes, his *uncanny* power to wreak destruction on anyone who thwarts him . . . This is very secret, *very secret*, but we are sure we are right. Fiorinda has been in the hands of her father, who was wearing the body of Fergal as a disguise; and it is Rufus O'Niall who is the Celtics' super weapon.'

Ax nodded. He could not trust himself to speak.

'You don't look surprised, Ax. Did you know this, about her father?'

He thought of the dark exercise yard in which he had walked with Fiorinda, unable to speak to her, unable to touch her, certain she was there. The wet heat of Central America fell on him like a shroud. He couldn't explain to Alain, the rationalist, the process by which he'd come to understand the truth his girl had hidden, and he'd refused to see.

'Just before I was kidnapped I'd realised Fergal had to be some kind of imposter. Sage had tried to tell me, more than once, that there was something weird about Rufus, and that the bastard was still after her, but I didn't believe it. When I was stuck in the jungle I suppose my mind was more open. I finally put the clues together.'

'Fathers obsessed with their daughters, the daughter who must be controlled, locked away, possessed, it's the fairytale of patriarchy,' said Tamagotchi. 'Always.'

'The worst crimes are family crimes,' said Mohammad, 'in all cultures.'

'Yes,' said Lurch, the young woman with a family background of stunning privilege, among the masters of the universe.

On the table in front of Ax was a blown-up detail from a satellite picture of central London. The English Free Army had been given emergency access to GPS: and so civilisation returns, in time to monitor its own final destruction. This was the reason why he had not been able to land at Heathrow. There was a bonfire piled up in Parliament Square, opposite the House of Commons. The picture was so clear that you could see the raw wooden steps leading to a platform on top, a pole sticking up, restraints. A roped perimeter surrounded the pyre; mounted police were standing guard. This construction had been in place for weeks. Obviously it was meant to terrify, but it wasn't a bluff. The bastards mean business. Any time, any day, they can switch on their rent-a-crowd lynch mob, and this is how she will die.

He stared at the image and his skin crept. *I dreamed of this.*

Put wood on the fire, Jackie, Good wood on the fire, Jackie—
I knew she was lost.

'We don't know how Rufus can be used as a weapon of

mass destruction,' said Alain, 'but our own research into the magic of the future, *la féerie scientifique*, leads us to believe that the potential is there.'

'Movie Sucre has investigated the occult,' said Tam. Movie Sucre was Alain's band: Eurotrash intellectual loonies. 'We can tell you. The world gets stranger, but magic is like telepathy, like the telepathy that has emerged through the Zen Self experiments. The phenomenon exists widely, but it is pitiful, like a vestigal limb. Rufus O'Niall is like nothing on earth. He is like the wild, crazy version of something that can only be created in a lab, and that we know to be awesome.'

'And he's Fiorinda's father,' said Mohammad.

'She has refused to confess that she is a witch,' continued Alain, 'But of course the people who are holding her know the truth. She is O'Niall's daughter; they are sure she has some of his talent. This is good because it makes her valuable, but equally, it means they will never release her into enemy hands; into our hands.'

'But if she has, uh, magical powers,' said Lurch, hopefully, 'why can't she use them to escape? I mean, in some secret way, that wouldn't be obviously weird—?'

Tam and Alain looked at the American impatiently.

'I doubt she'd do that,' said Mohammad. 'Not after the way she suffered, rather than let us know what Fergal was . . . No. She has her reasons. She won't take that road.'

'We have to try to break her out,' said Alain, after a silence. 'Your return has made the situation highly volatile; we cannot wait much longer. But when we stage our jailbreak, Rufus – who is still involved, we don't doubt – will surely intervene, and we will be helpless. The dilemma is even worse than it appears. I won't conceal from you, we don't know what to do. Our only hope is in the anti-Rufus, the White Rabbit, our Rambo—'

'Who is "Rambo"?' asked Lurch. 'Um, would a Hollywood human fighting machine be any use? I thought you said this was magic?'

'Tuh! Not Rambo, *Rimbaud*. The proto-rockstar poet, alchemist of the mind. We put our faith in that blue-eyed madman, our infant monster-genius—'

White Rabbit and Rambo were codenames Alain had used on the phone. Ax knew who Alain was talking about, but it was a false hope.

'Sage is dead, Alain. He's gone. I'm sorry, but *I know that*. He died months ago.'

Alain put his head on one side. 'Hm. You think so? I sincerely hope you're wrong.'

'So . . . we have to make a decision . . .' said Ax. But he had lost the thread. He was trying to find Fiorinda in his mind, but she was not there, she had vanished, blank—

'You must be worn out,' said Mohammad. 'There's no need to decide anything now. Let's get you to bed.'

'Me?' he said. 'No. I don't think I'll sleep.' He searched around the table for the faces of his friends. Where were they? Where's Allie, and Rob and Dilip? Where's everybody gone? I knew she was lost. He was startled to see his own hands, bandaged at the wrists, where the cuffs had galled. Am I free, or is this another dream? Alain got up and went to Ax's place. He had noticed, in the barrage at the end of the meeting next door, that the astonishing Mr Preston deeply did not want to be touched, so he didn't touch.

'You needn't sleep. Just eat something, take a little soup, and lie down.'

'Would someone stay with me? I'm afraid to wake up back there.'

'We'll stay with you, lad,' said Mohammad.

George and Bill and Peter were hiding in a drop-outs' hostel in Peckham. They were returned emigrées; they had entered the country unofficially. If they were spotted, they'd be arrested at once. For the others it was less clear-cut. Rob was at the Snake Eyes', lying low. Allie was living at the Insanitude, working there with a skeleton staff. The club venue was closed, but the Volunteer Initiative limped on; and someone had to look out for the Boat People in the North Wing. They met Dilip, who was living here, there and everywhere, in the back room of a pub in Vauxhall. This was not the Few's old drinking hole; it was another place, somewhere they thought was not under surveillance. Old habits die hard. They were still trying to spin the machine. Dilip was working on a poster campaign. He'd brought the roughs along for them to look at. Here's Fiorinda as Sita, the kidnapped princess at the heart of one of the great Hindu myths of the Good State. In the *Ramayana*, Sita is captured by demons when prince Rama and his brother/friend Lakshmana have been lured away; and then she's rescued by an army of heroes. Dilip had drawn Fiorinda in a garden, walls as high as a prison yard, proudly but chastely defying the leering advances of the demons – who bore close resemblance to Benny Prem and other luminaries of the Second Chamber Group.

Fiorinda had been moved again, this time to Holloway, which was scary because of that piece of conceptual art at Westminster; but good because the old dump was laced with *Myghter Arthur*, screws and inmates alike, so they were getting regular news. She's okay physically, was the word, but she's in solitary, and very low.

'She looks too *passive*,' said Allie. 'I don't like that. Couldn't she be more energetic?'

'I'm going for pathos.'

'Maybe you're right. Okay, let's go with this. Print it. Get it on the streets.'

'Flyposting after dark as if I was sixteen again. Oh yes.'

The sound system started to play 'Not In Nottingham', the single which DARK had recorded before their hurried exit; and somebody behind the bar pumped up the volume. Originally this song had been a cute number from the Walt Disney cartoon version of the Robin Hood story. The dyke-rockers gave it hell. *Robin's gone, Maid Marian's in durance vile, everybody is getting trampled by the bad guys . . .* The backroom clientèle smiled and exchanged knowing glances. We should find another pub, thought Dilip. There are too many Ax supporters in here; it's not safe for us.

'What comes next?' said Rob, when they could hear themselves speak again. 'After the demons we need the rescue scene, the happy ending.'

'Ah,' Dilip frowned. 'That's rather strange. She has to walk through fire.'

'The demons make Sita walk through fire?'

'Er, no. Her own people, when she returns to them. To prove herself.'

'Oh, God!'

'*Dilip!* For fuck's sake!'

'No, no it's fine. The fire-scene isn't a problem. Trust me. Sita is perfect for the Hindu community. She's the selfless protector, she's ideal womanhood.'

'*No!* Fuckit, we don't want Fio idealised and dead!'

They argued. Dilip agreed to think of another heroine; and they left separately. This is what happens. You expected to be taken out and shot. Instead you carry on like ghosts of yourselves, clinging to tattered fragments of your old routines.

The Heads were in contact with Alain, and with Richard Kent at Easton Friars, but they used the Oltech phones as little as possible. They stayed indoors a lot. Their natural faces had become a little too familiar to the public during the Triumvirate era, and you could get stopped by the police for wearing a digital mask. The news of Ax's deliverance came. Ax was flying into Heathrow, and elation gripped the secret resistance, although there was weirdly little excitement in the regular media. But the happy ending didn't work out, and the Heads found they weren't surprised.

'Occasionally,' said Bill, dryly, 'it niggles at the back of your mind that we are fucked. Fucking done for in some mysterious way that can't be beat, no matter what.'

Yeah, it niggles. The score keeps racking up against you, and you see that there's no chance, no hope, but you keep on until the lights go out, that's all. They were waiting to be told to go ahead with the jailbreak. Instead, they got a call from Olwen Devi. Olwen, who had vanished with her Zen Selfers early in Fergal's reign, was at Reading. She said to come and meet her there, in Travellers' Meadow.

They took the train (sitting in different carriages, and walking separately from the station to Richfield Avenue). Reading Site had been taken over, but the Meadow was an enclave of resistance. The van, which they'd left parked in its old pitch when they came back from Caer Siddi after Fiorinda was arrested, had not been touched. It stood there quietly, plumes of seeding meadow grass grown halfway to the windows. They let themselves in and powered up the systems, from force of habit and for old sakes' sake.

Olwen arrived a few minutes later with a couple of Zen Selfers. They let her in. The Selfers were dressed anonymously, not in their usual red and green, but Olwen had compromised: a terracotta choli blouse and a grey-green sari.

'What's going on?' asked George, when they'd done the polite greetings.

He couldn't get a handle on the expression in Olwen's eyes. He wasn't ready for it.

She sat at the kitchen table. 'You know, George,' she said, 'if somebody managed to reach the Zen Self, that person might have extraordinary powers. In theory, they might be able to manipulate this solid world as if it were the environment of a fantasy game. Like a magician, isn't it? We kept that idea very quiet, you will remember. The goal was far off, and we were probably wildly mistaken about what it meant . . . But that was my quarrel with Caer Siddi, long ago. For them, reaching the Zen Self was everything. I believed there was no purpose in the quest unless someone were to go, and come back.'

'Why bring this up now?' said George. 'What are you telling us?'

'Go to Rivermead, George. Go now, right away, all of you.'

So they went to Rivermead.

The Reading staybehinds were living with the situation. It would be harsh to say they were collaborating. George and Bill and Peter walked together, bare-faced. They caught glances of recognition, but you have to rely on your instincts, and they felt safe. The long-familiar scenes, revisited, seemed very vivid and full of detail: the faces like tiny portraits in a big Old Master picture, Breughel, maybe. There was a sorrowful gaiety in the air, a mirror image of the reckless anger and the joy of Dissolution Summer. Now we are grown, we know how terrible life is and that there's no way to fix it. But the sky is still blue, and the grass is still green, and we stick by the choice we made. We're staybehinds, we'll stay. The Rivermead complex was definitely in enemy hands, occupied and run by Benny's version of the Counterculture. But no one challenged them when they walked in. They went to Fiorinda's rooms, which felt like the first port of call, wondering what they would find. The door to the suite was open.

'Anyone at home?' called George, peering into the solar.

No answer. The room looked as if it hadn't been used recently, but it was clean and the plants had been tended. A mass of honeysuckle, trained over an arch, stood by the windows: flowers, foliage and green berries together. Someone stepped from behind it and stood looking at them, the living skull quiet and sombre.

'Oh, fuck,' said George. 'I thought no one ever came out of Caer Siddi.'

'No. Usually you can't.'

The time when they would have been overjoyed to see the boss was long past. They stared at him. 'What happened to you?' demanded George. 'We've been trying to get you out since Ax was kidnapped; why the fuck didn't you take any notice?'

'I didn't get any of your messages. I'm sorry. Just hang on a minute. I'm looking for something, and I don't know where to—'

He forgot to finish the sentence. They watched him walk around the room: a big, thin bloke in anonymous blue jeans, a biker jacket and an unmistakeable mask. The voice sounds like Sage's voice, and that looks like the way Sage used to move, but how could they be sure? He stopped by the grand piano, the skull frowning a little, and passed a skeletal hand over the polished wood abutting the treble end of the keyboard. The Heads saw a small recessed panel appear, where there had been none before. At Sage's touch (if this was Sage), it slipped aside.

'Oh shit,' he whispered.

He sounded so like himself they came to have a look, and that was a barrier crossed. The secret compartment held Fiorinda's saltbox, and an envelope addressed to the boss. He picked it up, as if it might burn him, and opened it.

Dearest Sage,
It's completely irrational to write to you, but Ax's letter might not get out of England, and anyway I'm not feeling rational. I want to tell you what I did and why, so that you can tell him when you see him. I know I was an idiot about Fergal Kearney. We all were but especially me, because *I knew*, and I didn't listen to myself. As you'll know by now, when you and Ax were both gone he came

and took me. I couldn't do a thing, because I won't use magic and anyway I didn't dare. He said if you tell anyone I will kill them. I knew that could mean like, the next second, so I kept my mouth shut and tried to think of an answer. It comes to me now that he'd made that promise in my dreams, so even though really I knew all along what was happening I couldn't tell, because Rufus would have killed you, killed Ax, and put you both in Hell. I know I used to dream about you two dead. Or being tortured. But maybe I'm just making excuses. Anyway, that's how I turned into Fergal's girlfriend. I lost some friends and I don't blame them, I was acting very strangely. But the Few stood by me. You must tell Ax that whatever they let happen and whatever they did, it was because *I said so* and they trusted me. Tell him I was trying to save lives, and keep my friends out of horrible trouble, and anything else was secondary. Like a chess-playing machine. Me, Deep Blue. No brain, no ideas, just simple objectives. For the record, I don't think there is a way out of this Crisis. I think we are all doomed, and it makes no sense to keep trying. But it made sense to Ax so I did my best, because I love him. I had hoped that Rufus would give up and go home, taking me with him: but don't get me wrong. Chip and Verlaine were right to do what they did. They didn't know the real situation because I hadn't told them, and they *did* rescue me. I hope someone keeps telling them that. Well, that brings me to where I am now. Which is not so bad. It's a lot better than the option I thought I was facing. I don't want to stop writing because I don't want to give up the illusion of talking to you, but I think I must, and now I'm going to hide this by magic; how irrational can you get?

If anyone's reading this it's almost certainly not you, so I won't get too sentimental.

I want to say always love me, but I don't want you to

be miserable. There, I said it anyway. Still your stupid brat.

Fiorinda

'Fiorinda—' He stared at the place where her pretty handwriting faltered as she wrote that Chip and Ver had done the right thing; then he put the saltbox and the letter in his pocket and turned to the band. They had accepted Fiorinda's secret compartment without a flicker of surprise, and he wondered at that.

'What the fuck happened to you?' repeated George.

They sat down together on the storm-timber chairs. 'I don't know where to start,' said Sage. 'The Caer Siddi people didn't tell me anything, because . . . It's a long story. Can it wait? We have to talk about a jailbreak; that's what I'm here for.'

George and Bill and Peter felt very unsure. This is Sage, but *it's not Sage*. George almost thought of asking the boss to unmask . . . The double doors to the solar, from the entrance hall, opened. Someone stepped in and closed the doors behind him. It was a young man with smooth golden-brown hair, in the red and blue livery of Rivermead, which the newcomers, the enemy, had retained. He looked at ease in his archaic costume; he should be happy with the way things were going.

'Rambo.'

Sage didn't seem surprised to be called Rambo. 'What is it?' he said, intensely.

'They know you're back, and they figured out what it means. I shouldn't tell you this, but . . . you'd better get to London. Right now. I mean, really quickly.'

Fiorinda had realised, without being told, that the news of Ax's return might have the ironic effect of ending her life. She hadn't been told that this was the day until they came to fetch her. No chance to choose a last breakfast, tuh. But she didn't mind. She went along with everything, thinking about animals in slaughterhouses, people in concentration camps; other prisoners the world over, guilty or innocent. You know you should fight to the last, but you don't. It's a hormone shift, and pity the people who are not wired for this blessing. Or who haven't had the experience to prime them for it. Fiorinda was lucky; she had already given up. It didn't even bother her that she would not see Ax. She'd been used to that idea for a long time. She was genuinely glad to be handcuffed, to get in the van, to hear the roaring and thumping of the other prisoners giving her a send-off. Outside, the noise kept going on. It reminded her of different rides, through different crowds, but most of all of the time when she and DARK drove into Newcastle on the Rock the Boat tour – playing Pictionary in the back of the bus while Tyne and Wear went berserk with terror of the immigrant refugee hordes.

Not shocked.

No, I'm not shocked that they'd do this to me. It was always in them, that was the whole point, the fact that we knew this kind of thing is in everyone.

So it's okay, Ax. Not new bad news.

She climbed the steps unaided. The bloke who strapped her to the pole wanted something, oh fuck, he wants me to forgive him. Okay, okay, now leave me alone. It was horrible, unbearably horrible, having her arms strapped up, but it won't be for long. Actually this is the good bit, so enjoy. Count the moments. Think of Ax and Sage. You must not leave your body (she remembered that she had made this bargain); but there are infinitesimal degrees just this side of the escape from time and space. You can find a tiny niche where it's possible,

where it's possible, even now,

to live, in one embattled island after another, and feel—

*

The state of affairs that morning at Westminster was chaotic. Inside the House of Commons the members (the ineffectual remains of the Lower Chamber) were debating whether Fiorinda should live or die. They knew what was going on outside, but they kept fighting this verbal battle, as if it were as vital as the other. On the way from Holloway to St Stephen's a mass of people had poured out of a fleet of buses to surround Fiorinda and her escort, giving belated support to the story that she'd been dragged here by an uncontrollable mob. This crowd collided with another violent crowd: Fiorinda's defenders, who had been alerted by the grapevine. The police, who were also piling out of buses (though many police had already been on the scene) defended the lynch-mob from the protestors, with measured insanity. Fiorinda's escort took her through. They set about their business in an orderly fashion, as if the rules had been settled and from now on barbaric executions could happen every day.

The police, mounted or in full riot armour, swayed to and fro. They did not fire on the crowd. Senior officers tried to delay what was going on at the pyre while the battle raged. Mr Dictator was in Paris. In a few days Benny Preminder and his junta would probably be history. The Metropolitan Police wanted no part of executing Fiorinda. But the drama had an unstoppable momentum. Fiorinda's defenders kept pouring in, but so did others: this second wave not hired to play a part, but voluntarily determined to see the witch burn. There were bursts of gunfire (the police still didn't fire on the crowd) as Fiorinda climbed the steps, as if of her own free will: it wasn't clear which side was firing. She was being fastened to the restraints. Her defenders were still fighting, hand to hand, but the water trucks that were supposed to be here must have been sabotaged, and somehow, however it happened, the bonfire had been lit.

Dilip was with Allie. They had been with Rob and Chip

and Verlaine, but they'd been separated in the mêlée. He saw the first flames; he heard the huge gasp of indrawn breath: the whole crowd, and the police too, stunned by this final enormity. The weather had been damp, but the wood was soaked in herbal oils, organic natural accelerant. Within seconds the pyre had flames running all through it.

'Green branches,' howled someone. 'Put on green branches, put it out—'

'Oh Sita,' he whispered, 'Oh *Sita*—'

Oh England, oh my country, how can any of us come back from this—

Allie, battered and trampled, her eyes burning from teargas, saw a tv crew in St Mary's churchyard, *still filming*. She stared, dumbfounded. Are people watching this on tv? In the places that have reception? In their living-rooms? Is that possible—?

The long grey van scattered the crowd as it slammed to a halt. Sage leapt down. But the flames were rising like a wall. George raced after him. 'Boss! No! Come back! It's too late, you'll kill yourself. It's no use. She's *dead*, Sage, she's already dead—' He grabbed Sage; Sage spun around, decked him savagely and raced on, going through the cordon of mounted police like a whirlwind.

He heard the crowd give a yell, but fuck them, and jumped onto the charred and flickering wooden steps. Thank God, in spite of the efforts of the people who were breaking green branches from the churchyard, there was far more flame than smoke. When the steps broke under him he launched himself upwards onto the platform where Fiorinda was hanging limply from the restraints. He cut her free and leapt down again with her body in his arms; had to dive through a wall of fire, but that's not hard, hardly even dangerous, it's a circus act. He was on the ground, and here's the water trucks at last: a cold onslaught caught him; he and Fiorinda were drenched.

Into the van. George slammed the door, Peter gunned

the engine. Out of here. The mob might have changed sides now they'd seen Aoxomoxoa, but take no chances. Sage grabbed the oxygen mask that Olwen Devi thrust into his hand and pressed it tight over Fiorinda's mouth and nose. He held her, upright against him, on the edge of one of the astronaut couches, in agonised suspense. It takes *so little time* for smoke to kill. But she was breathing, taking great gulps of the medicine. Her eyes opened. She saw the living skull and at once her whole body came alive, her smoke-scoured eyes alight with astonished joy. She reached up, still gulping at the oxygen and got her arms around his neck. 'Ah, my baby,' he whispered, rocking her, the skull's grin buried in her tangled, smoky curls, 'my little love, my darling. You will be all right now, everything is going to be all right—'

He laid her back and watched Olwen take over, with one of the Zen Selfers.

'You okay, George?'

'I'll live.'

'Didn't break anything, did I?'

'Don't think so.'

The city of London rushed by.

'She'll do,' said Olwen. 'She's going to be fine.'

Sage left the couch, and came and collapsed at the kitchen table, head in his masked hands. Water from his clothes puddled on the floor. Bill had pulled some vodka out of the freezer-womb. He poured a hefty shot and nudged Sage's elbow with it. The living skull goes *no* – a very familiar miserable-toddler headshake.

Bill nudged the elbow again.

'C'mon,' said George. 'Get it down yer. You'll feel better.'

He was still outraged. The assault on his jaw was nothing, and the bonfire stunt had convinced him this could only be his boss. But he walks out on us, he *deserts Fiorinda* and goes off on his own selfish trip, and then after a year, suddenly he's back, with no explanation, nothing . . . However, he took the shot glass and stuck it into the boss's hand, closing the crippled fingers securely, as he'd so often done in the past—

He started, and stared. The living skull looked back at him—

'Boss. Will you take off the masks?' said George, slowly releasing Sage's hand.

Sage nodded. He unmasked and sat there, head bowed, blue eyes downcast, his hands on the tabletop. 'Cack Stannen,' called Bill, 'have yer co-pilot take over. Get yer arse back here.' The Zen Selfer who was riding beside the driver took over. Peter came back.

They stared at the boss. 'You made it,' said George. '*You made it*, didn't you?'

'You reached the Zen Self,' said Bill. 'Oh, fuck. That's what Olwen was telling us!'

'No,' he said. 'No. Not all the way. I couldn't. Something turned me back.'

'You didn't go all the way,' Peter was shocked. Sage *always* goes all the way.

'So what happened then?' said Bill, after a moment.

'I was out for a long time. But I . . . I had to turn back. When I was reachable again, I found out how long I'd been away; and the people at Caer Siddi told me what had been going on in England. So I called Olwen, and here I am.'

He looked at the glass in his hand, knocked back the vodka, and choked.

'Shit. Sorry. That's the first time I've tasted alcohol in a year and a half.'

'You gone off it?' wondered Bill.

'No!'

Bill put his arm around Sage's wet shoulders and hugged him. George did the same. Peter, who was never comfortable hugging anyone, grabbed Sage's hand and shook it violently. His brother-Heads examined the boss, really looking at him for the first time. They were shocked at how thin he was. But not in bad shape, he's not been lying in a scanner plugged to machinery for a year . . . What the fuck happens at Caer Siddi?

'What was it like?' asked Peter, 'what was it like, nearly getting there?'

The boss smiled. 'It was good, Peter. 'Spite of everything, it was very fucking good. I'll tell you about it, if I get the chance. But not right now, I've got other things on my mind. I came back to do something. I'll see her safe, and then I'll get on with it.' He swallowed hard. 'Just tell me one thing. How long? How long was she . . . did that bastard . . . ? Shit. I can't say it.'

'My impression is he started hitting on her the moment you left,' said George. 'But she held out, and put him off. I think she had to let him have his way, to save our lives, after Ax's chip turned up and David died. That was last October.'

'We didn't know what was really going on,' said Bill. 'Fuck, how could we?'

Seven months. Sage reached for the vodka, poured another shot and downed it, with more success this time. 'I don't want to talk to Ax. Don't let me have to talk to him.'

'You *don't want to talk to Ax*?' exclaimed Peter. 'Huh? But what'll we tell him?'

'You'll have to do it sometime,' said George, compassionately.

'I can't. *What would I say?*' Sage put the glass down. He wiped away the tears with the back of his hand. 'What could I say to him, George? But I can't anyway. Ax mustn't know what I'm doing. I'll tell you, but you'll have to promise me you'll keep your mouths shut. Ax and Fiorinda mustn't be involved.'

*

Hours later, at the barmy army HQ at Easton Friars near Harrogate, he slipped into the room where she was sleeping. 'Do you want us to go?' whispered one of the barmy army medics who was watching by her bed. He shook his head. No. He'd just wanted to see her again before he left.

From Easton Friars he returned to London, to the roof of a tower in the City that belonged to eks.Photonics, his father's company. He had arranged to borrow a helicopter and a pilot from Joss Pender, before he went to Reading to meet the Heads and search Fiorinda's rooms. Olwen was there too. The rescue of Fiorinda was not enough. Ax was still going to have to invade, because Benny Preminder wasn't going to fold. The Celtics, damned fools, were eager to fight, and Fiorinda was *not safe*, though she was surrounded by an army of ruffians who would gladly die for her. Joss and his son, the skull-masked giant and the slight, dapper software baron, talked a little, about how things were shaping, and how Joss's low cunning had helped eks. to survive the anti-science backlash: polite nothings, to take the place of the things that should have been said.

Olwen stood to one side, hands clasped, her left hand cradling the many-faceted jewel on the ring. *This time you may not come back, my lady*, said the guru silently to her dear friend, wise mentor, second self. Serendip was going to go with Sage, to be his guide and guard. If the jewel did not return (and they both knew that she might well be destroyed, because this would be a very close fight), then the mainframe known as 'Serendip' could be recreated. But a clone is not the same person.

Our friendship will remain, answered Serendip, in the state of all states, where nothing is lost, my dove. We will never be parted there.

It would have to be enough. They had to risk everything.

'Thank you for this, Stephen,' said Sage's father, as the rotors began to turn.

That was a surprise. His sisters and his mother resisted the handle, but Joss had never called him anything but 'Sage' for years. He'd believed it was because Joss was very glad to pretend that Stephen, the sick child from hell, the teenage junkie, had never existed. 'For what?' he said. 'I should be thanking you.'

'For trusting me. For letting me help you, for once in your life.'

Sage took off the mask. 'Thanks for being my fixer.'

They embraced, tall Sage awkward as always with the transaction. Olwen came to join them, and gave him the ring. He put Serendip on his finger, hugged Olwen, and climbed into the machine. It rose and soared away.

The pilot turned and smiled shyly as Sage put on his helmet. 'Hi, Sage. It's good to have you back, Sir.'

'Hi,' said the Minister for Gigs, smiling in return. He relapsed into silence and they flew on, westwards. Sage thought of his band, of Ax, of his friends. Goodbye.

Fiorinda slept for twelve hours, woke feeling almost human and persuaded the barmy medics that she was fit to get up. She ate a big bowl of lentil soup with some very tasty brown bread to prove it while they found her some clothes. When she'd showered and dressed (her hair charred at the edges and still stinking of smoke, but never mind) she went in search of company. Easton Friars was buzzing. Everyone was too busy with the war effort to pay attention to a rescued princess. This put her out a little, but she found the Heads eventually, sitting around doing nothing in a bare, echoing games room on the ground floor. When they saw her they shot to their feet, their mouths open.

'Fiorinda!' gasped George. 'You're unbelievable, girl. You aren't supposed to be—'

'I'm not *ill*,' said Fiorinda. 'I was nearly burned at the stake, which was quite an experience, and I've no doubt I'm going to crash horribly when the reaction hits me. But for the moment I feel wonderful. It's amazing what not being in prison, and getting a little good news, will do for you.'

George and Bill and Peter sat down slowly, nodding.

'Yeah.'

'Incredible good news.'

'We was just saying that to ourselves,' Peter assured her, with transparent guile.

'Where is Sage?'

Three guilty faces. She discerned that Peter, at least, had been crying. Oh, God. Crash horribly. NO! This is not the moment to crash. 'Where the fuck is he,' she snarled, 'What's he up to? Don't piss around. Just *tell me*—'

'He's gone off to do something important,' said George, unhappily.

'Oh yeah? Like what kind of important? Does Ax know? *What is Sage doing?*'

'Ax knows,' said Bill, 'er, some of it. He may not have the complete full details—'

Fiorinda set her teeth. 'Oh fine. Absolutely *fine*. So, he's doing something stupid and he has not told Ax. Oh shit . . . has he gone off to assassinate Benny?'

'No!' The Heads looked relieved, though no less unhappy. 'No, no,' said George, reassuringly. 'He's not *daft*. Fuck, what's the use in assassinating Benny—?'

'Much as it would be a result—' put in Bill.

'It would be politically untenable,' said Peter, 'an' it wouldn't work either.'

'No, no. Fact is, he's gone after your dad, Fiorinda.'

'He's always wanted to,' Peter explained. 'An' he reckons now is the time.'

She sat on the scuffed and balding arm of a leather armchair. There was a well-hammered dartboard on the wall at the other side of the room, flanked by equally pockmarked portraits of nineteenth-century hoorays. Who were they? Did they come with the house, all these tatty old pictures? The world was shaking around her. This world which is still in blissful ignorance of what Rufus O'Niall is.

'Oh God. Oh, God. He can't do that. He has *no idea*—'

'Yes he does, Fiorinda,' said George, looking her in the eye. '*He knows about your dad.* He's got a plan. An' he wouldn't let us go with him, but he's taken Serendip. I mean, not a facet, Serendip. Olwen's lent him the ring.'

'Sage has a plan!' wailed Fiorinda, jumping to her feet, beside herself with rage and terror. 'Oh great. You know fucking well Sage never had a plan in his life, beyond *go for it until you got no armies left.* He has Serendip, oh wonderful. What could a fucking computer do? He doesn't need a *computer*—' Suddenly, she quieted. She stared at the three Heads, in wondering certainty. 'He needs me.'

The Heads stared back, guilty and hunted: Big George. Aquiline Bill, so aloof from the whole vulgar rockstar business. Peter, wrapped in his strange innocence. They were determined, but *in their dreams* they could keep her out of this.

'Okay, how bad is this? I was on that bonfire yesterday, and I know he was here last night. Has he left the country yet?'

'Not yet,' said Peter, eager to say something positive. 'Not 'til tomorrow morning.'

George and Bill glared at him, disgusted.

'Thank you, Peter. Right, I want the details. Everything. Come on, *now.*'

TEN

The Elephant's Child

Padstow Harbour at first light, one morning in July. The boats moored at the quayside, several ranks deep, were stirring with the dawn. The harbour was a more workman-like place than it had been a few years ago. Ordinarily there'd have been people about at this hour, but Mr Dictator's invasion was imminent and every port in England, even little Padstow, was under curfew. Sage moved around the deck, getting ready to cast off. The sound of a car's engine speeded him up, but didn't distract him. He could deal with anything Padstow Harbour could suddenly mobilise against him. A door slammed. The car turned and headed up New Street. Fiorinda stepped between crates and cables and stinking puddles of rape-seed engine oil, dropped over the harbour wall and crossed quickly, from deck to deck, to the sleek and dazzling white hull with the name *Lorien* painted on it. Sage looked up to see his rock and roll brat coming over the stern, wearing barmy army urban camouflage trousers and a drab teeshirt. He half-straightened, looking horrified.

'What are you doing here? How did you—?'

'I talked to George. I'm coming with you.'

The look of sheer horror at seeing her turned to deeper distress . . . 'Oh no, Fiorinda. *No*, darling. He's your father.'

'Sage,' said Fiorinda, advancing with menace down the

deck, 'I don't know if you ever noticed this, but the word father doesn't mean the same to me as it does to you, or to Ax. If the Furies decide to come after me, *they will get a piece of my mind*. I know Rufus is my father. If I knew everything that had happened to him in *his* life, maybe I would pity him. Maybe I even do. But leave aside what he did to me long ago. After you were gone, he took me in the body of a dead man, held me under threat of destroying everyone I loved, and he raped me in the body of a dead man for seven months. *Trust me*. I do not need to be protected from the trauma of helping to take him down.'

He did not seem to know what to do with his tall body, whether to stand or kneel or jump over the side. 'I wasn't there,' he gasped, between flight and desperate abasement, 'Oh, God, I wasn't there, and there's no excuse, nothing explains that—'

'*Yeah*. You weren't there. What's the difference? You would only have got yourself killed, and I'd have had to do exactly the same thing, stepping over your dead body first.'

He nodded, tears spilling, taking every word like a well-deserved blow. 'I knew that. I knew he was coming for us, and I couldn't beat him. I knew the only way I could save you, save anyone, was to reach the Zen— *but I didn't know he was already there* . . . I left you alone with him, I told you to trust him—'

'Oh, brace up. You didn't know, I didn't know. We were fucking stupid, we couldn't see what was staring us in the face, because we were having our guilty love affair . . . You weren't there and I got raped, but you're alive, you came back in time to save my life, and then you fucking RUN OUT ON ME AGAIN! Instantly! I can't believe it, I can't believe it! And how is Ax is going to feel, *you bastard*, when he finds out—?' She had reached him, shaking with fury and terror. '*Sage!* You can't kill my father. You cannot kill him! You – you have no idea. He will tear you to pieces!'

'Oh no. No he won't,' said Sage, pulling himself together. 'It's okay, Fee. He won't.'

On his tanned right hand he was wearing Olwen's ring. The white-gold jewel flashed sunlight. 'Oh, yes, they told me,' she yelled, and leapt at him, so he had to catch her. 'You have Serendip! Fucking wonderful! A *computer* isn't going to help you—!'

'Fiorinda, no, it's not like—'

She pounded at him with her fists. 'He will tear you to pieces. He will *tear you to pieces* and that will only be the start—'

'Fiorinda! *Look* at me!'

'You bastard! How can you do this to me? You fucking idiot!'

'Look at me. *Look.*'

He finally managed to get her attention and got her to look into his eyes. She gazed, and stopped fighting, and then they were kneeling, face to face, on the deck, his arms around her, her hands pressed to his chest. The time that passed in Padstow Harbour was very short, but when they returned, Fiorinda was smiling her starriest smile . . . She laughed; they both laughed, and hugged each other without a care in the world.

'Hey,' she said, tugging his head down to kiss him, kisses all over his face, 'let's not fight. Forget all that, it's stupid. We're together again, let's just be happy.'

'Good plan.' He held her tight. Fiorinda pushed her face into the hollow of his throat, breathing in his warmth. This is Sage, this is my Sage—

'George said you didn't make it.'

'Well . . . I didn't go all the way, or I would never have come back. But I got far enough that you are not alone any more, my brat: and Rufus is going to get a surprise . . . Now,' he unclasped her arms from around his neck, and kissed her hands, 'you have to let me go for a moment. *Not for long*, but I have things to do.'

'*Don't you dare run away.*'

'I won't.'

She followed him around in the daybreak-twilight, uncertain whether she'd made her point or not. Not that she'd know, but this seemed to be quite a toy. The silvery masts were arrayed with strange gleaming futuristic vanes that didn't even look like sails. The wheelhouse held so many screens and winking instrument desks it was like the bridge of a starship. 'Who does the boat belong to?'

'Friend of my father's.' He grinned over his shoulder. 'Can't help the name.'

'Do you know how to work all this stuff?'

'Nah. I have a facet of Serendip in the system. She'll sail the *Lorien*; I'll be taking orders. It's easy. C'mere, I'll show you. It sounds complicated, but you just have to follow the prompts.' Charts and radar, windspeeds, homeostatic systems . . . She leaned against his side, saying 'yes' occasionally and listening to the dear sound of his voice, watching the beautiful mobility of his face. The laughter lines around his eyes and mouth were deeper than they had been. His hair was cropped and he was cleanshaven, but she had the feeling he'd been living outdoors, gone through the second-degree-burns stage to get that tan, and a winter too: what *happens* at Caer Siddi? She noticed that he was wearing a nose-ring, something she had not known him to do for years. But what a lot of information— 'Hey,' she said, suddenly, 'why are you telling me all this?'

Deep in the boat's hull, there was a sigh and a murmur. Sage grinned at her. She looked through the wheelhouse windows and saw that the quay was moving. Padstow Harbour retreated smoothly, the foliage of the trees above that pretty jumble of buildings still dark under a depthless sky.

'We're leaving! Hey, what changed your mind?'

He shrugged ruefully. 'Can't think of what the fuck else

to do with you, my brat. I can't just leave you standin' there, and unfort'ntly there aren't too many people in Padstow, off the top of my head, would piss on Steve Pender if he was on fire. Let alone hold Fiorinda down, screaming, while he runs off without her—'

'*Again.* So you agree we're going after Rufus together?'

'We can discuss that. Let's get up the front end. I want to watch this bit.'

She sat on the rail in the bows while the Camel River slipped by, and Sage, with his arm around her, his cheek against her hair, counted off the landmarks of his misspent youth – which she had never seen before, because he'd never wanted to come back here. The Doom Bar, Brea Hill, Hawker's Cove, Trebetherwick: strange names that had fascinated her when she was a pre-teen Heads fan. There are the dunes where the famous beach hut used to stand, where Aoxomoxoa lived when he was writing *Morpho*. There's the place where the Hoorays used to have their wild parties, when Steve Pender used to sell them drugs, and experiment on their tiny minds.

The river opened into the expanse of Padstow Bay. The murmur of the *Lorien*'s engine cut out. They turned to each other and slipped down together onto the deck, hugging and kissing, until Sage was on his back, Fiorinda lying on top of him, propped on her elbows. 'What am I going to do with this horrible Sage?' she crooned, 'I will have my revenge. I'm going to eat his strawberries, nibble bits of his dinner, I might even *tidy his room* . . . Oh Sage, what idiots we were. The moment Ax had gone we knew how desperately much we loved him, and we were such *fools* we thought it was a disaster.'

'Instead of being the best news we ever had in our lives. Fiorinda, what do you think? Do you think he still loves us?'

'Don't be stupid. Of course he does. That was just a spat.' She put her head down on his breast, his arms held her gently and they lay for a while in silence, just breathing. She slipped her hand under his teeshirt to feel the warm beat of his heart. 'How thin you are . . . What happened at Caer Siddi, Sage?'

'I don't know what I can say. I was *out*, of this body, for a very long time.'

'Are you going to tell me how long?'

His left hand gently massaged her spine. 'When it scares me less to think about it . . . I had no idea. It felt like a single perception, there was no illusion of duration, no anxiety for what I'd left behind. I could have been gone for hundreds of years, Fee. I would never have known the difference—'

'But you were *there*, in the place where you are complete.' She propped herself up again, to look down into his face. 'What brought you back, my pilgrim? If it wasn't that you knew what was happening here? Miles to go and promises to keep?'

'*No!*' He grabbed her, bone-cracking tight, arms and legs, and rolled over, showering her with kisses. 'No! Don't you ever, *ever* believe that! I came back for my Fiorinda and my Ax, and a whole life that I love, and I would not miss one second of it. This is, *this*, holding my Fiorinda—'

'Okay, okay, I believe you! Knock it off, you're breaking my ribs!'

He relaxed. They lay side by side, gazing at the sky.

'Serendip says we're leaving the bay,' said Sage. 'Let's get up and look.'

The *Lorien* had left the last landmarks behind and entered a vast, stunning, transparent world of blue. Not a sign of human activity, only the seabirds. Hardly a sound but the slap of the waves against the hull. Sage looked up at the complex planes of the yacht's sails, shifting and adjusting to catch every lick of breeze, and consulted silently with the mainframe . . . 'That's it,' he said, at last.

'Everything's fine, perfect conditions. Nothing happens for hours, except more of this. The next incident should be Fastnet. What d'you want to do? There's food, d'you want to eat?'

She did not want to eat. She wanted to sleep; she felt as if she hadn't slept for a year, but neither of them wanted to leave the blue world. Sage went and fetched a rug and they lay down again together, indifferent to the hard bed, settling the way they always slept when they were alone: Sage wrapped around her back, Fiorinda holding his hand tucked against her breast. 'Sage,' she whispered, 'can I tell you the worst thing?'

He steeled himself. 'Tell me anything.'

'I think I killed my baby. Over the winter, I kept thinking. I'm afraid I killed my baby, to stop Rufus from getting him. I didn't know I was magic, but I knew he wanted the baby. I was only a kid, but I'd spotted he didn't leave me until he knew I was pregnant . . . I wouldn't have known I was doing it, I would have been just wanting to keep my little baby safe, oh . . .' She had started to cry. She turned in his arms, hiding her face. 'Oh, Sage it was *okay*. It wasn't as bad as you think, even the worst parts. I had my plan and I knew I could win and I was taking it a minute at a time. But I would lose concentration, and then I would accidentally remember that there was no other side, because I knew from the start I could bargain for other people but not for me. He kept on at me and on at me, even in prison. I thought he would get hold of me again, and I would be with him for ever, with the dead man, fucking me, oh dear, oh dear—'

'Hey, ssh. Hey, sweetheart, look at me, *look*. Don't go there, come with me—'

They escaped together, again, to the refuge she had found long ago, which had been barred to her since Rufus O'Niall revealed himself. *What is this new world?* she thought. *What are its rules? What will we do here, Sage and I?*

What a strange thrill, to think that perhaps I have a future . . .

'You know,' she whispered, with a tremulous smile, 'this could get addictive.'

'Mmm.' He grinned, incorrigible. 'Certn'ly a pleasant kick.'

'But I want to stay *here*. Only, my head is so full of hateful—'

She cried and he held her, telling her, you did not kill your baby, you loved your baby, little girl. You looked after him good. We know you did, you told me and Ax all about him. He died of pneumonia, accidents do happen. Hush, my brave girl. You did fucking amazing. You did fantastic. I am *so proud* of you, and Ax will be *so proud*—

'Am I spoiled meat? Will you and Ax never want to fuck me again?'

'Don't be ridiculous. Only reason I'm not begging you to fuck me now, sweetheart, is I can't bear it that Ax isn't here. I want him so much—'

'Yes,' she whispered. 'We want Ax . . . Sage, say *everything real is good*?'

'Everything real is good.'

'Will you sing me the Jigglypuff song?'

'Coming up.'

So he sang her a cartoon lullaby, and rocked her, and eventually she slept in his arms. Sage stayed awake, watching her sleeping face and seeing there the marks of suffering that had been hidden by the courage of her waking self. It's going to be hard, he thought, it's going to take time for her to recover, no matter what. But Ax would be there, and she would know that she was loved . . . The *Lorien* flew on, cruising at thirty knots under sail, like a knife through butter, what a boat. He watched the silvered alloy wings shifting, he watched the beauty of the ocean, and tried not to think of what he'd like to do to Rufus O'Niall, because that muddies the waters. No anger, no ultra-violence, just do what has to be done. It was late afternoon when the computer finally woke him.

'What is it?' There should be another hour of the crossing. 'Something wrong?'

'No,' said the voice Serendip used when she spoke aloud, welling strangely from the empty air. 'Everything's in order. I didn't want you to miss the dolphins.'

There was a school of them, a striped kind. They stayed for miles, surfing the bow wave as if the *Lorien* was a big ship: leaping up, bright-eyed, to beam at their whooping and cheering audience. By the time they left, banking off and vanishing to the south, the yacht had passed between Fastnet Rock and Cape Clear and changed her course. They were heading into Roaring Water Bay, at the southern tip of West Cork, with its skein of islands strung between the sailing ports of Baltimore and Skull – one of which, the hourglass-shaped Inis Oir, Island of Gold, was the private property of Rufus O'Niall.

Their perfect breeze was breaking up as they left the powerful calm of the open sea; and they were not alone anymore. There were other sails, and chugging ferries; fishing boats and little outboard-motored dinghies. They went down to the galley to look for food and brought back sandwiches of bread and sliced ham, and some red wine. The wine was extremely superior and wasted on both of them, but they ate, and drank it anyway, passing the bottle between them at the rail, looking at the traffic. It was very strange to see all these other people out at sea, just enjoying the beautiful weather: as if through a clear but impenetrable veil.

'Okay,' said Sage, 'given the situation at home, and given that this trip would be breaking contraband, even now, if there was nothin' else going on, this is the tricky bit. We can be sure there are suits in the *Dáil* who would be happy to hold our coats while we take out Rufus, because they know what he is, but officially the Irish government is neutral and we must not be caught. No need to worry about the radar on Mount Gabriel – that's Mount Gabriel, the hill above Skull – it won't spot the *Lorien*. But there're three Irish naval cruisers standing off Kinsale, which is a little too close, and Serendip's not sure what they're doing there. We seem to have sneaked by . . . just have to hope for the best. It's the right time to be coming into the bay. This is party central for West Cork sailing folk, it's hit the pubs hour and we are lost in the crowd. Fuck of a sight better than trying it after dark. We've got a fake radio identity, *Lorien*'s radar profile is non-existent. Once we get between the Calf Islands and Inishodriscol – that's the one over there—'

'You're very convincing, motor mouth. Is this all coming from Serendip?'

'Not all of it. I'm remembering some. I've been here before. My dad brought me on a sailing trip, when I was fourteen. Last-ditch bonding attempt.'

'Was that good?'

'Diabolical. I hated him; I couldn't do fuck around the boat, an' although I didn't count myself as addicted at the time it was my first experience of missing the smack, which he knew nothing about, an' he would have gone beserk—'

'I get the picture. Hey, shouldn't we be talking about what happens next?'

'Yeah. Let's get parked first.'

The *Lorien* slipped through the islands, the sunset behind her, looking no way out of place, just classy. On the land side of Inishodriscol they lost the crowd. They were alone as they passed Rufus's boat dock in the waist of Inis Oir, with the village climbing above it. About half a mile further, and they entered an inlet under engine power. There were no buildings in sight here, only rugged little cliffs, capped with a rising ground of gorse and heather. It was darker suddenly, without the great sky.

They went back to the wheelhouse.

'So,' said Fiorinda. 'What next?'

'Ah . . . Well. We're somewhat exposed. There's not much chance he doesn't know we're coming. But we have things in our favour. Rufus is a fearsomely powerful magician, but he's also been a superstar for forty years. He hasn't the sense he was born with. He can't tie his own shoelaces.' Sage grinned. 'As I would know. Also, if he's like any other senior rock musician I ever met, he's more than a little *deaf*.'

Fiorinda crossed her eyes. 'Eh?'

They laughed. But there was something wrong. Sage had been acting shifty since they left the ocean and turned towards the land . . . Oh, here it comes. He took her hand and led her to one of the sleek cockpit chairs. A solemn look. She realised they'd never had that discussion he'd promised.

'Sweetheart. I'm going on alone.'

'Don't do this to me.'

Never trust Sage when he gives in easily, over anything. 'Fiorinda please. *Please*, my baby, have mercy on me. How could I ever face Ax if I let you come along? You can't be involved. No one must know that you or Ax were in on this. I brought you with me because I realised you were as safe on board the *Lorien* as you could be anywhere, and I have been so happy with you today. But you're going to wait here. The *Lorien* won't be seen, even if someone comes looking. I have a mirror-routine running, sampling the light on the rocks and the water . . . Serendip won't let you leave the boat; she'll stop you by knocking you out if she has to, but she'll stay here as long as it's safe. If I'm not back when the next tide turns, or if for any reason it's time to go, she'll take you home.'

'You bastard,' said Fiorinda. 'I should have known.'

What could she do? Make things harder? No. She sat looking out at the inlet, thinking, this is *Ireland*, where I have never set foot . . . while he went below. When he came back, he'd changed into his sand-coloured suit. He looked amazing. She kissed him goodbye and watched him row to the cusp of beach at the head of the inlet. He must have been rowing for the fun of it, because as soon as he got out and shipped the oars the dinghy came gliding magically back to the *Lorien*'s side all by itself. He waved, blew her a kiss, and set off into the gold and indigo twilight.

She sat for a while, chin on her hands.

'Serendip. I'm very sorry I said that about you being only a computer. You wouldn't hold me here against my will, would you?'

'Of course not, Fiorinda,' said the empty air. 'And apology accepted.'

'Thank you. Tell me when I should go after him.'

He looked back from the ridge. The *Lorien* was invisible. There was nothing to be seen except the water and the rocks, and a couple of odd shadows. That's good, he thought, that's *very* good. He climbed down into the next bay, and here there was a real beach, a great wide sweep of golden sand, with romantic little cliffs and picturesque boulders; and the castle on the opposite headland, facing the west.

Nice pad, Rufus. Location, location, location.

He walked by the ebb tide, where the minor colours of twilight lay caught in the wet sand, thinking of the miserable fuck-up he'd made of his life, and how he'd failed his darling, again and again. But Ax trusted me . . . When Ax left, he trusted me to look after Fiorinda. He was wrong, but *Ax trusted me*, I remember that and it all falls away, the chances missed, the hope refused, all that sorry record. I'm all right now. I'm sorted.

The cliff was a piece of piss, likewise the curtain wall of the bawn, the outer defence of Rufus's castle. The stonework was new, but it wasn't sheer; the infra-red traps and the photo-opportunities were easy to miss. Once within the bawn he forced an ordinary Yale lock on someone's back door in the domestic staff quarters. Everyone was out, according to Serendip; for the moment, anyway. He sat gathering himself, looking around: at the kiddie art magneted to the door of the fridge, the ancient oilcloth on the table, the brand-new webtv sitting beside the cereal packets; the colour photo of a football team. A dog-eyed, sepia Jesus gazed from the wall, pointing to his Sacred Bleeding Heart . . . This palimpsest of histories that we live in. These human things, that look so precious, so vulnerable and fragile: but it's not true. A tiger is vulnerable. Trees, rivers, mountains, *they* are fragile. He wondered about the woman who ruled here. Did she have opinions? Or did she just live her life from day to day, not knowing anything except that she loved a few people? He thought he ought to have a clear head. Why am I doing this? To avenge my darling? To protect England? To save the billions? Are my motives pure?

I don't know.

I'll just have to wing it.

Serendip told him it was time to move on, warm bodies approaching. He went through the house, out the front door, and he was in the inner courtyard of Drumbeg – an open space surrounded by a handsome array of stone buildings, either new or much restored; and the tower.

It was half dark. There were armed guards, but they were avoidable. The dogs were more alert. Two Dobermans came trotting up, through the pools of shadow between the security lights: heads low, silent, trained not to give warning before they attacked. He put on the mask. '*I don't like dogs*,' he said softly, in the back of his throat. They took the advice and returned to their routine patrol. Sage had noticed, years ago, that animals seemed to *understand* the mask. The results could be unpredictable; it wasn't something he'd try again in a hurry on a nervy fucking big police horse, but dogs aren't dangerous.

Now he met a real obstacle, but it was the last. The door at the base of the tower was double-timbered, thickly covered with fanged studs of polished iron, and the lock was a massive, ancient thing, not amenable to high-tech persuasion. But he still didn't need magic, which was good. He wasn't sure of the limits of his new-found super-powers, but it seemed to make sense to conserve them. He took out a ring of heavy-duty skeleton keys and Serendip told him what to do.

And here we are, in at the front end.

The ground floor of the tower was surprisingly small. He had seen plans, and a video (an interview that the lord of Drumbeg had done in here, carelessly, years ago), but imagination is stronger. He'd still been expecting a big, English, baronial-style hall. The room had no furniture except for a mass of ancient weapons, lovingly displayed on the white walls. There were museum-quality rugs on the stone-flagged floor; a stone spiral staircase in one corner. Across from the entrance another, modern, door, promised different territory beyond. That was the way to the guardrooms. But Rufus's private army wouldn't come running unless someone raised the alarm. A big brass pitcher full of leaves and hothouse flowers stood in the cold hearth: the glossy magazine touch. On the wall above it there was a picture in an Art Deco frame, a soft-porn portrait of a very young girl, displayed on a woodland bank, her little breasts uplifted, her knees open, lips parted and gossamer wings spread wide.

The girl was Fiorinda, of course.

Someone came down the stairs, treading softly. It didn't sound like Rufus. Who could this be? When, apparently astonished beyond caution, this person had crept out into the middle of the floor, he turned around. A woman of a certain age stood there, dressed in a long green open robe over a slinky catsuit type thing: slim as fashion, long legs, a superb pair of tits, glossy, aubergine-coloured hair. She stared at him, wide-eyed. Ah, I know.

'Carly Slater,' he said brightly, bowing a little from his height. 'I think we met, once. You won't remember. Some fucking VIP lounge somewhere.'

She bolted for the stairs.

Sage followed, leisurely. He could hear music.

The source of the music was in the room at the top which, Irish-style, was the great hall, and here was the traditional rockstar castle stuff that he'd expected below: a minstrels' gallery, massive black oak antiques, a grand piano, costly knicknacks, fabulous paintings; and a stunning view, lost in evening, through broad windows all around. No sign of Carly. He didn't see Rufus either, at first. There was a wallscreen, maybe three metres across, hanging opposite the stair. It was showing the Inauguration Concert at Reading, of all things. Aoxomoxoa, skull-masked, in his sweeping black and white kimono, towers predatory over Fiorinda. Give me your hand, he croons, meaning, *I'm going to have you*, and she answers, pure as crystal, raising her starry eyes—

Vole et non vole—

Intimidated? Not she. She'll take the Don apart, this one—

'Can you remember the future, Steve?' enquired a man's deep voice, rich and musical, with just the trace of a Northern Irish accent.

'Me?' said Sage, grinning, strolling forward, hands in his pockets. 'I can't remember anything. Too many drugs.'

An armchair under the screen turned around (it didn't scrape on the floor). A big man was sitting there, relaxed and magnificent, shining black curls on his shoulders, a much photographed face, not so young as it once was. 'Aoxomoxoa,' said Rufus. 'How times change. Last time we met you were the fart-sucking faceless king of the lads.

Now you're the sex god that every man, woman and child in Ax Preston's little manor wants to *fuck*. Or be fucked by. But Aoxomoxoa, they say, loves only that grey-eyed slip of a girl who is the queen of England . . . I've been expecting you. Take a seat, make yourself at home.'

The screen had switched to 'Atlantic Highway'. Four skull-headed idiots bounced over the potholes in a terrible old wreck of a car, convertible, as in someone sawed the roof off; chief idiot sporting pink sunglasses and a Goonhilly Earth Station baseball cap. On backwards, of course. In a moment the masks will disappear. They'll cruise along Newquay seafront, all the tat edited out, and step out into a suave Cornish Riviera—

Sage folded himself into a black-oak baronial chair, facing the lord of Drumbeg, his hands still in his pockets, legs stretched out. 'Is this what you do with yourself these days, Rufus? Slob around in yer carpet slippers, watching my old videos?'

Rufus took a couple of draws on the cigar he was smoking. Then he decided to offer the box, pushing it across the massive, mediaevaloid coffee table that stood between them. No doubt these were very fine cigars. 'Please, help yourself.'

'Wasted on me, thanks. They make me throw up.'

'Really? But you're smoking a cigar in this video, a little further on.'

'It was a prop. I don't recall if anyone actually smoked it; I cert'nly didn't. Have you been studying my fucking videos as a *hobby*? Now that is sad.'

Rufus pulled the table closer to him, leaned down and spooned a quantity of white powder from a silver bowl, cut it deftly and offered a silver straw.

'What about a little blow? It's Bolivian, certified organic.'

Sage shook his head. 'Not my drug.' He noted that he was being offered, in some sense, fire and salt, and

414

wondered if there was a ritual significance. Fucked if he cared. No, in these circumstances, has to be the right answer.

Rufus leaned back. 'How old are you, Steve? Thirty-one, thirty-two? The perfect age for a rockstar. You've made the shitloads of money. You don't yet realise that no matter what the fuck you do now, you're on the downward slope. But all those people looking at you, they know. They've seen you take the step beyond the top, they've seen you topple. You can write your rock symphonies, fill the Superbowl, but you're *over* in their minds. Oh, you don't mind if I call you Steve?'

This earned a big sunny smile. I mind, if my opponent tells me he's rattled?

'Not at all. My grandad still calls me Stephen.'

'Maybe you'd like to see some pictures I took of her when she was twelve years old. The ones I took for the artist . . . She was very compliant, a real little professional.'

'No thanks.'

Rufus looked irritated. He crushed out the cigar in a chunky bronze sheelanagig ashtray. 'Then what *do* you want, Steve? If you're not prepared to accept my hospitality?'

'I've come here to kill you,' explained Sage, placidly. He took his hands out of his pockets and laid them on the arms of the chair, in full view. The jewel on his right hand caught shards of light from the fake-flambeaux around the walls. 'I'm gonna break your legs and peg you out and leave you for the tide. Anythen' else you need to know?'

The big man, in his dark, gold-fringed mantle, majestically filling that chair, drew a long, measured breath.

'Partly because of what you did to my babe,' Sage went on, 'I have to admit that, though I'm fighting the idea: because that would be revenge, an' I know it would be wrong, an' only store up trouble. Partly because *you won't stop*, Rufus. Everybody knows you won't. You're beat, you're not king of the hill anymore, but there's no way anyone can say to you, be a good lad and retire quietly, and you'll do it. You'll keep coming back, fucking everything up. And partly—'

Rufus laughed heartily. 'What, more? How many excuses do you need?'

Sage was reminded of something he'd had to face. The person he'd *liked*, in Fergal Kearney's body, though with a different voice, and eyes, and physical presence: the misfit, loser, but also a really clever and knowing guy, had been in some way Rufus O'Niall. God help me, of course I liked him. He is her father.

'And partly for your sake, Rufus. Because I've some faint idea what it might feel like, being where you are. Think of me as the doctor. I've come to get you out of the shit you are in. You don't have to die if you don't want. We could talk about other ideas.'

The two men looked into each other's eyes.

There was a silence.

Suddenly the magician surged to his feet, sweeping up the mediaeval coffee table like a mad, huge shield. 'Damn you to hell!' he shouted. He flung his shield and charged forward, unstoppable; stormed past Sage and rushed out of the room.

Rufus ran down the stairs to the bedchamber on the floor below, leaped inside and barred the door. He was very stirred-up, not at all concerned. He called the guardroom and spoke to O'Donoghue, his security chief. In rapid-fire he ordered everybody out: men, domestic staff, the lot. They could sleep in the village, or wherever the fuck they liked. He didn't want them around. For what was going to happen, he wanted a free hand.

O'Donoghue didn't question or protest. He knew better than that.

Rufus broke the connection, feeling profound relief. He

416

had stopped something that could have been a fuck-up. Now what? He paced up and down, lacerated by memory. The terrible shock, when he had seen her on stage at that fucking Inauguration Concert, for the first time. Oh God, *she's changed, she's changed*. Until then he hadn't cared what happened. He hadn't been fazed when she fought him off, the night when he had tried to initiate her. That was just girlish rebellion, very sexual, to be expected. He hadn't given a shit about the boyfriends. She was still his creature, he knew he could reach out and take her, any time. But when he'd seen her, on the screen, and he had known *she's changed, she's changed!* Oh God, the burning outrage. Those two bastards, they took her from me, they changed her. That doesn't go unpunished! They're going to be sorry they were born.

And he hadn't let it go unpunished.

He thought of Aoxomoxoa's little litany; well here's mine. I want Fiorinda back. I will make her mine again, and she will bear the child, *my son*, that only she can bear. I want the Celtic future, and I will help to make it happen . . . He laughed, full and hearty. Right to the last moment, he would have saved her. But he had been prepared to let Fiorinda die if he had to, for the sake of the larger vision: the more so because he'd felt she was dead already. It had not been his magical child, the broken-spirited thing, cowering in that prison. But she was alive – and without Rufus having to intervene at all.

Thank you very much, Steve!

Now I'm going to wipe that grin off your face, you insolent bastard.

He went on pacing, from sheer excess of energy, the space that surrounded the great bed. There should be fresh rushes in here, arm's-length deep. They say they can't find a supplier who will change them daily; it's maddening . . . She's alive. I will take her back. I will make her mine again. The English Celtics had sent him messages, warning him to expect an assault, because Sage had returned from Caer Siddi. They'd advised him to double his security, or get himself out of the way. As if they thought he *didn't know*. As if they could tell him what to do.

Like fuck.

The way I deal with this is mine. I take no pissant advice. This is MINE.

What shall I do with him? I can do what I like with him—

It was not a problem that Sage was within the gates. The tower was a mantrap. Oh no, having the enemy inside is no disadvantage; this place is custom-built for that situation. The chieftains who ruled here, five hundred years ago, never dreamed of a life without armed guards at the door. They weren't fools. They knew you can't have power without the accessories.

He grinned to think of how he'd wrecked that fantasy in Brixton.

'Thank you for saving her life for me, Steve,' he shouted. 'And congratulations. You trained her up to be a good fuck. She was a cold little fish when she was a child. It wasn't the sex that held me. She made all the running there. I loved her for her mind.'

Silence. But he knew the bastard was out there, listening.

'You can't kill me. If you had the power, you haven't got the balls. You can only kill when you're following orders, and master isn't here now. You're Ax Preston's dog. Everyone knows it. They laugh at you, all your old mates. Hey, how does it feel, bitch? How does it feel, taking it up the arse from a coloured boy, Aoxomoxoa?'

He wondered at himself. How *young* he felt. Like a teenager.

'You never talked to Ax much, did you?' came Sage's voice. Rufus listened carefully, placing him. 'When you were Fergal. I remember noticin' that. You knew he'd see through you. You were never afraid of me. I'm stupid. I'm a pussycat.'

Out on the stairs Sage sat crosslegged, whistling under his breath, arraying his weaponry. He'd been carrying his Roman legionary's shortsword concealed under his suit jacket. He laid it beside Fiorinda's saltbox. Doesn't look like much, but he had relied on Drumbeg being well-supplied, and he'd been right . . . And a handgun, the automatic from his desk in Battersea. Like George always says, it's a sin to ignore the obvious. So what was the plan? The plan was to come here, bullshit Rufus into accepting single combat, and then . . . er . . . win.

He liked this plan. It was simple. It had no moving parts. It was Sage-proof.

The other option, where the evil magician repents, was an offer that must be made, and Rufus knew that the offer was real. However, let's face it, not a serious contender at this stage. But it does seem to wind him up nicely!

He thought of wrestling with George, and how you should handle yourself with an experienced opponent who outbulks you by a margin, and who has a cunning mind behind the weight. Who can pin you down, if you let him. Be careful, be careful. A moment ago he'd been on the point of yelling, '*What happened in England, Rufus? You couldn't get past my babe, could you?*' God help me, I am such a fuck-up. Don't get him thinking in that direction. He mustn't start thinking about Fiorinda.

Be careful!

Shit, he had nothing belonging to Ax. Oh. Yes I do. I am Ax Preston's bitch.

He laughed. You think I don't want to belong to him? You think that's an *insult*? 'Hey, Rufus, you just sent your private army away. Why d'you do that? With a homicidal deranged intruder in the house? Wasn't that kind of a strange move?'

Oh, fuck. *Be careful!*

Rufus opened the door of the bedchamber. Sage fired instantly, at point-blank range. The magician should have copped two bullets in the forehead, and another in the chest, not heavy calibre but big enough to leave no doubt. Nothing happened to him. The bullets fell, spent, as if they'd travelled for miles, and chimed away down the spiral staircase.

'I have a charm against firearms,' he said, grinning like a barracuda. 'There is not a soul of them will harm me or anything of mine. Have you not heard the stories?'

'Worth a try.'

'Jaysus Fockin' God, that was poor. I expected better.'

Sage was breath to breath with the ghost of Fergal Kearney: a waft of carrion, sea-green eyes looking out of torment. Rufus caught him in the moment of shock and pity with a mighty cuff around the head, and followed it through with a twist of the arm and a thrust of such violence Sage went sprawling, tumbling out of sight around the curve of the stair. Rufus laughed. Not such an old man, Steve!

'I was pretty sure I couldn't shoot you,' called Sage. 'Maybe you're right an' I shouldn't have tried, without warning. Listen, we can talk. I *know* how it feels to be where you are. Are you sure you don't need help?'

'Are you pure in heart?' shouted Rufus. 'You'd fuckin' better be, Sage my darling. If you are not, then get out of here. Go. Because I'm going to tear your soul from your body, and put you living into Hell for all eternity. You can't withstand me. Believe it. *Are you pure in heart?*'

'Nothen' like. There's places in my heart it'll be a long time before I dare go near. But I'm on my way. I'm good enough to take you. You're not so tough, old timer.'

'My son would have been ten years old!' howled the magician.

420

He rushed to the landing below, his eyes aflame, his hair coiling like Medusa snakes, his good looks contorted into a mask so furious that even the king of the lads recoiled. Sage tried to run down another flight. Rufus leapt on him and dragged him into the room where the old chieftains had dispensed justice, which was a library now. Then they fought in earnest, Sage a few inches taller, Rufus broader and heavier: grappling and gouging, around the booklined justice chamber and the bigger room next door, a super-star's toy recording studio, leaving a trail of wreckage, shattering anything movable, no holds barred, two things becoming clear: Sage was trying to move the fight down-stairs, out to the beach, presumably, so he could carry out his promise. Though he fought like a madman, his intent was always to get back to the stair, get out of these rooms. But he could not succeed, because the other thing that became clear was that Rufus was stronger by far than the younger man.

And he grew stronger.

Whenever Sage could escape, he wasn't fighting, he was running away. He'd put the Roman sword under his jacket before he took those potshots; he never had a chance to draw it. Rufus was happy with no weapon but his bare hands. Around and around they went, until at last Sage escaped, and almost made it down the next flight. But Rufus was playing with him. He came on in another great rush, laid hold of Sage by the shoulders, wrenched him off his feet and sent him crashing against the wall. Sage was up again at once, only to be met by a tremendous lock around his neck and under his right arm. He couldn't do a thing; he was like a struggling child. The man's strength was monstrous.

'Now you start to understand,' said Rufus in Sage's ear, hot cheek pressed against the shorn fleece, '*now*—' He closed his teeth in Sage's scalp and gnawed, shook his head from side to side, spattering blood, and started to haul him back up the stairs, nothing in hell Sage could do, Rufus's grip was so inhumanly powerful. If he had managed to brace himself immovably his head would have been torn off, his arm ripped from its socket. So they arrived back in that room with the armchairs and the big screen and the expensive art.

'Listen, let me tell you,' said Rufus, with unhurried relish, holding Sage pinned beside one of the windows. Sage stared back, through the blood that was streaming down his face. He had no breath left for taunting—'You're gonna take a fall now. It's enough to break your bones. You can stop them from breaking, but you'll be draining your power, and you don't know how to open yourself to replenishment. I know you don't. I can feel it, and *I know you*. You don't know how to *take* what you *want*.' He shifted his hold to shoulder and thigh, unperturbed by his opponent's resistance, heaved back and took a swing, as if with a battering ram, and Sage went flying, crashing through the glass, out into the night and to the courtyard three floors below.

Fiorinda had reached Drumbeg while the fight on the stair was going on. She had found Carly Slater, in a little room above the entrance hall which had a hole in the middle of the floor where the old inhabitants of this place used to chuck down missiles at invaders . . . She had not been very surprised to find her aunt. She knew a lot about Rufus's present and past life thanks to her months with Fergal. She knew that Carly had been with him all the time; never been parted from him, not really, ever since the long ago.

When Fiorinda found her, Carly was sitting on a little stool, holding a doll made out of yellow straw and rapidly, urgently, picking it apart, while the sound of battle raged overhead. Now the figure was ripped to pieces by Fiorinda. Carly was up against the wall, wrapped in stone the way Fiorinda had been wrapped in the resurrected branches of the storm-timber chair. Fiorinda had found a tight curl of yellow hair inside the straw dolly, which she had kissed and put inside her teeshirt, against her skin. She preferred not to speculate as to how Carly Slater had got hold of a piece of Aoxomoxoa, maybe a long time before tonight; or in what circumstances. Not that she cared.

She stood listening, taking great breaths. The air felt thickened, richer, as if everything was giving off sparks. *What a rush* this magic is. It's a dreamworld. Everything's contracted. Nothing's in focus except what matters, but in that context, you can do what you like. Exactly what you fucking like—

Sage had not fallen. His exit from the window had not been much more of a challenge than what can happen when a stuntdive goes wrong. He'd recovered, and ended up clinging to the stonework, finding purchase with his fingertips and the toes of his climbing boots, flexible as dancing slippers. My name is Aoxomoxoa and I have superpowers, but I am not going to jump. For once in my life I am not going to ask for trouble . . . Keeping a three-point hold on the tower, he tugged the nosering apart with his free hand and sent a spider-wire thickening and spinning downwards. He secured the top end by thrusting the ring itself into the mortar between two courses of stone and twisting it so it expanded, a little chemical and metal explosive piton, locked in there. Who needs magic when you have Heads stagecraft? He wrapped his sleeve over his hand, with the line wound round it, kicked off and bounced, abseiling, down to the ground.

Another cheap round. He could feel none of the damage he'd taken; what damage? In fine shape, boiling with energy, he walked briskly to the front end of the tower again, the legionary's sword naked in his hand. He looked up. Fiorinda was looking down at him from the murder hole.

Her presence at once seemed very reasonable. Of course she's here!

'How's it going, babes?'

'Not too bad. I met Carly. I have her wrapped up for you.'

She dropped into his arms. He hugged her, laughing, the bare sword in his hand.

'You are a *bad* brat, and I am never going to trust Serendip again. D'you know, I think that computer's fallen out with me, she hasn't said a word since I started fighting Rufus. I detect tetchy vibes. Hey, Fee, what happened to jeopardising your immortal soul?'

'I d-decided my immortal soul can take a couple of knocks,' gabbled Fiorinda, her whole mind and body on fire, 'in a good cause. If I have one. It's a good cause, isn't it—?'

'I don't know.' He set her on her feet. 'I don't know anymore. Oh, shit, Fiorinda, this is dangerous stuff. I just this moment realised I am smashed out of my brain, and I didn't even know it, which is *not* the way I'd meant to approach—'

'I told you, I told you. *Fucking* dangerous, oh, my God—'

They grabbed each together, raining furious kisses, fused into one being, flooded with incredible arousal. 'Can we do this? Fee, can we do this, I mean Sage—' 'I *know* what you mean. I don't know! I don't know! I don't think I can stop.' 'God, this is amazing, I can't tell you apart from me—'

'We need Ax!' wailed Fiorinda, and then immediately, horrified— 'Oh no, no, no. I don't want Ax here. I don't want Ax to have anything to do with this!'

Her distress sobered them both, and the world came back: the ground floor of the castle tower, and air that was cold as old stone. At some point the lights had gone out. The weapons on the walls caught gleams from the summer night outside.

'Nonsense,' said Sage, earnestly. 'Ax was worrying me before he took off. May I say, both of you were getting me depressed, with your political differences, I fucking *hated* that. But he is okay. He is not a monster. We're the ones in danger!'

'I *know*,' said Fiorinda, with the same fierce urgency. 'I know he's okay. But for a moment my head is clear, so it was worth being scared. I am with you all the way, Sage. I'm not leaving you to do this alone. Just tell me one thing. Who is winning?'

'Me.'

He did not look as if he'd been getting the best of the fight.

'You're absolutely certain about that?'

'*Absolutely.*' He grinned like a tiger, stone cold sober, and took the saltbox from his jacket pocket. 'You'd better have this.'

Suddenly, Rufus was at the open doorway. Fiorinda and Sage sprang apart. What's going to happen now? How did he get down the tower? He didn't come by the stairs. Maybe he leapt from the shattered window of the great hall. He was clearly on fire as they had been, oh, *but much more so*. He had shed his purple mantle during the wrestling bout. He was wearing it again, wound and tied around him so as not to impede his movement. His still-beautiful face was transfigured, exultant. He looked at Fiorinda, one glance, and then ignored her.

'I have never had competition before!' he shouted, and swept weapons from the walls, testing and discarding. He tossed a second sword to his opponent, choosing a heavier model and a barbed trident for himself. 'You're right. This is the way to settle it! This is the Celtic way! Come on, bastard, fucking take me on, would you? Let's do it!'

Call that round one to Sage.

Sage leapt at Rufus. The battle was rejoined, a clashing and clanging of metal in the dark, sudden sweeps of whiteness across the empty courtyard as the security lighting woke, Sage running whenever he had the chance, as long as Rufus would come after him, determined to lure the magician away from his home ground—

Fiorinda stood clutching her head between her hands, seared by her father's glance, appalled by the traps that magic sets. Rufus wasn't supposed to know she was here! She had meant to be Sage's secret weapon . . . Oh God, I can't challenge him if he knows I'm here. *He's my father.* Such a coil of ancient fear and grief and twisted longing; how can I reduce that and come out winning? Sage was right, he's my father and I'm no use.

Carly dropped from the murder hole.

Oh boy. *Shit.* How did she? How *could* she?

'Have you got a phone?' demanded Carly. 'I'm going to call the police!'

She zoomed across the dark hall and started hammering a number combination into the lock on the inner door. Fiorinda chased after her. The door flew open. Carly hit a light switch and there was a big empty room, with common-room type furniture, tables and chairs, tall padlocked cabinets around the walls. An armoury.

'Where is everyone?' said Fiorinda, staring.

'Rufus sent them away,' gasped Carly. 'I think your fucking boyfriend made him do it. We've got to stop them, Fiorinda. They're going to kill each other!'

'Yes,' said Fiorinda. Carly had grabbed a landline phone from a table and pulled it to the floor. She was on her knees, stabbing at the keypad, the stiff skirts of her green robe ballooning round her, sheeny deep purple hair falling over her face. Fiorinda walked over, took the phone and threw it onto the stone floor. 'You're not going to call anyone.'

The two women stared at each other.

This is Carly Slater, procuress to the famous, who took the child Fiorinda to Rufus O'Niall's country house to be seduced. Unjustly blamed for this crime, in a sense, because she was only obeying Rufus. Looking at her, Fiorinda was eleven again. She was in the cold house where Rufus O'Niall had pursued his affair with the Slater sisters.

I didn't like you, Carly, but I liked all the treats.

'I once saw you in bed with my mum and Rufus,' she said. 'Do you remember that? I didn't understand that I was seeing magic, of course. But I was scared to death.'

Carly stared with large, grey-green eyes. 'Kill me,' she whispered.

'Not a chance. I want you to grow *very* old.' She twisted off the lid of her saltbox, flicked her wrist and sent a spinning curl of salt to fall around Carly's skirts, a circle around her on the floor. 'Try getting out of *that*, shit-for-brains. You're not going to help Rufus. You will not do any more magic tricks on my Sage. Got it?'

Carly made a keening sound and stared at Fiorinda out of the place where Fergal Kearney had been. 'For pity's sake. Kill me.'

Oh fuck.

Carly didn't look very different. Ten years isn't long, for a fashionable woman with access to every cosmetic aid. But there was a deadness in her features. Her face was a mask with something looking through the eyeholes. Her hand came down, slowly and as if stealthily – Fiorinda watching, fascinated – and swept a break in the ring of salt.

Fiorinda crouched, instantly shoved it back in place again, and felt an appalling rush.

What a rush. Her ears were ringing, her eyes darkened.

'My bossy little girl,' murmured Carly.

The hand came down again, same stealthy *intense* gesture.

Fiorinda made the ring whole again, thinking furiously.

She wasn't afraid to use the saltbox, although the box had originally been a present from Gran, which meant it was very dodgy. So what? All magic is untrustworthy, and hey, I can take over the means of production. I've read about that . . . But she could see where this was going. He moves, I move. I'm pinned down. If I break and run, I've lost him. I could kill Carly . . . But *I won't do that*. That would not be like me thumping Charm, that would be me murdering the horrible woman who is helpless. There, he's broken it again, and I fix it. The rush was indescribable; it tasted of metal and blood; it tasted of something huge beyond measure: but it's okay, I'm doing the hard thing not the easy thing, fixing not breaking, holding him off, refusing, no different from when I was in prison, only I *mustn't lose my concentration*.

She lost her concentration—

Carly rocketed to her feet and leapt over the ring. Her robe caught fire; she screamed and beat at the flames with her hands, but already, trailing little whirls of smoke, she was scrabbling the tables, the desks, searching for focus material – paper, pencil, wax, cord, anything a witch could use. Fiorinda had been knocked out, flung away somewhere. She came back, into her body, ran at Carly and caught her by the hair and saw, with a sickening delight, how the imprisoned creature looked at her: Carly's head pulled back, Carly herself still in there, mortally terrified, *just the way my mother was*— Oh God, Sage, this is dangerous. I will kill her, and when I've killed her there will be no way back. I will be what Rufus is—

Oh, my Sage, fight for me, and I will fight for you—

The swordfight went on and on, a hard, archaic slog. No one came near the castle yard, though the dogs in their kennel were kicking up a hell of a racket. Perhaps there are often strange nights when the dogs at Drumbeg yell their heads off and Rufus's peasants and his men at arms know just to stop their ears. Rufus pays well, demands complete loyalty, and gets obeyed: implicitly obeyed. It's nothing you can persuade anyone to talk freely about, but he's a very ill feller to cross . . .

Sage had taken a couple of slices, including a deep one in his right calf muscle that he'd copped one time when he had Rufus down for a moment. These cuts, like the bitewound in his scalp, were not worrying him, but they were bleeding freely. Rufus was unscathed. On the other hand, the fight had moved out of the bawn, Sage still falling back, and Rufus racing joyously after him. They were through the courtyard gates – which the duellists had found standing open, the gatehouse deserted, the alarms silent. Sage did not know if he had disarmed the system himself, or if Fiorinda had done it; or even Rufus, the better to pursue the joy of battle. All the magic runs together, as if to one end . . .

The fight was on the grey road now, that ran through the castle's grounds, along the top of the cliffs. Sage wanted to get down to the beach, and there was a path, but he couldn't get Rufus to take it. Never mind: he was on the right track, *he could feel it*.

What is happening here is that two men, each of them able to engage directly with the physical universe, yeah, the whole fifteen-dimensional kaleidoscope, are trying whose ability to change the world is greater. Their super powers cancel each other out, *almost*. This male-animal contest, the cut and thrust of the heavy weapons, the bloody, sweating struggle, is the form that they have chosen to decide the question. A sword fight has a rhythm that each partner tries to destroy: and that's essentially what's happening in all the dimensions. Whose rhythm will set the tune? Magic is a physical thing. Which of us has the edge? It's overwhelming, it's glorious, to argue your cause with the state of all states on equal terms. To be able to manipulate the world as if it's the contents of your own mind . . . But

Rufus has exactly the same power, though he came by it differently; he's been using magic for a long time, and he's not losing.

The Irishman was singing. Tears of emotion stood in his shining eyes and ran down his cheeks. He had no death wish. He was sure he was going to win – though he was beginning to realise he'd been disinformed. Sage chose to return to mortality; he did not *fail*. The bastard has much more control than he made out—

> When I lie upon my bed of slumber,
> Thoughts of my true love rise in my mind—
> I turn around to embrace my darling.
> Instead of gold 'tis the brass I find—

Sage didn't feel like singing. He was here to kill a man.

A lock. Aoxomoxoa and Rufus O'Niall, knuckle to knuckle in a clinch neither could break, Sage holding off that wicked trident in Rufus's left hand with his short-sword. Sage had put on the mask, for old times' sake. The living skull shone in the dark.

'When did you first know you were different, Steve?' demanded Rufus, his hot breath inches away. 'When you were two, three years old? That you were *more*? Richer, stronger, *too much*? You found out that the other kids couldn't *deal with you*. So you found your way up to the rock stage, which is the best theatre of power, *pure physical sexual superiority power*, in the whole fucking world, and you ruled—'

Rufus tried to force the disengagement. Sage wouldn't let him.

'So you're on stage in front of a million worshipping punters, and it's *already over*. It's not you they're seeing. You've become their meat, they're giving you *nothing*.'

'You shouldn't let it get you down,' said Sage. 'It's a well-paid job, with foreign travel, weird hours and good holidays. Think of it like that, an' you won't go nuts—'

He fell back, Rufus leaping after him, and felt the change from paved road to rough grass under his feet, and heard the sea, closer now. A thrill went through him, a recognition so deep he couldn't tell if it were joy or terror: and then he knew.

He was in the Zen Self dome, in January of the terrible year. He had taken a massive dose of snapshot, because he thought he could find out whether Rufus O'Niall really was a threat . . . Ax was in Amsterdam; Sage and Fiorinda were in despair. His eyes flew open, in the cold dark lab: and he knew.

So this is where I went. A clifftop. The dizziness of the blood I'm losing, the feel of these weapons, the sound of the sea at my back. The moon a blurred seal of silver in the overcast, not a star in the wide east, above that dark loom of rising ground . . . The details are not all the same, but *this is the moment* from which I came back knowing I'd been right about Rufus, and that the only way I could beat him was by achieving the Zen Self . . . I tried again and again to find out more, until there were no more visions, until the naked imperative of the quest took over. But *this is it* . . . Oh, shit, I'm here! I made it!

I'm on the wave now. I can't go wrong. And then he clung to the pure, sweet air on his face, the scent of gorse and peaty earth, ah, cling to this—

Sage had faltered. Rufus laughed, and hauled back for a gigantic swing. His opponent, instead of parrying it, dropped on one knee, caught him and cast him down. Rufus went flying into empty air. He landed in a heap, five or six metres below, and lay still for a long time, long seconds. Sage looked down. Slowly but inexorably, Rufus rose to his feet. There was a billow of darkness that must be shed blood on the dim sand where he'd been lying, but he laughed again, full and hearty, and stretched his arms. 'I could take on the world!' he shouted. 'Wouldn't you like to know how I do this, you bastard?'

'No,' yelled Sage. 'Because I know what it's cost you, an'

I think you're a fucking lunatic. Call yourself a rockstar? You can't even run a balance sheet.'

This is who I am. This is my completion. Now I leap—
—into the dark.

Remembering the future is the same as remembering the past; nothing stays the same; you never remember the same thing twice. He felt he should have jumped straight down, but no, it was a double somersault and a pike; he wished he could have made it three: partly to fuck Rufus up, partly to absorb some energy; jump straight down eight or ten metres, you'd snap your shins. He landed and rolled, arms spread, a weapon in each hand . . . and that's the end of the preview, don't know anything else, only that it's nearly over.

They circled on the sand, both men moving heavily now. I'm very tired. That's all it feels like, I'm very tired and I want to lie down. But I've drawn blood, I couldn't do that before. I can finish him. Thank God his power is divided . . . Thank God Fiorinda came along. I could never, ever have done this alone.

Rufus didn't even see the crucial stroke coming at him, the high sideways sweep that severed his vertebrae. He was thinking of something else. His blood leapt up like a fountain uncapped. The body stayed on its feet. The head had *vanished*. Where the fuck did it go? Sage dropped to one knee, leaning on the Drumbeg sword. The blurred moonlight was confusing, he felt very dizzy—

'Steve!'

He looked around. Rufus's head had landed on a flat-topped boulder, down by the sea. It was upright. The eyes and the mouth gleamed.

Sage got to his feet and made for the boulder. He was so tired he could hardly stand. So it's not over. He was fascinated by this head. 'Rufus,' he muttered, swaying. 'You're kidding. You can't come back from this.'

'Hahaha!' said the head.

Sage dropped his legionary's sword.

'You have her, but neither you nor Ax Preston shall enjoy her.'

Whatever. He took hold of the Drumbeg sword in two hands and heaved it over his shoulder. It felt heavy as lead. Raising it took for ever, but he was getting there, reaching the point on the arc where he could pitch forward, chop the fucking thing in two. His senses deadened by exhaustion, he didn't realise until the last moment that Rufus's headless body had come stumbling up behind him. He swung around and parried the body's swordstroke, but the barbed blades of the trident were thrust into his unprotected right side and twisted there, the weight of a big man's falling body behind them.

'Hnnh!' said the head, with deep satisfaction.

Fiorinda had realised that Carly was getting stronger. She had been exultant, and very frightened. She had to respond to the power turned against her; she'd known she would be destroyed, one way or another, if this went on much longer. But it didn't. The last bout was in front of the big cold hearth in the ground floor of the tower, under the picture of Fiorinda when she was twelve years old, the fairy girl with beestung lips and little rose-tipped breasts. In all the length of the duel they had moved only between the modern guardroom and this hall hung with ancient weapons. It had felt like light-years. She did not know if it was early or late, or if a whole night and day had passed. She cast yet another arc of salt (the floor was scrawled with them), completed another circle, and this time the magician inhabiting Carly had no riposte . . . She felt a different rush, a dying fall. Blue flames leapt from the circle like a flickering pelt. A flame-shaped creature clothed in blue fire stood there, enclosing Carly, and then whooshed away into nothing—

—leaving the woman's body lying on the floor, shuddering.

'Sage!'

She cast one glance at the picture of herself, dismissing it for ever, and ran: out of the hall, out of the bawn, found the path and scrambled down to the moonlit beach. She raced over to the tumbled bodies, shoved Rufus's body aside and bent over her lover. 'My baby, my baby,' she whispered, tears falling, stroking the bloody lamb's fleece.

The head sat on its rock. Its eyes were half-open and already sunken in the broad, deep sockets. It was mumbling fragments of words, some kind of threats, but it shut up after she'd filled the mouth with salt and sand. She lifted it by the hair and dumped it where she could keep it in sight.

Sage opened his eyes. He seemed to be pinned to the sand by an incredible weight, not pain, something more fundamental. Fiorinda was there, holding his hand.

'Hi,' he whispered. 'Cracked it?'

'Yeah, we cracked it.'

'You better get out of here, my brat, before the Gardia arrive. Take Serendip. The *Lorien* will get you home.'

'No. Olwen's coming with a helicopter. I sent for her.'

'Ah, that's good. Good you'll have company. But you should still get back to the boat.' He tried to raise her hand to his lips. 'Oh. I can't move.'

'I'm stopping you from moving, my darling. Don't fight it, lie still.'

'Right,' he sighed, smiling up at her. 'Make it last . . . But I can talk to you?'

'Don't talk too much. You know what I want to do after this, Sage?'

'Mmm . . . No.'

'I want to travel. You and Ax, you've been everywhere. There're so many places I haven't seen. I want to go to Milan. Will you come with me?'

'Why Milan? There's nothen' there but a few shops . . .

an' a Formula One course. Oh, okay, Milan . . . How long . . . d'you think it'll take them to get here?'

'About five minutes.'

Sage's eyes widened. '*Huh?*'

'Er, fact is they've been waiting on a Navy frigate out at sea that Richard managed to borrow for me. Hey, remember Venezuela! Did you think I would have come with you without back-up? We couldn't do anything for you going in; you had to be alone, you were right about that. But I reckoned it was okay for us to fetch you out, so I set it up and I didn't tell you because you would have argued. You are so dumb, Sage. Didn't you realise you might get hurt?'

He had realised. He had not expected to be alive—

'You're a very sneaky brat!'

'Hahaha. Me, Boudicca!'

His breath caught. 'How long did you say?'

''Bout four minutes now. Sssh. Hang on, my baby.'

'Talk to me.'

So they talked, softly, about the antics of little plastic armies on the kitchen table at Tyller Pystri, in the lamplight of an evening long ago, until Sage couldn't talk anymore, he could only look at her, and the seconds ticked by; and she knelt there by the tide, with his life in her arms, flickering like a candleflame in a draught—

'Will they get here, Serendip?'

'Everything's fine, Fiorinda. Don't let him go.'

When the helicopter landed, that's how Olwen and the Heads and the medical team found them: Sage lying at the edge of the sea, Fiorinda holding him, the magician's head beside them. Olwen Devi saw the great dark ragged gap under Sage's right ribs and stared at Fiorinda, open-mouthed, in appalled amazement.

'Just do it!' snarled Fiorinda.

They had his riven body onto the stretcher and an IV pumping plasma into him as swiftly as George Merrick's hands would move.

'Hi, George,' whispered Sage.

'Hi, boss. Got the bastard, did yer?'

'I did.' And at last he closed his eyes.

The helicopter rose and rattled away, eastwards, Sage's body hooked up to all the life support they had, Rufus O'Niall's head in a sack, and Fiorinda huddled on the floor, clinging to Sage's lax hand, tears streaming down her face.

God send each good man at his end, such horse such hounds and such a friend.

Six days after Ax's velvet invasion, as the media people were calling it, he was in Somerset, facing a pitched battle. At first everything had gone well. Benny Preminder's régime was in disarray. A hastily commissioned emergency Prime Minister had welcomed Ax's return. In Yorkshire and the North-East, people were celebrating. In London they were ringing the church bells and throwing street parties. (Amazing. The crowd that had tried to burn Fiorinda must've been aliens, popped in from another dimension.) But that wasn't the whole story. The Celtics were resisting wherever they held the balance of power, and in the South-West they were determined to fight. The success of an invasion is measured in hours, but the hours can stretch to days. Ax had walked into a ready-made situation not thirty miles from his home town, and it looked as if there was no way to defuse it.

The barmies were encamped on the north flank of the Polden Hills, facing the enemy across the valley of the Brue. Early on the morning of that sixth day Ax was in a canvas mess tent, with the remaining members of the Few, waiting for news. Kathryn Adams had returned to the US. Alain and Tamagotchi were not involved in this fight, and Mohammad was back in Yorkshire. His friends were noncombatants, and he intended to keep them that way; but they were safe enough for the moment.

The news that meant either peace or war would not reach them by telecoms. That was forbidden by the terms of their negotiations with the Celtics – and also because the Celtic netheads were as smart as any other kind of netheads, expert at using tech to defeat tech. They didn't know how the news would reach them . . . There was a plastic table, spread with a war-conditions rockstar breakfast buffet of bread and cheese, some very suspect sliced meat, and vacuum jugs of dandelion coffee. Chip and Ver, Allie and Dilip and Rob sat around it, making hopeful conversation. Rox was back in London. Ax studied a paper map. He'd been so savagely in need of his chip, these last days, that if he'd been anywhere near a working neuro-prosthetics clinic he'd have demanded a replacement over the counter, *do it to me!* Failing that, he had to learn the map and *think*, try to visualise, because it's always the detail that counts—

'We need to retake Reading,' said Dilip. 'If we could walk in there, and make it look never in doubt, that would swing it.'

'Yeah,' said Rob. 'We could do that. The town's ours. They may not love the rock festival thing, but they hate the fucking Celtics—'

Allie said, 'Ax. I have a briefing on Greg Mursal for you. Do you want it now?'

'Who's he?'

'He's the Prime Minister, Ax.'

He glanced over with a rueful grin. 'Sorry. Yeah. I'll get to it.'

The emergency Prime Minister, alas, was not a major issue. Most of the people who were in a position to control the future of England were probably to be found just about two miles away, in the enemy camp.

Put wood on the fire, Jackie. Good wood on the fire, Jackie—

'I'm going out for some fresh air.'

Outside the tent Ax's driver, a Welsh independent

volunteer called Bronwen Palmer, was sitting sideways in the open door of her jeep, feet dangling. *Stay with the vehicle* was the only way to hang on to mps – mobile power-sourcing, otherwise known as motor fuel. Take your eyes off your ride for a moment, even if you're driving the Dictator around, and it will get siphoned, or the fuel-cell will be drained, or it will vanish.

Ax nodded to her, took out a cigarette and looked north across the valley. There, beyond the Celtic position, lies the great mass of the Glastonbury Festival site, dwarfing the little towns of Shepton Mallet, Street and Glastonbury. Something like a hundred thousand people, who *actively want* to bear fifteen babies and see fourteen of them die; who *actively want* to keep their unfit in dogkennels and sacrifice them on feastdays, because Gaia has spoken . . . He didn't believe it. As the leader of the Rock and Roll Reich should know, it's all surface and moonshine. But the Celtic warriors wanted their pitched battle, it was their day in court, and either they would have their way, or Ax would back down, lose the initiative, and the invasion would be lost. He did not want the job of *dux bellorum*. It was the last thing he wanted, but he couldn't leave his supporters stranded. He had to make this work.

'What pisses me off,' he said, 'is the number of people who think I'm surprised it ended up like this. I am not surprised. And the other number of smug people who think this proves there's something fundamentally wrong with the Counterculture. There's nothing wrong with being green, or loving this beautiful country and not wanting to see it paved over. There is *absolutely fuck-all* wrong with the music; or with living the simple life. The Counterculture's not responsible for the Crisis. You know what Albert Einstein said, after the Second World War? He said it made no difference what weapons were used to fight the Third World War. He knew that if it happened, the Fourth World War would be fought with sticks and stones. As it turns out, the Third World War was fought with rotten money, and peasant soldiers in client states, over decades. But he was right.'

'You could duck this,' said Bron, 'and win a war of attrition.'

Yeah, he thought. Like your lot did, when *you* were the people who lived here, at the end of a tumbling empire. 'Nah. I'll fight. It can be won. It's the best option, when you look at the alternatives. What are you independent Welshpersons going to do?' he added, in her own language. 'Clear off back to the valleys would be my advice.'

'I don't know,'said Bron cheerfully. 'Taking a wild guess, we'll wait and see, and leg it for the winning side at the worst moment.'

'Right.'

'Of course, the Northerners'll do what the fuck they like. Hypocritical tight-arses.'

She had not expected Ax Preston to be like this, an unassuming feller with a few strands of silver in his dark hair, a demon for work and a distracted look. Didn't know what she'd expected, really. She liked the directness. He gives you the feeling he's not just moving his mouth to be polite to a minor player he'll never see again. He's talking to you. That's what I will tell people, she thought.

'Are you ever going to smoke that cigarette? Er, Sir?'

'No. It's Ramadan.'

It will be Yap Moss again, he thought, tracing the landscape with his gaze, fitting it to his plans. And they don't know. There were very few people in that camp over there who'd been in Yorkshire. They don't know what can happen in an afternoon. He felt sickened.

The command post of the Celtic forces was a prefab Iron Age roundhouse with a reed thatched roof. Fiorinda and the Heads drove up to it, Fiorinda in the front with

George. She was wearing the clothes she'd been wearing in Ireland, but cleaned up, and her hair was brushed until it glowed. The thing in the sack at her feet muttered, like something overheard in a bad dream. They parked a respectful distance away from the fully tooled-up warriors guarding the doorway. There were shouts of excitement in the distance, but the crowd here was silent, pressing close and staring: sombre, tattooed, pierced, wild-haired men and women.

'Rehearse me again,' said Fiorinda.

George repeated the Irish with her.

'I've got it.' She pushed back her hair. 'Shit, I wish I had some make-up.'

'You look terrific,' said Bill.

'Never better,' said Peter. 'I never saw you look better.'

'Knock 'em dead, my love,' said George. 'You're on.'

They were supposed to have a safe conduct. Unarmed, no panic buttons, no phones, nothing, they walked in, Fiorinda casually swinging the sack. Inside the roundhouse it was, unexpectedly, almost as light as day. There were ATP patches around the walls, between the posters and the flyers and the maps. Fiorinda grinned when she saw that. There was a trestle-table of pale raw timber across the centre of the house, and a row of people, mostly men, sitting behind it; others were standing on either side. She recognised several of the intimates of those winter evenings at Rivermead, but not Benny Prem; and some Scottish and Irish hippies, 'military advisors' from the less virulent 'Celtic nations' version of the Celtic Movement. They were not green nazis – but they damn well ought to know better than to be in this company.

'Hello, Jack,' she said brightly to the one she remembered worst of those who had seen her humiliated as 'Fergal's' whore, 'where's Benny?' She grinned. 'Is he not feeling very well? Hello Phil—' to Phil Maclean, who had been a friend of hers last time they met. 'How's the band?'

She emptied her sack onto the table in front of them, lifted Rufus's head by the hair and set it upright. A little salt trailed from the mouth; which moved, slackly, but no distinct sound emerged. The life in it was running down at last.

There you go. One dead magician. Think about it, boys. Those of you who know.

She said her piece, looking the chief of the Irish party straight in the eye.

'Coir paisean a bhi ann, agus nior fear, bean no leanbh sin Eireann Naofa, go dtabharfainn mise no mó churadh an locht.'

It was a crime of passion, and there is not a man, woman nor child in Holy Ireland, that would give me or my champion the blame.

There was a dead silence.

'Well?' said Fiorinda.

One of the men at the table (which of them was the first would be cause for endless speculation) stood up and bowed, without a word. Then another did the same, then one of the women. There was a rush. They were all on their feet. One or two even dropped on one knee. The armed guards around the walls decided to pitch in, going down in a wave.

Fiorinda drew a breath, and nodded.

'Good. That's very sensible.'

The tableau came to life. A babble of voices.

'No, I'm sorry,' she told them. 'Later. We'll talk. Now I have to be somewhere else.'

She walked out, the Heads forming up around her, into the waiting crowd. The bonfire at Westminster rose up before her and there was bile in her throat, but she raised her clasped hands above her head. 'It's peace!' she yelled. The warriors cheered. She and George and Bill and Peter leapt into the jeep and roared away.

While Fiorinda was pulling her stunt, Sage was on his way

from the Celtic camp to Ax's position, escorted by an enthusiastic crowd. Neither of them had yet seen Ax. They had come to Somerset straight from the South Wales Zen Self clinic, where he'd been patched up sufficiently that he could sit in a car. It was a tour de force but it was worth it at this juncture, when something like 'the return of Aoxomoxoa' could swing the balance. He was feeling the strain, conscious of pain and weakness under the drugs, but he was okay. All he had to do was sit and wave to the public, like dowager royalty. He was not afraid for himself, because all this felt like a dream anyway. He was afraid for Fiorinda, walking into that den of wolves without him. But he knew she would be fine. She could look after herself, and she had George and Bill and Peter—

The jeep coughed and died. They were on a little grey lane, eaten away by flowers and grass, that lead to Mr Dictator's camp. He stayed where he was, in the back with his Zen Selfer medical support, while the driver and his mate decided they'd run out of fuel, what a bust. The camp was just up the hill. Everyone in the jeep knew that Sage was incapable of walking anywhere, but the cheering crowd had no idea. They were mostly the Cornish Celtics, coming over to Ax's side because Sage had returned as a conquering hero. Shit. Fate has called our bluff. He hated the thought of being carried out of here on a stretcher, but that's what it might have to be.

There was a sudden commotion in the press of warriors and camp followers who filled the lane. Four young men came barging through the crowd hauling a great big roan horse, saddled and bridled in Celtic retro style. Everyone was overjoyed. What a great solution! The guys with the horse dashed right up, alight with excitement—

'Aoxomoxoa! Aoxomoxoa! Can you ride? Uh, Sir?'

So it's not over, because the answer to that question has to be yes.

'I don't know,' he said. 'I've never tried.'

If Olwen had been there she would have stopped him, but they'd decided not to send the weird-science guru herself into the Celtics' camp. The Zen Selfers wouldn't argue with Aoxomoxoa. He almost wished they would, but too bad. Can't let the punters down, not now. Got to act the part, one more time . . . So he climbed on board the horse, and the Cornish all ran along on either side of him, cheering, through a gate, onto a flowery hillside where crowds of soldiers from the barmy army, who had been watching and waiting up above, came racing down to join them, shouting madly: 'It's Sage!' 'It's Sage!' 'It's Aoxomoxoa!'

Ax and his driver stood and stared while waves of barmies swept past them whooping and shouting. The roan horse came up, surrounded by the tumult, and then the crowd stopped. Sage and Ax looked each other over, Sage leaning forward over the neck of the big roan. The horse took a few more steps forward. Sage slid down, very carefully, as if he was deeply suspicious of this mode of transport, and stood leaning on his steed's shoulder.

'Hi, rockstar.'

'Hi, other rockstar. How was Ireland?'

'Terrific. But I don't think I'll be going back for a while.'

Sage dropped the reins; Bronwen Palmer (what a story to tell) caught hold of them and stood there at the turning point . . . Mr Dictator and his Minister walked into each other's arms and the first rank of the crowd behind them took this as a signal. A small horde of barmy officers, war correspondents and close friends came rushing forward. 'Ah, *shit*, muttered Sage, head down, his face hidden against Ax's throat. 'Brother, get me out of this, *please*.'

'No problem. Leave it to me.'

Ax left him propped against the bonnet of Bronwen's jeep. He was shocked that Sage was so weak, and frightened again: when he'd seen his big cat riding up the field like that he'd thought, *thank God, he's not so badly hurt* . . . He showed no sign of these feelings as he advanced on the eager company. 'Okay, fuck off. He's *my* boyfriend. Have a bit of sensitivity. I talk to him first. You can have him later. Go on. *Get.*'

Everyone backed off very smartly. He returned to the jeep, smiling. 'See. Nothing to it. I could have been taking lessons from Aoxomoxoa—'

Sage wanted to tell Ax that he'd been sure he would die, on the beach at Drumbeg, and ever since then he'd felt as if he was living in a dream. But now he finally knew he was alive, and he wanted to say he was sorry, again, sorry, Ax, I fucked up, I didn't mean to do this to you. He wanted to explain so many things, but there was no time. There was blood in his mouth.

He stood on the cliff. He leaped—

'*Sage—?*'

Sage tumbled forward, so Ax had to take his whole weight, and felt the rigid body brace, and laid him down with terrified care on the bruised grass – his head thrown back, blood on his lips, wide-open eyes still passionately reflecting the blue of the sky.

'Sage! Oh shit, *Sage*! If this piece of theatre—'

Fiorinda walked slowly along a corridor in the Rivermead medical centre. The Reading Site had been in Ax's hands again since the battle of Glastonbury had been averted a week ago. She didn't think she'd ever feel the same about Reading, but the medical centre was okay. It was very quiet. She opened a door and looked into a pleasant room filled with summer daylight, simply furnished, and stood for a moment looking at two empty beds with the covers and pillows folded on them. Slight burdens; and lying very still. Then she turned from what might have been, to the world that she had made.

The third bed was also empty. Sage was sitting propped

in the windowseat opposite with his feet up, wearing white pyjamas and a shabby blue cardigan. His scalp wound was taped and he was holding himself oddly; he looked a little rough, but if you didn't know better, you'd never have guessed the state he was in . . . and that's why they were at Reading. The staybehinds had been able to protect a great deal by co-operating with the usurpers, including the cutting-edge medical clinic, here where Ax had provided a safe refuge for the future he believed in. This was the first time she'd been allowed to see Sage since he'd collapsed after that insane stunt at the battle ground, but *he was going to be all right*. He didn't need her tainted magic, not much: he didn't need to change the world. Good old-fashioned modern medicine would do it.

'Hello,' she said.

'Hi.' He had turned his head; he smiled at her dreamily. 'How are you?'

'Oooh, not too bad. Patched up again. Been through countless pints of other people's blood, as the synthetic kind don't work very well on me. Some of it Bill's and George's and Peter's.' His voice shook, his eyes tearing. 'I always d-did find it useful to have a band with the same blood group.'

'Rock and Roll feudalism can't be all bad. Does it hurt very much?'

'Nah, I'm fine. Got a shunt in my arm: I'm tanked to the eyeballs, an' I intend to stay that way.' He tried to laugh. 'You know, I don't understand Olwen Devi. One minute she tells me I must never, never touch any kind of recreational drug again in my life ever. Next thing she's giving me unlimited access to this *excellent* synthetic smack—'

Fiorinda had crossed the room. They looked at each other, silenced, solemn-eyed and almost afraid, because of what they had done together at Drumbeg.

'I killed your father, Fiorinda.'

'*I hope he stays dead,*' said Fiorinda, with feeling.

'Well,' said Sage, lightening up, 'if he doesn't—' he took his hands out of his cardigan pockets, and folded them around his knees, '—I'll just have to kill him again.'

'Augh! *Sage!*'

'What's the matter?'

'Your hands!'

'What, these?' He held them out, innocently, and Fiorinda grabbed these hands: these perfect, undisfigured hands, tanned from outdoor living, with long squareish palms, square-tipped fingers, strong thumbs set wide: instantly familiar, full of life, full of Sage.

'Oh, my God . . . Were your hands like this in Ireland?'

'Yeah. I *thought* you hadn't noticed, you strange girl.' He blinked. 'Woman.'

'*I had a lot on my mind* . . . Oh, Sage, how? How did this—?'

'I don't know. When I came back from the Zen, at Caer Siddi, these were my hands, that's all. I didn't do it, not consciously. I didn't even ask . . . well, shit, maybe I did . . . I just came back and these were my hands,' he repeated. 'Call it a side-effect.' His face broke up, like a little child's. He reached awkwardly towards her, without moving his rigidly held torso, his eyes blinded with tears.

'Oh, Fiorinda, I don't want to die. I thought I was going to die. I would achieve the Zen Self, and beat Rufus and I would die, I thought that was the deal, but *I don't want to leave you.* I want to stay with you and Ax, but I can't fix this damage, Olwen says I'd kill myself if I tried, I'm sorry, I'm so sorry, oh, and *I left you alone with him,* why am I such a fuck-up, why am I *always* like this? Oh Fee—'

She held his head against her breast; she had meant not to cry, but her own tears were brimming over, telling him, 'Hush, hush, poor baby, you are *not* a fuck-up, you are my Sage, you are my darling, you did fantastic, you are going to be all right, little Sage, baby Sage, we will look after you, poor baby—'

Ax had allowed himself to be waylaid because he wanted to give them space. The three of them were so shattered and battered it would be a while before the love affair was an issue, but he wanted them to know that he understood, and that it was okay. He walked alone to Sage's room, rehearsing what he would tell them, *I love you both very much. Whatever you want, that's what I want for you too.* They're the lovers, I'm their friend. We get that straight, from the start . . . He came through the door and saw his big cat in Fiorinda's arms, both of them sobbing like fools. His heart turned upside down; he was across the room in a second and taking Sage from her, completely unable to stop himself: *I'm never going to let you go,* he was babbling, *I'm never going to let you out of my sight again, either of you—*

'You shouldn't have left us!' sobbed Fiorinda. 'It wasn't his fault!'

'I know, I know—'

Ax held Sage's bruised and battered face between his hands, God what a *joy* to touch him, and kissed him, very tenderly and delicately, not to hurt him, but then, irresistibly, they were kissing each other deep, soul-deep—

Fiorinda got up on the windowseat, took possession of Sage's free hand and watched them, her heart filled with golden light. 'Maybe this is the moment,' she said, 'when I have to remind you he's off sex.'

'Oh really?' said Ax, smiling into Sage's eyes. 'For how long?'

'No time limit. Just until his new liver kicks in.'

'Shut up, Fee.'

'And the nanobots have picked out all the tiny bone fragments from his chest cavity and his right lung, so then he can have the artificial lung rem—'

'I said *shut up.* You are scaring me—'

'I was barely getting started.'

447

'I think we want you scared,' said Ax, fervently, 'I think we want you *terrified*. Listen, Sage. As soon as they'll let you out of here, we're going to Tyller Pystri. We'll stay there, the three of us, long as it takes to get you totally well, and then I don't know what the fuck we'll do, we'll do whatever we like. I'm quitting the Dictatorship anyway. But when we go to Cornwall, you have to promise me—' He broke off. They were both staring at him with strange expressions.

'Oh shit,' said Ax. 'I'm doing it again aren't I? I'm taking over—'

'You're quitting the Dictatorship?' repeated Sage, slowly.

'Yes. I know I haven't done my five years, but I want out. It's my decision, you're not responsible. I've had enough. I've realised what a wanker I was being—'

'Oh, hush,' said Fiorinda. 'Forget all that.' She held Sage's beautiful hand against her cheek. 'Er . . . these plans. Do they imply we're going to give our fucked-up, ridiculous relationship another try?'

'Aren't we?' said Sage, anxiously.

'If you'll have us, Fiorinda,' said Ax.

A short time later Olwen Devi, Dilip Krishnachandran and two of the Rivermead medical centre staff came into the room. Sage was in his bed, propped up high (it would be a while before he could lie down, his torso must be upright). Fiorinda was curled up on the coverlet, not touching, but very close. Ax was on the other side, asleep in a chair, holding Sage's hand. Carefully, Olwen checked the telltales on the back of Sage's left hand, the tube in his nose, the diamorphine shunt in his arm. She studied the array of screens, consulted silently for a moment with Serendip, and seemed satisfied.

'Should we wake Mr Preston and Fiorinda?' asked one of the nurses softly.

'No,' said Olwen. 'Make up the other two beds, and then we will leave them. Sage will come to no harm. I believe there are two people in this room who have more power over life and death than anything I can offer.'

Dilip knelt, lifted Ax's free hand from the arm of the chair and pressed it to his brow.

'And the third is just the king of England.'

He replaced the hand gently. Ax never stirred.